LOVE YOU BETTER

A Second Chance Romance Set in the Oakville World

KALLYN JONES

Love you Better

A SECOND CHANCE ROMANCE
SET IN THE OAKVILLE WORLD

KALLYN JONES

To SSL, thank you for your enthusiastic support and guidance in this story. I treasure your unconditional friendship and wisdom.
Also, to anyone who has ever felt not quite fill-in-the-blank. Your amazing self is enough.

Chapter 1

Ordinary World

BLAKE

Late again. A perfect score of tardiness, three weeks running. I hated it, had relentlessly lectured my employees on the virtues of timeliness in order to cure them of the rude habit. However, my boss voice wouldn't come out this morning. After releasing a cleansing breath, I approached my daughter's bathroom with caution. Thankfully, her charter school had been understanding.

She stood in front of the mirror frowning, bottom lip quivering.

I leaned against the doorframe. "Need some help, honey?" Her shoulders started shaking, and just like that, my nearly grown preteen morphed back into her toddler self in my eyes. Back then, a kiss cured her pains. Nothing I could do took away this heartache.

"Oh, Daddy…" Olivia burst into tears.

Dammit. Today's catalyst didn't matter. My girl was grieving, going through something no daughter should, especially a twelve-year-old. Her mother had died suddenly three weeks past. Should I coddle her or tell her to buck up—the dilemma of every parent? My instincts leaned toward the strict, so I did the opposite and pulled her into a hug. Besides, the concerned emails from her homeroom teacher had stopped last week, leading me to believe when Liv had a thorough, safe cry in the morning, she faced the day better, like when I hit a punching bag.

When Liv's sobs quieted to hitching breaths, I tipped her chin up, catching her gaze. I made a mental note to grab a frozen washcloth from the freezer for her puffy eyes before we piled into my SUV. She hated looking like she'd been crying when she was around her classmates. "Want to talk about it?"

"These knots in my hair won't brush out. I'm supposed to braid it before bed, but I was sooo tired last night. Now we're late again."

I had to handle a situation at work the night before. We were really late getting home. I needed to shut that shit down. Olivia was too young to stay home alone, and she lived with me full time now. She even fell asleep for a couple of hours in my office before I could leave. I tried to lift her without waking her, like when she was little, but those days were gone.

As the tears re-formed, I bent forward and kissed the top of her head. "Don't worry about the school bell, Sparrow. Your principal understands." I spun my daughter around and picked up her brush. "I watched some hair videos last night. One of them mentioned tangles. Let me have at 'em." I gathered her long dark hair that was a lot like mine—and like the smiling woman from my childhood dreams—brushing her hair from the ends up to Olivia's nape. I had learned the word nape the night before after researching the right way to do this. This wasn't our first snarly hair crisis, which was why I now knew about girl-dad YouTube channels. With a glass of bourbon in hand, they turned out to be surprisingly calming after a hectic day.

Olivia relaxed her tight shoulders. "You're not pulling on my scalp. Good job."

"Thank you." Another kiss to the top of her head gave me a tiny smile in the mirror. Then I parted her hair into three sections and continued slowly. "Meredith said silk pillowcases help. After school, she's going to show us how to make braids that won't fall out. Would you like that?"

"You told Meredith about my hair problems?" Her embarrassment reflected in the mirror.

I lifted my shoulder and tried to act nonchalant as I finished brushing. Inside, I was totally chalant, terrified I was a complete fuckup with my new parenting endeavor. The idea of letting Olivia down—not to mention her late mother, Gianna —was intolerable. "I asked for both of us, right? Now that my hair's down past my shoulders, it also tangles like a bitch… Oops! Sorry, Sparrow."

She giggled. Finally. "It's fine, Daddy. I won't yell at you like Momma did." She tapped her lower lip. "I might start a swear jar though. It could get me a pony."

"A pony?" A chuckle rolled through me, easing my tension. "In a condo? In downtown Raleigh? Do you plan to keep it on the patio?"

Olivia rolled her eyes at me in the mirror, looking exactly like her mother. "Don't be silly. It'll board at a stable. Sofia is taking lessons at an amazing place in Oakville. She said the instructors are soooo nice."

I picked up a hairband and said, "This your way of telling me you want riding lessons now?"

Liv's full smile graced her delicate features as she waggled her brows for an answer.

"Let's talk about it after school." Christ, as a restaurateur, my schedule struggled to meld with a middle-schooler's. How would I get away to take her to lessons right before the dinner rush? At least my restaurant, the Garage, was in our neighborhood and close to Olivia's school. She could walk over and do her homework in the extra office across from mine. My chef and partner, Felix, was a bonus uncle and cooked whatever she wanted for dinner.

With the tangles sufficiently tamed, I brushed her hair from top to bottom and gathered it into a ponytail. At least I could do that. It was my standard style lately, only with a manly rubber band. "How's that for now? Will it hold until Meredith?"

Liv sighed like the weight of the world clung to her tiny shoulders. She pulled her hair through the scrunchie one more time until it made something resembling a bun with the ends sticking out. She made another frown. "What if we just cut our hair? It might make our… transition easier."

"Give in? Are you kidding right now?" When I'd grown out my hair, it had been part of my self-discovery, and it worked. I finally felt genuine and no longer like I was pretending to fit in. Letting the gray hairs come in helped too.

If Olivia really wanted a fresh start, I would have made the appointment for her that afternoon, but this sounded like frustration talking. I gently tickled her side. "Do you doubt this old dog's ability to learn new hair tricks?"

"No, Daddy." Olivia shimmied away from my reach and laughed. Mission accomplished for the moment. "Do you think your family will want our hair to be long when you find them?"

My girl was certainly observant. I never told her why I grew my hair out. I guess it had been a reaction to the news that I was Navajo, after asking a social worker to investigate my case. The social worker had discovered as much as she could. It would still be a miracle if I ever put a name to my birth mother, let alone meet her.

Growing up, I was told that the young girl had been a

drug addict from the Cherokee Nation, but no one could answer which band. It turned out to be neither. If my adoptive parents had been wrong about what nation was mine, I wondered what else had been a lie. The woman I saw in my memory flashes didn't look high. More importantly, the feelings living inside me didn't jibe with the narrative. Only, what did I know? I'd been a toddler when my parents took me in.

Anyway, the importance of hair to Navajo culture had been the first thing I learned in my research on my true identity. Unfortunately, my free time had dissolved since then, putting a pause on new discoveries. As soon as life settled down, I promised myself and the woman from my dreams that I'd get back to it.

I laughed at Olivia's question. "Any family we might find will love you no matter what you do with your hair." I made a face in the mirror, making her smile. "I think it's gorgeous and worth figuring out, unless it's what your heart really wants. Anyway, Mer said it gets easier when you have the right products for the job."

"About Meredith…" Liv kept her eyes on the floor as she shuffled past me. "Sofia asked me to go to her house after school. Sorry, I forgot to tell you."

"But it's my day off." I cringed at the near whine in my voice. After the lesson, I planned to take Liv to a movie. At least she was in front of me and couldn't see my disappointment.

Liv padded down the steps without looking back. "Yeah, sorry. It's Sof's only afternoon off, and I have to see her. You know how it is for us kids. We're scheduled down to the minute."

Did I ever. Without Gianna as the point person in Olivia's schedule, I didn't know how I was supposed to keep up with her activities.

Once in the kitchen, Olivia stuffed her lunch into her backpack.

I snapped my fingers. "Oh, we're out of almond butter. Hope you don't mind cheese and crackers."

Olivia's face twisted as she bit her lip, like she was trying not to cry. Grief showed up at the most inconvenient times.

I pulled her in for a hug, set my cheek on top of her head. "I'm sorry, Sparrow. I didn't have time to hit the store yesterday. I used the brie you like… also put the fig spread in a little container. Is that all right?"

She nodded her head against my chest.

"I know Momma never forgot this stuff. I'm sorry."

Olivia sniffed as she nodded again. "It's okay."

My heart yearned to take away her pain. I stepped back and bent to meet her eyes. "No one will ever replace your mom. I know that better than anyone. There's nothing fair about what happened. I know I could've been a better parent partner." I brushed away her tears with my thumbs. "She was so good at being your mom, and I didn't want to look like a buffoon in front of you two. So I let Gia do too much. Promise to be better."

She gave me a sweet smile—the one that always melted my hard heart—and hugged me around my waist. "I know, Daddy. I don't know why cheese made me cry. It's like one more surprise and I'll break, you know?"

Hell yeah. I knew it well and silently promised to make it up to her. "We're not broken though. We'll find our new normal."

She mumbled something that sounded like I hate that phrase, and my heart squeezed some more. I had to try another way to lift her spirits.

We finally moved down the second set of stairs, toward the garage. "You ready to crush the day?"

"One good thing," Olivia said with a nod. It had been our

mantra since our world imploded. Finding one good thing in our current fog of crap days equaled a win.

After buckling up in my SUV, a text buzzed my phone as we waited for the garage door to rise. It was from my assistant manager.

JAY

Morning Boss. This is Jay's wife Alecia.

Um… bad news.

He was in an accident. We're at the ED now.

I texted Alecia back, asking her to keep me posted and promised to swing by the hospital as soon as I dropped off Olivia. Good thing she had plans with her friend. There would be no day off now. Just hoped Jay was all right.

"I'M NOT PUTTING A DAMN SCRUNCHIE IN MY HAIR. I'M NOT A girl."

"Don't you dare use that hair puller." Meredith slapped my hand as I reached for the plain rubber band that had been holding my ponytail. She'd just demonstrated how to make a regular braid, having me mimic her motions. She held up the rubber band I used and made a face at all the strands wrapped around it. Then she took hold of my ends and wrapped them in her tie. It was stupid to argue over hair, but it had been a rough day.

She gritted through her teeth as she worked. "It's a black, silk-covered band, you grump ass. Nothing girly. Helps prevent hair-pulling, is all." She pointed to the snarly knot on my desk. "I thought you'd want to hold on to as much hair as you can, given your age."

Not that I was going bald, but she had a point. Those little shits hurt when they came out.

She gave my new braid a little tug. "There… a nice, manly black one. Just like your heart. No one will notice, and your scalp will thank me."

She held up a mirror behind me so I could check it out. Mine wasn't as tight as Mer's, but it wasn't bad either. I liked it.

"I see you trying not to smile at yourself. Admit it… you feel better." She patted my shoulder. "Sometimes it's the little stuff."

I remembered the mantra that Olivia and I had—One good thing. I rubbed between my eyes while nodding. Meredith fell into the Chesterfield across from my desk. She had witnessed most of my shitty days. We were both worried about Jay, my manager. He would have to spend the night in the hospital, then stay home for at least a month to recover. Everyone at the Garage was grateful he'd survived the accident.

"You're welcome, Boss," Meredith quipped as she wrapped her long blond braid around her finger and pinned it into a bun at her neck with hairpins she kept in her apron pocket.

I rolled my eyes at her insinuation of my lack of gratitude. "What can I say? Can't wait for the day to end."

"Let me take the floor tonight," she said. "According to reservations, the dinner crowd looks light. I can divide up my area between the other servers and take Jay's load." She pointed her thumb over her shoulder at the boxes stacked up against the window wall that overlooked the dining area. "Working on that monstrosity won't be a picnic, but at least we can leave you alone."

I smirked at my head server. "Looking for a promotion?"

She popped her brows mischievously. "Perhaps."

I couldn't ask for a more loyal employee—or friend. A single mother, raising three daughters, I appreciated Meredith's drive and competence more than ever. Exhaling a long breath to release the day's tension, I steeled myself for the different pain those boxes held—the proof of my stupidity. "Thank you for everything. Extra time helps."

Mer stood and moved toward my office door. As she reached for the handle, I added, "We'll talk about a promotion as soon as the financial mess resolves."

A bright smile lit her face. "Thanks, Boss."

I stretched my arms, trying to find some way to relax as another issue from this morning popped into my head. "Olivia asked about getting a pony and riding lessons. I don't know how the hell I'm supposed to slip them into my 'pampered schedule,' so… yeah. Looks like you might need to step up soon."

Meredith tipped her head back and laughed, her dangling earrings bouncing against her neck. "Glad my girls are out of the pony phase. Although I always played the single-mother-working-for-tips card when they asked for shit like that. Don't worry. It's probably another phase for Liv."

I scratched my chin. "Hope you're right."

She stepped onto the balcony overlooking the Garage. The buzz of the kitchen and staff preparing for dinner floated up through the open doorway. Then she stuck her head back in. "Oh… and if you need another hair lesson, just holler. Especially with French braids. It takes a few times."

I growled under my breath, wondering if Liv was right about cutting our hair to make life easier. Only, my life wasn't simple during those years I was forced to keep it short.

Silence filled my office as the door shut with a solid thud. The boxes seemed to taunt me, like an enemy waiting to strike. Sorting out their contents was over my head, but I'd try. The one person I knew for sure who could fix my situations—the problems my bookkeeper dumped on us when he screwed me over—was also my ex-girlfriend. The one who had gotten away. She was also the best accountant I'd ever known. Except we had blurred the line between professional and personal. Then it bit me in the ass when she cut ties.

She could tear through this disaster like a bloodhound after a convict. Only, my pride wouldn't let me make the call. Blake Brady did the loving and leaving, not the other way around. No, I'd figure my money problems out another way.

I cranked up Pearl Jam and dug into the top box, making notes and highlighting for two solid hours. Until an alarm rang on a screen monitoring the restaurant.

A disturbance on the patio.

My intercom buzzed, and Meredith's voice cut off the music. "Sorry, Boss. We need you downstairs."

Chapter 2

It's Not Right, But It's Okay

CYNDI

"Well hello, Miss Sendaydiego. It's been a while."

I smiled at the hostess, dropping my eyes to her name tag. That's right, Meredith. "Wonderful to see you. Still here."

She dipped her chin. "Boss is the best."

I ignored the temptation to add, don't I know it? The owner of the Garage, Blake Brady, was an ex… ex-client and ex-boyfriend. Thankfully, he took Wednesdays off, so there was no risk of running into him tonight. Not that it would've mattered. I didn't pick the place. My official ex had done that. My ex-husband, Joel. He only patronized the best establishments, and the Garage was the best in Raleigh.

"Do you have a reservation? I don't see your name on the list?"

I looked up at the forty-something single mother, if memory served, towering over me. "It's probably under Williams."

"You got married?" Meredith asked with a gasp. "Congratulations!"

I almost choked. "Excuse me?"

"Mr. Williams mentioned meeting his wife for dinner."

I sighed. He would. "He's my ex-husband." Damn if the man still didn't get under my skin, and I couldn't explain why. I'd been contemplating this moment since he contacted me, asking for an in-person meetup. As usual, he wouldn't take no for an answer.

She did a double take and smirked. "I see." Meredith lifted her arm. "He's on the terrace. Follow me please."

On the terrace. I should've predicted that as well. Joel loved to be seen, even when visiting a town. Since he lived in Northern Virginia, he probably had local business acquaintances. Other than me.

As we weaved a path through the dining room, Meredith bent toward me and quietly said, "Love your hair. Wish I had the nerve to do something so fun."

"You're very kind. Thank you." The compliment came at the right time, bringing my swagger back. Women had been randomly saying similar things since I had my stylist dye the silver hairs framing my face blue. I stopped coloring my roots the year before and loved the sparkly "highlights" naturally forming in the front, but I also bored easily. A semipermanent fantasy color helped. "I'm sure Blake wouldn't mind if you colored your hair."

She nodded. "True. Boss doesn't freak out over such stuff. My family wouldn't take kindly to more change though."

I touched her forearm in support. Meredith was tackling emotional and physical mountains when I last saw her. "You look fantastic."

She blushed lightly and held out her arm. I adjusted my steps to match the beat of the Miley Cyrus song playing through the speakers. It put an extra swish on my hips and bolstered my resolve. Add in my platform over-the-knee boots and my five-foot-not-much frame felt ready to own this night.

Again, I wondered what the hell Joel wanted with me now. Not that I expected a fight, per se, but he'd refused to tell me what was so urgent we couldn't speak on the phone. Our divorce happened almost two decades ago. Aside from occasional texts—like when I sent flowers for his mother's funeral—we left each other alone. In any case, I for damn sure wouldn't arrive at the man's table unprepared.

Meredith cleared the roll-up door to the terrace—one feature of this former body shop-turned high-end dining experience in the heart of Raleigh's warehouse district—and my traitorous heart skipped a beat as my eyes landed on the man who had once been my world. Joel Williams still gave off Robert Redford vibes, now enhanced with a sexy, silver-fox bonus. The all-American sex god. He was speaking to an older woman at the next table. By the sparkling smile she wore, his charms were on full display. Curse him.

Do not get sucked in.

A potted red crepe myrtle tree made a rustling sound as Meredith's shoulder brushed it, and Joel turned his head, his thousand-watt smile landing on me. My steps faltered. Double-curse him. I inhaled deeply and covered the faux pas with a grin of my own. That was close.

Meredith pulled out the chair across from Joel, and I slipped into it, letting the prolonged smile suffice for a greeting. I turned my head back to the hostess. "Thank you."

"Great to see you again."

"You too."

Joel took my hand and pulled it to his lips, placing a slow kiss on my knuckles. "Cynthia," he crooned.

The woman next to us sighed, then leaned toward me and said, "You're very lucky." I turned my polite smile on her. No harm in indulging her fantasy for an evening since I knew better than most it was all show.

In the meantime, Joel's eyebrows rose, alternating one at a time—a rare talent that still made him look like a puppy. In the beginning, it was endearing. Now it was simply his way of assessing if I earned his approval. He leaned slightly forward as his eyes traveled down my chest and inside the silk blouse. I chose it because it was the same shade of blue as my hair highlights and it brightened the gray irises I inherited from my mother.

Leaning forward slightly, I allowed a better view. Heat from the lit candle warmed the tip of my nose. "It's an ocean-blue lace longline."

Joel's gaze flicked back to mine. "What?"

"The bra."

His eyes narrowed as his face filled with lust. "For me?"

I batted my lashes sarcastically. "For me."

Joel's eyes closed as a subtle shiver rolled through him. Triumph filled my belly. I was breaking my number one rule regarding men, but I didn't care. As often as I flirted, I never purposely did with a married man. Considering Joel's wife had relentlessly chased him while he was my husband, they both deserved it.

Finally, the real Joel, the one who used to be my universe, appeared. "You've changed, baby girl." He lifted his wrists off the table's edge. "It's not a criticism. Simply an observation." His finger slowly moved up and down. "The boots, the leather skirt, visibly sexy underwear… and your hair." His expression turned to disappointment, and I wondered how well his kids knew it.

Several responses to his obvious "criticism" of what I referred to as my power armor raced through my mind. Back when we were married, everything I did—from wearing preppy clothes to my ridiculous attempt at "the Rachel" haircut—had been chosen to make this man happy. My sole focus back then was to be the perfect wife. It took ten years for Joel to drop the bomb about his infidelities, letting me know how futile it all had been.

Meredith set a glass of iced water in front of me, then slipped away as I answered him. "Why are we here?"

He squeezed my hand hard—another power play memory resurfacing. "Straight to the point now?" Before he could say more, our waiter approached.

I remembered the young man from when the restaurant was my client. "Hello, Connor."

"Miss Sendaydiego? Nice to see you back."

Boy, I missed this place. The industrial-meets-rustic interior and the intimately beautiful patio. The Garage was a play on contrasts. High-end Southern dishes in a repurposed body shop. It almost made me regret ending the relationship.

Connor introduced himself to Joel and politely waited through our drink discussion.

"You want a red or wait… white?" Joel asked.

Connor cleared his throat and bent toward me. "Boss still stocks the French rosé you used to love."

"I still do. That will be lovely." I briefly touched my heart. "Thanks for remembering." Was it a dramatic gesture? Sure. But the kid didn't have to remember a detail like that.

"You're hard to forget." His cheeks flushed. "I mean… you're nice. Not like… yeah."

I nodded while watching Joel. He looked like he was doing relational addition in his head. The guy was flirting, but I had set the flirty tone back in the day. Joel seemed to realize my strutting entrance hadn't been just for him. Development of the skill had helped me heal from our train wreck of a marriage. This was how I moved through the world now, another part of my armor, so to speak. Besides, my relationship to the Garage and its staff wasn't any of his business.

He came back to his senses and glanced at the menu again. "I'll have the California Cab." He tipped his head back at Connor, and the charming persona returned. "A good old American classic."

A fire truck roared past, just a few feet away from us as the lady next to us settled her bill and left. When the Doppler effect faded, an intimate quiet descended over our table—the urban equivalent of an oasis, considering it was early for the dinner rush.

"Alone at last," Joel said, that smarmy look back on his face.

Dammit if it didn't start working on me, but there was a reason I'd fallen for the man. I opened my mouth to press the issue and keep from falling for real. He cut me off.

"I know…" He leaned forward, so I sat back. "You want to know why I'm wining and dining you."

I folded my arms.

"The thing is, I've been looking back… at my mistakes… the successes too, of course." I would've believed him if any ounce of contrition showed on his face. A crumb. Instead, it remained a blank canvas of practiced gorgeousness. Joel reached insistently and pulled my hand away from my body, stroking my wrist with his thumb. "I realized how much I missed you."

I blinked. Twice.

"Yeah, so… I'll just say it." His movements enlivened the perfume I'd sprayed there an hour ago, mingling it with his scent. "Since you're also single, what would you think about trying again? The magic's still there."

My eyes widened in shock.

"I feel it."

Our scents didn't blend. In fact, they clashed. Then I burst out laughing nervously. When Joel didn't return my amusement, I stopped cold, felt my face twist in disbelief. "You're not kidding."

His thumb moved again, like he was practicing some kind of mind control voodoo. My nose twitched, warding off a sneeze. "I made a mistake when I left you."

"Yeah, you did. Except, it's been almost twenty years. We moved on. How old is your son, by the way—the one who was born before our divorce finalized?"

Joel lit up at the mention of the apple of his eye. His legacy. "JJ's a senior. You'd be so impressed with him, baby girl. He's everything we'd dreamed about. A chip off the old block, as my dad says."

If he didn't shut up soon, the inside of my cheek would bleed from biting it. How could he not see what his words did to me? But that was us boiled down to our essences—me dying inside for a chance to please him and him oblivious to anyone else's needs.

Connor delivered our wineglasses, and I downed half of mine in one swallow. I looked back at him, and the waiter wiggled his finger toward my rosé, silently asking if I needed another. I nodded, then grabbed his cuff as he turned. "Can you bring me a French Connection instead?"

Connor's eyes narrowed as they assessed Joel. I wondered how close he'd been watching us. "Absolutely. Do you prefer a brand of cognac?"

I stared at my ex as I answered, "Your top shelf." I suddenly wanted to make Joel pay double for every minute of my time.

"Excellent. And uh… can I put in an appetizer for y'all?"

Joel picked up his menu. "Well…"

"The chef's board and grilled brussels sprouts with the balsamic drizzle," I blurted.

"Um, you forgot I don't like brussels—"

I growled low in my throat.

"Sounds good." Then Joel added, "And put in the smoked pork chop with sweet potato casserole for me. Cynthia?"

I waved my hand. "I'm still thinking. The appetizer will do for now. Thanks, Connor." My instincts had awakened, nudging me to make this fast and get the hell out before Joel burned the remnants of my heart.

"My pleasure."

When our waiter slipped out of sight, Joel started talking about the colleges his son had visited, like this golden-boy junior had already been accepted to them. Naturally, I deflected. "What about the other one? A girl, right?" As much as he'd wanted to father a son, back in the day, I'd dreamed of a daughter. A brood, really, but a girl or two had been my baseline.

Joel's features twisted with the disappointment I recognized. "She's just like her mother."

So she steals other girls' boyfriends then. I bit down harder to keep from being petty, then swallowed the rest of my wine, adding in a fake smile with a polite nod like I could relate. That comment would have thrilled me in another life.

Cognac or no, my instincts were now poking me hard, telling me to go. I scooted my chair back.

"I'm sorry, Cyn. So very sorry. I see everything clearly now."

I ran my hand through my hair. "What's clear, precisely?"

Joel mimicked my movements through his perfect strands. A tiny bead of perspiration dotted his still full upper lip, clean-shaven even in the late afternoon. "We had a good thing—the best thing—and I fucked it all up."

"I agree but—"

He slid into the chair next to me, leaning into my space. "Our flame burned so big. It can't have gone out completely. Tell me we can rekindle it, baby girl. We can get it back and have decades of fun... travel..." Joel's chair squealed as he scooted close to my ear and drawled, "Hawt sex." The earthy notes of his wine reached my nose as he pulled back, checking to see if I agreed.

Something niggled at the back of my mind, telling me to play along. I let my fingers walk along his forearms, exposed by the rolled-up sleeves of his dress shirt. They were softer than I remembered. Long hours working in finance could do that, along with hanging out at the bar with the boys. I scrunched my nose and leaned in, whispering in Joel's ear this time. "Why does it sound like you're having a midlife crisis?"

He caressed my cheek and hummed. "It's more like a revelation."

"You must know I won't be anyone's mistress. Especially not yours."

A barmaid set my cocktail down and slipped away at the speed of a seasoned professional. I wouldn't expect anything less at the Garage.

"That's the beauty of it," Joel began. "Karen and I are over. I meant it when I said we're both single. I have a condo in Fairfax now, but I could work remote."

Was he implying he could move here? The volume turned up on my instincts. Way up. The voices of my best friend, Kick, and my mother spoke in my mind, like support angels sitting on my shoulders. I pushed him away, no longer interested in this game. This wasn't funny. This man had humiliated me. No, decimated me. I wasn't anyone's joke anymore.

"Stop playing, Joel. Just… stop. We had our time. It was painful before Kar—your affair—but that killed what was left. We're over. Over, over. If you're single again, I'm sorry. Don't know what you did, but—"

"Karen's sleeping with her boss."

I bit my cheek again to keep from scoffing, tasted the tang of blood this time. "How original." She'd been Joel's loyal assistant back when we were married. I shifted in my seat, suddenly unable to get comfortable. Dammit, Joel.

"I know." He raised his hands, motioning to surrender. "I know. I see the irony. Believe me. But that's why I've been thinking so hard… making changes. It's hell being alone."

"Funny… I love it." A group of young women sat at a table on the other side of the patio. One of them laughed out loud, as if proving my point. Giving Joel one last benefit of the doubt, along with a little advice before leaving, I said, "Go to therapy. Find out who you really are before attaching yourself to another woman."

"But you're the love of my life." He reached for my elbow, and I leaned back, holding my wrist against my chest.

With abysmal timing, Connor set our apps on the table. The sharp spice of the balsamic-glazed brussels sprouts filled my nose, and my stomach rolled. Any other day, I would have devoured them. The waiter quickly left without asking if we needed anything or if I wanted to order. He must have predicted what was percolating inside me, probably saw it in my eyes. Joel had been the only person who couldn't read my face. In hindsight, he never cared enough to try. Didn't that make his calling me the love of his life even more ridiculous?

"Do you hear yourself?" I asked in complete incredulity. "I never did enough for you. I was never enough for you or your family." Not only did they expect me to act like old money—a learnable skill that I achieved, by the way—they wanted me to look like it. Me. An ethnically obscure girl with a Filipino father and an American mother of mostly German ancestry. If I had a dollar for every time someone in their crowd said, So you're Mexican… Chinese? What? I'd have an old money bank account.

Joel shook his head. "You're perfect. Thoughtful… Caring… You managed everything, even my mother. If it wasn't for the fertility stuff… but we don't have to worry about it now."

"Because you had your kids. Made damn sure of it," I declared, then took a steadying pull of my drink. The warmth of the cognac and amaretto gave me clarity. However, it didn't stop the feeling of ants crawling over my skin. I shifted in my seat again as I now saw Joel's agenda perfectly. As far as he was concerned, his kids were raised, so he could go back to the easy, submissive wife who lived only for him. Surprise, motherfucker. That Cyndi was dead.

"Exactly," he said, tipping his empty wineglass toward me.

"Tell me," I started, setting my elbows on the tabletop. "Do I look like the naive girl you married?"

Joel picked at the charcuterie board, popping a pickle in his mouth. "There's always room for change." He winked at me.

Changing back, he meant.

Our last afternoon together flashed through my mind.

Joel callously packed his clothes, throwing them in his suitcase as he cleared out the closet. My face burned from hot tears. My belly bleeding from yet another miscarriage—a girl. He'd just told me his assistant was six months pregnant with his baby. A boy.

"But I've done everything you've asked of me. I turned myself inside out to be your perfect wife, to never be a burden," I sobbed, nothing but a broken, tangled ball of confusion.

"And there's your answer," Joel bit out as he zipped his second suitcase. "You never asked me for anything." He had the nerve to pause his actions and ask, "Did you even need me?"

At that point in our relationship, I didn't know what I liked anymore. Even the baby quest had become just that—a goal, a checkmark to prove my worthiness. The mother to his heir. Instead, another woman beat me to it.

I scoffed at the memory as my foot bounced with energy. That last exchange had motivated my transformation. I vowed to never let another man decide those things again, and I liked —no, loved—this Cyndi.

A new couple approached a smaller table nearby. The man sat in the chair next to his date instead of across from her, like he couldn't get close enough. I knew couples like that. It helped clear my head.

Joel still didn't see the real me. Anger flared inside my chest at what was essentially his second rejection of me.

"Don't get me wrong…" He pressed, moving his pointer finger in my direction again. "You can keep this look for when we're alone. Not the hair, of course." He winked. "But maybe a wig like it… and the boots." He closed his eyes and did the shiver thing again.

As if a trigger had been pulled, I sprang out of my seat, knocking it back as I threw my cocktail in his face. I didn't give him a chance to say more. "As if I'd spend the rest of my good years on a three-pump chump like you. I'd rather spend my valuable time with my battery-operated boyfriends." The commotion caused an eruption of noise from the surrounding diners. Some gasped, some snickered. I couldn't have cared less. I leaned onto the table, letting him get one last, full look down my blouse, because fuck him. "Go find some dumbass twenty-nothing girl to screw over until you're ready for assisted living."

A table of women behind me laughed hard. One of them filmed us. Public embarrassment was Joel's worst nightmare. Still, I had one more thing to add. "You hurt me. Practically split me in half. But you didn't break me. I love who I am now and sure as hell won't compromise again… for you. Or any other asshole."

The women clapped. Well shit, I hadn't meant to be that loud, even if he deserved it. As I stormed off, Joel pleaded with me to calm down and come back. Was he more upset about my rejection of him or about the public scene?

It didn't matter. I'd said my piece. The million words I'd longed to tell him over the years boiled down to a few terse statements. I turned and charged through the interior of the restaurant with purpose and fury, looking down to navigate the labyrinth of tables and chairs and keep from catching a heel. Instead, I ran straight into a wall. A deliciously smelling, masculine wall. Of course he'd be there. Mr. Perfect. Everything I wanted. And feared.

Chapter 3

Road to Nowhere

Cyndi

"Sparky?"

Of all the people… his voice still curled my toes. Silky with a slight rasp, it held a slightly amused yet annoyed curiosity. Why had he used his old nickname for me? I gasped, as if the word stole the air from my throat. When I finally inhaled, my nose filled with his wood-and-leather cologne again. On him? The best smell ever. Asshole.

What a day—two-for-one exes.

"What's wrong?" he asked, his face pinched like he was set to defend my honor.

Only everything. Stupid Joel tried to suck me in again. Made a fool of me again. Except it's my fault for thinking time could mature him. And now you're here on what's supposed to be your day off. But it's apparently not. Dammit.

"Sorry about the scene," I mumbled.

Blake Brady's addictive brood—the opposite of Joel Williams's manipulative fits—was not what I needed either.

Why did these two worlds have to cross each other? It was like the men messed with a time-space continuum, throwing me off-kilter. I stepped back and wobbled off the side of my heel, almost twisting an ankle, making me triple angry because Cyndi Senday-fucking-diego could run in heels let alone stomp in them. Double dammit.

"Whoa." Blake grabbed my upper arms to steady me. His soothing tone morphed into a growl. "Go up to my office. I'll take care of your... guest."

Yeah, not happening. "It's all on me," I argued. "Joel... he behaved himself. Let him eat in peace." He was probably waiting for me to leave before making his own quick escape.

I swung my forearms around, breaking Blake's hold. He bristled with a deadly energy as he stared me down, his Adam's apple bobbing while he processed my words. He'd grown his hair long. It hung in his face, making his warm brown eyes look like night. Desire washed over me at this incredibly inconvenient time, but we never lacked chemistry.

Nope. Not going there either. "Why are you here?" I blurted, incapable of saying anything helpful. But I'd only agreed to this fiasco of a dinner because it was supposed to be... Blake's. Night. Off.

The corner of his mouth lifted. "It's my restaurant."

It didn't matter. Nothing did. I just needed to get the hell out of there. Home. "Everything's..." A hot mess, but you can't fix it. "It's fine, Blake."

I stormed past him, the safety of my car now my life's goal.

"Come on, Spark," he called after me. "Cyndi!"

But I kept on walking. Screw all men and their perfect bone structures.

I UNZIPPED MY BOOTS AND THREW THEM DOWN THE HALL TO MY bedroom before shutting the front door of my house. Watching them fly through the air felt like throwing away my old self. Who cared if Joel didn't approve? Our visit showed me he never would. The real Cyndi was awesome, and he could go to hell.

I opened my streaming app and played Vivaldi, needing the lift the Four Seasons always brought. The moment felt like a big change in mindset. I went to the wine fridge and opened a bottle of my favorite rosé. "Take that, Joel. It's not one of your stupid Cabs, thank you very much." Not that there was anything wrong with Cabernet Sauvignon. It was the way he raved about them being superior to any other.

My best friend's ringtone drowned out the Vivaldi, and I answered, "Hey."

"What happened?" she asked, her soothing tone telling me she had one of her visions.

I let out a cleansing breath. "I'm over him, Kicky. I really am." As hard as the evening had been, the revelation hit me like a blessing. So freeing. I lifted my left arm and twirled.

"So you did see Joel."

Kick Harrison and I had been like sisters since we roomed together during our freshman year at Michigan State University. By the end of the first semester, it was obvious she had a sixth sense about the people she loved. It never helped her prevent a disaster, but she knew when we needed her.

"The one and only." I sank into my plush love seat, curling my feet under me. I sniffed at the tingle in my nose, and my voice dissolved into something resembling a mouse's. "I had dinner with him tonight."

"Well shit. Why? And why didn't you take me with you?" Her words were loaded with concern and knowing. She'd been with me through my disaster of a marriage. When it all had circled the drain, I flew down here and stayed in her guest room in Oakville. It helped me decide to restart my life here.

"Because I'm a grown-ass woman. Besides, I'm not afraid

of him. I thought time might change him. You know? Soften him."

Tears crept down my cheeks as I caught her up on the cringe details of my failed dinner date. About thirty minutes later, I felt better and inhaled a full breath. This must've been why it rained the most in spring and autumn. It wasn't enough for the temperatures to change. After a harsh winter or summer, the ground needed cleansing too. Like my soul.

"I'm proud of you," Kick said.

I scoffed into my headset as I walked around my house, watering my collection of succulent plants. I never had kids or pets. These little pretties were my babies. I spent good money matching the right container to the plant and made villages of them. "You're proud of me for falling for his shit again? I almost got sucked back in."

My best friend clicked her tongue. "You never would have. When you two blew up, I could tell you were about ready to leave anyway. But you needed to grieve the miscarriage first. About today... hold on a sec." Kick spoke to her husband, Thomas, then came back. "Anyway... for whatever reason, I think inside you wanted to prove that you're in the right place now. And you did it."

For whatever reason? "I know why, chica, and it's part of why I'm mad at myself."

"Yeah? Tell me."

I shrugged, the watering can still in my hand, as if Kick could see me. "We're gonna be fifty." I watered the plants around my soaking bathtub as I waited for Kick to answer.

"No, we're turning forty-nine." Her chuckle held an edge. "Besides, you went through a turning-forty crisis. I won't allow another one... especially a year early."

I sighed and sat on the tub surround. "It's not a crisis, per se, but my retirement person eludes me now. Since you remarried, it won't be you anymore." I tapped my chin. "I should place an ad on the city social media page."

"Seriously?" Between soft chuckles, she added, "What about the number of times you told everyone you put the 'sing' in single? How you don't need anyone."

"I'm obviously a shitty wife, so another marriage is out. You and I could go on a trip or two together, but you also have Thomas. Ergo, I need to find a retirement buddy. Preferably a woman who wants to share a house of some sort. We could help each other keep track of our appointments and shit."

"How long have you been thinking about this?"

Uh-oh. Kick was well-versed in my kooky tendencies, but it must have been the first time I'd verbalized that train of thought. "Since your wedding, I suppose. It's not like it came together all at once," I said, trying to sound casual. "So a year-ish?"

I leaned into my mirror, catching sight of a wiry hair, and plucked it from my neck. It was the kind that showed up overnight, already two inches long and gave me witchy vibes.

The phone line stayed silent as I made my way back to the kitchen and poured another glass of wine. I didn't press Kick to talk. She was a thinker and purposeful advisor. When given the time to process, her wisdom was golden.

As I opened the door to my screen porch, she surprised me with a sniffing sound. "I'm sorry for being so self-focused."

Shit. "No, Kicky. I've always been team Thomas." I settled into my chaise, grateful for the late-summer breeze across my screened porch. "A retirement buddy will never replace you. Guess I'm thinking about preparing."

"You're anxious about it or it wouldn't have come up," Kick observed. "I can't believe you're giving up on finding your man person. I've always figured you held men at arm's length because of Joel, and today was a victory. Give it a few days. You'll feel better and might even finally find your prince."

"Maybe, but I doubt it." I took a pull from my wineglass and set it on the side table, watching the clouds change colors during the sunset. I chuckled at the idea of me with a prince. "It feels like I've kissed all the frogs in Raleigh and Oakville. Even licked some. They're just toads. Besides, I'm too old for a prince."

"There's always Chapel Hill or Durham. A doctor at one of the medical centers. A professor Thomas might know. A widowed king."

"Please… don't even." I chuckled. As usual, Kick lifted my spirit. "Besides, in my mind, Raleigh represented the whole triangle." I leaned back and closed my eyes, letting the breeze wash over my skin.

Then my phone beeped with an incoming call. "Hey, Kick, I have an incoming. If it's my dad, I need to take it."

We dropped our call, and I clicked over to the new one. Since my mom passed away last winter, we checked in on Wednesdays and Sundays at the minimum. With all the hulla-baloo, I'd forgotten about calling. But it wasn't my dad.

"Sparky, it's Blake. Look, I'm sorry to bother you and possibly make your evening worse, but your date's still here."

The clouds lost their pink hue and shifted into a deepening purple as the sun sank behind my neighbor's house. "And?"

A ragged sigh came through the line. "He moved to the bar after you left… Well, he's toasted now. My bartender tried to call him a cab, but he'd only give us your address, which set off my alarm bells. Did he mention where he's staying? Or do you want him delivered to your address? I caught enough to know he's from out of town."

Aggravated, I stomped back into the house. So much for relaxing. "Leave it to that idiot to assume he could spend the night," I muttered. "Can you hold him somewhere safe until I get there? I'll see if I can check him into the Marriot." It was the closest hotel to the Garage. Or the no-tell motel on the seedy side of town. One with extra roaches.

Chapter 4

Better Days

BLAKE

Despite her annoyed expression, Cyndi lit up my restaurant as she walked through the entrance. She smiled at Meredith, laughing with her escort as they made their way to the bar. It's why I'd called her Sparky. Despite her tiny size, Cyn exuded a feminine warmth while also carrying a take-no-prisoners air. I shifted my shoulders as I tracked her, shrugging off the knowledge that after three years, I still wanted her.

More casual than earlier, Cyndi strutted to the bar in jeans and a Pearl Jam T-shirt with a motorcycle jacket. Her platform gym shoes made me smile. I'd never known there were such things until her. I bet the woman wore platform slippers, not that I'd ever stayed the night with her to find out.

She found me watching her from the corner of the bar, and her brow cocked. "What's so funny?"

"Your shoes."

"What?" She lifted one to assess it. "They're comfortable."

"They're you."

She stuck her finger in my face, waving it. "Don't." Then she shook her head, like she was telling herself no. "Where's jerk face?"

I tipped my head up. "Sleeping on one of the sofas in my office."

Cyndi folded her arms over her chest, doing wicked stuff to Eddie Vedder. She'd cut the shirt neckline into a deep V. "What would it cost me to let him spend the night up there?"

"Would that I could, Spark." I drummed my fingers on the bar. "Would that I could." I'd slept in my office plenty of times before, but Cyndi didn't know about Olivia and me.

I blamed it on the overwhelm of seeing her, like the stress of it had been my last straw. With no plan or thought, I blurted like a dumbass, "Why'd you ghost me?"

She briefly flicked her wrist. "What are you talking about? I set you up with Al. He's the best around for established restaurants. I focus on start-ups now."

I narrowed my eyes at her, knowing that was a lie.

"Fine," she acquiesced, "I still take care of Kick, but she's like family."

Ouch. That stung at my real question, not to mention the scandal we were doing our best to smooth over. Movement of the bar staff stalled in my periphery. I leaned down toward Cyndi's ear and growled, "You mean Al, the man who's stolen hundreds of thousands from me? Risking my livelihood and my employees'. The feds are breathing down my neck because he fled the country and left me looking like a guilty schmuck? That Alan?" I didn't blame Cyndi, but she needed to know. He'd had access to my books because of her recommendation.

Cyndi stepped back as if I'd pushed her. "No!" Her hand flew to her mouth.

I clicked my tongue before biting my lip. It was such an embarrassing shit show, more words escaped me. I could only nod.

"Oh, Blake. I'm so sorry." Her demeanor crumbled with guilt, which I couldn't tolerate.

I shook my head and gestured toward the stairs. "Let's go get your husband settled somewhere."

Cyndi flinched and turned on her heel, her head and shoulders fallen, leaving me feeling like shit. I touched her shoulder right before she moved. "Hey, I'm sorry. That was uncalled for."

"As much as I hate to admit it, Joel was my husband. I'm the insecure, nitwit who fell for a guy like that." She took the first step.

I found her hand and squeezed it. "You were young. I'm sure he swept you off your feet." I looked up at the window wall of my office. Not that I could see in. It had a one-way film on the glass. "Guys like him always do that kind of shit."

Her gaze followed mine, eyes narrowing before turning back to me. "You never did."

For a second, my Cyndi came back. I wanted to tell her I'd take care of this guy and any other who'd hurt her—who'd put that haunted look in her eyes. I recognized her self-rebuke. But if I had baggage back when we were together, it was now tripled. A huge part of Cyndi's appeal had been her carefree spirit. She'd never let herself get tied down with my problems. Yeah, this was my shitty situation talking.

I looked over my shoulder to keep from saying something truly foolish and caught Meredith's eyes. I shook my head to reassure her all was okay, lying to myself as much as her.

Up in the office, Cyndi's ex was out cold. When we finally got enough coffee in him so he could stand, the guy nearly crushed Cyn. I jumped between them and threw the asshole's arm around my shoulders. "Guess we're going for a walk."

"Where?" He screeched the question as we made our way to the freight elevator in back.

"To the Marriot across the street. You're lucky the nice one is the closest."

"I want to go to Cynthia's," he whined as we stepped into the box.

Cyndi made a gagging noise, and I had to agree. "The lady says no."

She touched my arm and whispered, "Thank you."

I let out an exasperated exhale. I couldn't let her stumble around with this asshole. Not even fifty feet. He'd hurt her in this state. He clearly wouldn't care if he did.

Thirty minutes later, we stood in front of Cyndi's car parked at the curb. She had bought a room for Williams while I played personal leaning post to the man. On the way back, in the elevator, out on the warm sidewalk, we kept silent. My thoughts flew through me at the speed of light. Everything going on—work, my daughter, being on my own, screwing it all up… mostly work and how I needed to clear my name.

It was clear Cyndi's mind raced too. Her purse slid off her shoulder as she tipped her head back to the stars and said, "Please let that be the last of Joel Williams."

"Gotta say…" How would I put this? "It's odd that he still gets under your skin. When we were… you know." I cleared a seed of bitterness from my throat. "You didn't seem so affected by anyone."

Cyn bit her lip as she stared at me. "First, I'm over him. Thoroughly. For ever and ever. Amen. Second, maybe we have different definitions of what it means to be affected."

A couple who were regulars at the restaurant walked by and nodded to me. I barely acknowledged them back, my attention focused on Cyndi. My fingers ached to touch her since she'd done her little catwalk thing into the restaurant. I wanted to feel—no, hold her again. Let her body help me feel better. Ease the ache. But she'd made it clear that I wasn't the one. I didn't miss her annoyance at running into me earlier. At least she gave the gift of letting me know I'd been different from her ex. Better.

As desire warred with despair, I reached for Cyndi, then clenched my fist, keeping it between us. She opened her mouth, but I blurted, "Come back to work with me, Cyn. Help me clear my name. Please."

Chapter 5

Hello

Cyndi

It took a week to clear my schedule, yet it seemed like only minutes had passed when I found myself back in Blake's office, staring at his collection of Star Wars paraphernalia to avoid getting lost in his soulful eyes. There was an aspect of the man that had reminded me of a dog at a shelter labeled a troublemaker. When I looked in his eyes, I saw pain and a plea for hope.

"I figure Kramer left these files behind because he believed no one would understand them. Or to stick it to me." Blake had given me admin access to his bookkeeping system and other relevant software.

"Maybe both," I said, feeling awful for putting him on Alan Kramer's radar. Blake didn't deserve this. Neither did the other Triangle restaurants the man had stolen from—six in total over two years. Blake's part of it came to a little over $430,000.

A year into their association, Kramer recommended a new point-of-sale system. The fancy device housed software that deleted certain orders, creating a fraudulent sales record, and funneling the extra money to an account owned by Kramer and the software creator—his cousin, no less.

I scrolled through pages on the laptop Blake let me use. "I bet the actual books are with him." I pointed to an unusual set of numbers. "This already doesn't add up. My guess is they stashed the money in multiple places."

"What do you mean?"

I moved the laptop so we both could see the screen and pointed. "Here. These look like IBANs for international bank accounts, but they don't have country codes. He probably has those on another system."

His brow furrowed as he stared at the entries. "I don't use international banks."

I nodded. "Exactly."

"And?"

I stretched my arms over my head. This would take a while. "It means keep digging."

Blake slammed his fist on the desk, his expression part feral wolf, part that dog in pain. "We're lucky the AG and governor are regular customers. They're doing what they can to help me, but it can't look like favoritism either. The bottom line is my name was on those documents. I'm already making interest payments."

I slid my hand over Blake's, steadying his tapping fingers. "It'll help." Seeing the man so stressed cracked the part of my heart I'd hardened regarding him.

His hair had more silver in it than back then, and I figured this was the cause. Not that it looked bad, damn him. It was quite delicious to stare at, so I looked down at the screen.

Blake slumped some, the world on his shoulders. He was on the hook for over $700,000—more, if the district attorney wanted to make an example of him. I didn't think that was the case, even before Blake mentioned he was a patron. The authorities were more interested in Kramer and his cousin. The Feds were after them for income tax evasion and theft. But the owners were still responsible for the unpaid taxes. When money was involved, sympathy for the naive business owner only went so far.

"Did you called the lawyer I recommended?"

Blake's jaw flexed before giving me a friendly smile. "We're meeting this afternoon."

Two weeks later, I ended up working in the spare office next to Blake's. The Garage's new, legitimate point-of-sale system and accounting software setup was almost finished. Since there was only so much I could do from my home office, I had to finish on site. So here I sat, a few feet from Blake. I swear I heard every inhale he made and hoped it was calming him, considering how they distracted me.

The night he had helped me with Joel, Blake asked why I'd ghosted him. Thankfully, it was to deflect his question in the moment. How could I explain how he unsettled me. I still had to get through the forensic phase of this project. As hard as that would be, pretending Blake didn't get to me proved harder. Still, I felt like I owed him. Plus I kicked ass with this kind of stuff. It had nothing to do with any lingering feelings or wondering what might have happened if I hadn't freaked out three years ago. Besides, Blake was polite, grateful, and—thank God—distant since I came back.

I set my computer glasses on the desk and rubbed my eyes, the twinges of a headache coming on. An ice tea would restart my brain.

"Oh!"

I looked up at the startled voice. "Hello?"

Putting on my progressive frames made me start too. "Well, hello to you." A smile automatically stretched across my face at the pretty pixie staring at me. "Aren't you adorable? If not a little young to work here."

I wasn't an expert at kids, obviously, but the girl looked like she belonged in middle school.

She giggled at my question. "I come here after school and do homework until it's time to go home. Unless I have practice or go to a friend's instead."

"And I am using your desk, aren't I?" I waved my hand for her to come near. "I'll scoot over. You can pull up the chair from the corner. It won't be long. I'm almost done for the day. Would you like a drink? I was just about to get some tea." Now I was prattling on. To a child. Except there was something about her. Like a little angel had taken a moment to check up on me. Or my guilty conscious for the situation wouldn't shut up.

She laughed and held up a to-go cup that had been down by her thigh. "Aunt Meredith gave me a soda when I got here."

That still didn't sit well with me. "Speaking of... a restaurant seems like an odd place for after-school care. Are there more young people coming? I guess I could pack up, but I wanted to finish this piece of my project today. It's for the owner. And important." Why was I defending my actions to a girl? Again, with the guilt.

She tipped her head side to side in the way puppies stared at funny humans. Like they were trying to make sense of them.

"My dad is the owner," she said, as if that explained everything.

"You're..." The photos in Blake's office came to mind. The shelves running across the back wall, filled mostly with Star Wars figurines. Also, framed pictures of him with a baby, then a little girl and her mother. His daughter. "Olivia?" Her whiskey-brown eyes sparkled just like Blake's. With the same light that had made me panic three years prior. "Aren't you supposed to be like nine or something?"

She laughed as she set her drink on the desktop. "I was three years ago."

Right. I hadn't met Blake's daughter when we dated. He shared custody of her, so two weeks of the month were his daughter's and the other two had been mine. It had been wonderful to not worry about him smothering me. Then he asked me to meet his daughter. Olivia.

"Which explains why you're bigger than the girl in your dad's pictures." I clicked my parched tongue, desperate for that unsweet tea with lemon. With a shot of bourbon. Only, why did I care about meeting her now? Blake and I were just working together. We'd committed to stay in the friend zone on my first day back. "This must be your father's part of the month. Except… don't you go to your mom's after school?"

Olivia dropped her backpack and stared at me, her chin quivering fiercely like she was fighting to steel herself. She quietly answered, "I live with my dad all the time now." A tear dripped onto her cheek. She viciously wiped it away. "Momma… she died last month."

"She…" Oh shit. This poor baby. Olivia sniffed hard, a tell before a full-on sob, which I knew well. All my defenses dropped. "I'm so sorry. I met her once. She was very nice."

Olivia's breathing hitched. "She had asthma."

Well, hell. "That must have been so scary." I thought there was medicine for it.

She fiercely brushed another tear. "I also have asthma."

I stood as she sniffed again. More tears dropped, and I held out my arms to her. I wouldn't let her crumble in front of me. Motherhood might not have been for me, but I wasn't cold-hearted. She had to be at the height of grieving. "Would a hug help?"

Olivia stepped into my hold and set her head on my shoulder. She was already almost my height. As I wrapped my arms around her slight form, her first sob broke free.

"I'm so sorry. Let it all out." She cried for a while as I rubbed her back. "It's not fair, is it?"

"No," Olivia answered as she shook her head against me, voice a little hoarse.

"Do you have an inhaler with you?"

I felt her nodding on my shoulder as she sniffled.

"You know your dad will make sure you have the medicine you need, right?" Suddenly I understood exactly how much weighed on Blake. He was a full-time single parent now. Mentally I took it upon myself to make sure he came out of this fiasco financially better than he went into it.

"I guess." Olivia's cries turned into whimpers.

It was hard enough losing my mother last winter, but she'd at least lived a long and happy life. At the funeral, even though everyone was sad, there was a celebratory aspect of the day. I couldn't imagine what it would have been like to bereave at twelve.

"From what I know about your father, you are always at the front of his thoughts. He's going to make sure you grow into a healthy, happy-go-lucky girl. Okay?" Another nod. I pushed Olivia back enough to wipe her hair off her face. "I hate you had to learn about life's pains so young. Have you been holding your tears in all day?"

"I s'pose." Her shoulders raised on a huge, ragged sigh. "I don't know why today was so hard."

"Did somebody say something rude? Sometimes kids can be dumb and don't realize they're being mean. Grown-ups can also be guilty of that, to be honest."

"No, not really." Olivia expelled several hitches as she sighed. "There's a mother-daughter fashion show next month. It's a fundraiser. Since my mom was a baker, she used to lead the refreshment committee. This week's newsletter asked for a new parent volunteer."

Well, shit. What to do now? Olivia bit her lip, like she was trying to hold back another round of tears. I squeezed her hand and rubbed the top of it with my thumb. A futile attempt at support.

My best friend, Kick, would know how to help. "That sounds tough. Not that you ever need a reason to grieve. The process works itself out in its own time. I can tell you this… these moments will jump out at you many more times. It's totally normal when they do."

The corner of Olivia's mouth tipped up, accepting my words. She opened her mouth to speak but was interrupted by a man clearing his throat. I exhaled in relief, thinking Olivia needed him more than me. That was immediately followed by panic as I feared how Blake would react to my trying to counsel his daughter. Sure, I was close to my best friend's kids and supported them through similar circumstances. But they were stuck with me. Otherwise, I didn't hang out with kids and didn't want to overstep.

I jumped back a step, certain I'd crossed a line. "Blake… sorry. We were just—"

Olivia stepped into her father's side like a little magnet when he held out an arm for her. As he kissed her head and rubbed her arm, his eyes stayed on me. I relaxed when he mouthed thank you.

"How long were you standing there?" I asked, running a shaky hand through my hair.

Blake tipped Olivia's chin up to meet his gaze. "Long enough to hear about the fundraiser. Sorry about that, Sparrow. Want me to see if the restaurant's baker can help?"

She gave her father a sweet, sad smile. "No. It's probably best to let another family take over now. Not that they'll ever make anything as tasty as Momma's."

Blake returned a devilish smile. "Bet they'll bring store-bought treats."

I pretended to gag, which made her giggle. He pulled Olivia in again, wrapping both arms around her. My heart flipped at the sight. I'd always known Blake was an attentive dad. Seeing the proof up close made my rusty, nonfunctioning ovaries ache. Not that it mattered. I was back for business only.

"Listen, Liv, I spoke with Mrs. Page this morning," Blake said. "She'll pick you up in an hour and take you home. You'll have dinner with her. Then you two will go back to our condo. Mrs. P. plans to stay with you until I get home. How's that sound?"

Olivia narrowed her eyes. "It sounds like I have a babysitter."

Blake turned away from her, a look of exhaustion on his face. "What if we call her what she is—a caring neighbor?" Olivia scrunched her nose and stepped out of her father's hold. Blake tried again. "Come on. You'll help each other. Mrs. Page has her friends and hobbies, but she misses the mothering gig, you know? Since Mr. Page passed and her daughters live in different cities, she's lonely. Frankly, I'm afraid she'll spoil the shit out of you. You do like her, right?" Blake grimaced as he asked the question.

Olivia rolled her eyes. "Sure, but—"

"I'll be working late for a stretch, Sparrow. There are issues here that"—Blake raised his hands—"I swear you don't need to hear about the boring details, but they require my attention. I can't focus on them if you're home alone."

Olivia folded her arms, throwing her weight onto her hip. "What if I want to go to Sofia's house after school?"

"Text me and Mrs. Page." He pulled his phone out of his pocket. "I'll make a group chat now. You're old enough for some freedom, but it comes in stages, honey." He finished typing and snapped his fingers. "Oh, Mrs. P. also agreed to take you to riding lessons, if you're still interested. Apparently, her daughter used to ride at the stable you mentioned. Carol and the owner are still friends."

Olivia lit up at the words, and I snorted a laugh. Girls and horses. Some things never changed. Growing up in rural Michigan, I began lessons as soon as I walked. We had a barn on our property and three horses as part of our menagerie. Both Bradys looked at me curiously, so I shrugged. "Sounds like a great gig for you both. Besides, falling asleep up here, only to have to wake up, go home, and fall back to sleep will be a pain. You don't want to do that every night."

"Exactly," Blake said.

Olivia bit her lip. "I suppose." She wrapped her hand around a messy braid. "It is hard on my hair."

"So…" Blake raised an eyebrow. "Can we try it for a month?"

She raised her eyebrow with the same mischievous lift as her father's. I ducked my head to hide a smile.

"You said Mrs. P. will make dinner?"

"That and then some. If I were a betting man, I'd lay money on her spoiling you big time." Blake moved to the front of the desk and leaned against the edge. "She's excited about it." He winked at Olivia. "You've hooked another one under your spell."

That was easy to believe. I'd been in a room less than fifteen minutes with Blake's daughter, and I was already thinking of ways to make her smile again.

Blake pulled me back to reality when he said, "Go study in my office, Sparrow. I need to speak with Ms. Sendaydiego."

Chapter 6

All the Small Things

Blake

I watched my daughter disappear into my office, forcing my heart rate to slow. My protective instincts had jumped into overdrive the second I heard her sobbing. I ran up the stairs, ready to protect my little girl. Like a gut punch, it hit me that her tears came from grief. Then my pulse raced for another reason. Not for the first time, I wanted to throttle Gianna, Olivia's mother. If only she'd told me she'd lost her healthcare. Hell, I would've married her if needed to put her on mine.

Finding Cyndi comforting Olivia floored me. Her ease with Liv's tears was a reminder of what a shit I was with feelings. I'd been doing anything and everything to make my daughter's tears stop. Cyn instinctively knew it was best to let her cry.

As expected, you screwed up your business, and you'll wreck your daughter by the time she's grown.

I shook off the old man's voice in my head and willed myself to settle down. It was easier after witnessing how much Olivia's tears had helped her. Did that mean she was afraid to grieve around me? She tended to hold it in around me until they burst forth. Message received, Sparrow.

"Thank—" I stopped when I noticed Cyndi wasn't paying attention. She was staring at her laptop screen, lost in thought, a grimace on her face. Please don't cry too. I cleared my throat, making her jump.

"Oh! Right." She slammed the computer closed. "What do you need?"

I chuckled and play-knocked on the doorjamb. "You texted me, remember?"

She shook herself, like her mind held her in a far-off place.

I pointed toward my office, adding, "I'd forgotten about Olivia coming here after school." I tapped my head. "Having a hell of a time keeping it all straight in here."

Cyndi's hard exterior softened. Since the Garage had become her client again, she'd gone overboard to stay distant and aloof. Given the unresolved circumstances of our breakup, I understood. Or were they only unresolved for me? Watching her let my daughter in made me… unsettled. You could add on peeved. But I'd agreed to our friends-only status to save my restaurant. My people.

She waggled her phone. "I bet her momma kept track with a calendar app. From what I know of a young teen's life, no parent can be expected to keep track of a kid's comings and goings in their head."

I scratched the back of my neck. "Don't I know it?"

"I could ask my friend, Kick, what she used to manage her kids, but the calendar on your phone is probably a good start."

"Yeah." I pulled my phone out of my pocket. "I'll check it out."

"Anyway…" Cyndi opened the computer, and as quickly as she logged back in, the hard edge returned. "I think I found something you'll like."

I leaned against the edge of the desk as she spun the laptop around. "My radar says Kramer's in the Caribbean, but we need to bring in a pro to be sure." She tapped the desk and grinned triumphantly. "Fortunately for you, I know the biggest, bad-ass-iest investigator in town."

My brow furrowed as I studied the screen. "Why the Caribbean?"

Cyndi held up a finger before giving me a sassy look. "First, it's awesome. Who wouldn't want to hide out on a beach, drinking rum punch? Second, several Caribbean countries don't have extradition treaties with the US. If you were in a hurry to get out of dodge but had also done all this bullshit to concoct a posh life for yourself, where would you set it up?"

I shrugged. "Somewhere beachy, yeah."

"You do get it." She highlighted a line from the restaurant's credit card statement. "His last charge with one of your cards was at a gas station in Florida. It's across the street from a marina."

"How do you know it's—"

"Google maps." A bright smile crossed Cyn's face. She bounced in her seat as if she was dancing to a song in her head.

"You think he chartered a boat?"

"No way would he stay in the states when the Feds are on him."

I nodded. "The cops said as much. That's why their hands are tied."

She pointed at the file on the screen. "Then there's my third point. These numbers keep repeating and only after he installed the old point-of-sale software. They look like reverse IBANs, if that makes sense. Like he made a code, albeit a simple one."

"They're international bank account numbers?"

"I'm just not sure which banks he used. That's why we need Angel Security to take over the forensic accounting." She clicked through more pages with the suspicious numbers high-lighted.

Cyndi caught me grinning when she glanced back up. "What?"

"You said 'we.'"

"I promised to get you out of this mess." Her gaze darted out the door, telling me she was thinking of my daughter. "Now that I know the full extent of what you're carrying..." She bit her lip. Seriously, woman, don't cry. "Against my better judgment," she said, then whispered, "I'm in."

A shiver washed over me like I'd been hit. Against her better judgment? "What did I do to you?"

Cyndi winced like I'd hit her. Something I'd never done. "Nothing."

"Argh." I growled while walking to the window wall. Would it help to dig up the past, or should I be grateful someone else was on my team? Not that I wanted Cyn to take on my burden. The dumbass who had trusted too much was me, letting Alan Kramer butter me up with all his bro talk. I believed he was my buddy and had my best interest. Like a sucker.

"You'll never amount to anything." Shut up, old man. I couldn't let my adoptive father be right about my loser status. Despite his death a few years back, I still had to prove him wrong.

Downstairs, the floor crew made last-minute table adjust-ments for a large party. This was all for them. And Liv. Since Cyndi had come on the team, the burden had been eased. That's all that mattered. I exhaled, feeling fifty pounds lighter.

I walked back to her and bent down to reexamine the screen over her shoulder. Before I could stop them, irrational emotions flooded me. Guess I did need to do some digging. So I stuck my foot in my mouth. "Why'd you ghost me?"

Cyndi shoved me like she needed the distance even if only

a few inches. My frown shifted into a grin with the idea I could wiggle under her skin again. Good.

"How the hell is ghosting the term for a breakup? A ghost is someone who sticks around when they're supposed to be gone. Therefore, I didn't ghost you."

"We never had a breakup." I made air quotes as I glared at her.

In a calm, indifferent tone, she said, "I admit to disappearing." She spread her fingers in front of her. "Poof. But it needed to happen."

I pointed at her. "There. What happened? Is it so terrible that I want to know why?"

"Fine," she said, stiffening her spine as she rolled the chair back. "We were a dead end from the start." She huffed and ran her fingers through her hair. "When I married Joel, I became Cyndi Williams. You know, like the actress from the seventies sit-com? I watched reruns long after it ended. Anyway, the jokes were never-ending. No way would I put up with being Cyndi Brady for the rest of my life." She vigorously shook her head. "No Blake. Just… no."

I jumped like I'd been shocked. "Are you fucking kidding right now? Did I mention marriage? Ever?" Not to mention who watches that show anymore? Then again, since I knew who she referenced, anyone older probably did too.

I ran my hands over my face, not believing her for one minute. I'd asked Cyndi to go to the North Carolina State Fair with Olivia and me. She'd always been up for an adventure, so I figured the rides, animals, food, and such were a shoo-in. Liv had been nine and in that golden age where she could go on all day without a nap and still believed her dad was cool. I'd envisioned a great time. Cyndi didn't have the decency to say no. She just never returned my text. Or the next twenty. Not to mention the calls.

I charged back to the window wall, furious with both of us.

Why couldn't she be straight with me—then or now? Why couldn't I let it go?

Watching the dinner crowd didn't help calm my temper this time. After shoving my hands in my pockets to keep from punching the glass, I counted to ten. All right, maybe I wondered if we had the potential to be a family back then. I might have hoped Cyndi would fall in love with my amazing daughter and vice versa. With no rush though. It was enough to be excited about the possibility.

Hell, I hardly knew Cyn when she split. I just knew I liked her. A lot. Really liked who I was with her. For the first time in my memory, I'd had a goal that hadn't involved proving a point to my old man. Apparently I ended up not being enough for Cyndi either.

When my breathing slowed, I said, "The name's not even mine. Why would I care if you changed yours?"

A few sniffles came from her direction. "I'm sorry. You didn't deserve that. Forget my shitty reasons."

"Are you sure there wasn't more?" I looked over my shoulder. "Hell, if you had just taken my calls. Left a message or something. Do you have any idea what I was thinking? At first I wondered if you were in an accident."

She bit her lip and nodded yes, her eyes shimmering. She blinked several times as she stared off again, making me feel like an ass. So I stopped pressing. God knew I didn't need another thing on my plate.

She sniffed like she was crying, and I pressed my eyes shut. "Shit."

Relief spread over me when Cyndi cleared her throat and asked, "Give me time, Blake. Please drop it for now. I'm here, and we're doing great as friends. Can it be enough?"

"Sure." I spun around, resolved to be true to my word. We were better off friends. I placed a smile on my face and walked back to her. Offering my hand, we shook like we were making a gentleman's deal. I did my best to school my expression when our hands clasped. Nothing gentlemanly raced through my thoughts or my body. I ignored it. I would need to do that a lot for this to succeed. "Let's get my damn money back."

"Mmm." I closed my eyes and savored the flavors bouncing around my mouth. They reminded me of the good part of growing up. Mrs. Page had gone all out for her first dinner with Olivia. Grilled pork chops over red cabbage, topped with homemade chutney, and sweet potatoes on the side. The cabbage was cooked with champagne vinegar, balancing the sweetness of the chutney. Add in the smoked char of the meat… well, I almost begged her for the recipe. It would fit perfectly with the high-end Southern food Felix made at the Garage.

My chef and partner, Felix Jackson, won culinary awards and was working toward a James Beard. His kitchen fed me well, but I'd been too busy to eat earlier. Thankfully, Mrs. P. made extra for me. I bit into another forkful and sighed contentedly, my shoulders loosening as I swallowed the bite. "I should have hired you in my kitchen."

Mrs. Page smiled behind her cup of chamomile tea. "Flatterer."

"Really. This dish gives the Garage heavy competition."

She blushed as she took her cup to the dishwasher, placing it on the top rack. I hadn't expected her to do the dishes, but the sink was spotless. The machine was only waiting for my plate.

"You know my cleaning lady will run that, right?"

She waved me off. "It's full now. Let her unload it."

"You didn't need to do all this, Mrs. P." It felt a lot like taking advantage.

She glared at me like I was still a young teen. "Call me

Carol. Please. Besides, I had so much fun doing this that I feel guilty about taking your money. It's not like I need it. I'm a Page." Her late husband had been from one of Raleigh's founding families, making her old-money rich. "When I moved into my condo, do you know how thrilled I was to learn Gracie Brady's boy lived two doors down? You told me if I need any help…" She bit her lip. "I've never lived on my own, and having you close made me feel safe."

I ducked my head. "I'm glad." Our little neighborhood looked out for each other. Still, we ended up in an amicable stand-off now. My gratitude for her eagerness to bail me out melded with the rest of my stress, and suddenly I was shaking my head to fend off a flood of emotion.

"It did my heart good to see how well you've done. What a fine man you became, despite… you know. But Blake, dear…" Carol sat down and touched my arm in a motherly way. "Don't take this the wrong way, it's just you don't look good. Talk to me."

Well, bless her heart. I chuckled under my breath at my joke, then took a chance. "Gia's death isn't the only thing weighing on me." After filling her in on the theft and my part in it, along with my assistant manager's accident, I looked up into eyes filled with… forgiveness? Understanding? I couldn't tell. "Anyway, filling in for Jay is one thing, but I have got to find a way out from under this legal cloud. My staff doesn't deserve the instability, and neither does Liv. If her mother were here, I'd probably ask her to take my weeks this month so I could get through it as fast as possible." I grimaced at my run of confessions. It sounded whiny to me. "Anyway, you're a life-saver. Can't thank or pay you enough."

She slapped my hand. "It's my honor, especially now that I know the whole story. Thank you for seeking me out, and don't you dare pay me. Like I said, money isn't my problem. Boredom is."

I rubbed my temple. "How do I not pay you? You're—"

"Pretend I am family."

I would have, happily. Carol was the opposite of what I knew family to be.

"Speaking of… Where's your mother in all this? If one of my daughters ended up in your situation, wild horses wouldn't keep me away."

I waved off the sentiment. "Ma'am isn't like you. She's… she was different when I was little. Pops, though…" A memory resurrected from the deep. My mother cheered me up with a sucker after scraping my knee. I still had the scar from falling off the monkey bars while my adoptive father played baseball. He knocked the candy out of my mouth, taking a baby tooth with it. You don't reward boys for clumsiness, Gracie, especially one like him. My mother kept her head down and said nothing. It ended up being her MO with my old man, but I couldn't blame her. Not anymore.

"Your father could be difficult."

I cocked an eyebrow at her unnecessary restraint. Mr. Page had been Pop's friend. Carol was the second Mrs. Page, who entered my parents' orbit when I was in middle school. While my mother kept herself buttoned up tight and at least a decade out of date the way my father wanted, Carol had always been a modern woman. She scandalously wore shorts on hot days. My mother and her friends gossiped about that and more. In hindsight, Carol's youthfulness probably threatened her. Not to mention her ability to have kids.

"Anyway, my mother doesn't like leaving the Villages anymore. Living with the old man's outbursts all those years… routines make her feel safe." While my mother hated leaving Florida, I despised visiting. Someone always called the police on me.

I stretched my arms over my head. Memories had a way of tightening my back. "She doesn't know about the restaurant.

Ma'am freaked so badly in the lead-up to Gianna's funeral that I caved and told her to stay home despite Liv and I needing her support."

"I wondered why she didn't come."

"You were invaluable, thank you. And you're right about Liv needing a grandmother figure. If you don't mind the term. I hate being gone from her so much now. But——"

"Bless your heart." Carol squeezed my hand. "You're doing your best. Above and beyond, if you ask me. I would love for Olivia to think of me as another grandma." She chuckled softly. "I live for the day one of my girls has a baby."

I moved to the sink and rinsed my plate, making sure my back stayed turned to keep from seeing the sympathy in Carol's eyes. It was overwhelming. After letting my guard down with Cyndi this afternoon—and coming out covered in emotional garbage—my nerves were frayed. Still, there was something else on weighing on me.

"In the middle of all this, I'm searching for my birth mother," I mumbled, my eyes staying on the sink. It felt good to share it with Carol. "Or I was. The search has stalled." I figured I might let it go. My Sparrow could be enough. She was my world.

"Does Gracie know?"

I shook my head as I turned around, pressing my hands into the counter behind me. "Talk about her freak-outs."

Carol sighed. Her face filled with understanding. "Carrying another burden then."

"Perhaps." I tried to look as factual as I sounded. "The social worker discovered some things about me." I gave her a sarcastic grin. "I was born in Arizona and not in Western North Carolina like I'd been told. Then her trail ran cold. I took a DNA test in case a relative happened to, so… who knows?" I shrugged.

"Oh?" Carol's eyes widened. "Did you find anything?"

I let my head hang as my gaze fell to the floor. "Nothing worth reaching out for." I blew out a long breath. "I had to press pause on looking further since the fraud and… Gia."

"You're being too hard on yourself." Carol slapped the table for emphasis. "You are a fantastic father. And man."

I bent toward the dishwasher and set my plate on the bottom rack, pausing before adding soap. Carol's words were so unfamiliar to my ears they grated. I instinctively waited for the sarcastic punch line, but it never came.

She continued as I hit the Start button. "I don't understand why no one woman has snatched you up."

A vision of my time with Cyndi came to mind. Except the interest hadn't gone both ways.

"In my day, women would've fallen over themselves for a man like you. Ambitious… providing… devoted father…" She popped her eyebrows as I returned to my seat. "Handsome as the dickens."

I scoffed at her comment. "In high school, the girls who liked me did it to piss off their parents. Surely you understand that."

"I do. Sorry, dear." Carol settled her chin on her hand, looking guilty, which I hadn't intended. "My Mellie's dating a young Indian man… South-Asian-wise, you know? I mean—"

I raised my hand and smirked. "I get it."

She flushed a deep pink. "The point is… I only care about how he treats her. Does that make sense?"

One hundred percent, except… I leaned into my hand and dug my fingers into my temple. Bringing up Carol's daughter made me think about my little girl dating. My head wanted to explode.

"Olivia hasn't had the same issues as I did." No one ostracized or bullied her for being Native American. Of course, she was also half Italian. I chuckled. "One teacher made the wrong assumptions when she started school and greeted her in

Spanish for a month." I wondered if it would happen again in high school since Liv's current school went through eighth grade.

Carol had mercy on me and changed the subject. "I can't wait to take Olivia to her riding lesson next week."

"That's right." I'd forgotten about my daughter's latest obsession. Carol's mercy extended to Liv's newest extracurricular activity. "At least she's over ballet. I could never get the hang of a tight bun."

"That's what I mean by devoted." Carol lifted her brow to prove her point, like making crappy buns qualified me for the father of the year.

How could I not give everything to my little girl? From the first time I held her, she filled the gaping hole in my heart that longed for roots. Despite my terror and cluelessness at how to be a dad, she stopped crying when I held her and cooed. Her perfect mouth opened like a little bird's when she looked up at me. That's where the nickname came from.

A child is a man's hope for the future. I didn't realize until then that my daughter would also be the link to my past. As she grew, Sparrow's features became more like the woman I had dreamed about for as long as I could remember. Maybe she wasn't an illusion like Ma'am claimed, but a memory.

"Momma!" Liv's keening cracked the quiet along with my soul. I froze. The irony of it happening right when I was thinking about the woman who might have been my mother made a chill race up my spine.

Carol touched my shoulder. "Is this common?"

I held my head and nodded.

"Olivia was weepy at bedtime," she whispered. "Rubbing her back let her relax and drift off. She wants reassurance she's not alone."

The cries turned into whimpers. Still, I couldn't move. It was like she was an infant again and Gianna criticized anything I did. Carol gave my shoulder a squeeze. "Go to her, honey. Pat her back and tell her you're here."

I looked at her. "That's enough?" Olivia wasn't a newborn anymore. She suffered real world problems now.

"It's everything, dear."

Chapter 7

Cult of Personality

"Stop grinning like that." Kick's eyes darted around her coffee shop in her mother hen way before giving me her full attention. "It's kinda creepy."

"Maybe I missed your face." I licked a bit of foam at the corner of my mouth as I set down my cappuccino. Nobody knew their way around an espresso machine like the crew at the Perked Cup, and it had been too long since I'd indulged. It helped that drinks were always free given my best friend was the owner. Plus I missed her. After making big strides at the Garage in the past week, I could afford a few hours of Cyndi time.

I tugged at the beaded lotus drop earring in my left ear. I had made them for my mother's birthday, but she passed first. "It's also good to take a break from—"

"I knew it." Kick cut me off, grinning wider than I was. "Lightning strikes twice. When you mentioned working with the Garage again, I knew sparks would fly between you and Blake Brady." She snapped her fingers in rhythm.

I cringed. "Please don't say his last name." When I told Blake about my Brady Bunch hangup, it wasn't a total fib. Hell, the show still aired on cable.

She singsonged and shimmied. "Be-cause-you-want-him. Admit it."

Want was the problem. I furrowed my brow at Kick and grunted. Her manager, Deana—a master multitasker—heard us as she served a customer and chuckled deeply from her belly. It was such a warm sound that it always made me smile—even coming at my expense.

"Blake and I agreed to be colleagues. No more. In fact, I'm on a man hiatus. After the run-in with Joel, I'm all about Cyndi." I batted my lashes playfully to throw her off. "Putting the sing in single again."

Kick waved her hand in front of my face. "Hello? Who are you? And what have you done with Ms. Sendaydiego? It was obvious he got to you back then." She grabbed the ice tea she kept on the back counter and took a pull from the straw. "It's like you're trying to be me or something."

I lifted my shoulder nonchalantly and sipped from my cup. "Probably the 'or something.'"

"Right," Kick drawled skeptically. Her gaze continued to follow the action in the dining room. It was a leftover habit from some difficulties she'd lived through a couple of years past.

"It's all good, chica. I only mean it's fun dating myself. When I find a moment alone, that is."

The truth was, the more time I spent at the Garage, the harder it became to stay away. Not only did I have to fix Blake's problem, hanging out with the restaurant staff was like having coworkers again. I often left the transom part of the window wall open in order to hear the bustle below as I worked.

Normally, I did the bulk of my work in my home office. Back when Blake and I dated, I didn't spend as much time with him as I had these past few weeks. It surprised me how much I liked being friends with him. It gave me hope we could keep our working relationship going.

"Anyway, Blake's new system should be running by Halloween. It's like what you're using, except you know… bigger." I spread my hands wide to show the difference. "Plus, if I finish on time, I can spend my birthday with Tatay."

We met in our first year of college, when we were assigned to each other as roommates. She quickly learned some Tagalog words and phrases I'd grown up with. By the end of our first week together, she knew Tatay meant my dad. Her openness to a culture I had barely known was a big part of why we grew close. In fact, she tagged along to my first Filipino American Student Group meeting on campus so I wouldn't feel alone.

Kick stuck her lip out in a pout. "You won't be here for the party."

If she'd been closer, I would've smacked her. Instead, I imitated her mom glare. "I can't believe you still do them." The Perked Cup almost went out of business after a spoiled man-child sabotaged her annual Halloween party. All because he was obsessed with her daughter, Rachel, who had politely turned him down, even after she broke up with her boyfriend. Suffice it to say, the kid didn't take kindly to hearing no.

"That was two years ago. We're stronger than ever in the community now."

"True. It's just…" I finished my cappuccino. "The memories still give me PTSD. I can't believe it doesn't trigger you."

Kick folded her arms and clicked her tongue. "You weren't even here. You ditched me, remember?"

As if I'd forget. "That might be the problem." I'd been

having my own party with a guy who seemed to have potential. Big surprise… he didn't. The signs of perimenopause had just started, and I wanted a distraction. So I'd blown off Kick's party. Not that I could've stopped the chaos, but I still felt like I'd let her down.

This year would be my forty-ninth birthday, and I was grateful to be alive. I guess losing my mother had shaken some sense into me. I also had a feeling my father was hiding something. When we FaceTimed, he always said everything was fine, but his body language didn't concur. I feared the loss of my mom affected him physically. Unfortunately, Tatay was also a retired family doctor. When it came to his health, he wouldn't listen to me.

I changed the subject. "Anyway, my cousin, Berno, thinks Tatay's struggling. I set up appointments with all his doctors so I can go with him and assess how he's really doing."

"Well, shit." Kick swept a curl off her forehead as she ducked her chin. "Sorry for being selfish. It's a great idea. If there's anything I can do to help, let me know." She snapped her fingers. "Want me to see if the jet's free?"

My earrings bumped my neck as I shook my head. How Kick's life had changed in two years. Her first husband had been an NFL star receiver, yet she still had never uttered the words our jet until Thomas Harrison. Kick's new husband shared one with his business partners. I waggled my phone in the air. "Already bought my ticket. Thanks though."

"Certainly. Next time ask me first. You'll probably go back to Michigan more now, and the jet can land at municipal airports. You won't need to drive so far like with a commercial airport."

"True. Thanks, chica."

"Anytime. Seriously. You're family." Kick finished her tea and put the glass in the dirty dish box. "Ooh, it's almost five o'clock. Will you please pick tonight's song? I'm out of ideas."

The Perked Cup—well, Kick—had strict study hours from three to five so the kids who hung out after school could do their homework. She always played classical music during that time because of an article she'd read about how it improved cognitive function. At five, Kick queued up a lively song and encouraged the kids to dance and shake out their cobwebs, so to speak. They loved it, even when she played "old" songs, like an early 2000s song—insert eye roll.

Before I could say more, the café door chimed and in walked Olivia Brady with her caretaker, Mrs. Page. I blinked to make sure it wasn't an illusion. "Why, it's Miss Olivia." She saw me and ran into my open arms for a hug. "Hey, gorgeous."

I looked over her head and smiled at Mrs. Page before extending my right hand. "Mrs. Page, right? I'm Cyndi." My grin widened as I looked back at Olivia. "I'm Mr. Brady's accountant."

"Hello, Cyndi. Call me Carol, dear." She shook my hand with a steady grip and a warm smile. Despite her blond pixie cut's somewhat disheveled appearance, her hazel eyes beamed. I attributed that to hanging out with the young girl next to me. Liv glided over to the register, and Carol bent down toward me, adding, "Thank you for helping Blake. I hate what that horrible man did to him."

I hadn't realized he'd shared his situation with anyone else. The Blake I knew always kept his cards close to the vest. I leaned closer and said, "I promise he'll get out of it better than ever."

"If there's anything I can do…"

I looked at Olivia, letting her know she was doing a whole lot already. My shoulders surprised me by relaxing. Discovering Blake kept another confidant eased some stress I'd been holding.

Carol and Olivia placed their orders, then sat on stools to

my left. I'd been planning to leave and check in with another client, but not anymore. Kick must have picked up on it because she slid a glass of iced water in front of me.

"What brings you two in?" I asked.

"Car trouble." Carol pointed out the window. "We made it inside the parking lot, thank goodness. Then this one saw the café sign and suggested we finished waiting for her father inside."

Olivia sipped on her Italian soda. "I finished my homework in the car, but then I had to pee." She turned her head from side to side. "Speaking of…" I pointed out the hallway with the restrooms, and Liv trotted off, shouting, "Thank you!" That girl was a ray of sunshine when her cloud of grief cleared. I hoped her new riding lessons helped with that.

I introduced Kick to Carol. We made small talk while my bestie filled another order.

"Betsy is my neighbor," she told Carol. "In fact, my husband and I board our horses at her stable."

"Ooh, which ones?" Olivia asked as she slid back onto her stool.

"Thomas has a feisty black rogue with a star here." Kick pointed to her forehead as if showing where the white mark was. "His name's Eddie. I have a sweet palomino named Anabelle."

"I rode Anabelle!" Liv was so excited she bounced on her stool. "And I brushed her."

Kick leaned down and reached for something under the counter as she gave Olivia a motherly smile. "I'm so glad. She's perfect for new riders." She straightened, holding her trusty bottle of cleaner.

Carol spoke as she typed on her phone. "Your horse has a nice temperament."

"She does." Kick pulled a clean cloth from under the counter, sprayed one side, and wiped as she spoke to us. "It makes her wonderful to ride, though the real reason we picked her was for my husband's horse. As nice as Anabelle is with kids, she won't take any guff from that scoundrel."

"Y'all talking about me?" Thomas asked, a smirk firmly set on his face as he rounded the corner from the back hallway.

"Might as well be," Kick muttered through a grin as she tracked his path. Thomas made his way behind the counter and kissed her on the cheek. "We were describing your horse," she explained.

"Ed's no scoundrel." Kick scoffed at Thomas's mock defense. "He can't help it if he likes your hair."

She touched the base of her skull like it still hurt. "He bites at it."

I never understood how Kick's wild mane of soft brown curls could be mistaken for hay, but along with braiding her hair, I had recommended wearing a cowboy hat in lieu of a riding helmet. It was a trick I learned growing up around horses.

"I remember him," Liv said. "I walked close to his stall, and he nipped at my hair too." Her hand moved to the back of her head.

"This is Olivia, and she's taking lessons at Betsy's place," Kick explained to Thomas. "She road Anabelle."

"A new equestrian?" he asked. "How nice."

Liv beamed. "YesIt'sBig!"

"Uh-oh. You're awfully young for high school speak." We all laughed at Kick's term for the way teenagers talk in squished sentences. She swore each of her three kids had picked it up the first week of ninth grade. "Let me guess... you have a teenaged brother or sister?"

"No—" I started, but Liv interrupted.

"Well, my best friend's sister goes to Raleigh Central. We've been besties since preschool."

"I knew it," Kick said, looking at the girl with motherly

warmth. She had a way of doing that with all the kids who frequented her café.

A new customer came in, and Thomas slid over to the register. "Hey," Kick protested.

"Stay with the ladies, darlin'." He made a shooing motion with his hands. "I've got this. In fact, grab another tea and take a minute."

Kick checked her phone and grimaced. She scanned the dining room as she harrumphed.

"What's wrong?" I asked her.

"It's almost time for the five-o'clock dance, and we never picked out a song." Her eyes narrowed expectantly as she leaned toward me.

I raised my hands as I shrugged, like I was trying to give back a chore. "What are the kids even into these days?"

A group of girls at a large table erupted in laughter, catching our attention. Kick tipped her head as she regarded them. "Believe it or not, they want eighties and nineties movie tunes." She bounced her wedding ring finger on the counter, making a little tapping noise as she thought. "What's the song from the movie you loved? You know, with the boom box guy?"

"Seriously?" I propped my chin on my hand. "You mean 'In Your Eyes' from Say Anything?" I sighed. My mind went back to the night I saw it for the first time at a theater in Northern Virginia. Joel and I were engaged. "I was dumb enough to think Joel was like Lloyd." It turned out they had nothing in common.

"Oh right." Kick's nose scrunched. "Not very danceable, is it?"

"What's this?" Carol asked.

I shifted back to include Carol and Olivia in our huddle. "We were talking about one of the most romantic movies from the eighties, Say Anything." I sighed again, reflexively. Back then, I wanted to live the film and the song. "It wasn't demeaning, like so many other teen movies from then." I continued, filling my audience in on the story of the smart girl catching the eye of the creative, worldly boy. How they overcame their obstacles and grabbed their happily-ever-after. In hindsight, the end was more of a beginning, and I wasn't so sure about them anymore.

This time everyone sighed wistfully. Olivia added, "Lloyd sounds like my dad."

I tossed the visual around in my head. The kid had a point. Could have been why he came so close to my third rail when we were together. By then, I knew the soul-consuming love that Lloyd and Diane inspired only happened in fiction. Reality was… well, reality was Joel Williams. It drained while giving nothing in return. Taking every drop you had until you were dead inside.

I snapped my fingers. "You want a party song, right?" Kick nodded. "What about 'Cult of Personality'? It's on the sound-track and a proper headbanger."

Kick's eyes lit up. "Nice. Love the message. Yeah."

"What's a headbanger?" Olivia made a face at us.

I did a double take, my eyes wide in disbelief. "Surely you know about head-banging and hair bands." Someone needed to revoke Blake's Gen-X card if she didn't.

"Nope." The stinker made the P pop audibly because her lips were wet from her soda. I had a feeling Miss Olivia Brady had a flair for the dramatic. My kind of kid.

I shivered at the grossness of her chewed straw, then looked back at Kick. "Is it time?"

As if all our talk of romantic movies and who was like whom had summoned the man, Blake entered the Perked Cup with his typical cool swagger and furrowed brow. My face suddenly heated. Darn it.

"Daddy!" Olivia plowed into him.

Blake one-arm hugged Carol, then squeezed his daughter

as he kissed her head. "So relieved you two are all right." His eyebrows popped up when he noticed me. He smirked and tapped my shoulder. "Why, it's my good friend Sparky."

I rolled my eyes at him. He had been going out of his way to emphasize our friend-zone status. "Yo… pal."

Kick stared at us, a questioning look crossing her face.

"Wait…" A light bulb seemed to turn on behind Blake's eyes. He held out his hand to Kick. "You're the best friend, aren't you?"

"I am," she proudly admitted and shook the offered hand. "Kick Harrison. Nice to meet you."

Thomas sidled up to Kick and greeted Blake. "Hey, Brady. Happy to see you on our side of town."

"You know each other?" I asked, my gaze moving between the men.

Thomas explained, "The Garage has the best Southern food in town. My team likes it so much we only book the private room for our outings now."

"I'm honored," Blake said with a slight bow.

"Ooh, shoot. It's almost five. We need to get the party started," Kick cut in as she put her phone in her apron pocket.

I clapped. "You found the song?"

"I did." She carefully removed her scrunchie from her hair, letting those wild curls billow around her face.

"Come on, gang. We'll show the kids how to head bang." I hopped off my seat and grabbed Olivia's hand. "Carol… you coming?"

She waved us on. "Go ahead. I was organizing PTA bake sales when you girls were shaking your heads."

Blake called after us, "Where are you taking my daughter?"

I spoke back over my shoulder as we passed the counter. "To the stage. Come join us."

Kick cued the song and encouraged the kids who'd been

studying to stand by their tables. Blake's face lit in recognition at the opening bars.

I waved him over as I helped Olivia take her ponytail down. "Your pretty hair must be down for this." The top layers of my bob were long enough to demonstrate tossing mine around to the beat. Liv caught on quickly and joined Kick and I as we rolled our heads while spinning in circles.

Blake stepped up on the little platform—his hair already out of its confines—and threw his noggin around while adding an air guitar. The proper eighties male response to a hair band.

The girls and I pretended to back him up as we bopped, shimmied our shoulders, and tossed our hair until Olivia dropped from dizziness. The rest of the kids had smiles on their faces as they joined in. By the end of the song, my face ached from grinning. The room erupted with cheers and clapping. I wondered if Blake felt the same. All the weeks of worry and grief seemed to fade for a few moments as he high-fived Olivia.

"Should we put this on the repeat list?" Kick asked the crowd. The space filled with noise again from the kids answering yes. She returned to her work area, and the rest of us took our seats.

"It's decaf." Kick slid an ice tea in front of me and grabbed one for herself. "You deserve it. Great choice."

Blake watched us. "Is this a common thing?" He wiped a bead of sweat off his brow, his eyes still twinkling with joy.

"Monday through Friday, five o'clock," Kick said while fanning the neckline of her T-shirt. "The kids should learn that life can't be all work."

"We should do that at the restaurant," Blake said. The visual made me laugh.

"You're working too hard," Carol observed. She squeezed Liv's shoulders and said, "Great job, honey. You caught on fast."

"ItWasBig!" Olivia air-banged her head a few times, then let it collapse on the counter. "Now I'm soooo hungry. And thirsty."

"Can you stay and eat, or do you have to get back?" Thomas asked.

"Well—" Blake started.

"Please can we eat?" Olivia cut in. "I'm starving," she added with a preteen's emphasis.

Blake's eyes danced as he assessed her antics. "Sure, Sparrow. Why not?" He turned back to Kick. "I saw the signage outside… Is everything gluten-free?"

"No." Kick pivoted, pointing out the two display cases as she spoke. "We offer both. The coolers were just upgraded, so we have more gluten-free options. The sign lets our customers know we take food allergies seriously."

Blake bent over the displays, studying them. "It's all labeled?"

"With potential allergens, yup," Kick answered with pride in her voice. "It reassures customers, and my staff doesn't have to answer the same questions throughout the day. A win-win, really."

"Sounds like a lot of work," Blake said, his brow furrowing.

Kick shook her head. "New product gets a file on our computer system, then we print out the card. The payoff has been bigger than we expected. Word of mouth spreads fast on gluten-free and allergen social media pages. We used to close on Sundays, but the extra business led to us making a seven-day schedule. You'd be surprised how far families will drive for a weekend treat they trust."

"For a coffee and scone?" he asked skeptically, straightening as he rubbed the back of his neck.

Watching Kick's passion for the allergen community in action heightened my pride in her. Thomas also sported a grin matching mine. Her enthusiasm for the allergen-safe food was contagious. I predicted Blake would end up another convert by month's end. I planned to nudge him, of course.

Kick tucked a curl behind her ear and went for a full-court press. "I speak from experience when I tell you how hard it is to navigate our restaurants after a food allergy diagnosis. Our culture is based on food and socializing in restaurants. Yet those of us with allergies get treated like spoiled, over-indulged whiners instead of medical patients who literally put our lives on the line to hang out with loved ones as we pray a kitchen staff takes our requests seriously."

Blake's brow creased almost to the bridge of his nose. "You can't be serious. What about people who make a big deal about a wheat-based pasta, then turn around and order cake for dessert?"

"Oh boy." Thomas blew out a long breath.

Kick touched his forearm comfortingly. "It's all good, Cowboy. Mr. Brady hasn't said anything I haven't heard many times." She turned back toward us. "I've personally never had a customer do that. It's more common to have a mother stand in front of my counter in tears because she can finally take her kid out for a treat. To get an idea of what I'm talking about, look up the health risks of undiagnosed celiac disease. I'll also tell you it only takes about twenty minutes for me to feel the effects of a tiny amount of cross-contamination—that's usually before a meal even ends."

"Or on the way home," Thomas added. I had a feeling he was remembering their first official date.

"Right?" She continued, leaning against the counter to get a little closer to us. "As hard as it is on me, it's hell for kids who don't understand why they're left out." She tapped the top of the display case. "I'll leave you with this—it will be a major marketing point if you're ever interested in doing this at your place. I can help, along with those in the local allergy alliance. Word of mouth works in reverse too, especially when staff not only refuse to help, but they also literally ask why you bothered to come to their business."

"No." Blake stepped back, aghast.

"Multiple times." Kick sighed sadly. "I could go on, but we better feed Olivia."

Liv exhaled loudly. "Finally."

We all chuckled as Kick pointed out what was left. She glanced at Blake. "Nothing fancy like you're used to."

He waved off her comment, chuckling. "That'll be perfect. Being around Chef Felix's food doesn't mean I only eat five-star." He spoke to Liv and Carol. "Pick out what you want, ladies."

He pulled out his phone and started typing on what looked like a note app. I figured he was sorting through his thoughts from what Kick had shared and hoped he'd take it seriously. The Perked Cup's recovery from efforts to run it out of business was practically miraculous, in large part thanks to Kick leaning into this niche.

While he still looked pensive, I elbowed Blake and said, "Go grab a table."

"Are you eating with us, friend?" he asked cheekily.

"Yeah. Pleeeasssse?" Olivia added.

I pressed my lips to keep from laughing at her. It was hard to not fall for her adorableness. Not that I was falling or anything.

"I'll stay for a bit. I have to get back." Apparently she was already hard to say no to. I leaned around Liv and pretended to glare at her father. "This dude I'm working for is a real ass… uh, hard nose."

Kick touched my hand before I could leave the stool. She said under her voice, "You're good with her."

I tipped my head back up at the ceiling and sighed. "Not you too." At this stage in my life, I knew better than to let myself fall for either Brady.

Chapter 8

Everything You Want

Blake

The words in Felix's email blurred as I read them, adding in a funky wave action for kicks. I dropped my computer glasses and rubbed my eyes, feeling a headache coming on. I'd been glued to my desk since Olivia's morning drop-off. Hours were spent handling my lawyer's requests for copies of reports Kramer had filed for the past two years. I forwarded them to Cyndi as well. Updates trickled in from Angel Security, the company hunting down Alan Kramer for me. A guy named Wes was on the case. Then my phone binged with a text from Liv's school counselor. She had another crying event, but it only lasted thirty minutes. I considered it as a win. Any small win would do these days.

Then there was Felix. My executive chef and partner had taken my suggestion to research an allergy policy as an insult. His current note contained a list of the ways his kitchen was a proven, tightly run ship that didn't need "upending."

My hand reflexively moved up to my temple and rubbed

the tender spots. Felix's resistance was an unnecessary nuisance, considering I'd win eventually. I had already investigated the cost versus profit of other restaurants who had implemented a system like Kick's. I liked what I saw and planned to ease Felix into it. My team didn't call me Boss for nothing though. I'd go full-on asshole if needed. Promoting a niche beyond upscale Southern comfort food would benefit the Garage and my staff. It was the key to taking us beyond our legal issues and into the realm of award famous.

All those things paled in comparison to the real reason I couldn't stay on my game today. I sighed as Cyndi hit a high note to a song called "Trouble." I think. Off-key. With her earbuds in. She'd been at it all afternoon, saying it helped her concentrate. It did the opposite to me, only I wasn't annoyed. Cyndi's bad singing made me chuckle. Catching a whiff of her lingering perfume in the hall made my pulse dance. Watching her bounce up the stairs in another pair of platform shoes was like experiencing a work of art bring happiness to the world. No, I enjoyed having her around too much. And I didn't know what I would do about it.

I grimaced every time her beautiful, tan face popped into my mind, let alone actually walked into my line of sight, because I dreaded the day our arrangement ended. As my eyelids closed, memories filled my mind of how she liked it when I kissed the tender spot behind her ear. Her supple curves in my hands had been heaven. She still was my fantasy woman, and I couldn't do anything about it. Cyndi promised to stay on as my accountant after my case was settled, both a blessing and a curse. She would stay in my life at arm's length. The friend zone sucked. Like I had time for more anyway.

Friends.

I inhaled again, raising my shoulders as high as they'd go before letting them drop. I stretched my neck, and—

"I'm trouble y'all." More singing drifted in.

A fuck ton of trouble. I chuckled and shook off the notion.

Embarrassment would wash over Cyndi if she knew I heard her warning the masses of her badassery. She might stop singing altogether. It wouldn't have been so bad if I heard the actual music. I imagined her dancing in her seat in her otherwise silent office. Her office. It had become Sparky's office in my mind. What would it be like when it was empty again? What would the restaurant be like?

Teasing her about our friendship pact became my way of reminding myself to hold back. It surprised me how much I liked being Cyndi's friend. Sure, I missed the orgasms we gave each other—fuck, I missed those something fierce. But this was great in a new way. She was funny, spunky, and lit up whatever room she occupied—the reason I called her Sparky to begin with.

Common sense me sent a warning to my dick—dick-me, if you will—to calm the fuck down. My two sides had been at war since I pressured her into taking up residence in the Garage. It had been too long since my dick saw any action outside my morning shower, and it had to stay that way for a while longer.

However, if dick-me managed to change Cyndi's mind, I was sure I'd lose our friend status forever. That would be worse than blue balls. Far worse.

Cyndi moved on to a sultry song. The words to Sade's "Your Love is King" barely floated in, but they hit straight at my heart. Had anyone ever loved her like a king? Didn't take a genius to know the feeling eluded her like it did me. I had tried to settle Olivia's mother into that place in my heart, but it wasn't a fit for either of us. We'd been a parenting team, but we'd never reached the soul level.

I pulled on my collar. It seemed to have shrunk while I was wearing it. I rescheduled a breakfast meeting for the next day and reserved time in my gym. Then I texted a few sparring buddies to see if they were available. The sweat and muscle exhaustion of man against man would do me a world of good. I had to pay more attention to my physical health, for my daughter's sake as much as my own. But first I had to get through this day.

Lately it seemed impossible to get out from under the watch of the authorities, not to mention the tangential heat from being a federal witness. This stress needed an outlet, and I'd been letting it stew. I bet if I slipped my arm into one of those blood pressure cuffs at the pharmacy, it would read high. Not good.

I stood and straightened my waistband after deciding to get a change of scenery. A tight spot on my back released. Still, something drew me closer to Cyndi's presence. I stopped at the threshold of her door, pivoted, and moved to the balcony railing to clear my head instead.

Noise from the kitchen reminded me of Felix's email, so I decided to head downstairs for a chat. However, my feet wouldn't move. I just stood at the balcony, contemplating the house below. We'd come a long way from our days in a food truck. Someone stroked my arm with a tender touch, and I started.

Cyndi also jumped back, landing on one platformed foot with the grace of an athlete. "Sorry, Jefe. I didn't mean… Um, are you okay?"

"Heff-A?" I raised an eyebrow in question.

She casually tossed her hair. "The crew calls you Boss, right?"

I felt my mouth match her small grin. "They do."

"Jefe is Spanish for boss. Well, el jefe, but…" She shrugged, then settled next to me. "Anyway, you were brooding so hard I felt it from the office." She rubbed her fingers together, like she was feeling the air.

I dipped my chin. "Probably."

"Anything you want to talk about?"

Everything? Nothing. "I'd rather forget." How do I keep you here? "Do you have any good news for me? Could use some."

Cyndi's shoulder bumped against my arm like she was about to make a joke about it not being all that bad. Then she paused and looked up at me. "Wait. What's wrong?"

Ah, so my face really was broody. I scoffed, not wanting to go into detail. Besides, didn't she know it all already? Most of it anyway.

"Come on, tell your little buddy." She coaxed, making me laugh.

The noise from below caught Cyndi's attention. Meredith was seating two women wearing business clothes. The hum of the restaurant in action usually relaxed me, but anxiety continued buzzing along my spine.

Cyndi sighed before turning back to me. "I'm trying to be your friend." Her eyes flashed wide. "Wait, is it Olivia?"

"Yes, but the counselor helped her through it. I didn't have to pick her up."

"There's a victory. Not that her grief will go away, but it's progress." Cyndi's gray eyes lit with warmth. I liked how they did that whenever the subject turned to Olivia.

"All true." I spread my arms wide, presenting the restaurant and my frustration. "We could use some progress here."

"You're in luck, Jefe." She bumped my hip. "Your pal came through early." She shimmied her shoulders as she snapped her fingers. "The new point-of-sale software is ready to test."

"No shit?"

"All. The. Shit." She sang while doing a subtle snake move with her shoulders and hips.

Man, those hips.

I let my gaze take her in, allowing a moment of good. The site of Cyndi Sendaydiego was definitely good. From her sleek, dark bob with silver and blue highlights to her silky dress that was dyed red on top, fading into a gray tone perfectly catching her eyes and ending just above her knees. Her pretty cleavage peeked out from the neckline without being inappropriate for work, while the bottom hugged her… well, fine-as-hell bottom. I could have stared all day. Then there were the boots. Her over-the-knee boots drove me bananas. She'd bought them back when we dated and once worn them and only them while I fucked her. Talk about focusing on the good stuff.

Cyndi had also come through for me in a huge way. My chest puffed out in relief. I picked her up and spun her around as I whooped, then said, "Thank you." Two stupid paltry words that weren't nearly enough and meant the world to me.

Her squeak of delight and fear snapped some sense back into us. A few people down below looked up at us. I set her down, swiftly guiding her back inside her office, my hand on the small of her back. Cyndi's shoulders made another little shimmy, making me wonder if she wanted to be touched too.

"Sorry about that, Spark. Did I frighten you? You know, I'd never—"

"I wasn't afraid, just surprised." She reached for my wrist, preventing my hand from wrapping around her neck and pulling us closer. "I trust you. Friend."

I exhaled loudly, like a popped balloon. She trusted me. The words were a curious gift. What I needed. More than the news about the new software. Those words made both logical me and horny me throw a party. I reached for Cyndi's jaw, cradling it in my hands like the treasure it was. I needed this celebration and hoped I'd read her right. I bent down and pressed my lips to hers, relishing her softness, her taste. I deserved this—we both did. We deserved to celebrate.

Cyndi sighed as she melted into me, letting me wrap my arm around her waist. I lifted her and walked us to the closest open surface—the glass wall. She hoisted herself higher, crossing her ankles at my back, rubbing her heat against my dick. I grabbed the hem of her dress and pushed it up so I could feel the soft skin of her perfect ass.

In an instant, we went out of our minds, forgetting all sense of propriety. We were celebrating something we deserved.

Cyn directed as much as she gave. Her hands floated up my chest and wrapped around my neck as she adjusted the angle of our mouths. Her tongue teased my lips, and I accepted the eager invitation. I'd take whatever she offered. All the worries from the day, not to mention the past months, dissolved as our tongues reacquainted, dancing to a beat that felt both familiar and new.

"God, Blake," she breathed as my fingers eased inside her bikini underwear, stroking through the silky wetness there. Why did her quiet drawl of my name make me feel like a king?

"I've got you." Our hips moved together as our bodies came alive with pleasure. I'd give her anything, do anything to keep feeling this way. A text alert buzzed in my back pocket, but I ignored it. We finally found our moment, and nothing would stop it. "What do you want, Spark?"

"This," Cyndi answered, pressing her pussy hard against my aching dick. All sense of time and place disappeared. "Now," she demanded.

"On it," I said, my mouth smirking in between demanding kisses. I pressed my leg into the wall and reached for my belt. The buckle had sprung free when my phone rang with the ringtone for Olivia's school. "Fuck."

Chapter 9

Crush

CYNDI

The sense I was being watched made the hairs on my neck prickle. The delicious, manly scent was proof Blake had caught me. Boy, did we need to talk. I couldn't avoid him forever, but our slip of control from the other day still addled my brain. One minute we were talking as friends and the next we were about to take our clothes off. It only meant I should make an appointment with my battery-operated boyfriend. Blake's woody smell hit my nose again, and it was clear my dry spell wasn't the problem.

Don't look. Keep working, Sendaydiego.

I didn't trust myself to talk through the other day. Regardless of my confusion, I wasn't stupid. Cyndi time was my priority, dammit. Not the revival of a silly crush.

Thank God for Olivia's school. The situation made Blake get the hell out of dodge, allowing me enough time to gather my wits. Then I escaped the Garage by working from home for a few days. Somehow he knew to back off. I bet he was as confused as I was.

Blake cleared his throat in a way that sounded like he was smiling. Time to face the music.

I spun in my chair to face him, a friendly smile on my face. Curse him for looking so devilishly broody as he leaned against the doorframe, hands in his pockets like he was bored. "Hello, Jefe." I hoped the title would be a reminder of our working relationship. Maybe we could both realize our kiss had been nothing more than a small slip.

Blake didn't pelt me with questions about my disappearance as I expected. Instead, he walked to the chair in front of the desk, sat, and scooted it until our knees touched. He pressed harder until I moved my legs apart, until they were essentially hugging his legs under the wooden top. An unseen embrace. Curse me for loving it.

Blake placed his elbows on the desktop, settling his chin in his hands. He wore an amused expression on his chiseled face, the corner of his mouth ticking up mischievously and making my belly flutter.

I ran my fingers through my bob, tucking a few strands behind my ear. Still, he stared. "What?" I finally asked, a little loud.

"Problem, Sparky?" The smirk grew into a smile.

I pointed at him. "Stop that."

Blake sat back, pressing his lips together like he was trying to keep from laughing. He stretched his legs, tangling his ankles with mine. Yet he didn't say more.

"Fine." I raked my fingers through my hair, lacing them at the back of my neck. "I poofed again. I'm sorry." I kept my gaze firmly on the grain in the wooden desktop. "I—"

"Poof? Oh right… no ghosting."

I lifted my head, and the man had the gall to wink at me. "Pardon?"

"You like me." He held his elbow and rested his chin in the thumb and forefinger of his other hand. We were inches apart and eye to eye, like besties sharing deep secrets instead of ex-lovers who almost became de facto lovers. I considered bolting. It wouldn't make me feel any more immature than I already did.

"You like me, and for some reason it freaks you out." Blake's warm brown eyes softened. "That's why you keep poofing on me, as you put it. Isn't it?"

I blinked. Twice. "Well, shit."

"Not analyzing." He reached for my hand, giving it a gentle squeeze. "Let's figure out where we go from here."

"How's Olivia?"

"She's fine. Don't change the subject."

"You are bossy," I muttered, scratching my forehead with my free hand.

Blake flashed me a roguish smile. "We're a great team, professionally speaking."

"True," I drawled hesitantly. My promise to stay on as Blake's accountant was the reason I came back today, hoping to sneak in—I'd even worn my running shoes. The staff had to start training on the new point-of-sale software. I figured Blake would leave me alone if I was busy with the crew. I'd been about to head downstairs when I sensed him hovering. "I'm keeping my word in that regard."

"Appreciated." He adjusted his position but kept hold of my hand. When I tried to pull it free, he stubbornly winked again. "We're also great"—he cleared his throat again—"personally speaking."

I opened my mouth to argue, and he raised a finger for me to hear him out. "We can have both."

"How?" I sat back, folding my hands in front of me, making a weak defensive wall. Blake watched my movements like he knew exactly what I was doing. As hard as he could be with his team, he didn't push or call me on my pitiful protective measures. Is that why he kept freaking me out?

Blake tapped his fingers on the surface of the wood like he was practicing scales. I wondered if he ever played the piano. "I drop off Liv at eight fifteen every morning. I started working out at the gym again, but I could skip a day or two for other reasons."

"Other... Me? You want to"—I swallowed hard—"schedule nookie on the down-low?"

"I'll bring breakfast. We can talk too." He shrugged and gave me his handsome smile again. The crinkles around his eyes did bad things to what was left of my ovaries. "I enjoy spending time with you, Spark. My days are booked to the minute." He lifted my hand, staring at his thumb as he stroked soothing circles there. I pressed my lips together to keep from purring into his rough touch. "Our chemistry ignites as soon as we enter each other's orbit. Scheduling time won't douse it."

I didn't agree with Blake, but he'd piqued my curiosity. "Where do you see these wild, rationally irrational events happening?"

"Nice description." He stopped the rhythmic movements and pointed at me. "This is why our chemistry works."

"No admissions of chemistry were made, and you didn't answer me."

Blake gestured around the room. "What about here? The cleaning crew starts upstairs so they can finish my office before I arrive. They won't bother us." He resumed the circles.

He had a point. Both of us had been coming in early to crank through our projects. About the time I was ready for people, the kitchen staff showed up, their pleasant voices floating up to me through the window.

I bit my lip, considering his proposal. My promise to quit mixing business with pleasure made it painfully difficult to meet new men. By the time I finished work and hit the gym myself, I was tuckered out most nights. Plus I had recently made some medical decisions that caused the men I usually picked to think twice about dating me. My dry spell had become a desert.

"Let's try an experiment." Blake stood, keeping his grip on my hand. He pulled me into him when we reached the end of the desk. His hands came up to my jaw. "Such a lovely, delicate face." He leaned down and kissed me deeply. In no time, I flamed like the other day. Blake did the same, according to the sounds he made.

Our tongues dueled at first to make our own points. He growled into me, and that was all it took for me to melt, our tongues now dancing, caressing, as our hands roamed over each other. "Mmm." He hummed as I stroked his dick over his pants, lost in the sensation and need.

Chemistry had never been our problem though. I pulled back, my ears warmed. Had the air-conditioning broken? It was suddenly unbelievably hot in the office. As if he could read my mind, the daring smirk came back. "Our problem was too much chemistry," I argued. "All you've proved is that I've gone a long time without a lover."

"Really?" He grabbed my ass, pulling me right up to his erection, and rubbed. God, it felt good. Wanting it didn't make it a good idea. He chuckled roughly into my ear.

"Promise you won't fall for me."

"Wow." Blake's eyebrow lifted.

I stuck my finger in his face. "You did before, admit it."

"I wanted to. You didn't give me a chance." An alert chimed on Blake's phone. "Damn. Hang on. I'm expecting news from the private detective." He pulled his phone out of his pocket. A confused expression crossed his face. He stepped back, sinking into the chair again.

"What is it? Something with Olivia?" I asked.

"It's an email from the DNA website."

"You did one of those?" I leaned forward. "That was smart."

"Yeah." His eyes briefly lifted to mine before returning to the text. "I'm trying to find my birth mom. The social worker I hired hit a dead end and suggested it."

I moved to give him privacy, except I didn't know if he wanted a friend nearby. So I let my gaze travel around the room. I'd brought a beaded tree I made as the only personal touch from home. Despite the mostly empty bookshelf and general emptiness of the room, I liked it. A smoky-gray film covered the outside of the glass wall, creating a one-way effect. It also gave the space a coziness, along with the exposed brick wall behind me. The other two walls were painted a medium blue, reminding me of the sky at dusk.

"Well?" The suspense got to me.

Blake dropped into the chair before rubbing a hand over his jaw. "A woman in Phoenix thinks I'm her cousin."

Chapter 10

What I Got

Blake

"Doesn't the test confirm if you're a match?" Cyndi asked.

"Yeah," I answered, half aware of her question. I couldn't believe what I was reading.

I had a cousin named Blake, but he's dead. You and your mom—my auntie—disappeared when you were three. We eventually had a funeral and everything. My mother is your mom's older sister. Oh my God! Gran will be over the moon.

"This can't be right," I said, lifting my gaze to Cyndi, letting her steel-gray eyes center me. "Her cousin disappeared when he was three." I showed the supposed match to Cyndi. "I was adopted when I was two and a half, but the results show up as a first cousin."

"You still have a grandmother?" Cyn asked, handing the phone back.

I shrugged, letting my hands rise with my shoulders. "Sounds like it." My heart pounded a beat so fast I struggled for breath.

"This is huge." Cyndi's eyes widened, like she was more excited than I was. She walked around the chair and bent to wrap her arms around my shoulders. She squeezed me before speaking into my ear. "You found your family." She kissed my cheek with all her sweetness.

I read the message again.

"The age thing though." I'd have to ask the social worker about it. Liv had been the only toddler I ever spent time with, but my memories were clear regarding how much she'd changed between two and three. I shook my head in disbelief before reluctantly chuckling. Did we have blood family? Suddenly fear washed over me like a tidal wave. What if they hate me too? I grabbed Cyndi's arms like they were a life preserver.

I'd taken the test to find my birth parents, but this woman, Sherry, claimed my mother was dead. What happened to her? Or us?

Hell, I just wanted someone to love me for me. One person would do. Why was it so hard to find? I leaned back against Cyndi, closed my eyes, and pretended it was her.

AFTER REWRITING MY RESPONSE THREE TIMES, I SENT THE message off to Sherry, hoping she was right. Fortunately, my schedule required me to compartmentalize and put those hopes on hold. So I made a meeting with the owner and executive chef of the Victorian, a local restaurant that set the standard for dealing with food allergies. Kick Harrison had hooked us up for ideas on improving the Garage's allergy awareness. As I researched best practices, it became obvious this was the way to get an edge as well as win the award Felix desperately wanted. The chef at the Victorian had celiac disease, like Cyndi's friend. Touring his kitchen encouraged me. Our kitchen wouldn't require an overhaul. Minor remodeling would do. We'd still have to find time to shut down for about a week, but my gut told me it would be worth it in the long run.

Right before heading down to the dining room, a new email came in from Sherry with a photo attachment. A young woman held a smiling baby. It was supposed to be my mother and me as a baby. She looked so young—like twenty. The face that had often forced my memory to not let it go for as long as I could remember stared back, flooring me. The baby though… He—I—favored Olivia. Gianna always said she looked like me, but I never had anything to reference until Liv was three. I scrolled through my phone to a baby picture of my girl.

"Holy shit." She looked like the baby in the email. Me?

"What's going on?" Cyndi asked as she walked through the door, her laptop bag over her shoulder.

"This." I gave her my phone with the picture of baby Olivia and gestured toward the photo on my monitor.

She pointed at the screen. "This you?"

I chuckled in amazement. "According to Sherry. You remember the email from yesterday?"

"Of course." Cyn's features softened as she scanned the two pictures. "That girl is your mini-me." Her voice softened. "You were adorable." She came closer and squeezed my shoulder. "Your mother is gorgeous."

"Was," I clipped. She flinched and my body sagged in response. "Sorry. Didn't mean to sound angry."

"No, you're right." She leaned against the edge of my desk, looking down at me with a sympathy I hated. "You've found her and lost her on the same day. It's a lot."

"They believed I was dead, but I'm very much alive. What if she's also out there somewhere? I've been reading about missing and murdered Indigenous women. What if she's missing like me?"

"Oh honey." Cyndi rubbed circles on my shoulders. "She's more likely in the murdered category now. I'm so sorry to think it." She circled her arms around me and bent down. "Start with these people and go from there."

I let go of the hopeful breath I'd been holding in and held on to Cyn's arms.

"You've got a crap ton to deal with." She gave a squeeze, as if to say see ya, and stepped back. "I should leave you alone."

"Oh no." I pulled her hand into my lap. Removed the bag from her shoulder and swiveled to set it behind me. "These emails don't negate our arrangement. Sharing them with you helps. As far as I'm concerned, we're still on."

"Who said we'd solidified an arrangement?" she asked, making finger quotes in the air. However, her mischievous grin said she was in.

Despite everything, or maybe because of the overwhelm of it all, I craved her. Since she'd walked back into my life, she softened all the blows that had been thrown my way. I needed one good thing that was just mine. I longed to touch her, hold her, lick every inch of her. Make her scream so loud it echoed in the dining room.

"You're not getting out of it." I shifted Cyndi so she straddled me. She wore a pair of flowy slacks, and I wished like hell it had been the dress from the other day. Still, I grabbed her hips to grind her on my dick. We both hissed at the exquisite contact. The temptation to strip her and have her almost won out, but the buzz of the dinner hour crept through my transom window, meaning I was late. Fortunately, no one had called up looking for me. Yet. It took a moment to gather my wits, but I reluctantly slid her off me. After standing, I kissed the top of her hand. "Breakfast tomorrow. Right here." Her pupils dilated as I playfully slapped her bottom, telling me what I needed to know.

"Again with the bossy." She clicked her tongue, one side of her mouth ticking up in a sassy smirk. "Almost makes me want to see what you'd do if I stayed home."

Yeah, we both needed to let loose. I laughed as I met her mouth for a quick goodbye kiss. "I can chase you across town, but I'd rather chase you around my desk." Her sexy inhale of desire almost made me come in my pants, like a pubescent boy. "Oh, and Spark?" She picked up her bag and turned back to me. "Wear the boots."

Chapter 11

Training Season

Cyndi

By ten o'clock, I was reading in bed when a text from Blake alerted on my phone.

BLAKE

I forgot to tell you something…

> Waiting with bated breath.

BLAKE

Shit. That sounds hot.

> How horny are you?

BLAKE

Soooo

Ugh. So was I.

> Ask your question.

BLAKE

Right. It's not a question. Kind of.

!!!

BLAKE

Yeah. So, since we were last together. <cough>
I got a vasectomy. Thought you'd want to
know. It was confirmed by the doc. <So fun> If
you still want me to wrap it up, I'm your man.
Just figured I'd give you the option.

Blast him. Surely he planned to destroy me. My contraceptive situation was the main reason for my lack of dates. I pulled at the collar of my sleep shirt and made a mental note to have my HVAC guy come out. It had been impossible to keep cool lately.

I racked my brain to think of the best response—didn't want him to feel bad about his honesty.

I stopped taking BC pills last year because…
well, just needed to. It's a big part of the reason
for my hiatus. Still technically infertile.

BLAKE

You've been on a hiatus?

I'd told him in passing already, but we didn't get into the reasons.

Does it matter?

BLAKE

No. I've been in a dry spell too. Friends treat
me like I'm having an existential crisis because
of it.

I hear you.

BLAKE

The younger women I've met expect babies,
and I'm done with that.

> I don't blame you. Going off birth control made
> dates "complicated" on my end.

BLAKE

I get it. Anyway, I'm also clean. I get checked
with each physical, and that was two
months ago.

> Aww. You say the sweetest things. Lol. Same
> here.

BLAKE

So?

Right. His question. The idea of a safe bareback sex with Blake was almost too much to handle.

> Leave the condoms. Bring the cannoli.

BLAKE

Nice! The Godfather. You do know me.

> I couldn't think of a Star Wars quote that fit.

BLAKE

Forgiven. Can't stop smiling.

He sent me a bunch of smiley face emojis with an eggplant for good measure to prove his point.

BLAKE

Any requests for me?

After only a second, I think of one.

> Leave your hair down.

BLAKE

Really? *Should have grown it out years ago.*

Running my hands through it when we kissed had been an erotic surprise. My stomach tightened at the thought of doing it again. A bead of sweat traveled between my breasts. What the hell was wrong with the air-conditioning? I had to stop thinking about sex and go to sleep so I could get the real thing in the morning.

Night night, stud. Need you fresh for duty in the morning.

Blake sent one last horse emoji. This scheduling nookie idea wasn't so bad after all. Except my body was hot for other reasons now.

I slept without any covers.

I tiptoed up the Garage's back steps like a naughty teenager. The realization made me mad, but I kept on going. Pride or no, I wanted to avoid getting caught by the cleaning crew. Why I cared so much now—a grown-ass woman—when I'd owned my agency for years, I didn't know. I'd gone back on resolutions many times. A woman's allowed to change her mind. But this felt different. Then there was Kick. Her voice played on repeat in my head, along with her laughing at me. I'd be damned if Blake ended up different from any of my other dates. Hell, I had friends-with-bennies arrangements from time to time.

But if I hadn't been in denial, I would have strutted my stuff right up the front stairs and pretended Blake and I had an early meeting. But I had woken up with my head in a mess. It didn't help that I'd been too hot to sleep well.

Blake Brady had me off my game. If only I knew why.

Netflix and chill? Sure. Dinner and a nightcap? Of course. Bagel and a bone? This was new.

At least the souls of my over-the-knee boots stayed quiet. I reached the top step without making one squeak on the wooden stairs. I unbuttoned my trench coat and pulled at my wrap dress. Geez, it was hot up here.

Wear the boots, he'd said. I'd show him. I took his words literally. After making it to the second level, I turned toward my office to stow my stuff and remove the dress. A strong hand unceremoniously yanked me into Blake's office, making me squeak in surprise.

"Where do you think you're going?" Blake glared like he was perturbed.

I made a warning stomp next to his foot and dropped my gear. "Don't make me regret this with a case of your surliness."

"Sorry. I…" Blake stepped back and closed the door. "You were late. Was afraid you'd changed—"

Well shit. Suppose I deserved that. "What do you think now?"

His jaw dropped when he turned around. I had untied the dress, letting it and the coat slide off my arms, puddling behind me. I stood before him wearing a matching black silk bra and string bikini panties. Along with the boots. Boy, had I missed my shapewear walking in, but I figured if Blake wanted to play out a fantasy, he'd get one. I put my weight on one hip and angled the other leg, striking a pose. This might actually be fun.

"There was an accident on Capital Boulevard." My excuse for the lateness.

"Oh." Blake rubbed his jaw, tucking what hair he could behind his ears. He slowly walked around me, fingertips touching where he passed. First between my breasts and along the underwire of one side, down my arm, to the string holding my bikini panels together. The caress sent shivers up my spine, yet I stayed still, letting his eyes get their fill.

Mine did the same with him. I looked over my shoulder. "Your hair's down."

"As requested."

His erection made an impressive tent in his sweatpants. When I woke up, I'd texted one last time, asking him to wear gym clothes. A little fantasy for me. Ooh, did he deliver.

The sweats pooled a bit at his ankles. I wasn't sure if it was part of their design or because of Blake's height. Not that he was short. He just wasn't one of those ridiculously tall men. Another aspect of his perfection in my mind. When we stood together, he made me feel like a real woman and not a child. No, average-height men were highly underrated.

I still looked up to meet Blake's gaze when I wore my platform shoes. Besides, nothing else about him was average. His broad shoulders and finely cut abs testified to his workouts. The man was meaty in the best ways.

He stepped up to me from behind, his erection settling against my ass. I wiggled my hips, letting him feel my approval. One of his hands turned my chin as he licked his lips. "I—" His mouth devoured mine. I wanted to spin into him, but his other hand roamed down the front of my body. It dove inside my underwear and gripped my sex, pressing me against him. He made a low, approving rumble in his throat as his fingers slid through my folds. The pumping of his hips behind me and his fingers inside me had me rocking to his rhythm.

Already keyed up, it didn't take long to begin my climb. "This is the most brilliant idea," I breathed.

"I'm a genius," Blake said, moving his kisses from my mouth to my jaw, down my neck. "Just one thing." Before I could respond, the hand that had been cradling my chin moved to the back of my bra and unclasped it. I shimmied out of the straps, letting my head fall against Blake's shoulder as he palmed my breasts.

Every nerve in my body practically jumped to meet his touch. My movements grew as he slid more fingers into me, adding a circling movement on my clit. Then he pinched my nipple. "Need you to come," Blake demanded, his voice gravelly. "Need it bad."

The grumble of his chest against my back as he made his request set me off. My knees weakened when the waves swept through me. Blake held me up by pressing me harder into him while still pulling on my nipples, drawing out my orgasm with lighter caresses of my pussy. He remembered exactly how to make the bliss last.

"Beautiful," he said as he watched me come undone on his hand. To keep me from falling to the floor, Blake moved us to a Chesterfield flanking his desk. He knelt before me, deftly removing my bikini underwear while leaving the boots on. The action brought me back to my senses. He'd been about to put his mouth on me, not that I'd object. Far from it, but it was my turn for a show.

"Uh-uh-uh." I ticked my index finger back and forth before moving it up and down. "Now you."

He stood back, a cocky smirk in place, and grabbed the back of his muscle shirt. Up and over. It landed somewhere near my clothes. I tipped my head in challenge to see if he would pose for me. His eyes dropped to the floor for a beat, and the edges of his ears darkened. Not fair. Bossy Blake was sexy as hell, but a shy, possibly insecure Blake? Utterly irresistible.

My gaze moved over Blake's body, traveling across every cut plane, waiting to see what he would do. The man managed to get better with age. His body—including his dick—had been perfection when we dated. It still stood proud, the head of him peeking out of the waistband. He caught me looking, and the corner of his mouth lifted. "Is this why you requested the sweats?"

I fanned my face as I pretended to swoon. "Gray sweats are…" I inhaled as I licked my lips.

"Really?" He softly chuckled. Already in bare feet—so hot—he removed his sweats in one smooth motion, suddenly standing before me in his blessed, naked awesomeness. The dusting of closely groomed slightly salt-and-pepper hair across his chest made him more scrumptious, like he dared the aging process to try to take over. I licked my lips as my eyes admired every plain and groove, wanting to taste each inch. We hadn't planned for that kind of time.

The sparrow on his left pec—over his heart—still moved me. He'd told me the story of it early on, how it represented his love for his daughter. She was as much a part of him as his still-sculpted abs and strong thighs.

Don't you dare freak. I couldn't cut and run again. I'd forever feel bad about doing it to him the first time. So I stayed and played. Indulged. Friends with benefits. Ooh, I benefited.

Blake must have had his own self-talk, because he placed his hands on his hips, lifting his proud chest in a pose. For me. Such a lucky lady.

Now, I wasn't dumb. I knew my body wasn't twenty anymore. Hell, it wasn't forty anymore. I never pretended to be. My curves had softened more than I preferred. But I worked hard for what I did have. So I let my body stay on display for him. Even placed my foot on the edge of the sofa, exposing myself to Blake.

His eyes hooded as my hand slipped down to my pussy and stroked it some. He made that low, growling sound in his chest as his hand came up and pulled on that magnificent dick. Overcome by the sight and sensations, I let my head fall back.

"Cyn," he warned.

He wanted me to come on him this time, and the climb

had begun again—more like it hadn't left. I would wait for him. I wanted him in me bad. I'd had a hard time getting to sleep last night, thinking about this moment. However, I also felt naughty. I bit my lip to tease him.

"Don't you dare," Blake growled.

Oh yeah, this was a fun way to start the day.

"Hey." He pulled me up, grabbed a blanket from the back of the other sofa and spread it out on the cushions behind me. Then spun us around and sat, bringing me between his legs. Thanks to the platform boots, Blake nuzzled into my boobs and let his hands roam my back, paying particular attention to my ass. He tipped his head back and caught my eye. "Climb on."

"Yes, Jefe." Blake scooted back as I moved over him. He guided the head of his dick through my wetness, making me gasp as it grazed my clit.

"Take it."

I eased onto him, appreciating the blissful stretch no battery-operated boyfriend could achieve.

Once seated, I set a slow pace, drawing out our pleasure. I squeezed on my way up and slammed on my way down.

"Damn, woman." He threw his head against the back of the sofa.

"Good?"

"So good."

We both held on, relishing the sensations of our bodies working together, our grunts and moans the only sounds louder than our skin slapping. Total heaven. Then the climb began again, and I scrambled off him.

"Hey." Initially surprised, Blake caught on when I held on to the cushions. He grinned and stood, lining himself up at my pussy. "Want it rough?" I groaned for an answer. He slammed into me, and we both cried out. I had loved him this way before, and he didn't disappoint.

Blake reached around and fingered my clit as he leaned toward me. "Need you to come, Spark."

I looked over my shoulder and said, "Slap me."

His eyes glazed over at the request before giving me what I wanted. My pussy tightened at the sting of his hand. I tipped my head back and moaned. "Again."

He growled his approval and complied on my other cheek. It was enough to set off the contractions. Enough to make us come together, lost in the frenzy of our bodies joining. For a second, I wondered how I'd ever let this man go to begin with. No one had ever given as much as he'd taken with me.

We collapsed onto the sofa, gasping for breath, boneless and enjoying the elation our chemistry created. Blake pulled me against him, face-to-face. He traced the edges of my mouth with his finger. "You're so beautiful."

I took it all in, wanted to accept it and keep it in my heart. Except my heart was asking, what happens now?

Chapter 12

I'll Be

Blake

I made myself get up and poured us each a coffee from the thermos on my credenza. We both had packed days. Besides, I didn't want to get caught. Maybe it was the perceived naughtiness of a work tryst. Or how broadly Cyndi had declared we were only friends. Or was it the murmurs among my staff regarding bets on how long it would take us to do what we'd just done? No, I quickly recognized the selfishness in wanting something for myself, and Cyn was my pick.

I added creamer to Cyndi's cup and handed it to her before producing the bagels I'd picked up on my way in. She set the food on the end table and stretched out her legs, sitting opposite me. For someone so petite, this woman had legs for days. She raised one in the air, unzipping the boots she still wore and sliding one off before doing the same with the other.

The first sip burned my taste buds. "Damn, that's hot."

"Yeah?" A corner of her mouth lifted politely, like my

exclamation hadn't registered. Cyndi settled back into the cushion, staring at the coffee she held in both hands.

I nudged her with my foot. "Everything all right?" God, if the word regret came out of her mouth…

"You called me beautiful," she quietly said, still looking at the mug. "Twice."

She couldn't be serious. I scratched my chin. "Is this new? I can't be the only one."

Cyndi shrugged off my question. "I'm usually too… fill-in-the-blank… to be someone's definition of beautiful. Or I'm not enough of fill-in-the-blank. You know? Too Asian. Not enough European. Too short. Not meek enough." She scoffed. "Joel had the nerve to tell me I was too agreeable the night he left."

If I ever saw that man again, I'd kick his ass. "He justified his betrayal by blaming it on you." I grabbed one foot and massaged it so she'd relax.

"I know. Just trying to explain I've never measured up to the standard of what a woman should be." Cyn drank from her cup and almost choked when she chuckled. She cleared her throat. "If I had a dollar for every time someone asked what I am or where I'm from. Hell, if I had a nickel, I wouldn't have to work."

"No shit." I laughed. "When you say you're an American and they counter with, 'But where originally?'" I bit into my bagel, chewing while we made fun of our shared experiences. "Gianna's grandfather was convinced I was Sicilian. Since I'd also been adopted, nothing I said changed his mind."

Cyndi tossed her head back. "But you look Native American, not Mediterranean." I liked that she saw the differences. She added, "Growing up in the middle of Michigan, people would argue with me about being Asian. My dad is mostly Malay and distinguishes himself from more recent Asian immigrants to the Philippines. The differences were never understood here. In high school, my ability to tan was a superpower. White girls were so jealous, but my dad's sister found it embarrassing. She was obsessed with white skin, and I refused to lighten mine."

"Lighten it?" My eyes grew wide. My hand shifted back to her leg, caressing and squeezing it. "Your skin is beautiful." I also had vivid memories of local girls basking in the sun for hours to achieve a skin color like Cyn's.

She bit off a piece of bagel and set it down. "It's just Auntie's way. Not that I fault her. It's the standard she grew up with."

"She shouldn't make you feel bad for it." I squeezed her foot, hoping she felt my sentiment as well as heard it. "You're stunning."

"Thank you." Cyndi dipped her head like the attention embarrassed her. "My auntie means well. I suppose all the others who call me 'exotic' mean it as a compliment. At least that's how I learned to take it."

"Smart." I winked at her before closing my eyes, taking a moment to acknowledge how much I needed this. How nice it was to be with a woman I had so much in common with. I could've stayed there all day, but the restaurant was waking up. Fortunately, Felix was scheduled to receive our deliveries this morning. The perks of being the boss. I'd asked him to text if he needed help, under the guise that I was pulling together information for my lawyer.

"Speaking of people meaning well," I started with a chuckle. "When all this settles down, I'm thinking of taking Spanish classes." I circled my face with my finger. "All of a sudden, something about this look makes folks around here assume I'm fluent. They just walk up to me, speaking it a mile a minute. Then they get mad when I say, 'No habla Espanol.'"

Cyndi giggled at my story. "I hear you, except I'm good for a quick interaction if they slow down." She poked my stomach with her foot. "Has it really only been recently?"

"Yeah." I grabbed the foot, tried to tickle it, but couldn't get her to flinch. This new piece of knowledge fascinated me. A new challenge. But everything about her fascinated me. Thoughts tracked to old issues. "Growing up, everyone knew exactly who I was... The Brady's Indian boy. Racist terms flowed freely even from our closest friends." I sighed heavily. "If they did it around my parents, I was expected to laugh, though it often put the old man in a bad mood. But I never was mistaken for Latinex."

"Geez, that's horrible." Cyndi's brow furrowed, like she was angry on my behalf. A new sensation. I'd do anything to keep that feeling around. "I want to hug little you. You had to have been the cutest kid in town."

I waved her over, lifting the blanket so she could snuggle up. She hugged me with her whole body, knees pressing my legs. Even her thighs tightened around me. How had I let her go three years ago? Her head tucked under my chin, and I inhaled deeply, letting the exotic floral-coconut scent relax me.

Cyndi made a sweet, little moan, expressing exactly how I felt about having her soft curves pressed against me.

"I wish we could've been friends when we were kids," I whispered.

"We'd have kicked their asses."

"Yeah." Thumping bass tones from the kitchen floated up to my office as the kitchen staff prepped for the day. We didn't so much hear the music as feel it in a slight rattle of the window wall. At the same time, my dick started to come back to life.

"Blake..." Cyndi's tone warned, but she wore a grin. "We have to get going."

The air filled with the notification of a text before I could answer. "Hang on." I reached for my phone on the side table. "I told Felix to text if he needed me." Instead, it was from Carol Page.

Cyndi moved up onto an elbow. "What's wrong?"

"Carol's sick and can't stay with Sparrow tonight." I shot off a response, telling her no problem, I hoped she felt better soon, and to let me know if I could bring her food or medicine.

"What are you going to do?" Cyn ran her fingers through my hair.

I closed my eyes to visualize the night's schedule in my mind. With a heavy sigh, I finally said, "Guess Liv will have stay up here. I could run her home after the dinner rush and make sure she calls me before going to bed."

"When does Jay come back? You've been working nonstop since his accident."

"Tomorrow afternoon, thank God." I fingered Cyndi's hair, enjoying the softness of the silky strands. Is that why she did the same with mine? "Once Jay's at one hundred percent, I'll stagger the schedule again. I don't like relying on Meredith constantly closing since she's a single mom."

Cyndi pulled a face on me. "You're a single dad too, you know."

"But I have Carol. I lucked out."

She placed a kiss on my chest. "I could hang out with Olivia at the condo."

I did a double take, shocked by the offer. "She's a kid. You don't like kids."

"Since when?" Cyndi popped back up on her elbow, leaning over me.

I blinked. Isn't that why she broke up with me? "Three years ago, I asked you to hang out with me and my daughter, and the next thing I knew, you were gone. Unreachable."

She winced, then quietly said, "It wasn't because of Olivia, but if you don't want me near her, I totally understand."

The memory of her comforting Liv in her office raced through my mind. Cyndi knew what to say to make her feel better. I was still practicing how to be an emotionally open father. I squeezed her shoulder. "It would help a lot if you stayed with Liv tonight."

I never would have expected her eyes to light up so much at the chance. What I would give to figure this woman out.

"Thank you. Should we order an early takeout and head to your place?"

"Put in an order with Felix. He lives to spoil my girl." I shook my head as I laughed. A warmth spread through my body, settling in my heart before heading to my dick. Was this happiness? I knew what it looked like and how it felt with my daughter, but I'd never noticed this with a woman before. Not like this. I was probably wrecked mentally. It made me vulnerable. Regardless, my erection continued to grow, ready for round two.

I rolled Cyndi away from me, lifting her top leg over mine.

"Don't we have to get to work?"

"Shh," I nipped her earlobe. "We've got a few minutes."

Chapter 13

Dreams

CYNDI

Considering I spent the morning having sex, the day flew by. While I trained the last of the waitstaff on the new point-of-sale software, Olivia buzzed by on her way to the soda station. Her hair was in two French braids. Apparently the popular girls at her school were into braids. Blake had shared that tidbit one morning when he came to work grumpy from being late thanks to his "clumsy fingers" not quite getting it yet. Since the two plaits were still tight and even, one of them must have figured it out.

Liv's uniform blazer was clipped to the top of her backpack. Despite what the calendar claimed, summer still had its grip on North Carolina. Her poor short-sleeved button-down shirt had sweat spots on it. A possible topic for our evening.

"Hey, little chica! Did your dad tell you I get to hang out with you tonight?"

"Uh-uh," she answered, shaking her head as she drank

through the straw. "The office only gave me a message to come here after school. Is Ms. Carol okay?"

"She's under the weather and doesn't want to risk passing it to you."

"Hmm." Olivia's face scrunched like she was upset.

My heart fluttered in my chest. I pulled at the collar of my blouse. "Would you rather hang out here this evening?" I asked cautiously.

"Hmm?" Liv's expression seemed to clear. She blinked a few times, like her mind was some place else. "Oh no. Going home is better, I guess."

"Is everything okay?" I wondered why she seemed so distracted. Then I remembered she was a pubescent girl with emotions and hormones swirling inside her like a tornado. Olivia was in puberty, wasn't she? "Anything happen at school?"

"No. School was fine. It's just... You think my riding lessons will be canceled tomorrow?"

"Oh. Oh!" My self-absorbed meter jumped to ten. There was no reason to care so much about Olivia's approval anyway. "I bet Mrs. Page is resting hard so she can to be ready for your lesson."

Liv gave me a small smile before sticking the straw back in her mouth. "Yeah. Bet."

"Anyway... you can put my laptop on the shelf in our office and use the desk for homework."

"I was going to work in Daddy's unless he's busy in there."

"Sure." I ran my hand through my hair, nodding vigorously. "He's at a meeting now. I'm sure he won't mind. Sounds good." Nice going, nitwit. To stop myself from blabbering, I patted Olivia's shoulder and turned back to my clipboard to see who needed training next. She was a few feet away when I remembered our plans. "Olivia?"

She turned around and gave me a little huff. Again, I hoped it was the hormones talking.

"Felix is making our dinners. What time would you like to eat?" I asked. A small bead of sweat formed on my upper lip.

Seemingly out of nowhere, Blake walked up to me, placing his hand on the small of my back. I instinctively shimmied away from his hand while he called his daughter over to us. Whether he noticed my reaction to his display of affection, I couldn't tell. He drew Olivia into his arms and kissed her head. The way she tried to wiggle out of his hold made me bite my lip to keep from laughing. She must have hit the "too cool to like grown-ups" stage after all.

"What are you up to now?" Blake asked Liv.

"Homework, I guess." She shrugged nonchalantly. Then her eyes narrowed. "I can stay home alone, you know?"

Blake inhaled audibly before letting out a wheezy breath. "I'm not ready yet. The neighborhood is—"

"Safe," she pressed.

"Busy," he countered. They lived a few blocks away, on the edge of the warehouse district. It was halfway between the Garage and Olivia's school. Aside from the few empty nesters, like Carol Page, the neighborhood was mostly made up of young professionals who still liked to party at night. I understood Blake's hesitancy. He didn't so much as glare back as he stood firm, not letting his gaze divert from his daughter's.

She rolled her eyes. "Fine. But can I work in your office?"

Blake and I both chuckled at Olivia's sense of negotiation. "If you don't mind using the couch. I have stuff to finish so I can take off early tonight."

Olivia's eyes lit up. Finally. "Will you be home before I go to bed?"

Blake's shoulders fell. I wanted to rub his back and reassure him, then mentally kicked my ass. Don't let one romp reel you back in, amazing as it was.

"That's the plan," he answered. He gave her a squeeze and added, "Go get settled, Sparrow. I'll be up after a check-in with the kitchen."

She sent him a quick smile and bounced off to the elevator.

Blake rubbed the back of his neck as he turned to me. "Everything going all right here?"

"It's trucking along."

"Thank God something is," he said with a long-suffering sigh.

I almost touched him again. This time on the forearm. This itch had to be reined in, or the fun stuff would have to end before it really started. I gripped the clipboard with both hands. "Was it your meeting?"

Blake shrugged as if to say not really, but his jaw clench gave him away. "I hate this whole thing. Have to go round up more receipts for the audit."

"That's my job."

"You're handling the reboot and the post-bullshit audit. It's enough."

Stubborn man. "Please… forward the requests to me. If I can't get to them, I can probably tell you where to look."

"Fine." Blake leaned toward me before taking a step back. "Thanks, Sparky."

"Boss…" Felix interrupted us. "Quit your yacking, yeah?"

He subtly entwined our index fingers. "Catch you later."

Chef Felix hooked up Olivia and me. She had his famous cracklin' buttermilk biscuits with shrimp and grits. Oh, to be able to eat that many carbs in one sitting again. I didn't suffer though. My plate was filled with Felix's pimento cheese on a homemade baguette and a house salad with smoked mozzarella on top. I ended up saving more than half the salad for lunch the next day. It had been filled with greens, heirloom tomatoes, pickled onions, the aforementioned cheese, and grilled chicken strips. I was stuffed.

"What should we do now?" I asked Olivia. "Do you have more homework?"

"Uh-uh," she answered, along with another head shake. This girl hadn't completely filled her vocabulary with weird teen speak, but she sure did rock the grunts and nonverbals. "It's done. Can we watch a movie?"

"Sure." I gathered up the dirty dishes and set them in the sink, wondering what twelve-year-olds watched nowadays. I figured they stuck to scrolling on their phones. "Do you know what you want?"

"Can we see that one from your friend's coffee shop? The one you said was your favorite in the eighties."

I put the empty boxes back in the takeout bag. It took me a minute to remember that afternoon. Kick had asked me to pick out the five-o'clock song. I smiled at the memory of dancing on stage with Olivia and Kick, Blake reliving his teens on an air guitar. "You mean Say Anything?"

She casually lifted her shoulder. "Guess so."

After throwing away our takeout garbage and wiping down the table, we settled in the media room. The condo was a newer design but in the style of an old brownstone. The garage, an office, full bath, and this flexible space were on the first floor. The second held the kitchen, dining room, living area, and another bathroom. On the top floor were two more bedrooms, both set up as owner's suites, with walk-in closets and bathrooms attached. Blake's room also had a sitting area and a rooftop deck. It overlooked the small yard below and had views of downtown Raleigh through the trees. I adored my private, wooded backyard, but this was also pretty cool.

A ginormous, navy, U-shaped sectional anchored the media room. The cushions were so deep that my feet wouldn't touch the floor if I sat all the way back. The plush chenille material threatened to lull me to sleep if it wasn't for the precious girl in my care. I sat in one corner and pulled my feet under me. The screen filled most of the wall we were facing. Speakers of various sizing scattered around the room made the space scream man cave. All except for the young girl in the corner opposite me, holding a soft pink pig. She'd changed out of her uniform and into pajama pants and a T-shirt, looking ready to relax.

We both brought down glasses of water that we placed on a rustic coffee table, filling up the center space. The ceiling was painted a dark gray, the walls a lighter shade of the same color, giving the room a cozy, movie-viewing vibe. I pulled a throw blanket over my feet.

"So how is school going?" I asked Olivia a bunch of questions as I searched for the movie in each of their streaming services. "Do you like your classes?" I hoped it didn't sound nosy. While she hadn't talked my ear off over dinner, Liv was polite and sweet. I liked her and hated how she still gave off an air of low-level, constant emotional pain. It made me want to fix anything else that went wrong in her world.

"It's fine," Olivia answered. Like most teens, I discovered fine was one of her favorite words. "Math is getting tricky, and my teacher can sort of make fun of a kid when they get the answer wrong. But I haven't been a target. Probably because of… you know," she whispered. She sipped her water and added, "The teachers have been extra nice this year. I just… I hate it when my friends are picked on in math."

"Of course you do." I was outraged for her. No child should have to put up with that behavior or witness it. It harms everyone in the room. I put the remote in my lap. "If you need any help with math, let me know. I've always been good at it. Okay?"

Olivia nodded.

"Encourage your friends to tell their parents about your teacher. I bet they don't act out in front of other adults, right?"

"No. She's like a different person around other teachers and parents."

"Is it possible they don't know about her?"

Olivia shrugged. She leaned forward and took another drink of water before snuggling back and squeezing her pig. The essence of a girl on the edge of adulthood, straddling both worlds.

I leaned forward with my hand stretched out on the cushion between us. "They need to know, sweetie."

She gave me a small smile and nodded again. I wasn't sure if she believed me. Blake would definitely hear about this when he came home.

"Here it is." I found our movie and hit Play.

I was immediately back in the headspace of my younger self. Olivia didn't believe me when I told her about going to plenty of parties like the one on graduation night. I delicately described one particular bash we had in the woods every fall, wondering if Blake did similar things back then. Who was I kidding? I bet boys like him definitely did. Probably got up to big trouble at one of those bonfires.

I changed the subject by sharing how I wore similar clothes as the characters. Liv rolled off the sectional sofa, belly laughing. The hairstyles didn't help either. She also made fun of the cars and phone cords. I marveled at how far technology had come in my short lifetime. Still, we managed to live and love with our "pitiful" cassette tapes and reliance on pay phone collect-call shenanigans.

I giggled at the memories.

An awkward silence settled over the room as the credits rolled. I looked at Olivia. "What did you think?"

"Lloyd reminds me of Daddy."

"You said that before. How so?"

She slumped into herself, then bit her lip. "No one believed in Lloyd, even his close friends… other than him being nice, which was great… but he was more than nice."

The kid blew me away. "You think people underestimate your dad?"

"Gramps did," Liv answered without batting an eye. Her brow furrowed, like she recalled something awful.

What had she witnessed? I didn't want to pry, but thanks to her emotional response, I reached for her hand and squeezed.

Words spilled out of her like they needed to release. "Gramps always said mean stuff. He never cared who was around either."

"I'm sorry, honey." I stroked the top of her hand with my thumb. "That was so wrong." My former in-laws treated me similarly, but at least I could count on my parents. The revelation put Blake's actions into a new perspective.

We had time for one more quick show, so we cued up a teen series. As the credits rolled, Olivia quietly asked, "You think I'll have a boyfriend like that someday?"

I did a double take, wondering if I heard her right. It seemed a little early for such questions, but it had also been a lifetime ago for me. "Absolutely. You're the best catch, ever." I thought of her father and added, "Not for a while though, okay?" She sighed and shrugged. Uh-oh. I delicately pressed the matter forward. "Do you have an interest in someone?"

Olivia ducked her head shyly. "A boy kissed me."

"What?" I forced myself to be calm, betting Blake didn't know about that. "Where?" I shook myself. "I mean, were you two alone or in front of people?"

She sniffed, like her nose was stuffy. "We were in line for lunch."

I felt my face scrunch up, didn't like the Me Too implications of this. "Did he ask permission?"

"Uh-uh," she answered in her typical Liv way. Another sniff.

"You're not getting sick, are you?"

Olivia shrugged. I vaguely remembered Kick's daughter doing a lot of head shaking and shrugging at that age. I wondered if hormones interfered with word-making. She finally said, "I have to take medicine before I go to bed. For allergies and asthma." Another shoulder lifted. "That kind of stuff."

"I see." I rubbed my chin. At least I didn't have to take her to the after-hours urgent care. However, Blake would have wanted to go instead of me. "Wait. About this boy—"

"He's fine." Liv picked up the end of her braid. It was looking rough now. She removed the band and started taking it down with her fingers. It had been ages since I could do that. "He didn't ask, but the attention was nice. It's just…"

"It's okay," I encouraged, feeling the weight of Liv's recent loss. "I won't judge."

She inhaled with her whole body and let it out like she was getting ready to meditate. Or confess. "A girl in eighth grade is preggers."

I winced at the words, noting how Olivia used slang, like a silly word would keep the situation from being real. "Poor kid. She's staying in school then?"

"The other girls say her parents make her go. Like it's her punishment or something." Liv hugged her pig.

I knew better than to believe childish gossip. The truth is easily manipulated by people with nefarious intentions. "How do you feel about it… about being able to have a baby so young?"

"It's scary." She pulled her feet up against her bottom, reminding me of a roly-poly bug. "I can't… do that yet anyway."

I stretched out my legs in her direction, not sure if it was appropriate to snuggle up on her. Our feet had plenty of room to rest side by side. That would be enough to reassure her of my attention. "You haven't had your period yet, you mean?"

Another sniff. She pressed her lips together before shaking her head. "There's stuff down there, but it's not blood." Her gaze lifted and peered into mine, pleading. "Is it… normal?"

"If you mean it's clear and slick to creamy and sticky, yeah. It's totally normal. That's what happens in the run-up to your period. Didn't they tell you about that at school?"

"I don't remember." She grabbed the end of the other braid and started taking it out. "It was embarrassing."

"I see." I let my head fall for a moment, trying to remember what it was like back then. "It sounds like you'll probably start your period soon."

A look of terror washed over Liv's face. "When?"

"I don't know." I felt my face mimic her terror before slapping on my best attempt at a soothing smile. I hadn't expected this level of girl talk. "How long have you been living with these questions?"

"I don't know." She looked so sad. I couldn't take it anymore.

I moved to the middle cushion and held out an arm. "Can I give you a hug?"

Olivia slid into my side like she'd been waiting all night to do it.

I finger-combed the waves in her hair. "Is it safe to assume you don't have period supplies yet?"

"I'd say it's very safe," she said into my shoulder. I already loved her wit.

"Want me to get you some things? Or would you prefer Ms. Carol to?" I asked, rubbing her arm.

Her eyes came up to mine. "Would you help me?"

I smiled into her gorgeous little face, still full of a baby's softness, making it hard to believe she was on the verge of womanhood. "Kid, it would be my pleasure."

"'Kay." Olivia snuggled back into me.

I spoke over her head. "I'm going to give you my business card. Carry it in your backpack. Even with a period kit, if you have questions, or need me, text me. Okay?"

"What's a period kit?"

"Did anyone mention it in school?" I asked, hoping I wasn't overstepping. Praying Blake wouldn't kill me.

Olivia shuffled against me. Probably another shrug. "Maybe."

"Didn't pay attention?" I jokingly jostled her.

She whispered, "Figured Momma would take care of it."

Dammit. "I'm sorry, little chica." I pulled her in tighter, spent a few minutes rocking her slowly, clueless about what else to do. Finally I made a mental list. "Let's see… period kits have probably changed since the olden days when I was your age. Now you can choose between disposable pads and period underwear. We should pick up some of both so you can experiment with them."

Olivia sat up a bit to look at me. "Can I get unicorn ones? Fairies would also be good. Just no princesses."

"Unicorn what, honey?"

"The underwear and pads. What designs do you buy?"

This girl. My heart twisted. "I wish. It's a great idea. Unfortunately, that stuff doesn't really have designs. Colors, yes, but I've never seen any fun patterns."

"Oh." Olivia sat back, retreating into herself, disappointment falling over her face like a window shade pulling down.

It brightened up when I shared an idea. "We can look for a pouch with unicorns or fairies on it. Would that work?"

"Mm-hm." Liv nodded as she pulled her hair over her shoulder. I interpreted it as a good sign.

"We'll put some pain medicine for cramps in it and a sealable bag in case you need to change your undies." Olivia's chin quivered, and I pulled her back into me. "I swear you'll be okay."

"Pain?"

I sighed heavily. Did these people teach her anything? "It's different for each girl, but possibly. The medicine helps a lot." As I rubbed her arm, another idea popped into my head. "My friend let her daughter take the day off school on the first time her period came. It wasn't a typical sick day though. They went to lunch, had mani-pedis. Made a ladies' day of it, like a celebration. Want me to ask your dad if we could do that? Or I bet Ms. Carol would love to if you'd prefer her."

"You would do that for me?" Liv held so much hope in her eyes as she asked.

I was playing with fire, but in no way could I disappoint this angel. "Miss Brady, it would be an honor."

She bit her lip and quietly added, "What if it doesn't come for a long time, but I still want to do those things?"

"You'd want to hang out with me?" Now I pressed my lips together to keep my emotions at bay. As long as I looked at her the way I did my goddaughter, it would be fine. I'd talk to Blake about having Liv call me Aunt Cyn. That would help.

She casually lifted her shoulder. "Sounds like fun." I could see excitement hiding behind those indifferent, deep brown irises so much like her father's. The little stinker.

"It sounds amazing. I'll clear it with your dad."

"Clear what with me?" Blake said, as he entered the room from the garage. I don't know how we didn't hear the car pull in.

Olivia jumped up and shook her head at me, silently imploring me to say nothing. I tipped my head to the side, letting her know I wouldn't keep secrets from him, but I'd give her this. For a minute.

"Tell you later," I said.

It didn't matter. Liv jumped over the back of the sectional and slammed into her father.

"Hey, my Sparrow," he said, laughing. He kissed her head. "Take it you had a good evening."

"Mm-hm."

Her grunts amused me, but what did that mean?

Chapter 14

Crash Into Me

Blake

I snuck up behind Cyndi, wrapping my arms around her, enjoying the weight of her fabulous tits in my hands as she loaded dirty dishes into the washer.

"Better stop," she said with a smile. "My pal, Blake, will be down any minute."

I leaned down and nibbled the back of her ear. "Cute, Sparky." After sending Liv to bed, I changed out of my work clothes into a T-shirt and lounge pants. They totally displayed the semi I sported, but Cyn already made it clear she didn't mind. Besides, I couldn't help it. Seeing those two hanging out, getting along, even sharing some kind of secret, made me happy. Who knew it would be an aphrodisiac?

I figured I'd make the most of my semi situation and ground against Cyndi's sweet ass.

"You should tame that fire," she said, looking over her shoulder. The smirk told me she didn't mean it. "No playing when your princess is in residence," she added, pointing up to my daughter's bedroom.

Like I would do that. I'd never had a sleepover when Liv was with me. "Believe me, I know." I could still have some fun. God, it had been so long since I had a steady anything. This morning's pair of orgasms wasn't enough. I pulled Cyndi's hips harder into me. "Give me a minute." God if she didn't press her whole back against me, taking from me as much as she gave.

I kissed her shoulder and stepped back before we got out of hand. "Seeing her smile tonight… it made me happy." I adjusted my "happiness" and moved over to the kitchen table. "Can't thank you enough. What exactly did you do anyway?"

"We chatted about girl stuff," Cyndi said while she filled two glasses with water. She sat across from me, passing one of the glasses my way. "She's terrific, Blake."

Didn't I know it? My gaze moved up to the ceiling. "That baby girl is the best thing I'll ever do." I drank some water to clear the choke in my throat.

"That's just it…" Cyndi tapped an index finger on her chin. "She's not a baby anymore. You kinda need to prepare."

"I know." I sighed reluctantly, letting my head fall against my hand as it rested on the table. "She's growing too fast."

"She's about to get her period, Blake," Cyndi said, jumping straight to the point. The words hit me like a slap.

Was this women's intuition? "How do you know?"

"I stumbled upon it," she started. "Liv's probably been dying to talk to someone about it. The bottom line is…" Cyndi held up a new finger to tick off each of her points. "The breast buds, for one. In fact, someone should take her shopping for a training bra. If her uniform shirts get wet, it will probably cause a crap ton of teasing."

I almost swallowed my tongue and coughed to recover. Kill

me now. In the back of my mind, I'd known it was coming but figured my daughter would ask for one when she was ready.

"Don't wait until she's in tears over being bullied about it."

Alarm bells clanged in my head. "She's being bullied?"

"No, no." Cyndi raised her hands in a stopping motion. "I was mean-girled though. I doubt seventh graders have changed much."

"Ah." I sat a little easier in my chair. Still, I didn't like hearing about Cyn being bullied either.

She cleared her throat and sighed heavily. God, how bad would this get? "Liv shared enough to tell me her hormones are waking up. Add in the moods—"

"How long?" I cut to chase. Couldn't take much more.

Cyndi reached for my free hand under the table as I wheezed a weary breath. "This month, next month, the one after… can't say for sure, but it won't be long."

My eyes dropped to the table's surface. My stomach roiled. "Think I'm gonna be sick."

"Honey, if I thought you could, I'd say you're turning green." She rubbed the top of my hand with her thumb. Then she sifted my hair off my forehead, beckoning me to look at her as she cradled my jaw. "If you're upset about this, your girl's terrified. One foot is still firmly planted in childhood while the other one feels like it's rushing into a scary, adult world."

Without thinking, I groused, "Dammit, Gia."

"Hey," Cyn soothed. She scooted her chair closer to me and rubbed circles on my shoulder. "You're doing great. You're not alone either. Those instincts were spot on when you reached out to Carol Page." She grinned at me. "You have your awesome friend right here."

She was awesome. Too awesome maybe. "What do I need to do?"

"To start, don't freak out when I tell you the next two things."

"Aw, fuck, Sparky." How could a day begin so spectacularly only to go so far downhill? My meeting with the lawyers had been torture. Then a meat vendor told Felix he had to raise his prices. Since I was committed to their quality, I promised to work it out in the budget. Now this.

Cyndi grabbed both my hands and leaned in. The distraction of her pretty cleavage helped. "This all started because an eighth-grade classmate is pregnant. It sounds like the middle schoolers are reeling from the news." I groaned wearily in my throat, couldn't imagine what the girl's parents were going through. But she wasn't finished. "Also… a boy kissed Olivia in the lunch line at school. It was out of the blue, not what she'd planned and—"

My protective growl kicked in. Cyndi shushed me, placing her finger over my lips to keep me quiet. "How am I supposed to stay calm about this?" I snapped. "Who is the little asshole?"

"She didn't tell me, and I didn't ask." I wanted to scream, why the hell not? Cyn squeezed my hands, giving them a jostle. "This is why I decided to tell you. You can't go off around Liv. She'd see it as overacting, not love. She needs you to listen and hold your tongue. When she wants advice, she'll ask for it. It came out of her because she's confused. Growing up is suddenly real to her, and she's not sure she's ready."

"Makes two of us."

"Exactly." Cyndi stretched back in her chair. "It's coming, regardless."

"What do I do?" I couldn't shake the scowl off my face. It didn't help anything to stay mad at Gianna for dying on us. It was an accident. Liv would have needed my support anyway. What if her period came when she was staying with me?

Cyndi introduced me to the concept of a period kit, volunteering to put it together. It was clearly time to step up. I didn't want Olivia to end up settling for a douche who was squirmy about the natural happenings in a woman's body because I couldn't deal. Didn't that notion make my stomach curdle?

We decided to go as a threesome over the weekend, early in the morning. Weekends were hell to get away from the restaurant, but Jay was doing lunch on Saturday to ease back into his schedule. Of the three weekend shifts, that was the lightest.

I could get away for Sparrow. She needed to know she was supported and surrounded by love. I busted my ass to get the restaurant back on track for her as much as for my employees. My lawyers were confident I wouldn't do jailtime. None of the local or federal authorities I'd spoken with had mentioned it, but the fine was going to be a whopper. I'd lost sleep over where the money would come from, especially if we never recovered the stolen funds. But I'd figure it out for Olivia and my crew.

Cyndi had command of the shopping in her head, but I still wrote everything down on my phone just in case. My chest softened to hear her sound all-in about this. Hell, she'd given my daughter a big hug when Liv went up to bed. They shared words out of my earshot, and it lifted my heart. It helped to see evidence that Olivia and I wouldn't wander alone. But past experience taught me to stay prepared.

Cyn never explained why she'd disappeared in the first place. I'd only asked her back because I didn't know anyone else who could help me dig out of my financial hole. I was leery of trusting her with my daughter's heart and resolved to stay grateful for whatever Cyndi gave us while making sure we didn't rely on her.

The same applied to my dick. We had a world of fun in the morning, but it wouldn't—couldn't—be a priority.

As if she read my mind, she stretched out her legs and set them on my chair, crossing her ankles next to my thigh. Her foot flexed, like she'd planned to flirt with it, then changed her mind. "One more thing before we get to our next issue." I lifted an eyebrow. Not sure I was ready for one more thing tonight. "If it's okay with you, I'd like to let Olivia take the day off school if her period comes during the week. We can hang out on the weekend if that ends up being the case." Cyn giggled. "Come to think of it, I don't remember a single girlfriend starting her first period on a Saturday."

She explained the concept of a ladies' day and how Kick Harrison had done it with her daughter to celebrate her periods instead of dreading them. It didn't sit well with me. Cyndi wasn't Liv's mother, though she made it clear she didn't mean to be.

"Shouldn't I do it?" I asked, leaning back in the chair, mirroring Cyndi. "You know, for support."

"No. I think it should be a woman. Carol could, if you prefer, but Liv asked me if I would."

"Why—"

Cyndi held up a hand to stop me. "I remember parts of my first one." She shook her head as she laughed. "I was furious with my mother, like she'd done this to me. No one portrayed it in a positive light either." She propped her arm on the table and leaned into her hand. "By the time my father came home from work, I wanted him and no one else. He must've read it on my face because he sat in his favorite chair and let me snuggle into him while we watched my TV shows. We hadn't done that in years, but it helped to find reassurance I was still his little girl despite the chaos I perceived in my body."

I rubbed my chin. "So come home early… expect Liv to need a cuddle."

"It would help." Cyn gave me a shy smile. "At least be ready to listen."

"Gotcha," I said, reassuring myself with several nods in a fake-it-till-you-make-it way. "Please tell me that's all."

Her foot rubbed my leg now. She moved her finger back and forth between us. "Where do we go from here?"

"This morning was a helluva lot of fun," I said, letting myself indulge in squeezing Cyndi's foot.

"Agreed." She let out a cute little sigh. "Now what?"

"Friends…" I pressed my thumb into her sole. She bit her lip to keep from making the moan from earlier, the one I'd heard in my head the rest of the day. "…have fun."

"The office isn't a good idea."

"Come here after drop-off," I insisted.

"I have an appointment tomorrow."

I laughed. "Didn't mean every day. But I like the way you think."

"Well—"

"What if we meet here the morning after tomorrow?" I winked at her. "We can play in my room and…"

A pretty grin spread across her face. "I like and. All the and."

"Annnd," I emphasized with a smirk of my own. "Afterward, we can see where our schedules match. I'll phase back into a normal schedule next week."

"When Jay comes back."

I pressed her foot into my reignited arousal. I wouldn't put my future hopes on Cyndi, but I'd sure have fun with her while it lasted. "Can't wait."

With that settled, I walked Cyndi to the door, buzzing with renewed energy as she put her shoes on. She didn't regret our morning. More than half of me expected her to call it off. But she agreed to be my—what? Fuck buddy? Guess so. Not like I had time for more in my schedule, let alone the emotional room in my head.

Cyndi slid her arm up around my neck and pressed a quick kiss to my lips. "Thank you for today. And for trusting me with your precious girl."

Maybe it was her words. Or my body was finally crashing after being on edge all day. I didn't let her go when she shifted to step away. Instead, my arms wrapped tight around her tiny curves as I tucked my face into her neck. Peppering kisses there, the faint scent of coconut in her perfume, lotion, or whatever filled my nose. I inhaled deeply. "Can we—"

"That bad of a day?" she asked, pressing her body into mine.

I sighed into her. "Yeah."

"I should've waited to tell you about Olivia." Her hands slipped under my shirt and lightly massaged my back as I pulled up her tunic and gripped her ass through her leggings.

Did she need this as much as I did? I had to get over this consuming desire to touch her skin. "Am I an asshole for wanting to get off this hamster wheel once in a while?"

People kept saying the fraud case wasn't my fault. Neither was Olivia losing her mother. Yet I was the one dealing with the fallout. I ceased another selfish moment and ran my nose along Cyndi's skin.

"Considering everything on your plate, not at all." Her fingers moved over my back muscles, like she appreciated what she found there, making me shiver. Might have moaned. Even these small touches were good. So good. She tipped her mouth up closer to my ear and whispered, "Wish I could let you take it all out on me."

Damn her words. I groaned and ground into Cyndi, neither of us daring to do more.

"You know, even hamsters take time for themselves," she added. "Two mornings. Then we'll crawl under the sheets and disappear."

I leaned back and peered into her eyes, the low light in my entryway making them look almost as dark as mine. "You had a hamster?"

"My godson did." Her eyes sparked with a smile.

Cyndi's involvement and interest in kids that weren't her own added to the attraction. I moved my hands up to her tender jaw and kissed her hard. She responded with a breathy whimper, opening her mouth to me when I licked her lips. God, this was nice. Our tongues danced together, tasted each other, giving support as well as taking it. Maybe we could—

"Mommaaaa!"

Another one of Olivia's nightmares broke the spell.

Chapter 15

Something to Talk About

Cyndi

"You promised you wouldn't change Big Mama's recipes."

Felix's outburst caught my attention as I worked through an early lunch a sous chef named Susana made for me. Blake and his partner had been going over ways to make the Garage allergy friendly. Things didn't look good from my seat.

Chef leaned aggressively toward Blake, a finger pointing at a spot across the kitchen. By the set of Blake's jaw and flare of his nose, I could tell he was working hard to contain his temper. Boy, it did things to me. His physical power didn't scare me, quite the opposite, in fact. When I clenched my pussy, a shiver ran up my spine. Not a good look in public.

I shook myself and tried to get back to my spreadsheet, but my gaze wouldn't stay away from the arguing men. Part of me wanted to "help," certain Felix would come around if I shared my experiences dining out with friends with food allergies. My circle added new food issues regularly, and I figured it was new normal. Hell, I'd been given orders to eat more protein and fewer carbs. I moved to stand and caught Blake's eye. He lightly shook his head no.

He said something that caused Felix to flinch, like he'd been slapped. It was impossible to make out Blake's words, but the growl sounded like a dog's warning.

"Fine. Boss." Felix spat out the words and stormed off. Blake and I jumped at Fee's angry use of the moniker. They were partners, not employee-employer. In fact, the staff started calling Blake Boss as a counterpoint to Felix's Chef.

Blake stormed over to me and slid into the other side of my booth. "What are you doing down here?"

I jumped again but quickly calmed when my eyes landed on his pained expression. "Testing a dish the kitchen is working on. Susana wanted to try it out on virgin taste buds," I explained, pointing to my empty plate.

One side of Blake's mouth ticked up, quivering, probably at my use of the word virgin. At least his frown disappeared.

I shifted my finger and aimed it at him now. "Not a word." This time he bit his lip. I did the pussy-clench-shiver again, wishing he would bite me. This man could be an addiction if I wasn't careful.

He probably already was. After only two weeks, we'd carved enough time out of our morning schedules to have sex in almost every room in Blake's house. Today we'd left a trail of clothes from the entryway up the two flights of stairs to the bedroom. Then he pinned me up against the door wall, my legs wrapped around his waist, while he said the yummiest dirty words in my ear. The man loved his vertical surfaces. And colorful praise. Memories and aftershocks from our tryst had distracted me all morning. That was why I came downstairs.

I cleared my throat. "Looked intense over there. You okay?"

"It's fine," Blake answered, flicking his wrist. "We knew Fee would buck the idea. He'll come around."

True. It almost made me feel bad, since I'd suggested it. Blake wouldn't press this hard if he didn't believe in it. He'd also never jeopardize his partnership.

"Anything I can do to help?"

"Uh-uh." He drank some of my ice tea. "Fee needs to stew on it. Always does. He hasn't visited the Victorian yet either. They'll help him see it, like they did for me."

I slid the glass back and sipped, liking the familiarity of sharing, knowing I damn well shouldn't. "What was he saying about the recipes?"

"The Garage's reputation is built on the foundation of his heirloom dishes." He stretched his neck, like he needed to release the tension. "I get where he's coming from. When we went into this, I promised Felix he'd be king of the kitchen and I'd handle the big-picture experience. But this is part of that… We have to grow our reach to stay relevant." Blake took the glass with a wink. Despite the argument, he was testing me, pushing the boundaries of our promise to stay a secret. Instead of angering me, it made me want to laugh. Maybe that's why Blake did it. He pressed his fingers into his temple, his expression serious again. "I asked Felix what his grandmother would've done with those recipes if anyone in his family had been allergic to them."

"Ouch."

"Naw. He needed to hear it." Blake scratched at his ponytail. His hair was growing fast. "Felix is madder about it making him rethink his reality. It'll work out."

Blake might have been confident Felix would come around, but his fingers tapping on the tabletop gave away his troubled emotions about their argument. I could relate, hating every minute of the rare fights I'd had with Kick.

He lifted my glass and finished the tea.

"Hey!" I protested, like I didn't have access to a bottomless supply.

He raised an eyebrow in challenge, acting like he really wanted me to acquiesce and take the private part of our relationship public.

I leaned in and whispered, "Stop." Sometimes a woman needed to float in denial for a while. It was a welcoming river for a scrambled head. I planned to ride the current as far as it would take me even if I ended up stuck alone on an island—or pulled under some rapids.

"Please. No one's fooled, Sparky. I could stand up right now, announce that we know each other carnally, and the crew wouldn't be surprised."

My nose tingled and my ears burned. But it didn't matter. I knew how to stop this dangerous train of thought. The best way to tame Blake's rakish fire was to turn the subject onto his daughter. "Did Olivia ever pick out a Halloween costume?"

His long-suffering sigh made me laugh. "We bought the fairy one you two found online." He pinched the bridge of his nose, grumbling, "Still think it's awfully sexy."

"Above-the-knee skirts are normal now. Sexy is 'I can see your undies.'" He glared at me in protective father. It was like glaring in Southern—a skill I'd learned since moving here—but with extra testosterone. I knew it came from a place of overwhelm and not possession.

I slipped off my pump and rubbed Blake's ankle with my foot, hoping no one would see my attempts to soothe him. "Want me to talk to her about adding leggings? I could blame it on nighttime temperatures." With her ankle boots, Liv would look like an adorable pixie. I wished I could see her in costume.

"Please." His foot moved over to my leg, returning the under-the-table flirt action. "Still can't believe you won't go with us." He waggled his brows. "We could play sexy Lord of the Rings afterward."

My stomach whooshed at his words. Desire quickly turned

into alarm. "With little chica in the house?" The man wanted to break his own rule now.

"She's spending the night at Sofia's."

Oh hell. I swallowed hard while images of Blake dressed as a hot elf came to mind, his silky hair falling around pointy ears. I reached for his ears and snapped my hand back, remembering we were in public. Colleagues didn't touch each other intimately. Ooh, this was hard. But I wouldn't go back. I couldn't.

He tilted his head, cautiously asking, "What are you thinking?"

"You'd make a gorgeous elf." My own ears heated at my words.

Blake's lips twitched. "Here I thought you had secret hobbit fantasies."

"Is that a short joke?"

He snickered and pressed his fist to his lips. "Don't the females wear corsets?"

"You're thinking of a wench."

"Nope." His eyes glazed over.

I snapped my fingers in front of his face. "Like either of us do body hair." I shuddered at the image. "Not that I would hold it against anyone." My shoulders shook as a belly laugh tried to erupt, threatening to draw attention to us. I bit my lip to keep it in.

"We could glue fake mustaches on our feet."

"Stop." I laughed and slammed my hand over my mouth, causing Blake to also chuckle. Staff members on the floor stopped and looked at us with knowing smiles. Damn him for making his earlier point.

He schooled his features and dropped his voice. "This is why you need to stay. You make me laugh. You make me forget."

I grumbled, torn between spending time with Blake and

my plans with Tatay. The real problem being more than amazing orgasms. I liked hanging out with Blake as well. We had fun together. Admittedly, it still scared me. "No, Jefe." I hooked his ankle and pulled. "I won't apologize for spending my birthday with my dad. He needs me too."

"You're right." A smoldering grin replaced Blake's chastised expression.

"What?"

"You said 'needs me too.'" He singsonged. "You think about me and Sparrow."

I rolled my eyes, deflecting, because, yeah, they were on my mind. All. The. Time. "I think about all my friends."

"Wait…" Blake leaned in, concern filling his tone. "What's wrong with your father?"

Chapter 16

Daughters

CYNDI

"Come on, Tatay. Order something other than the one-pound BLT. Considering what your doctor just said—"

The doctor hadn't liked my father's blood sugar numbers—no surprise. He'd battled it a few years now. His cholesterol had also ticked up. Except his normal, blow-it-off attitude held an edge that scared me. I didn't need a psychologist's diagnosis to tell me my dad was depressed. It was expected after losing his wife and best friend.

What I hadn't counted on was how poorly he had been taking care of himself. Diabetes was no joke in our culture and could be missed because Filipinos often didn't fit the profile of an average American diabetic. Dad usually kept a close eye on his numbers and managed his health with diet and exercise—usually. I suspected it all went out the window when my mom's cancer rebounded. Understandable, but I wasn't ready to lose another parent.

Tatay slapped his hand on the table. "I'm a doctor."

"And the world's worst patient." I narrowed my eyes at him, and he mimicked my glare before breaking into a warm chuckle.

"All physicians are, iha."

"I'm not a little girl, Dad."

"You're not my wife either."

Woo boy. I'd flown to Mid-Michigan for my birthday. Turning forty-nine made me miss my parents, especially since this was my first one without my mother. It hit me hard to think my time with Tatay might be running short as well.

I used the visit as an excuse to tag along to his doctor's appointments, hoping for reassurance he was as healthy as ever. Instead, my suspicions he was making light of growing health issues were confirmed. We ended up bickering over it on the drive to lunch. I should've taken him somewhere with a healthier menu, except those places were an anomaly here.

My father's eyes scanned the vast menu at Antonio's Restaurant, a landmark Italian restaurant, famous for its one-pound BLT sandwich. Many travelers on the interstate made a point to stop in and fill up before finishing the drive "up north" or shopping at the nearby outlet mall. For us, it was the nicest place in town.

We sat in a booth by the window, the ever-present smell of bacon mixing with red sauce. Antonio's offered a wide variety of dishes. The bright light from outside bounced off the laminated menu, so I left my sunglasses on until I decided what to order.

I had tried the big BLT sandwich once when I was young, after a boyfriend dared me. I finished it, then threw up. Thankfully, I made it to the bathroom first. It was a rite of passage for most of the local kids.

Tatay treated it like a mark of his manliness, but his BLT days were over. He sighed like his manliness had ended as he set down the menu. "What would you order, jefa?"

My father occasionally used the nickname on me when he found me amusingly annoying. This time it made me think of Blake since it was his moniker at work. It didn't help that everything brought him and Olivia to mind, even from across the country. I shook it off and forced myself to focus.

After scanning a few pages, I found what I wanted. "I'll get the stuffed tomato." It was a tomato with chicken salad in the center and a side of fruit. I ordered it the last time we visited here—right after my doctor had declared me borderline for type 2 diabetes—and I wanted to cut back on carbs. It turned out to be delicious. I read the description again, my decision made. Hell, I'd leave half the fruit. A birthday cake from my auntie waited for us at home.

My father pulled a face like a spoiled little kid being forced to eat his vegetables. After more back-and-forth, I talked him into getting the perch dinner. It bothered me how our roles had suddenly swapped. My heart broke for my father, especially since there was no way to fix his grief. Yet another reminder to keep my heart to myself.

Our conversation moved into an easier category as we caught up on my auntie's family down in Detroit. Or I hoped it would until Dad's face crumpled again.

"What's wrong now?" I asked, relieved to see my tea show up. It gave me something else to focus on.

"The condo next to Star is for sale. She wants me to buy it and move down there."

It wouldn't be a bad idea if my auntie weren't such a busybody. "What does Berno say about it?" My cousin, Bernardo, was a successful realtor and Aunt Star's son.

Tatay scoffed. "It was his idea."

"I bet." I took a drink from the straw to keep from laughing. Auntie Star made interfering with Berno's family her life's work. He was essentially trying to take the heat off him and put the heat on my father. As if Auntie didn't know how to multitask. Also, there was a reason my father lived almost two hours away from his sister.

"It won't come to that." I tapped his hand. "We'll figure it out."

Three days later, I was back home, celebrating a belated birthday with Kick and her daughter, Rachel, on my screened porch. It was still warm enough for my succulent plants to hang out there. This time of the year used to be hard on me. As much as I liked snuggling into a thick sweater, I hated the shortened days and gray skies. Now summer temperatures were holding on with the stubbornness of an exhausted toddler about to throw a fit. We hadn't been this warm this long for years, despite the leaves displaying their peak color. I was determined to enjoy my beloved heat while welcoming the breeze from my ceiling fan. I stretched my linen top away from my belly to catch the air.

The flavored cigar Kick had brought over as part of my present relaxed me. Smoking wasn't something I did regularly. I'd learned to smoke cigarettes in high school but quit easily enough in college—easier than most anyway. Thank goodness. However, partaking in an occasional cigar came in handy when entertaining clients, especially since I never learned to golf. Kick had introduced me to hazelnut-flavored ones due to her silent partnership in a smoke shop she had inherited. In fact, she'd been the one to give me the idea to meet with clients in the lounge at the shop—recently renamed Dexter's Smoke Emporium, after the manager-partner.

Kick and Rachel shared a sofa while I sat in a lounge chair tucked into a corner. Our feet rested on a big ottoman in the center of the space. I tipped my head back and blew out another satisfying puff, grateful for the break from family and work. The setting sun peeked through the linen curtains tied to the sides of my porch, blocking the view to my neighbors' homes. The back "wall" was left open to my yard and the woods behind it, adding to my sense of serenity.

As the sky moved through various shades of pink and purple, I suddenly wondered how it looked from the patio at the Garage. I bit the inside of my cheek to shift my attention back to my guests—my found family. That darn Blake Brady. No matter how hard I tried to stop them, my thoughts kept drifting back to the man. And his sculpted cheekbones. I had hoped some distance between us would cool my jets regarding our trysts. It didn't work.

"Berno is a great guy," Kick said, bringing me back to the porch.

I turned away from the sky show, my ears slightly burning. "Sorry. What?"

"Your cousin… Berno," Kick pressed, a knowing smile touching her lips as she dragged from her cigar. "You were sharing about how he ran interference between you and your auntie."

"Right," I said, nodding as I tried to recall the rest of our just-spoken words into my brain. My trip to Michigan.

Overall, it had been a good time, even if visiting my hometown didn't fill my cup the way it used to after losing my mother. It didn't matter if I stayed in my childhood home or traveled to the center of town, memories of her jumped out at me constantly. Sometimes they lifted my spirits and made me smile. Other times they dropped across my shoulders like a weight, reminding me of the hole she'd left.

No matter what I did to cheer my dad, he was obviously experiencing the same thing on steroids. On the flight home, I concocted a plan to convince him to spend the winter with me. I'd start with Christmas break first, then use the overwhelming tax season as a cry for help. My father had one hell of a hero's complex, especially for his iha—his little girl. If that didn't work, I would become jefa and demand he come down.

I shivered at the memory of our afternoon at my Aunt Star's house and said, "Berno saved my bacon when his mother went all auntie on my ass. She decided I must move back to Michigan to take care of Tatay. Like I don't have a vibrant business here." We three modern women shook our heads in united disbelief.

"What about the condo next door?" Kick asked, referring to Aunt Star's efforts to bring my father down to Detroit.

I curled my upper lip. "Star wants us both to move in and be one big, happy family."

Kick barked a laugh. "She can't be serious."

"Sounds like Gran's sister, doesn't it, Mom?" Rachel observed.

"A bit." Kick took an understandably long pull from her little stogie. Where my family could be misguided and meddling, Kick's family's disfunction started with judgment and ended with a meanness bordering on evil. "Aunt Eileen emailed me the other day to chew me out over Bobby. No surprise since I won't take Eileen's or my mother's calls anymore." Kick's hand shook as she tucked some of her long curls behind her ear. "They both know to call the nurse case manager Thomas hired if they need anything." She tipped her head toward me. "The difference is Star knows when to back down. She's genuinely concerned about her brother."

I blew out a puff of smoke and let the nutty scent calm my blood pressure. Kick had been through hell and back thanks to her mother's family. Her comment relieved the guilt I'd been feeling since the afternoon at my aunt's. She and my cousin loved my father. Their long drive from the Detroit suburbs placed a burden on them that was only slightly easier than mine. The distance worried them like it did me. "Can you send me information on that nurse case management company?" I asked Kick. "It might help settle my family's concern."

"Sure. Hold on, there's a card in my purse." She jumped up in search of her bag, leaving me alone with my goddaughter.

I pulled my feet under me. "Tell me all about your glamorous, new life, Snow." She'd been recruited to Broadway after college and had recently joined a touring company for Wicked. Rachel was in line to play Elphaba when the current actress's contract expired. She winced and nervously played with the ends of her ponytail. "Something wrong with the show?" I asked.

The musical was about to do a two-week run in Raleigh, and she used her afternoon off to hang out with us. Boy, I missed her. She and her brothers had been a huge part of my life since I moved to North Carolina. I was feeling some of Kick's empty-nest syndrome. We hadn't seen Rachel since her mother and I traveled to New York to see her in an off-Broadway show last winter.

"The musical's great," she said. Her eyes darted inside my house, tracking where her mother had gone. "It's that wretched nickname. It's…" She sighed in frustration.

I moved across the porch and slid into the empty seat next to her. "Makes you feel like a baby, perhaps?"

"And then some." Her eyes fell on the ashtray holding our cigars. Rachel's ashed out after a few quick puffs, and she showed no interest in relighting it. Her shoulders dropped like they were tired. Even last winter, it was obvious something big had changed in her. The eternally positive girl had disappeared, and I wondered if it had to do with her latest breakup. Rachel had been in a string of messy relationships with both men and women. The one thing they had in common was cheating. On her. I wanted to injure them all.

In that way, she reminded me more of myself than of my

bestie. Without trying, Kick had found herself two princes who adored the shit out of her. I loved that for her, considering how hard the rest of her life could get. I, on the other hand, only found those toady types. Young ones, old ones, it didn't matter. The lessons managed to help me find myself and love myself enough to make sure no one ever wrecked me again.

I gently tugged Rachel's hair, thinking she might need some frog-kissing tips. "Do you have time for a life outside of work these days?"

She pursed her lips in her sassy way. "You mean, am I seeing anyone?"

"Perhaps." I feigned innocence before breaking into a chuckle.

"Kinda?" Rachel pulled at her lower lip. "He heard my brother call me Snow and used it against me. It was just a disagreement. Nothing serious. He had a point though."

"Uh, who is this 'he'?" I already didn't like him.

She leaned over, making sure her mother was out of earshot. Now my hackles shot up. Rachel whispered, "It's kind of secret… because it's early."

"Really?" I looked through my empty kitchen for Kick. "You used to share secrets with your Auntie Cyn."

Her hand lifted to the diamond pendant she always wore to keep her late father, Shane, close. He'd bought it for her eighth-grade graduation. "It's fine. He's separated, so we have to be careful."

Separated. As in still married… Don't freak, Sendaydiego. Did I mess up her judgment somehow? A breeze blew through my hair, cooling my blood before it boiled. "Have you at least told…" I hooked my thumb toward the kitchen.

Rachel shook her head.

"Well, shit." I scratched my nose. "When is the divorce final?"

"We're busy." She scrunched her face and murmured, "That's why it's private for now."

I bet. I relit my cigar to bolster my nerves. The girl was walking on my third rail, but I knew her. It was out of ignorance… and probably a search for a father figure. I scooted my chair closer. "To a certain extent, you'll always be your mom's little girl. And mine." Rachel opened her mouth to protest, and I raised a finger to stop her. "However, when your dad came up with your nickname"—Shane had called her Snow White because she matched the description of the Disney princess—"I gave him a hard time. He was barbecuing and singing along to the Eagle's 'Witchy Woman,' and I pointed out how the song's subject shared the same physical description of the cartoon. My point to him then and to you now is… you don't have to be boxed into a persona you don't identify with."

"I feel so much… more."

"Exactly. You can be both. Or something totally different." I brushed a few waves off her face. "For your mom, it's a way of saying she loves you and honoring Shane. However, it doesn't mean you're doomed to be a princess forever. If anyone tries to put you in a box, don't let them. Break the damn box if you must. Whatever it takes, honey."

The wind blew Rachel's hair off her face, exposing the depth of her self-doubt. "Why is this always so hard?"

"Sometimes we go through the same trials until we finally learn the lessons."

"I suppose." She tipped her head back, letting the breeze flow over her.

"I don't know how much you remember from when I was married, but my ex and his family smushed me into a box that never fit. I've tried getting over it, sometimes meeting men who wanted to box me right back up. You know what I discovered?"

"What?"

I held up a finger. "One… each instance taught me a new lesson. And two…" I shimmied my shoulders. "I'm amazing."

We both laughed.

"Seriously." I reached across the sofa cushion and squeezed her shoulder. "Self-love and grace are the crux of a woman's beauty. Don't let anyone else dictate your worth, Rach."

"I'll try," she said after a long sigh. Then she tipped her head toward me. "Thanks, Aunt Cyn."

"Anytime, sweetheart." I smiled at her and scooched closer, pulling her in for a hug. "You can always come to me. Promise I'll listen." She smiled in acknowledgment, but it didn't reach her eyes. Whatever bothered her was locked up tight.

I'd learned the hard way that sometimes our loved ones had to keep riding their rough waves while we waited for them on the shore, ready to pick up the pieces. It never felt like enough. I wanted to swim out and rescue her, dammit. I didn't know how Kick handled it. I was just the bonus mom, and it tore me up.

Kick returned with a plate of macarons, a pitcher of tea for refills, and the business card for the nurse case manager. She sat in the chair I'd vacated. "Everything okay?" she asked suspiciously.

I squeezed Rachel's shoulder, letting her know I had her back. "Rach was sharing about Wicked."

Kick beamed with pride for her daughter as she reached for a cookie. "Tell Cyn what the director said about your voice."

As Rachel recounted the story and all the funny happenings with the show, my phone buzzed with a text. Afraid it might be about my dad, I pulled it out of the pocket of my bicycle shorts.

BLAKE

Are you home yet? Can you talk?

After a quick check, he reassured me there was no emergency. I let him know I had company and would be available soon. An hour later, Kick drove Rachel back to her hotel in Durham.

I filled my watering can before calling Blake back. Talking to him might take my mind off my worries about my goddaughter and my father. But the man also had the power to consume my focus. The spike of joy I felt when the text came through had been a warning. Taking care of my succulents while we spoke would keep me from going over the edge. From losing myself in him.

Despite my plan, I sighed deeply at Blake's warm, "Sparky" greeting. As much as I tried, I couldn't resist the emotional pull. He sounded equally relieved to take my call.

"Hey, Jefe, what's going on?" I made sure my voice sounded unaffected by his smooth tones.

He blew out a long breath. "Remember the cousin I found?"

"Sure." I moved from plant to plant, giving them their precious water. Each bloom was taken as an expression of love and contentment. I shared the sentiment.

"Well, she and I emailed a few times. Then we called each other."

My big, diverse family had been a source of comfort when I was down. I hated Blake had the opposite experience. Was thrilled when his cousin reached out. It meant the world to have him share parts of this experience with me. "Have you learned anything new?"

A low rumble came through the speaker. I couldn't tell if it was about good news or bad. "You have no idea."

Chapter 17

Alive

BLAKE

The time had come. After a few weeks of sorting our schedules so everyone could be here, Olivia and I were about to meet my birth family with a video chat. I pulled her into my lap for security as much as to fit us both on the camera and accepted their call with a click of my shaking fingers.

Did I look all right? Did we look like them? Would they like me? God, I hoped no one cried. Holy hell, there were a lot more people on-screen than I expected. Was everyone part of my family? Smiling, hopeful faces filled my monitor. Part of me wanted to run. The other part felt oddly at home. Finally.

For a second, I wished Cyndi was sitting next to us, lending support. Except we weren't like that. Her pep talk from earlier would suffice. As grateful as I'd been for Cyn's—and Carol's—help these past months, Liv and I were on our own now. My knee bounced as I waited for these beautiful people to unmute.

"Can you hear me?" A voice I recognized from past phone calls with my cousin Sherry came through the speakers.

"Yep. Sounds good. Do y'all hear us?" I said back.

An older woman giggled. "He says y'all."

I bit my tongue to keep from sarcastically saying, What did y'all expect? I'm a Southerner. Except I wasn't. Not anymore. Sherry gave the lady a stink eye. Guess we were all on edge.

"Hello, everyone. I'm Blake—"

The older woman gasped. "He kept his name."

"I told you," Sherry said, frowning back at her. They had the air of a mother and daughter. Thanks to my small window in my monitor's corner, the resemblances were undeniable. Our eye shape, cheekbones, full bottom lip. My nose had a bump on the bridge from breaking it in a fight when I was a teen. Otherwise, it would've been straight like theirs. My eyes were lighter though.

"Yeah." I ran my hand through my hair. "It's about the only thing I remember from then… my name. My adoptive parents used it for my middle name, but I switched it back when I became an adult."

Olivia watched me speak with her eyes wide. Guess I never told her that story. We needed to spend more time together. I gave a quick smile and a tickle to loosen her up. "This here is my angel girl, Olivia. I also call her Sparrow."

She waved at the camera. "Hi."

"Aren't you gorgeous?" Sherry declared, her eyes shining. She sounded as overwhelmed as I felt, then looked at me. "I can't believe Baby Chunk turned into you."

"Baby Chunk?" I laughed, incredulous. The earliest photos my parents had of me were of a skinny toddler.

Sherry nodded vigorously. "The chunkiest. I used to pull you in a wagon." She wiped her brow. "But you were too heavy for an eight-year-old girl to carry. You were àwéé tsoh."

"What?" Olivia giggled in my lap as the hole in my heart wove itself together.

"It means chunky baby," Sherry answered. She proceeded to handle all the introductions at her end. The older woman was her mother, Donna—my mother's older sister. Thanks to earlier emails, I knew my birth mother's name had been Debra, and everyone called her Debbie. They had an older brother, Joe Jr., who was a Vietnam veteran and had kids of his own. More cousins. As I scanned the crowd, it didn't look like Uncle Joe made it to our party. I didn't mind. The group was big enough for now.

Sherry's husband, Gabe, waved hello and stayed in the background. Her daughter, Juniper, and her son, Canyon, were both there. Juniper lived near her mother with her fiancé. I was honored she'd made time in her busy schedule to come over.

Canyon lived with his parents in Phoenix and was a student at the community college. He planned to go into business with his father, who had built a hospitality company out of a fry bread food truck. Now they ran a dozen food trucks, two bars, and two brick-and-mortar restaurants of various Southwestern cuisines.

Embarrassed by my problem at the Garage, I said little about it. Not until I was out from under the shame of the investigation.

Juniper and Canyon asked Olivia a ton of questions about her school, hobbies, and friends. I had mentioned Gianna's passing in one email to Sherry to avoid having this visit take a dark turn for Liv.

Juniper, though, was a competitive hoop dancer, besides going to school and planning a wedding. My daughter was fascinated with the description of the art form and couldn't wait to learn more.

"Enough you two. It's auntie time." Aunt Donna pushed her way past the kids and filled the camera lens. Her eyes examined every inch of my face. "I can't believe the world's pudgiest baby turned out so handsome. I mean, you were always a beautiful baby, and you slimmed out as soon as you started walking. Well…" She chuckled as she quickly spoke. "The moment you balanced on two feet, you began running." She clicked her tongue, then leaned into the frame and stage-whispered, "And still single? What a crime. The girls will line up to get a piece of you when you come to visit, don't worry. Auntie will take care of you."

I shook my head, laughing. It was easy to eat up her rushed words about me as a baby. All my life, the earliest years were empty, like I was born a toddler who could speak a few words.

But what was this auntie stuff? Was Donna's mind stable? "That's all right I'm…" I couldn't finish the sentence. Technically, I was still single. With a special friend. Not to mention busy. Plus… did they say visit? I hadn't planned that far ahead.

"Yeah…" She pointed at me, nodding her head knowingly. "I can tell how you play it."

I coughed, with no idea how to respond to her in front of my twelve-year-old daughter. The words fuck and buddy screamed in my head, and that was where the words stayed. Thank you, Auntie.

Aunt Donna pointed at her temples. "You should brush in that gray-away, honey."

Olivia snort-laughed at her while I cleared my throat. "I thought it looks distinguished." Truthfully, I didn't think about it at all.

"Will you leave him alone, Ma?" Sherry pushed her mother out of the way, saving me. "Your auntie energy is new to him." My cousin turned to me, looking a little sheepish. "Sorry, Blake—"

Before she could say more, Aunt Donna cut back in. "That's how you do family… you throw them in the deep end.

Besides, what's he going to do?" She turned to me with a devilish smirk. "I know where you live now."

I liked Aunt Donna.

My gaze shifted to Olivia, who seemed to wear the same overwhelmed-but-awed smile I did. Then the group parted as a much older woman made her way into the frame. Donna vacated her chair and stood behind her, lovingly easing her long, silver hair over her shoulder.

The woman reached for the screen and Sherry said, "It's Blake, Gran. Do you remember him?"

I swallowed around a massive lump in my throat. Blinked my eyes several times. This woman was regal. Fragile yet made of steel. She seemed to hold the world's knowledge in her piercing gaze. And she was my... grandmother.

She did a double take at Sherry, her face contorting. "What do you mean, do I remember my beautiful Blake?" When she turned back to us, a tear tracked down her cheek. "I never forgot you, shitshói." She gasped when her eyes moved to Olivia, then back to me. "I've dreamed of you."

"Shi..." My brain raced back through time to see if the word was familiar. I was desperate for it to be, but nothing came.

My grandmother pulled back her shoulders, not that she'd been slouching. "You are my shitshói. My daughter's child."

I stared speechless at this ethereal soul. Grateful to have her —them—and angry about being taken away in the first place. I'd missed so much. As I sniffed, the sound echoed on the other side of the call.

I longed to know what she'd seen in her dreams, but I was terrified to ask. What if she saw the things that I worked hard to forget? The dark times motivated me, pushed me to be better. It didn't mean I wanted to talk about them. It was stupid to think my grandmother knew what my adoptive father had said to me or the way my teachers treated me, but something in her expression told me she'd seen it all.

I sniffed again. "Can I ask your name?"

My grandmother smiled warmly. I swear, a spark of a memory bloomed in her smile. Not the one from the visions that lived at the edge of my memories. My spirit knew this one. "I'm your Grandma Rose." She declared it with warmth and dignity, like she wasn't just introducing herself, she was introducing the family. Formerly.

This time my eyes and Olivia's widened with surprise. We both shook our heads in amazement. Then I said, "Olivia's middle name is Rose." Gianna wanted the name because they were her favorite flower, and it sounded pretty to me. Did I have a memory of it somehow?

Aunt Donna's hands flew to her mouth as she gasped while my grandmother smiled proudly. Then she said, "You are Blake Joseph Nez. Born for the Salt People clan. Your grandfather is Towering House People. I don't know the rest, but it's enough. When you visit, I'll teach you the Diné words."

The lump in my throat wouldn't go away as I was introduced to the real me. I stared at the floor while Olivia spoke for me. "Nez?" She turned to me with her face scrunched. "Do we have to change our name?"

Our room and the other one fell silent as I squeezed her. "One thing at a time, Sparrow." I looked at the camera. "Right, everyone?"

Sherry smiled at her. "That's right, baby girl."

Then I did what I did best and changed the subject. "What's this about me being a big baby? My adoptive parents have photos of me as a tiny two-year-old."

Grandma Rose, Aunt Donna, and Sherry exchanged looks before Donna said, "That's impossible, honey. While you slimmed down in your second year, you were three when you were taken."

My brows rose into my hairline. "Wait, what now?" My heart raced as my throat dried. Was I older than I'd been led to believe?

"Yes," my grandmother continued. "You spoke well for a little guy. Could read some words also. You were three."

Olivia squirmed out of my lap as I rubbed my temple. The world had gone fuzzy. Had I turned fifty without knowing it? "Anyone want to tell me when my birthday is?"

Chapter 18

Shivers

Cyndi

The rapid clicks of a keyboard told me Blake was in his office, sounding like he was beating the crap out of it. I popped in before dropping my gear in my office. It was hard not to call him this morning and find out how the video call had gone. I had to stay focused on early meetings with other clients and was proud of myself for waiting until the afternoon to check in.

"How did it go?" I asked.

His brow furrowed so deep that his eyes looked like black holes when he finally lifted his head. "I'm fifty, Sparky."

"No, you're not." I chuckled, nonplussed. If I remembered right, his birthday was in April, roughly six months before me.

He grumbled as he pushed his hair back. "I've been corresponding with the social worker investigating my adoption, as well as an acquaintance who is a child psychologist."

"What's going on?" I slid onto one of the Chesterfields. Today's tone scared me.

Blake rubbed his temples. "My birth certificate says I was born on April twentieth. Turns out, that's around the time I disappeared. Most likely, it was the day I was found."

"Okay. When's your actual birthday?"

"According to my family… September second."

"Ooh, a Virgo. Nice."

"That's what you get out of this?" Blake asked. I was trying to make him laugh, but his scowl only deepened.

I lifted my shoulder. "So you missed a birthday—"

"My fiftieth." He growled. "The bastards estimated my age. Again, as my family tells it, I was three."

"I don't understand. Wasn't there a search?"

His mournful sigh broke my heart. "Apparently not. After I pressed her, the social worker sent a photo of me in the sheriff's office." His head tipped up to the ceiling. "I looked like hell, Spark. My friend said I looked traumatized. He also said it explained why my birth family has different memories of my verbal skills than my adoptive parents." He waved his hand. "Whatever happened probably caused me to shut down."

"Oh, honey. It's a blessing you don't remember." I bit my cheek to keep from crying. "Is there anything I can do?"

"No. Thanks." He gave me a sad little smile and shook his head. "At least the laws were changed to make shit like this harder to get away with."

I tipped my head to the side. "What do you mean, harder? Didn't the Indian Child Welfare Act put an end to taking children from their families?"

"Some private adoption agencies exploit loopholes to go around the law."

"What? So would a baby like you still end up in the same circumstance?"

"My family doesn't think so. They're adamant that I would've been raised by my aunt—Sherry's mother." His demeanor finally broke as he spoke about them. His stoic face twitched with amusement. "She's a trip."

I stood and moved toward Blake's desk. The distance was painful. "Who?"

"My Aunt Donna. Or auntie, as she called herself."

I palmed a small hairband as I passed the corner of his desk. "I know all about aunties," I said, chuckling as Star came to mind. She'd recently sent me a realty listing for the home next to my cousin's. I knew exactly what he was in for. Blake hummed as I let my nails skim his scalp. I loved the feel of his silky strands flowing through my fingers. "I have a particularly charismatic aunt."

"If that's your euphemism for nosy, I'm in the same boat," Blake said, his shoulders bouncing with amusement.

"Nosy, meddling, presumptuous… yeah." Blake chuckled at my description. I explained, "They consider it key to their role in the family. Mothers are revered, especially with my family's Catholic background. A momma don't put their kids on the spot. That's where tiyas come in."

"Tiya?"

"It means auntie. We use the English word too. Anyway, an auntie can be any older woman you're close to. I'm a tiya to Kick's kids." I worked Blake's hair into a braid. It was getting long and luscious, testing my libido's willpower. "Let me guess… she had plenty of words for your single status."

He carefully looked over his shoulder. "How'd you know?"

"Oh, Jefe." I tied off the end of the braid, folded it over, and secured everything in the band. "Mine has ridden my ass about being a spinster since the divorce. With much love, of course." With his hair done, I rubbed Blake's tight shoulders. "Geez, you're like a rock. Poor buddy." He moaned under my touch, lifting my spirit to know I could help somehow.

"Actually, after Joel left, aside from Kick, no one had my back like my Aunt Star. I mean, my parents loved and supported me, but Star wanted to call out a posse." I laughed at the memory. It was one of the few good ones from back then. "Ever since, she's been convinced my 'problem' would be solved by finding a good Filipino man." Find yourself a good American boy. I bet Tatay would eat those words now if he could.

"Star? That's an interesting name."

"It fits her." I found a big knot and pressed hard with my thumbs. Blake exhaled hard as the muscle released. "It's really Tala, which means star. When she came here, Aunt Star perfected her English skills by watching soap operas. One of them had a character named Star. She changed it to the English version soon after, but I liked Tala. I always wanted to use it for a daughter if I had one."

"Sparky." Blake grabbed my hand and brought it to his lips.

"Stop the sympathy, buster." I tapped his shoulder. "I play the cards as they're dealt, but if I can't talk about it, then I know something's wrong. Just because it didn't go as planned doesn't mean I don't enjoy what I have."

He kissed my fingers again. "Point taken." He shifted his head from side to side and moved his shoulders in circles, testing their new looseness. "Thanks." He pulled me around so I faced him, his woody scent filling my senses. "For everything."

"Anytime." I leaned against the desktop. "What are you going to do about this birthday stuff?"

Blake's eyes narrowed, making me regret my question. "My lawyer's looking into it." He rubbed my leg. The gesture seemed unconscious, like it soothed him or helped him think. Or both. "It's easiest to leave it as is, but that feels fake. I haven't decided."

I pressed my hands onto the edge of the desk, leaned into them, and let Blake get an eyeful of my cleavage. The way his pupils dilated told me it worked. Hey, anything to get him into a better mood, especially since I had to get working soon.

"In conclusion, embrace your auntie…" I paused for him to fill in her name.

"Donna."

"Auntie Donna's energy." A grin stretched across my face as I imagined what she looked like. Warm, mysterious, and gorgeous like her nephew. The smile grew as I studied Blake's collection of Star Wars paraphernalia on the wall behind him. A string of LED lights focused on Luke, Han, Leia, and Chewy. The little boy longing for a connection. For meaning. After all these years, he'd found it. "This is good. Really good."

"It is." He absently squeezed my calf muscle. I liked it. A lot. Giving Blake comfort without a happy ending seemed more intimate than if I'd dropped my lacy underwear and jumped on his lap.

His lips lifted into a shy smile. "We might go visit them over Christmas break."

My breath caught in my throat as I wished for a beat that I could go with them.

"Uh, Cyndi, the dinner service is starting."

I jumped at Blake's words, then checked the time on my laptop. "Shit. I'm so sorry." I'd been engrossed in my new spreadsheet and lost track of time. Hey, that's another symptom to put on the sheet. I squeaked at the notion he might see my work and slammed my laptop shut, startling him.

Blake looked at me suspiciously and slid into my side of the booth. "Why'd you do that?"

I had moved down to the dining room during the lull between lunch and dinner, taking advantage of the tea station. Plus it was cozy in the big booth at the back of the house.

"I'm so sorry I lost track of time. Meredith…" I called out to her as she passed the table. "Next time give me a shove."

She made a face like she didn't know what I was talking about, and Blake waved her off.

He wiggled his finger at my computer. "What's on there. Is it about the Garage?"

"Sure." There were open tabs regarding my work for Blake, just not the top one.

He narrowed his eyes in warning. "Sparky."

"I was working on our project." Emphasis on was. I deflected with a perky smile.

Blake shifted, turning to face me. "Then why hide it?"

"I…" It was so embarrassing. "Hell. Fine. After I finished for the day, I made a spreadsheet of my symptoms."

"A spreadsheet?" He seemed impressed.

"Accountants love spreadsheets."

Blake leaned closer. "What symptoms?"

I shrugged. "Random ones… figured if I track them, they might make sense. It's what Kick does when she thinks her health is tanking."

"Are you sick? Why didn't you say something?" He grabbed my hand and squeezed it.

"I'm not." I pulled our clasped hands under the table so the staff wouldn't see. "I'm not sick, per se. I just feel weird sometimes. Unusually hot… headaches… sluggish. They're not scary. Only new." I opened the laptop and entered my pin. "Since I'm seeing my doctor next month, I figured I'd track them." I rubbed his hand with my thumb. He had rough hands from boxing. No pansy business hands for this man. "I'm sorry about taking up Meredith's table. Should probably add brain fog to the… list." I pointed at my laptop.

"This is Collin's section tonight, and it's fine." He brushed a piece of hair off my face. "I don't like the idea of you being sick."

His intimate gesture amped up my nerves. "Quit with the PDAs or the staff is going to suspect we're…" I moved my finger back and forth between us.

Blake set his elbow on the table and rested his head in his hand. A devilish smirk brightened his face. "They suspect, Sparky dear." He tipped his chin at my computer. "You should put that on your spreadsheet."

"What?"

"Cluelessness." He winked at me.

Darn it. That counted as brain fog. My brows rose to my forehead. "They can't know."

"Why not?" He checked over his shoulder. "They won't object."

"We said 'friends'," I insisted.

The fingers of Blake's freehand mimicked tiptoeing up my thigh. "We are."

"Then we added fuck buddies on the side. On. The. Side. Blake." I pressed.

His eyes crinkled with a silent laugh. "I won't ravage you on this table." His fingers traveled up my arm. "Even if flirting with you makes me want to. Besides, best friends make the best lovers. It's a twofer."

"Best friends?" I squeaked as Blake nodded slowly. "Kick's rack is impressive, but it's not my thing," I said with a smirk.

"Touché." He chuckled but didn't relent.

"So you want to make this more official?"

"Maybe."

"And you want to tell Olivia about us?"

Panic replaced Blake's flirty gaze.

I bit my lip, soaking in my gotcha moment. I shook my head. "No worries."

"It's just—"

"I get it." I motioned toward my computer. "How about we finish settling your books and reassess our status in the new year? Then you'll get a glimpse of what it's like to see me rarely during the winter." Blake would still be a client, but it seemed easier to give him my personal time if he wasn't taking so much of my professional focus. It also allowed me to put off thinking about the real reason I'd broken us off in the first place. If he changed his mind, I wouldn't have to think of it at all.

Blake leaned back in the booth, like he was practicing being close without touching. "I remember your tax season. All right, you win." He stretched his arms overhead. "Are we still on for tomorrow morning?"

"Wouldn't miss it." I chuckled at his one-track mind, not admitting how much I needed it too. Blake had a way of clearing my head of noise that had recently taken up residence. I quickly typed brain fog and bloating into my spreadsheet.

"Good. Oh…" Blake ran his hand over his head. "Thanks for the braid contraption, by the way."

"Yeah?" I bounced a little from the compliment. "You like it?"

"It's cool." He moved his head from side to side. "Plus the chefs prefer it tied up. Felix has been giving me hell about wearing my hair loose in the kitchen. Where'd you learn to do it?"

"It's a secret." I batted my lashes. "My hair was long when I was young. Those mad braiding skills don't just disappear." I didn't want to tell him I'd done a little research online. It would mean admitting I was thinking of him more than I should have.

"Come on." Blake made a pouty face. "I was hoping you'd teach me." Then he popped his brows mischievously. "Unless you promise to do it for me every day."

Well, shoot. I folded my arms and narrowed one eye, assessing him. "I adapted it from a show called Dark Winds, okay? The main dude's hair is longer than yours, but when he did it up, it reminded me of you. Only, he had a legit cloth way of tying it. I finagled it with the band. Good call on the silk covering, by the way. My old hairbands used to get so much hair wrapped around them." I rubbed the top of my head, swearing my scalp suddenly ached some from the memory of pulling them out.

Blake lifted an eyebrow. "Dark Winds?"

"Oh yeah. You should check it out." I nodded enthusiastically. "If you want to go up to the office, I could show you what I did." I quickly saved my files and shut down the laptop. I waved my hands at Blake. "Well, let's go."

"Hang on." Blake blocked my attempt to shuffle out of the booth. He wasn't a mountain of a man, but he sure was solid. "Chef and I finished the holiday plans this afternoon. Felix plans to cater a few Thanksgiving dinners, but they'll get picked up first thing in the morning. We're holding a private dinner here with friends and family of the staff on Thanksgiving afternoon."

"Aww. That's really sweet." This was why I was determined to make sure Blake came away clean from his legal situation. He didn't deserve what Alan Kramer was putting him through.

His ears darkened as he shook his head. "I'm trying to ask you to join us. The staff thinks of you as part of the team. Liv is dying to see you again." He leaned toward me and lowered his voice. "And I want you there for me. I know you usually go to Kick's, but I'm not afraid to pull the my-mother-will-be-in-town card. Could use a friendly face when she's around."

I felt my face crumple as my heart tore in two. Running interference with challenging mothers was my specialty, and I was close to certain I'd be nicely rewarded for my efforts afterward. "Dammit. I'm sorry, Jefe. I can't."

Chapter 19

Always Something

BLAKE

I pulled into the circular drive at the Hilton near my place, frowning as I peered up at the cloudy sky. It was an omen. A bright day might have eased the tension rolling off my mother as she struggled to climb inside my SUV. Who was I kidding? The sky wouldn't have helped her, but it could've lifted my mood.

Humid air filled the space along with my mother's signature Chanel perfume. Both essences battled with the spicy scent of the leather conditioner for dominance.

I inhaled deeply and tried to channel the nicer memories my mother's bouquet elicited. At least the driving rain had stopped. She arrived late the night before because a severe thunderstorm delayed her flight. Instead of catching up over dinner at her favorite restaurant like I had planned, she demanded to be taken straight to her hotel.

"Good morning, Ma'am." I waited for her to settle in the

passenger seat before leaning over and kissing her cheek. "How was your night?"

"The bed is soft."

It wouldn't have been if you'd taken my room instead of insisting on staying at a hotel.

My mother preferred complaining about a bad hotel experience to risking the possibility she was an annoying house guest. Plus having to ask which cupboard I kept the dishes in had freaked her out the one time she came for a visit. She spent the afternoon rearranging my kitchen because the woman didn't understand how my needs could deviate from hers.

"I don't understand why you live in such a small apartment. You're a father, not a bachelor. You can afford a decent house with a real yard and guest bedroom." She clucked her tongue as she loosened the bottom of the seat belt and shifted in the seat like she couldn't get comfortable. It didn't matter that I would've happily slept on the futon in my office or on the sectional in the media room. Or that my daughter and I lived in a condo I owned.

There had been a time when Gracie Brady, my adoptive mother, smiled often, kissed booboos, served juice popsicles to the neighborhood kids. The years with her husband, Kurt, erased that. Nothing pleased the old man. Not naming their long-awaited "son" after him. Not keeping a spotless home at all hours, despite said rambunctious son. The only thing predictable about my old man had been his volatility. Eventually my mother craved security and stability above all. By the time I was a teen, we related to each other the way cellmates in prison did—or that was how it felt. Despite Kurt's predictions, I never ended up in jail. Gracie, however, only found her "parole" after he died. As such, she fought changes as fiercely as a freedom fighter crusading for justice.

Case in point, her hair. Growing up, my mother moved

through the popular styles and trends of the sixties and on, like the other women in her circle. After they retired to Florida, she reverted to the bouffant she wore when she and Kurt met, complete with a dark dye job every two weeks to cover her silver roots. No one was fooled into thinking she was young. Well, maybe her new "man friend" was. I hadn't asked.

"I still don't see why you and Olivia couldn't come down for Thanksgiving."

When my old man died last year, Gracie's neighbors in her expansive retirement community took her safety as a single widow seriously. Initially, the attention eased my concern for her, given our distance. However, someone called the police on me the last time Liv and I visited. Twice in one day. The second time, my daughter was in the rental car. It didn't help that my mother never displayed pictures of me or Olivia at her house. Not one. That had been another directive from Kurt, but she could've framed some afterward. Instead, they stayed in an envelope in a drawer. I doubted she ever mentioned us.

Liv huffed in the back seat, and my mother turned her head toward the sound, adding another cluck to a disappointed sigh. Yeah, it was better that she'd spent the morning at her hotel. I'd offered to pick her up early for breakfast and watch the parade on TV. After my daughter woke up in a bad mood, I breathed a sigh of relief when my mother texted to cancel. I let Liv hang out in her bedroom while I read instead. Olivia's moodiness was becoming a daily event.

I plastered on a smile for both of them, wishing Cyndi was here. She had a way with persnickety family members. Hell, she probably would have won Kurt over if he were still alive.

"I couldn't get away from work this week, remember? The restaurant is booked for private parties. You and Liv can spend time together tomorrow and Saturday." We pulled up to a red light, and I gave her a quick smile. "Carol Page is excited to see you again. And to show you how well our girl's doing with her riding lessons. You remember Carol, right?"

She gave me a look—the gentle scold—telling me to stop being dumb. I knew it well. "Is Carol still hot to trot?"

"Excuse me?" I laughed as the light turned green and we picked up speed. My foot almost fell off the pedal in shock.

My mother waved her hand—another of her you-should-know-this moves. "All the husbands were jealous of Mr. Page when he remarried his young girl. I suppose you wouldn't have noticed since you were a boy." She leaned toward me. "Some of the other wives let themselves go, but I worked hard to stay pretty for your father. So that Kurtis would be proud of his wife. And you."

I caught my flinch at the word father. I didn't like it since I'd never felt it. But it wasn't her fault. She didn't give him the son he craved, and I couldn't be white.

I changed the subject. "You look pretty, Ma'am."

She lifted her purple satin blouse at the neckline. "This old thing?"

I laughed, knowing full well it was new, probably bought for this day and wouldn't be worn again. Gracie Brady might hate change, but she loved new clothes. "Anyway, we're glad you agreed to come up for a few days. Right, Liv?"

"Uh-huh. Hi, Gigi." Instead of Grandma Gracie, Ma'am preferred the term Gigi. She claimed it didn't make her as old as grandma did despite the fact she was well into her senior years when Olivia was born. I watched my daughter in the rearview mirror. She didn't take her eyes off her phone.

"Are you going to allow this disrespect the whole time I'm here?" My mother's face flushed.

I tried not to roll my eyes as we turned the corner to the street the Garage was on. Hang in there. "She's twelve, Ma'am. From what I'm told, it's a hard age for any girl. I'll err on the side of indulgent considering Liv's been through hell these past few months." I shrugged. "We were lucky to get a response from her at all."

"You need to parent her right, especially since you're the only one she's got now." I winced at the words. She'd hit on my rawest nerve—ruining my sweet girl. Still, I wouldn't apologize for being a father who refused to scream. Or hit. It's not like the old man had won me over with those tactics. He lost my respect long before the age of twelve. Ma'am continued, "In my day, children obeyed their elders above all else. If they couldn't do it naturally, they were given what-for."

No shit. That's why Gianna and I let Olivia express her moods and feelings. That spread to letting her decide who to hug and when. We believed respect was earned, and a gut instinct was something to hone, not suppress. It wouldn't help anything to say that. I'd been defending my parenting style ever since my daughter was born, but Olivia was the only thing I'd ever had that was truly mine.

Until I found my birth family.

We pulled into the employee lot behind the Garage. Finally. I put the car in park and leaned toward my mother, letting the engine drown out my voice from the back. "Don't take it personally, Momma. Liv's mad at me. I expect our party will cheer her up."

My use of the word Momma eased her sourness. At this point in our strained relationship, the word was a gift from me. I recognized the shitty manipulation and leaned into it anyway. Couldn't help it today. Her eyes brightened. "What did you do to anger her?"

Hating the practice of gossip but believing it might help, I checked the back quickly to make sure Liv wasn't listening. She stayed focused on her phone. "I missed an equestrian showcase last weekend. It was the first one she'd been in and was a big deal."

"Why didn't you go?" Like the other women her age, my mother drank up this kind of tea with gusto.

"Work. We hosted a wedding reception. It had been on the books for a year. Plus my assistant manager was in a car accident, and he's still easing back into full time. That's why I couldn't take the time off to see you."

That was a half-truth. I still caught the sweats anytime a memory traveled back to that day we visited her. The cop pulled me over for looking suspicious, then forced me out of our rental car while Liv cried. No matter what I did to comply, he kept yelling and threatening me. When he slammed me against the window, my baby's face filled with terror. I'd never get that image out of my mind. If Denny, my mother's new companion, hadn't come along, who knows how that afternoon would've ended. I never wanted to go back there.

"You provide a home for that girl and jobs for your staff. That's what a man does. That's what Kurt did. How can she be mad about that?" My mother pivoted in her seat. I braced as she scolded Liv. "Stop whining and grow up. Everyone has hard years. At least you still have a dad who loves you." That last bit was a dig on her own childhood.

My eyes shifted to the rearview mirror, and my shoulders released their tension. Liv wore her earbuds and hadn't heard us. I almost laughed. If Ma'am had hurt her, I would've taken her back to the hotel. As it was, I saw why my girl had been hurt over my absence. I'd been putting my career before her to prove to a dead man that I was capable. A dead man who wouldn't have accepted me if I'd been perfect.

I shut off the SUV, reached back, and squeezed my daughter's knee. She looked up and pulled out the bud. "We're here, Sparrow."

"Big. Is Miss Cyndi here yet?"

Shit. I muttered, "I wish." I could almost conjure up Cyndi's coconut-and-floral fragrance, making Ma'am's perfume dissipate. Thinking of it dropped my blood pressure a notch, especially since the visual images it inspired involved her naked and making sweet noises in my ear. A full sensory experience, that woman. Unfortunately, our schedules hadn't overlapped before she left to spend the holiday in Michigan with her father.

For the fourth time since we arrived at the Garage Thanksgiving party, Olivia erupted in a belly laugh. Thank you, Meredith's daughters. They were in high school but had graciously folded Liv into their circle. The girls' paths had crossed over the years but hadn't seen each other in months.

Meredith elbowed me in the ribs. "Stop being so bossy, Boss."

"You don't want me to be me?" I asked as I stared her down. Guess I was on edge.

"You want to kill somebody? Because that's how you look."

Great. "I was thinking." About my mother's grimaces.

She entertained a lot growing up, so I set up our feast in part to show her a good time while defusing our usual stresses. Instead, the tension was amped up when we walked into my restaurant. I never learned the art of masking my emotions, hence the slightly condescending nickname Boss.

I never minded the combination of tongue-in-cheek razzing topped with respect. But I'd never considered whether my moods affected others. The day I discovered Alan Kramer's theft, the restaurant had a great night. In fact, the revelation bonded my staff and me more. Had I been taking their good humor and maturity for granted?

I inhaled a ragged sigh of acknowledgment.

"It's technically a day off, so relax," she encouraged. "Hell, it doesn't even matter if the food is up to Felix's standards. We won't complain."

"My mother would," I explained, letting my eyes dart to her place at the table. My mother's approval meant more than a food critic's glowing review. "But you want me to loosen up?"

"At the least." She picked up a tray of mashed potatoes from the service counter. I carried an uncarved turkey to its spot at the end of our buffet, letting it rest while Felix finished the sides. "We did this to make the holiday easy and fun. Remember?"

This was also my way of apologizing for acting asshole-y lately. My staff wasn't to blame for the theft or that I'd let it happen under my nose. Add in Gia's death and Jay's accident, and I'd been on edge for a while. I tried not to take it out on them but often failed.

It stuck in my craw that I could have treated them the way Kurt would. I always knew when his job as an assistant plant manager went tits up by the way he treated Gracie and me.

"How's this?" I plastered on a big smile as we walked back to the kitchen for more sides.

Meredith rolled her eyes. "Now you look happy to kill."

I would be happy to witness Kramer receiving his comeuppance. Then I envisioned that scenario.

"There!" Meredith pointed at my face. Approval spread across hers. "Much better. Whatever inspired it, keep it up."

What the hell? I scoffed as a sous chef loaded up a tray of mac and cheese.

"We know it's been a hard year. We hate it for you and us." She touched my upper arm. "Don't add your mother to the mix."

"That obvious?" The sun finally appeared, which helped. Normally, we'd lift the overhead door and bring the cool air inside, but that might give the impression we were open for dinner. "I shouldn't have insisted she come up. Except we won't see her for Christmas, and that seemed cruel." After a quick video call with my Arizona family earlier, we decided to spend Christmas with them. It was the easiest way, given Olivia's school break, and the Garage was closing for renovations. It meant I wouldn't oversee each step, but I trusted Felix's with it.

"You haven't mentioned them to her, have you?"

My head dropped in shame. "That's why I wanted her to come to my place for breakfast. She could've met them and seen how great they are." And ease my guilt regarding the search.

"Regardless…" Meredith tipped her head from side to side. "If your momma can't have fun with our crowd, let it go. I don't know what to say about the rest, except if you need an ear… I know all about hard conversations with family." Then she rubbed her hands together as the last of the side dishes appeared on the serving counter.

How I wished I could imitate her hard-fought-for carefree attitude. A middle-aged transgender single mother, she knew the ins and outs of fighting through hardships to find happiness. I admired the hell out of her.

Meredith grabbed the sweet potatoes, and I picked up the tray of Felix's famous mac and cheese. My eyes traveled to my mother, who was in a deep conversation with the mother of a waiter. With impeccable table manners engaged, she smiled politely at the other woman. Whether it was genuine, I wouldn't know until the gossip began tomorrow at breakfast. Hopefully, I could divert that. I'd take the improvement even if it was only on the outside.

We set the trays down and lit the cans underneath them. "All right, you win." I gave Meredith my actual smile. I'd rather take my motivation from authentic heroes. "Thank you. I'll keep you posted on the rest."

• • •

"Can we go shopping after my riding lessons? Didi told me about a shop in North Hills with cute bras in my size." She put her hands together. "Please, Daddy?"

Bra shopping? The period kit adventure was bad enough. I failed to hide my wince.

"Who's Didi?" my mother asked. We'd finally coaxed her over for breakfast the following morning. I did it by picking her up for Black Friday shopping at Dillard's at dawn.

"She's Meredith's daughter. From yesterday's dinner. Remember Meredith, Gigi?" Olivia bit into her French toast. My chef skills would never compete with Felix's, but I made a damn fine breakfast.

I added another slice of freshly cooked toast to the pile, planning to freeze the leftovers. A yawn practically cracked my jaw, and I drank from my coffee mug. I should ask Cyndi where Kick gets her coffee. At least it was a sunny day. The sunrise had been a beautiful treat.

"You're too young for brassieres," Gracie declared.

Olivia's face fell. I'd semi-forgotten about shopping for one, but Cyndi's warning about what could happen if my daughter's uniform shirt got wet haunted me. Liv finished her toast, then perked up. "Could we go out with Cyndi again? Like we did for the period kit."

My mother raised her cup for me to refill it. It was a move I'd watched Kurt do as far back as I could remember, only the gesture would be for her to serve him. I quietly chuckled, thinking about the ways people influence each other. "Who is Cyndi, and what in heaven's name is a period kit?"

"Cyndi is Daddy's friend. She's helping him with—"

I forcefully cleared my throat to cut her off. Olivia didn't know all the problems at the Garage, but she knew more than Ma'am did.

"His accounting." Her mouth slid into a dangerous smirk. Guess I hadn't hidden as much as I'd hoped. Olivia carried her plate to the sink. "Anyway… Cyndi thinks my period will be here soon, so she showed Daddy and me how to make a kit for my backpack. That way, I'll be prepared if it happens in school."

My mother scoffed as she waved her hand. "Who prepares for a curse?" She cackled oddly. "It's a rite of passage. Growing up should be difficult. Right?" She pointed at me. "You had erections in the front of class."

I choked on my coffee as Olivia snorted. Thanks, Mother.

"Olivia needs to face the humiliation of staining her skirt in public. That's how a girl learns." She added milk to her cup. "Why do you think it's a curse? Eve betrayed Adam, and we pay the consequences."

I turned back to the stove so Ma'am wouldn't see me roll my eyes, but Liv's quiet whine hit me in my hackles. I pulled her in to my side as I flipped the last piece of toast. "We'll talk to Cyn," I whispered, then kissed her head. I tipped my head toward the stairs. "Miss Carol will be here soon. Finish getting ready for your lesson while I talk to Gigi."

"'Kay."

I watched her disappear up the steps, then turned my attention to the cabinet with storage containers. All this to stall as I formed a plan. I had hard things to bring up, and her take on Liv's impending puberty didn't help.

Meredith had left me with a piece of advice last night that had stuck with me—dig down for the good even if it's deep. Covering those times in shit doesn't mean they're gone. I hoped she was right.

After putting the French toast in the fridge, I made two glasses of iced water and set one in front of my mother, just in case. I swallowed deep, then I offered her a boon to my bane. "Momma…" Her features softened. "Please don't scare Liv about growing up. It's hard enough when a kid has support."

Her brow pierced as she opened her mouth to respond, but

I quickly cut her off. "I know you think I spoil her, and I don't care anymore." I ran my hands through my hair, catching all the unsaid words on that topic as they reflected in her eyes. "There's no Gia to take the lead anymore. It's on me to bring her into her womanhood. Me, Momma. And I won't apologize for trying to make that girl's life a little easier." I sat back in my chair. "Besides, according to Cyndi and Meredith, periods aren't as scary as they used to be. The kit idea made sense. At least the products sound better." I took a drink of water, letting the cold liquid cool my emotions as much as it did my internal temperature.

She tucked her lower lip under her top one as she contemplated the glass and mug in front of her. I wondered what memories had grabbed her attention. Without taking her eyes off the drink ware, she finally said, "Preparation is a good, Kurtis. Nothing wrong with preparation." Her use of my first name snapped my head back, except I should've been prepared for it. I had taken away their endearments when they refused to honor my switching back to my real first name. Of course, she'd use the gift of calling her momma to dig in her feet. Then she pivoted like the expert gossip I knew. "Who is this Cyndi woman?"

"Like Liv said, she's a friend." The sun peeked out from behind a cloud, brightening my kitchen, warming the sage-green walls. It looked like spring in the space. I had let a designer pick the colors when I bought the condo. The word masculine often came up in discussions I hadn't cared about at the time. I wished I'd known better. Cyn's buttery kitchen space with the warm wood cabinetry came to mind, and I smiled.

"Uh-huh," Momma murmured. "Friends don't put that look on your face, mister." She popped her brows. "Haven't seen that smile since your college girlfriend. What was her name?"

"Tina."

"What's she doing nowadays?" She finished the coffee and stood to place the mug in the sink.

"No idea. We ended before graduation. Remember?" Tina had been my first love and my first true heartbreak.

"But this Cyndi—"

"Is my accountant and a friend. Leave it at that."

She opened the dishwasher door and started loading the breakfast dishes. "You want more from her."

I sighed and tipped my head back, looking for answers on the ceiling. "I'll give you this one, Momma. Yes. But I'm taking it slow. There's so much going on right now."

She righted herself and leaned against the counter. "You need a mother for that girl upstairs."

"What?" I grumbled under my breath. "Jesus Christ. It's not a job. You can't just slide one woman in for another. Gia will always have the spot. It doesn't mean I won't take help where I can get it. Cyndi, Carol, and Meredith are all going overboard to be there for Liv." Then I realized my mistake.

My mother's chin quivered as our unspoken reality slapped her in the face once again. It wasn't my intention. It never was. Before I could apologize and clarify, she pivoted yet again. "I got to say… I was impressed with your friend yesterday. You'd never know he was a man."

Fuck my life. "Momma…" I slumped in my chair. "Meredith is a woman."

She lifted a skeptical eyebrow, shoved her hand on her hip. "You're so stubborn. I don't know where this indulgence of yours comes from. I bet you go along with this woman-man… whatever, just to spite your father."

Fury made me shoot to my feet. My mother's wince halted my approach and doused my heated emotions. No matter what, I wouldn't be like Kurt Brady. He didn't hit often, but we never knew what would trigger a punch. I moved to the sink and rinsed a dish, then handed it to her.

"I've learned to listen to people, Momma. Equally important is believing people when they tell you who they are and what their life is like." I handed her another dish.

She scoffed at my words.

"Seriously," I pressed. "Kurt wasn't good at walking in other people's shoes. The repercussions of his refusal taught me the importance of doing so. You see?"

"I suppose."

"Thank you for being polite to Meredith yesterday. But you should know… Mer has taught me a lot about not giving a crap about what others think. She's happy in her skin and really wouldn't care if you like it or not." If I knew who had gossiped about Mer to Gracie…

My mother stopped her work and turned toward me. "That doesn't sound like respect… sounds like veneration."

"She is one of my heroes." I nodded slowly as I thought about it. "I'm still working on the fine art of not giving a fuck."

"Kurtis!" Momma snapped a towel at me, making me laugh.

The clock over the table caught my eye. Carol was due soon, and I was allowing my mother's tangents to keep me from what really mattered. I gestured toward our seats and said, "There is something we need to talk about."

As expected, the tension hummed anew in her body. After all these years, it was her default demeanor.

"Momma…" I lowered and slowed my voice to ease her reticence and cut to the chase. "I found my birth family."

Her gasp confirmed what I'd always suspected—that she'd hate the idea. "So you have your real momma now?"

My nose stung from the truth. "Not exactly. I have cousins, an aunt and uncle… and a grandmother. My b-birth mother is presumed dead. In fact, the family believed I was dead this whole time as well."

"Really?" Her face twisted with confusion.

My temper piqued again as my questions bubbled to the surface. In the meantime, Gracie seemed relieved to know Debbie wasn't alive. "What did you know about them? About my family?"

She shook defensively, like I'd slapped her with words. "Only what your father had told me. You were found alone in a car. Alone, Kurtis. The authorities suspected you'd been there for days."

Past fights with the old man over the same topics flew through my memory. "Did those authorities tell you they were from Arizona and not Western North Carolina?"

"What? No. Your mother had overdosed. What kind of girl does that with a child in the car?"

I leaned across the table. "Who told you this?"

"The lawyer!" My mother's chin trembled with fury. "Kurt. The social worker. Sister Mary Charles, who put you in my arms."

I'd forgotten about the nuns. "They lied to you." I bent my head. "Wonder how much Kurt knew, or if it was between the lawyer and the sheriff's department. But after my social worker hit a wall—"

"You hired a social worker and didn't tell me?"

I tipped my head toward her. "Come now. You can't blame me for poking around." My mother huffed a big breath of air in an effort to make me feel guilty. She didn't know I'd dealt with guilt a long time ago. "Anyway, I hired a private detective who found a mostly erased record."

"If it was erased, how can you—"

While she spoke, I swiped to the photo on my phone and placed it in front of her. She covered her mouth with her hand, swallowing a gasp.

"That's me shortly after I was found, in the sheriff's office." Her finger traced my face in the photo. I cleared my throat and quietly asked, "Did you know I was actually three? Almost three and a half."

She vehemently shook her head. "You were two, Kurtis. Your birthday is March thirtieth."

"That's the day I was found, Momma." I reached for her hand and gestured toward the photo. "The little guy there shows classic signs of trauma. The social worker told me it can cause regression. According to my family, I talked well by then."

"Your…"

"My cousin. My aunt. They're wonderful people… not addicts, like we were told. Just a great, hardworking American family. My cousin and her husband are in the hospitality business like me. They own several restaurants, in fact."

She stubbornly pressed her lips together, but I also pressed. "They're dealing with the reality that I was stolen from them."

"No." My mother's eyes filled with a furious defense. "You needed me. When Sister put you in my arms…" Her eyes shimmered, telling me I'd gone too far.

"Momma?" She stared at the photo, her face filled with love and confusion. I didn't know what I'd do if she cried. Except there was one more thing she needed to hear. I swallowed hard. "Momma."

Her gaze reluctantly met mine. I exhaled and blurted it out. "Olivia and I are spending Christmas in Arizona."

Chapter 20

Close to Me

Cyndi

The heat from my cousin's firepit warmed my toes. I finished the last bites of Aunt Star's barquillos and set my dish on the table next to me. My tummy was now as happy as my toes.

The air held a chill, though it was warm for late November in Michigan. I pulled the chair closer to the fire's brick surround. This was the first Thanksgiving in my memory where my family could sit outside after sunset. Bernardo had built a fire when his girls asked for s'mores. If the weather trends kept up, it would make a nice tradition. The sweet tang of burned sugar from the marshmallows hung in the air, mixing with the woodsmoke.

Most of the boats on Cass Lake, where Berno lived, were in storage for the winter, giving me a clear view across the water. Add in the lights from neighboring homes made a fiery contrast as they reflected off the black water.

My gaze moved to the flames in the pit as they cycled

through the colors of a rainbow. Bernardo had sprinkled that stuff on the fire to make it "look like magic" for his daughter Addison. He lived to make his girls smile. He reminded me of my dad in that way.

Addy was the younger of Berno's two girls. She currently snuggled in her mom's lap, her heavy lids fighting the urge to close for the night. The oldest, Willow, slid onto my lap after cleaning off the roasting sticks. As I pulled my fleece blanket over Wills, I filled up on her bubblegum-shampoo-scented hair and her stories from sixth grade. She was handling the transition to a bigger school brilliantly, making use of the confidence she inherited from her father.

She was a year behind Olivia. Throughout the long weekend, my thoughts kept bouncing back to the sweet girl and her sexy father back in Raleigh. An intoxicating pair, they were, even if I didn't like how they lived rent-free in my brain. Or my heart. It didn't help that Blake and I texted frequently. He shocked me by checking in to ask about my dad and the visit without trying to sext or flirt. The way he easily focused on our friendship as much as our benefits was new to me.

In return, I worried about his time with Mrs. Brady. Blake didn't say much about her, but what he left out told me all I needed to know about their tension. I hoped the visit wouldn't discourage him, hating the possibility of anything making those proud shoulders fall.

Part of me wished Blake and Liv had come up to Michigan with me. I hadn't noticed it until earlier, but a niggling voice told me they would fit in with my family. The clarity with which the scene played out in my mind unsettled me. It was another dumb fantasy.

"Why are you grumbling, Auntie Cyn?" Willow asked.

Dammit. I pushed silky wisps of her hair off her face. Her button nose was disappearing, growing into a woman's. "Sorry, Wills. I was thinking about something annoying." I tucked our fluffy blanket around her more. "Tell me about your elective." Her school had hired a new art teacher who added jewelry-making to the schedule. Since I had a side hustle selling beaded pieces, Willow knew me more for that than as an accountant. She was also one of my biggest fans and had jumped at the chance to learn. It made my weekend when she told me why she'd picked the class to learn how to make pieces like mine.

"Well… my projects are Christmas presents. It'll spoil it if I tell you more." Willow wiggled in my lap, her bony little bottom poking my thighs.

"Gotcha." As I adjusted her position to get blood flowing back in my legs, Star interrupted us.

"Stop torturing your auntie and go put on your jammies, iha."

"But—"

Star gave Willow "the look," stopping her words cold. I kissed her head and sent her off. A chill settled over me with her absence, even with the blanket. I'd been hot so much lately I welcomed the sensation.

My aunt sighed heavily as she settled in the chair next to mine. "You look so good with her. A natural."

Here we go. Surely I was old enough for this to end already. I sipped the holy basil tea sitting next to my empty plate. "You've been saying that since Willow was born." We were entering the part of the evening that focused on my relationship status. Or lack of one. It was as much of a family tradition as her desserts. It always happened after the girls were sent to bed, so it didn't surprise me.

"A daughter would have been wonderful, but"—I leaned toward my aunt and touched her arm—"I'm happy with my life. I'm proud of what I've achieved." It took long enough to get to this point. Finally laying to rest my issues with Joel helped.

"Good to hear," my father said. He appeared on my other

side, startling me. He pulled up a chair, blocking the light breeze moving over the water. My family didn't gang up on me the way some did. Instead, they saw themselves as showing "collective concern." It was their way of supporting me and reinforcing their negative opinions of my ex-husband. "I thought a nice American boy would give you the best life."

My dad had drilled that into me as soon as I was old enough to date. He'd been as broken over my divorce as I was.

"Regardless of his heritage, Joel wasn't a nice boy, Tatay. That's on my naivete, not yours."

I was about to explain further when Aunt Star cut me off. "A Filipino man wouldn't have left you all alone. You could've adopted—"

"One did. Besides, I haven't been—"

"What about you?" my father asked Star in warning. They leaned toward each other over me, slipping into their familiar siblings' report as if I wasn't there. "I was afraid you'd end up trapped like our mother, but you got out in time." His gaze moved to Berno. As if it were a beacon, my cousin walked over and joined us, settling on the edge of the brick wall. "Raised a good man."

Auntie Star dropped her feet to the patio and pointed at my dad. "You should have let me find her a match." The fire crackles almost drowned out my aunt's voice, like it was on my side.

God help me. My chilly skin warmed with every word. I threw off the blanket and almost pulled off my cashmere sweater. "My life isn't anyone's fault." I looked at my father. "Not yours." Turned toward my aunt. "Definitely not yours." I finished my speech as I looked at Bernardo. "I've dated men from all backgrounds, even ours. And I've learned from them. Regret nothing. Not even Joel." My aunt and father gasped at his name, but it was the truth. Life could be hard. It could also be beautiful. Both the good and bad made me who I was. "Just because I'm taking a break from the dating scene, it doesn't mean I've given up."

Aunt Star's face brightened. "She has someone, and she's keeping it from us."

Good grief. I rolled my eyes as my cousin chuckled. I could have used his help, but he was here for the entertainment.

"Who is it?" Star asked my father.

"She tells me nothing." Daddy answered like I wasn't there. "Not that I want to know."

Damn straight. I gulped down the rest of my warm tea, then stood as I threw the blanket over my arm and grabbed the plate. "I love y'all to the moon." I kissed my dad and my aunt on their cheeks. "But I'm not a project that requires fixing."

I stepped out of my shower, the events from the previous week still swirling in my mind. My father ended up passing out on Friday. So I stayed with him for several more days until I was certain he had stabilized. The stubborn man had refused to go to the Emergency Department since he claimed to know exactly why he'd experienced syncope. What he wouldn't say was he didn't care. I already had a list of pros and cons for him to move down with me. I intended to counter each of the cons at our Christmas visit. I couldn't drop everything for him once tax season was in full swing. What still eluded me was a draw, something other than me to entice him to move south. But I'd figure it out. My stubbornness came from Tatay after all.

As I ran the epilator over my legs, my body started sweating profusely. I quickly finished and grabbed my towel to dry off a second time. It was an annoyance that had showed up in the summer. I would shower, dry, apply a progesterone cream, then my face regimen, etc. By the time I was ready to dress, I usually dried myself again. Sometimes a third time.

All my frustrations came to a head in that moment...

family issues, my body, Blake. A strong wind bent the trees in my backyard, so I opened my windows, hoping it would cool me off. With everything else going on, I couldn't afford to be thrown off by my dumb body temperature. The breeze didn't help much, not like it would if I were in the backyard.

Dammit. I decided to get ahold of this before moving on to my to-do list. If I'd been in a better mood, I would have made a joke about sweating over my succulents to save money on water and checking off my first item. But not this day.

A blog post I'd read about perimenopause relief mentioned orgasms helping hot flashes. This didn't feel like the episodes my friends had described, but I wondered if there were different ways the flashes manifested. During recent "dates" with Blake, I noticed my skin tended to heat and find relief after his brilliant Os. It couldn't hurt to experiment.

I slid my arms into my silk robe—there was no point in dressing until my skin cooled, retrieved my phone and trusty wand from the nightstand, then headed downstairs to my screen porch. The ties in my privacy curtains needed tightening. No sense in giving the neighbors a show. Still, the space was fully open to the back, thanks to my wooded yard and the acres of more trees abutting my property. I stood in the middle of my porch, taking a moment to let the air caress my skin. The air swirled around me like a mini tornado, testing the ties on my robe. My skin was hot, but not as bad as it had been upstairs. This might work.

After connecting the speaker on my porch to my phone, I cued up The Cure's "Close to Me" to get into a groove. I fired up my purple battery-operated boyfriend and eased down into the lounge chair. The wind swept over me like a caress as the silicone tickled my sex. I went slowly, edging multiple times, so when I crossed the finish line, I'd have a day's peace.

By the time the next song started, I was so caught up in the sensations that I didn't notice or care what was playing. Stevie

Wonder's "Superstition" barely registered. Instead, the breeze continued to cool my skin as the wand helped my hormones settle. I closed my eyes; everything disappeared but the build in my core.

Each burst of air felt like Blake's breath on my skin. Images of him over me, beside me, filled my mind. The vibrations of the toy became his fingers massaging me. Taking me higher. It was so real that I could swear I even smelled his cologne. I let out a whimper and gave in, letting go. Finally ready to take my relief.

Then I heard a moan that wasn't mine.

Chapter 21

Simply Irresistible

Admittedly, I should have kept knocking on Cyndi's front door, but her car in the driveway told me she was home. Without thinking, I pressed the door latch, and it opened for me. In my defense, I knocked as I called out her name. Three times. The loud thumping of a Stevie Wonder song drew me to the backyard like a pied piper. It was also why she didn't hear me. I was half right.

Cyn's house was as bright as I remembered from when we first dated. Blue denim furnishings, red pillows and throws, and butter-colored walls. Seagrove pottery from local artists filled a cabinet in her dining area. Cyndi possessed every inch of her home. It made me think of her warm smile, her perky confidence, her style.

The layout of the first floor quickly came back to me. She did most of her living on the first floor, with an owner's suite and office to the left. The upstairs had been set up for Kick's kids, and I'd never gone up there. They were lucky to have an extra caregiver after their father died in a car accident.

I turned right, moving through her dining room and family room, past the kitchen to the breakfast area, heading for the back porch. I followed the sound of music like a mouse in a maze looking for its cheese.

And stopped cold.

The glimpse of Cyndi's pussy did me in. I hadn't intended to creep or unintentionally fill my spank bank with images of my favorite subject. She was grinding on a buzzing toy as if her life depended on it. If only I'd kept my shit together. Watching her undulate against the purple wand was one thing. Seeing her sweet pussy deepening in color and glistening, getting ready to come, sucked the breath right out of my lungs. Nearly swallowed my tongue as I let out a ragged wheeze, like a dog craving a bone.

"Blake?" Cyndi popped out of her chair like it electrocuted her. "What the hell are you doing here?" The dildo flew out of her hand, end-over-end, heading straight for me. Instinctively I grasped it and shit… it was coated with her arousal. I swallowed hard, almost taking my tongue as I used all my willpower to keep from licking it. Don't sniff it. It had to be somewhere beside my hand. I set it on the side table. The buzzing noise grew as it bounced on the hard surface.

Panic washed over me.

"Press the middle button," Cyndi ordered. She stopped the music and faced me.

Our heavy breathing was louder than the billowing curtains straining against their ties. Wind blew apart the sides of her thin robe, putting her spectacular body on display. Soft curves. Tawny skin. Bright gray eyes lit with fire. Late-afternoon sun filtered through and between the fabric, lighting her from behind. Every one of my middle school wet dreams realized. Who was I kidding? She played the lead in my wet dream the night before.

Cyn faced off with me, her expression fierce, her spine straight, making no attempt to cover herself. It reminded me of the warrior princesses in the video games I used to play when I had free time. Except for her tiny size and her bare feet. Like this, she barely made it up to my chest, but damn. She threw her shoulders back, claiming an air that made me feel like the small one. Who could blame her? I'd surprised her.

No way would I apologize though. I wanted to thank Fate's representative that set me on this unplanned path. That entity deserved a shrine. I'd clearly been blessed. Only something was wrong with Cyndi.

I pointed my thumb over my shoulder and said, "I knocked," like it explained the intrusion. I cleared my throat, scratched my temple, searching for words. My brain refused to work. "The door was unlocked… and I-I heard Stevie Wonder." Like that gave me permission to barge in. Truth was, as soon as I cottoned on to what my eyes beheld, I'd been spelled. Time and purpose disappeared. I whimpered again, wishing we could get back to the Cyndi-about-to-come show. A few brain cells fired again, and I added, "If you'd been playing bow-chica-wow-wow music, I could've taken the hint."

"I was." The wind whipped Cyndi's hair across her face, and she flicked it back, annoyed. "The playlist jumped to this one, and the rhythm fit my… Oh hell." The star of my show stomped her foot. "You can't just show up out of the blue!"

"Yeah." I rubbed my temple as my thinking brain stayed on hiatus. It's what happens when all your blood rushed to your dick in two heartbeats. I shifted my hips as if that would return my circulation to normal. Cyndi's gaze dipped down, checking me out as her eyes followed my movements. The chaos mixed with heat in them didn't help my situation.

I swallowed around another lump in my throat. "That

analysis you're working on… last month's figures compared to the previous two years… The la-lawyers want to see your report." Cyndi lifted an eyebrow. I sighed in frustration, unable to string together a complete sentence. What the hell. I whipped my shirt over my head, letting it fly into a corner behind me. "Can I join?"

Her nostrils flared as she breathed in harshly and set her hands on her hips, keeping the robe behind her body. "Blake," she breathed. God, the inhale made her tits sit up higher, those tight, brown nipples taking all my attention. Luscious curves softened muscles she worked hard to maintain, like her body was at war with itself.

Given all my efforts to age gracefully, I could relate.

"You interrupted my private time with a question you could've texted. Why aren't you at work anyway? And what's with the bandanna?"

I pointed at the do-rag I'd wrapped across my forehead and shrugged. "Keeps my cowboy hat clean?" Despite everything, she'd noticed me. I wondered if I was starring in her fantasy when I walked in. The corner of my mouth twitched. "Left the hat in my SUV."

"Of course he did." She lifted her eyes to the ceiling before returning them to me. "You work on Saturdays."

"Right." The statement finally clicked in with my synapses. "I, uh… have the morning off to watch Liv's riding lesson, but her group went out on the trail," I answered in a rush before letting out a breath I'd been holding since the drive over because I'd been angry with myself for screwing up again. "I didn't read the schedule close enough. Carol asked me twice if I was sure I wanted to take Sparrow." My neighbor's insistent messages made sense now. I sighed. "Anyway… there was nothing for me to do at the stables, so——"

"You came here."

I popped my eyebrows. Hell yeah. "The law firm's email

came through when we were parking. Figured I'd check on my buddy, Spar—" My words faded into the breeze.

That was the problem.

Cyndi wasn't sparkling. Not with her confidence and poise. Her skin was covered in a light sheen, but her bright gray irises looked… defeated. I stepped toward her. "What's wrong?"

"Aside from you barging in on a highly personal moment?"

I nodded while silently thanking Fate. No way did I regret witnessing what my eyes beheld. Besides—I reached for her and swept my finger across her flushed cheeks. "You've been naked and… playful in front of me before. That can't be what's snuffed out your fire."

She groused at my words. "Fire's the problem." Cyndi tied her robe, except the slick silk immediately slid open, catching on her pretty, taught nipples. Another burst of wind blew the bottom halves away from her hips. She briefly closed her eyes and her shoulders dropped. "I had a doozer of what I think is a hot flash upstairs."

I tipped my head to the side, biting my lip to chase away a growing smile.

Cyndi scowled. "What's so funny?"

I touched her glowing chest, enjoying the sensation as my finger traveled between her breasts. This was what a hot flash did to her? "You sound like a superhero… The Hot Flash." I gave her a wink, but her chin wobbled.

"I don't like this, Blake." She turned and padded toward the corner of the screened porch, then spoke to the woods. "It feels like every time I finally figure out who I am, life throws me a plot twist." She shook her head. "Wish this one would hurry the hell up and move on." The wind kicked up a notch, and Cyndi held the robe away from her body like it was a sail. So the wind brought her out here. The shadowed outline of her form against the satin was as carnal a vision as when she had faced me. Still, she wasn't enjoying it. I couldn't allow that.

I stepped up behind her, leaving enough space between us for the air to circulate. I pulled the raven and platinum locks off her cheek, unable to keep from touching her. "Your hair's soaking wet. How long has this flash been going on?" No wonder she was miserable.

"No, it's…" Cyndi let out a long-suffering sigh. "For some reason, showers trigger bad ones. Lately I end up toweling off multiple times." She looked over her shoulder and quirked her eyebrow. "That's why I didn't put clothes on. I'll need a change of clothes if I dress too soon."

"Ah." At least it didn't sound as bad as I'd pictured. Annoying? Yes. But I imagined her achy, like she had a fever.

Cyndi's head dropped, and she spoke to the floor. "I'm losing myself again."

If that statement had anything to do with her asshole ex, I'd put the bastard in the hospital if he came back here. I pulled the robe away from her shoulder and kissed her dewy skin. "Orgasms help then? Is that why you were out here?" I kissed her again, tasting coconut and… almonds. The scent of her bodywash or lotion was strong. "You're ruining me for dessert." I licked her shoulder, letting her flavor linger on my tongue. "And Stevie Wonder."

"Blake…" Cyndi drew out my name, a hint of a giggle in her throat.

"Do. Orgasms. Help. Sparky?" I repeated, accentuating each word with a kiss.

Cyndi nodded rapidly while exhaling. "Yesss."

I lifted her wrist and pulled. "Come." We moved to the lounge chair, and I settled on it, kicking the ottoman back as I placed her in front of me.

"What are you—"

I lifted her foot and tucked it against the back of my thigh, opening her sweet pussy to me. My eyes drifted closed for a split second when I glanced at her still-wet sex. How'd I get so lucky? I picked up the wand and raised an eyebrow. "Is this what you want?"

Cyndi bit her lip. "Please."

"This is what it takes to make you polite?" I scooted forward, pressed the middle button on the wand with one hand, and palmed the back of Cyn's thigh with my other. As I peppered her stomach with open kisses, the toy came to life. I looked up at her beautiful face, peering down at me with eagerness. Those lightning eyes hadn't sparked back to life yet, so I gave her a wink and set to work, licking her tight clit as I let the wand tickle her lips.

"Mmm." Cyndi purred, her hips immediately moving against my mouth as I explored more with the toy. She must have been close when I interrupted her. I moved the wand to her clit so I could watch her come undone. So gorgeous.

Cyndi inhaled roughly as her body found a groove on the vibrating head, her back arching in ecstasy, nipples tight and dark. It used all my control, but I wanted—no, needed—to witness her come back to herself.

"That's it," I praised, massaging her ass with my free hand, my hips moving with her rhythm. "So beautiful."

"Blake—" Cyn's breath caught in her throat. Something held her back.

I pulled her down to my mouth. "Need more, honey?" My patience snapped. The voyeur's curiosity morphed into a need to take part. It spurred an ambition to help her come like she'd never done before.

"Please," she gasped.

I stood and moved behind her, keeping her foot on the cushion. Reaching around with one hand, I turned up the vibrations and pressed it up into her. "How's—"

"Yes." Cyndi hissed as she shoved her head into my shoulder. "God, yes." My other hand grabbed her tit, massaging hard and pulling on her nipple. She rewarded me by letting go, dissolving into a series of cries that grew louder until Cyndi bit her lip and forced air through her nose.

What a gift. I'd been having a blast with our hookups, discovering ways to make Cyndi's body hum. Hell, we'd even touched an exhibitionist rail with our playtime against the windows. But this was the next-level vulnerability I hadn't experienced before.

I didn't care that my dick was still tucked away either. It strained against my zipper, but my senses, my thoughts… everything focused on her. I needed to see her satisfied, at peace. See those eyes light again.

As what seemed like the longest orgasm in history—at least from my experience—continued, Cyn couldn't hold back from crying out. Catching on to a sense of overwhelm, I eased up on the toy before bringing it back gently to draw out her pleasure, determined to make this the best one she'd ever had. Her yells turned into hums and sweet moans. I lost track of time and place, watching her become a goddess in my hands. It made me feel like a god myself to share it with her. The world narrowed to the two of us, creating our own tempest on a screen porch.

And Cyndi became more to me. More than my fuck buddy. She let me in. Still over my head, with the world pressing down on my shoulders, but I was a new man now. Together, we were special. I wrapped an arm around her waist to hold her up as her legs became jelly.

I switched our positions, settling back in the lounge chair and pulling the ottoman over with my foot so I could prop my legs. Then I stretched her out on top of me to recover and waited for our heartbeats to return to normal. I wondered if she'd also changed and kissed her head reverently, silently begging her to.

Later, when I settled in my bed alone with the wind blustering against windows and lightning cracking overhead, I knew I'd fall asleep to the memory of the sexiest woman I'd ever know panting in my ear. The smell of coconut hair products. The taste of her sweetness still on my tongue.

As the wind blew over us in the lounge chair, Cyndi sighed in contentment. Her skin broke out in goose bumps, telling me I'd done her right. I brushed her hair off her face. It was mostly dry now. Dark brown, silver... and a few highlights of blue were like silk threads sifting through my fingers. Her expression became peaceful, blissed even.

"Better?" I asked around a voice rough.

Cyndi tipped her head back and laughed as she tucked her hair behind her ear. "So. Much." She kissed my chest before quietly adding, "Thank you." She stilled and tracked something beyond me in the yard before she started giggling.

"What?"

She shook her head. "A rabbit stopped in the middle of the lawn like he was checking out the commotion. Then he hopped off like he was disgusted with the show."

"Or he's searching for Mrs. Rabbit after being inspired." I waggled my brows. "I've never seen you hotter."

Cyn's head dropped as if embarrassed.

"None of that." I wrapped my arms around her.

She relaxed and snuggled into my chest. Good. If she kept looking at me, I risked declaring the words neither of us was prepared to hear.

Instead, I cleared my throat and said, "Good to have you back, Spark." I spoke to the porch and the house, looking through the sliding door into her breakfast nook. "You're not losing yourself. You're not going anywhere. If you feel lost again, tell me. I'll find you."

"You would, wouldn't you?" Cyndi asked as she drew circles on my chest with her finger.

As long as you'll let me. A persistent noise competed with the sound of our breaths. "Hold on." I shifted her and dug out the still-buzzing sex toy from under my back. I held it up, focusing all my power on the center button to get it to shut up. Cyn giggled.

I studied the wand drenched in her arousal and couldn't resist holding it to my nose and inhaling. Her eyelids fluttered as she watched me. I'd become addicted to her scent and taste. "Oh, what the hell." I licked the thing clean and flashed her a satisfied grin. The latex head didn't measure up to kissing Cyndi's pussy, but the heady look on her beautiful face made the action worth it.

It reminded me that my dick was still raring to go. I shifted to ease the discomfort. Cyndi gasped and pushed up off me. The silver in her eyes sparked with mischief as she stared at my junk while licking her lips.

Her new position allowed me to palm her lush breasts. I could've touched her all day and sighed with contentment. This lady was becoming my addiction. Not just her body either. I enjoyed spending whatever time we had together, whether it was business or pleasure. But her letting me in like this? I'd play the friend game through the holidays, but that's all she'd get.

"Your turn," she declared, peppering kisses on my chest, then lower. I hadn't expected reciprocation. Still, I wouldn't turn her down. The idea of her full lips around my dick made my head dizzy, though I really wanted to come inside her. In the end, it didn't matter. As she unzipped my jeans, my phone rang with my daughter's ringtone.

Chapter 22

How Bizarre

CYNDI

The Perked Cup's bell chimed on my arrival as I stepped through the doors. It was a refuge, drawing me in like a magnet this morning. I had questions only my best friend could answer. Kick and her crew had transformed it for the holidays. Warm woods decked out in garland, with dried fruit and spices tied to it, greeted me as Dean Martin sang a jazzy Christmas tune.

My eyes roamed the dining room in search of Kick. As expected for midmorning, a few people hung out at bistro tables with their laptops and drinks. Miss Ginger Cookie read a holiday story to six little ones and their caregivers. They snuggled on floor pillows on the stage, listening to a tale about kittens building a snowman. Miss Ginger's green with white snowflakes holiday sweater complemented her festive red hair. My hand instinctively sifted through mine as I considered what color I wanted to use on my highlights. It was time for a refresh.

Without coming to a decision, I bolted to the counter for

my therapy session. My head was messed up over what happened with Blake. Any new decisions eluded me. Did I even want to keep my silver sparkles, or did I want to go back to dying the roots? I couldn't say.

"Hey, shug. Y'ight?" Deana Douglas, the morning manager, had become a friend, thanks to our connection to Kick. Her head tilted from side to side as she assessed me. She had a special talent for catching everything.

I gave her a quick smile as I swapped out my sunglasses for my readers. "I'm fine," I lied, feeling my scrunched-up face give me away. I perused the case of pastries to avoid eye contact.

Dee propped her elbows on top of the display and rested her chin on her hands. I stayed bent over, waiting for her to ask me if I wanted my usual. When the question didn't come, I stood and faced the truth.

"You done?" she asked, mixing a concerned expression with an amused one.

I sighed and tugged on my beaded earring. "I'll take a peppermint latte, I guess."

She chuckled from her belly as she grabbed a large mug from the rack.

"Kick around?" I asked when she moved to the espresso machine.

"I'm afraid not," Dee said over her shoulder. "She and the professor went on a morning ride."

"Okay." I settled on my favorite barstool so we could keep talking. Kick and Thomas often rode their horses together, but they did it before work started.

Deana must have recognized the confusion on my face. She continued, "The dog went along, right?" I nodded, knowing this was also typical. "And she ran into something or over something... Anyway, she was cut..." Dee moved her finger over her shoulder, showing where Kick's rescue hound, Macushla, had been cut. "She's at the vet, getting stitches."

"Poor baby."

Dee finished making my coffee and brought it over. "Yeah. Kick took her in so the professor could finish a big experiment."

"You know he's not a professor anymore, right?" I asked before taking a much-needed sip of my drink.

Deana shrugged. "He'll always be the Prof. to me."

Admittedly, the moniker fit him. I mirrored her shrug and smiled before taking another pull from the cup. The velvety texture and not-too-sweet minty flavor made my stomach do a happy dance. It helped me relax, and I exhaled a long, slow breath.

"Tell me what's going on." Dee leaned against the back counter, letting me know I had her undivided attention whether I wanted it or not.

I gave in and collapsed onto my elbows. "Do orgasms help cool hot flashes?"

She chuckled through her answer. "Didn't expect that question today." As the chortle settled, a distant smile spread across her face. "Yeah, they can."

"Okay." I dropped my head into my hand as I continued processing what had happened.

"Let me guess." Deana leaned down to meet my eyes, keeping our talk private. "You had a flash in front of your silver fox and he"—she pressed her lips together for a second—"took care of it."

I dropped my chin to make my hair fall over my heated ears.

Dee continued, "You don't know what to do about it." Her tone sounded surprised, like she'd made a revelation.

I shook my head and practically scrunched into myself to become smaller.

"What's wrong with that?" She touched my arm, then interrupted me before I could answer. "Oh! You don't know about your feelings." She clicked her tongue. "You and Kick are cut from the same cloth."

"Pardon?"

"It was obvious you caught it bad for the man the first time you dated him." She played with the pendant around her neck. Her husband had given it to her for their anniversary. "When Kick mentioned you both were here a few weeks back, I figured you were in it for real now."

My fingers found my earring again, and I rolled the beads with my fingers as I spoke. "We bumped into each other here. We didn't come in together."

"Semantics." Dee waved me off. "Kick told me about the dance-off y'all did. I didn't need to see it to know what's going on."

My brows drew together. As much as I tried, my face wouldn't relax. "We're supposed to be friends."

"Really?" Deana lifted her eyebrow sarcastically.

"With benefits." I looked around the dining room to avoid seeing her smirk. Miss Cookie said something to make the kids erupt in giggles.

"Have you ever been best friends with a man?" Deana asked.

Her question startled me. I spun around. "A what?" This was a new concept for me.

"Best friend. A. Man." She let the phrase hang in the air while she poured herself an ice tea. "You know, Gordon's my ride or die." If we could all be so lucky to have a marriage like Deana and Gordon.

A new customer came in, making the concept swirl around in my head a while longer. After they left with a to-go cup, Dee returned, her expression expectant for my answer.

I tucked my hair behind my ear. "It never occurred to me

to have a best friend of the male variety." I reluctantly finished my latte and set it on the saucer.

"You know Thomas is Kick's person now, right? Nothing against you. It's just what happens." She swirled the ice in her glass with the straw. "Could be why you're out of sorts. Have you never gone there before?"

I stared at the dried foam clinging to my empty cup as I pondered her question. Joel always had his buddies. They obviously knew plenty of stuff about him I hadn't been privy to. I had Kick and other close friends during my marriage. They never mixed. After the divorce, I occasionally brought a date around to meet Kick. I remembered the few serious ones. We never connected that way. "Guess not."

"Hmm." Deana scanned the room before leaning down again. She quietly said, "Tell me about your hot flash."

I filled her in on how it started after my shower, going down to the porch, and Blake walking in. The way he acted vulnerable. Listened. Put me first.

"Oof." She fanned her face. "You're making me bothered. Where's my man?"

I sighed. "It was… intense." Some of my unease came from not having reciprocated. Blake and I both almost cried when his daughter called. But he didn't act cross with her or me—only made a self-deprecating joke about it, like he hadn't intended to finish himself to begin with.

Then he invited me to go to lunch with them. Not once did he act cock-blocked, and the man grumped about plenty. Blake's commitment to fatherhood, though, was at the top of his sexy attributes. Right up there with his chiseled cheekbones and soulfully brown eyes.

Dee tapped a stylus against a tablet as she studied me. I felt myself looking at her with puppy eyes, asking for help, craving her wisdom.

"You opened up to him out of desperation and he came

through." She tapped the counter. "This is good. It's beautiful."

"Then why do I feel so… off my game?"

"You gave one man everything, and he used it selfishly. I understand why you've been reluctant to go there again. Doesn't mean it's what you need. Maybe keeping men at a distance has run its course. You see?" She gave me a scolding look. "And it's not fair to project your ex's betrayal onto this one. Sounds to me like your fox is special."

"Umm. Ouch."

"You talk to me…" Dee spread her hands wide unapologetically. "You get the truth."

I bowed my head. It was what I asked for, but ooh, it stung.

She pointed at my mug. "Can I get you another?"

I drummed my nails on the counter as I considered what I wanted next. "Sure. A scone and green tea please?"

"I didn't chase you off then." Dee dipped her chin. "Good to know." Her dark brown eyes smiled at me like I'd made her day. She plated my snack and drink and served some new customers while I sat with my feelings. When she came back, I was ready to burst.

"What do I do now?" I asked, eager to settle the nervous energy thrumming inside me.

"You and Kick." Her eyes danced as she drank her tea. "Weren't you the one who told her to jump, or do I remember that wrong?"

"This is different. Unlike Kicky, I've been dating this whole time, and it's only made matters worse."

Story time ended, and Dee said goodbye to the kids and moms as they left the shop. When we were alone again, she grew serious. "A'ight. You might have been in the water, but you only hung around the shore. How about swimming a little deeper? You know, trust your silver fox with a little more of your awesomeness. Your real self."

"Just because we fool around, it doesn't mean we're more than friends." I broke off a piece of the scone and popped it in my mouth as I stared out the window. The moms loaded their little ones into car seats. Miss Ginger ordered a latte to go and waved at us as she left.

Deana tsked. "You sound like your girl again." She picked up the tablet. "I told Kick you had caught feelings for the man the first time. Told her to stage an intervention when you let him go. But she wouldn't." I braced as she tapped out a rhythm with the stylus, matching the driving beat of a Mannheim Steamroller carol. "Do what you got to do, Cyn. It sounds like this man is good for you or you would've shut it all down when he walked in on you. If you ask me, you're good for him as well. Not to mention… all that motherly love inside you and him having a young girl who needs it. Y'all deserve each other in the best way. Should be shouting 'hallelujah' instead of moping at my counter."

The pastry bits I'd eaten turned into a globby goo in my stomach. Dee didn't understand the problem, but I did.

Chapter 23

As It Was

Cyndi

"What are you two doing here?" I asked Kick and Thomas. They occupied my favorite booth at the Garage. Blake and Felix sat across from them. Kick shifted her gaze to me and smiled.

Fee slid out of the booth and gave me a quick hug. "Good to see you back. How your daddy do?"

"He's... stubborn." I had spoken to my dad again on the drive in, and still he wouldn't budge on spending the winter with me. He used my mother's horse as his excuse this time. I planned to press the issue next week when I went back for Christmas. I was working on a boarding arrangement for Mom's horse at a neighbor's stable. I also hadn't booked a return flight home in the hopes Dad and I could drive his car down together. Considering how much I craved certainty, I didn't enjoy leaving the back end of my plans open, so it had to work.

As I hugged Felix, I caught Blake's sour expression and

worried they might have scratched the kitchen upgrades. Fee squeezed my shoulder and teased. "Sounds like someone I know."

"Are you talking about me?" I joked while pointing at my chest. Most of the table laughed. Blake grimaced after checking his phone.

Felix spoke near my ear. "Glad you're here. Boss is in a mood."

No kidding. Only, I didn't know how I could help. Deana's words of wisdom from the other day came to mind, but instead of reassuring me, they increased my stress.

I slid into the spot Felix vacated next to Blake. The corner of his mouth ticked up briefly. Blink and I'd have missed it. It beat a frown in any case. I rubbed the soft leather seat, like a kid self-soothing. Maybe Blake was as freaked out about last Saturday as me. The idea eased my anxiety some.

"So… what's up?" I asked Kick, avoiding Blake's eyes.

It seemed like every time I looked at the man, we were back on my porch, emotionally spent and running scared. We obviously needed to talk but didn't know where to start.

Kick pointed at a small stack of papers on the table. Kitchen plans. I blinked at them as if they'd magically appeared. "Last-minute checks before the renovations begin."

"And?" I tugged on my earring, waiting for the but.

Instead, Kick smiled. "Everything looks great. Blake and Felix took the Alliance's suggestions to heart. I think it's going to be a hit."

"Alliance's… suggestions?" I must have missed something along the way.

"I'm here as an advisor… newly representing the Allergy Awareness in Hospitality Alliance of the Triangle. Blake is my first client."

"The allergy alliance's acronym is… AAHAT?" I asked sarcastically, unable to resist a chance to needle my best friend.

I also hadn't heard the full name of her new group, as if she didn't have enough on her plate.

Thomas snorted. "I call it 'aa-hat'." He flicked the edge of his fedora as Kick bumped his shoulder, making them both laugh. Blake quietly joined them.

Their playful goofiness eased my pent-up tension, seeing the evidence of their best friend status. Dee had been right, and I was surprised to find myself happy about it. Kick had plenty of room in her heart for extra love. Besides, no one deserved it more.

She slid a pastry box toward me. "I also brought these for Felix."

I lifted the lid and inhaled the rich, buttery flavor. "Southern-style biscuits?"

"Gluten-free ones." She shimmied in her seat like an excited little kid. "My baker has been working on them." A smile spread across her face. "They passed the Fee test. He's going to call her about an exclusivity arrangement."

"Fee?" I turned toward Blake and said, "He has come a long way if Kick has 'Fee' privileges."

The golden flecks in his warm brown eyes lit. "Guess so." The amusement disappeared quickly, but he stayed in our conversation. "We're ready for the shutdown."

"Excellent." I patted my leather bag. "I have stuff for you to peruse before work starts." The restaurant would close for renovations the day after next.

I looked at Thomas. "Why are you here? Not that I mind."

"We're going dancing at the jazz club after this." He kissed Kick's cheek. "A little date night before our big holiday family fun time." He waggled his eyebrows sarcastically.

Kick and Thomas planned to spend Christmas in Michigan with her extended family. In fact, my crew planned to join them for an evening in Detroit as Rachel's special guests when she played Elphaba for the first time. Add in my family, and we were going to fill two rows.

Kick rubbed Thomas's biceps. "He's a teensy bit stressed about all the Allen hang time."

"No..." Thomas started. Then his shoulders dropped. "Fine. Yeah. We were supposed to host Burt and his kids in the mountains, and—"

"And then our girl had this opportunity come up," Kick said.

Thomas's eyes softened as he looked at his wife. "Yeah."

Blake huffed at Thomas's words. So that was the reason for his grumpiness. He'd told me about spending the holidays with his birth family. It didn't require a PhD to guess it would be stressful.

"So we booked a rental near Burt and will do the holidays in the D."

"I rented a condo in downtown Phoenix. My cousin's house sounds big enough, but I don't know..." Blake said as Thomas nodded knowingly.

I made a note to ask Blake about it later and changed the subject. "I can't believe you two still go out dancing after... you know." I bit my lip to hold off the panic that ensued whenever I remembered that night.

"You really haven't been out since Ducky's, have you?" Kick reached across the table and squeezed my hand. "Why don't you come with us?"

I waved her off casually. "Like I want to be your third wheel."

At the same time, Blake asked, "What night? What happened?"

"Uh..." I squirmed, like my dress had suddenly become a sackcloth.

"Two years ago..." Thomas cleared his throat. Yeah, he didn't want to think about it either. "Kick and Cyn were roofied right under my nose." He bit out his last words, still blaming himself.

"Hey, you saved my life," I insisted. The man would forever be my hero for that and more.

Blake's posture tightened even more. If men had hackles, his would've stood tall. "What do you mean?"

"It ended up being nothing. It's what could've happened that messes with all our heads. Anyway, Kick fought the guy off. It was in the paper." I looked around the open space to keep Blake from seeing the truth. I'd been scared shitless when I came to in the Emergency Department, and it still affected me. Hence the not going to clubs anymore. "As soon as Thomas figured it out, he drove us to the hospital."

"Not nothing, chica. You were unconscious." Kick's chin quivered, and I grabbed her hand.

"Who?" Blake's eyes changed from their whiskey color to black. "Where?"

I let go of Kick and patted Blake's biceps. "We're fine."

Thomas added, "It's taken care of."

"He in jail?" Blake asked.

"Dead. And I'm still pissed that what happened wasn't illegal due to a technicality," Thomas grumbled.

"Thomas…" Kick stroked his arm. "Our incident helped change the law."

A state law had recently passed, making it illegal to drug a drink even if the victim didn't end up assaulted. I still couldn't believe it had taken so long for it to go through.

Blake's voice dropped. "Are y'all talking about the shooting? That stuff in the paper."

I winced like I'd heard the shot. I hated thinking about Kick in the hospital. I'd only spent a few hours in the Emergency Department after our night at the club, Ducky's.

"It's related. Yeah." Now Thomas was brooding.

I wanted to punch my own face for bringing it up. I was

used to people—even strangers—knowing about those events. It never occurred to me Blake hadn't heard about it.

Kick leaned into her husband and kissed his cheek. "Like you said, it's over. We're good." She settled into him and looked at me. "We won't let those assholes take away dancing."

The wheels turned in Blake's mind as his eyes moved around the table.

Thomas broke our uncomfortable silence. "Before we take off, man… I was hoping to reserve your event space in January for my staff's yearly kickoff."

"Sure." Blake pulled a napkin from the holder and jotted down notes as they compared dates. "I'll have to check the calendar. I think you're good though." He did a double take my way as he wrote. "What?"

I shook my head, not wanting to look like we were fighting in front of my friends. Especially if it ended up starting one for real.

Kick slid out of the booth. I took a quick sip of the ice tea I'd poured on the way in and stood to give her a proper hug. She kissed my cheek. "Thomas's protective instincts always go into overdrive when we're out dancing." She popped her brows at me and whispered, "Makes for a fun night." I almost choked on my tea and rubbed circles on my chest to make it go down. "Think about it," Kick singsonged as her eyes flicked between Blake and me.

I made a shooing motion with my hands before giving Thomas a quick hug. "See you in Detroit."

He huffed and gave me a quick good-bye kiss on the cheek before taking his wife's hand and maneuvering toward the door. I returned to the seat across from Blake.

"What's wrong?" he asked.

"I was going to ask you the same thing," I said from the corner of my mouth. I should've sat next to him. We could talk quietly and not worry about eavesdropping. When Blake just stared at the back of his phone, I pressed. "Is it your trip to Phoenix?"

Blake blew out a long breath. "And then some... Olivia's turning into someone I don't recognize."

"Uh-oh." I sipped from my straw. "Does she not want to go? She seemed so excited to meet everyone."

"It would've been Gianna's year to have her for Christmas, so her sister decided Sparrow should stay here with them." He ran his hand over his hair. A thin strand fell out of his braid. "If she'd brought it up earlier, I would've happily swapped Thanksgiving. Now Liv's caught in the middle and taking it out on me." Blake flexed his hands like he couldn't keep them still, so I slid my glass over, offering it to him. "Thanks."

"It's not like you find your long-lost family every day. This is important."

"Right? That's what I've been telling Olivia and her aunt. Except... I yelled at her this morning. Our tickets are purchased, and the condo in Phoenix is rented, you know? It's a done deal." He looked so angry with himself. If we weren't in public, I would've hugged him. Instead, I found his hand under the table and squeezed it. After finishing what was left in the glass, he continued. "Now she's ignoring my texts. I don't know if she's home at her friend's house or what."

Not cool, Liv. "It's been hell to think about Christmas without my mother. I can imagine what's going on inside Olivia. Why don't you look for her? We can go over these papers when you come back."

He pointed to the napkin. "I need to check the calendar and email Thomas with those dates before I forget."

I didn't realize I was growling until Blake sighed. "What now?"

"You should hire an event planner," I blurted. It wasn't our first talk about adding more people.

"What am I to pay this person with? Felix's famous hush-puppies?"

"It can be part-time to start." I leaned toward him. "Your plate is overly full."

"Which is my fault. One obstacle at a time, Cyn. I'll consider it when we're on the other side of this mess."

"Then bring on an investor. Or two." Another point of opposition between us.

"In the middle of a fraud investigation? Come on." His voice almost grew louder than the buzz of the staff preparing the tables. "I'm a shitty bet."

I hated it when he talked negatively about himself. His words made it sound like a character flaw and not his terrible circumstances. "I told you I'm looking for a smaller venture for some of my money. The Garage would be perfect."

"And how would that look with the lawyers?"

I exhaled slowly to keep my composure. "With the new guardrails I've put in place, it would be a simple loan. Or is this about trust? Because I vanished before."

He lifted an eyebrow. "It's not like you've been available since…"

"Yeah. I know." My ears heated, and my hand lifted to my earrings. My feelings about our afternoon on my porch still ran the gamut. Or maybe I fought against their logical conclusion. I didn't know.

"Did I do something wrong?" This man really had the weight of the world on his shoulders, and I wasn't helping.

I whispered, "I'm not used to being so…" My hands made lifting motions as if of their own accord.

Blake's eyes seemed to smolder. "Hot?"

"Vulnerable," I countered. "Exposed."

"Hey." It was Blake's turn to squeeze my hand under the table, out of sight. "It was an honor to be there for you like that."

"I've never been so out of sorts before."

The corner of his mouth twitched into a smirk. "I like to think I helped sort you out."

"You did." I felt my face match his desire-filled expression as I remembered that afternoon. "You also had me at a disadvantage."

Blake's thumb stroked the top of my hand. I briefly closed my eyes, accepting how good it felt. "The next time I feel overwhelmed, how about I call you?"

"Promise I'll come running." I tucked my hair behind my ear.

"Will you look at me?"

I tipped my head up, thinking about what Dee said about not treating Blake like he was Joel.

"No more disappearing—emotionally or physically—all right? With everything else going on… it's too much."

I pressed my eyelids shut to keep from crying and nodded. "Promise. Again, I'm so sorry." The tables were filling up around us, intruding on our bubble.

"I want to kiss you, you know?" Blake casually leaned on his elbow as his other hand squeezed mine. I opened my mouth to respond, but he cut me off. "I know, after the holidays. But when we get back, Spark… we're talking through our shit. Got it?"

I smiled at his gruff description of romance. "Merry Christmas to you too."

"Just need to get through the next three weeks."

Chapter 24

A Long December

Christmas morning with my dad turned out to be especially difficult without my mom. She had been one of those Christmas women who decorated every inch of the house. I blamed Frankenmuth, the tourist town next to where I grew up and where she was raised. It was Christmas year-round there, thanks to a giant warehouse of a store that called itself a Christmas wonderland. Mom had worked there for years, including playing Mrs. Claus.

Dad and I woke up drowning in heavy grief, like she'd passed the day before.

"You haven't finished your pancakes, Tatay." He had more than half of his two flapjacks left.

"I ate the egg." He tried to hide how often his gaze drifted to the empty chair to his right. My parents sat next to each other instead of across the table. That way they both looked out across the fields while they ate in the breakfast nook.

It had never slipped past me how often they held hands

under the table. As a girl, I made faces and teased them for it. Now I knew it's what I'd been looking for all these years. Seeing my father's pain, it looked like I'd been spared.

"Okay. Why don't you grab your shower before we head down to Star's?" I kissed my father's cheek and walked his plate to the sink. After rinsing, I put them in the dishwasher and added the soap packet.

"Stop. It's not full," Dad said from over my shoulder.

I pressed the buttons, closed the door, and turned around. "I run my washer when it's half full, otherwise it smells. It's part of living single. Sorry."

My father grimaced as he stared at the machine.

"Hey." I reached out and squeezed his shoulder. "You sure you're up for today?"

"Yes, jefa." He gave me a small smirk that didn't reach his eyes. My heart broke more at the evidence of how hard he was trying to move on. "If we don't get to Star's on time, she'll send Bernardo for us."

I laughed. "Good point." I grabbed the cleaner and sponge to wipe down the kitchen.

Dad finally left to shower and nap. He'd been napping more lately. I hoped it was okay but didn't know who to ask. His doctor always said his tests were normal. Only, normal didn't necessarily mean healthy.

The yellow warbler from the wall clock went off, letting me know it was ten o'clock. I wondered if it was okay to check in with my pal, Blake. I told myself he could use a friendly voice with all he had going on, but the truth was, I wanted to hear him. I activated my earpiece and dialed.

"Everything all right?" Blake's words came out gravelly when he answered his phone. It was the opposite of the bourbon-like smoothness I'd expected and grimaced. I should have known better.

"Shit. I woke you up. I'm sorry." I picked up the sponge I'd dropped and moved to the table to wipe it down. "I'll let you go."

"Don't go. Talk. Please. We landed late is all. Didn't get to sleep till two."

"Well, hell. You should go back to bed." I knew he never slept in, but maybe he'd made an exception for their vacation.

"I'm trying to tell you I've been up. My voice is rough from lack of Zs, but I'm awake. Making pancakes for Sparrow and me, in fact. She's in the shower, so I could use your voice in my ear."

I stacked the local newspaper Dad still had delivered each week and set it on the bench by the back door. "I made pancakes too. Now my dad's up in the shower."

"Hmm. How's he doing?"

I was about to say good, then remembered Blake could understand. "It's tough. We're trying to keep some of our traditions, so it's not so different. Putting up all her decor though…" My voice broke, and I swallowed hard. "Mom liked to turn the house into a veritable North Pole. I talked my dad into putting out her most favorite decorations and one tree instead of six. It still ended up being a lot."

"Six?" Blake's chuckle eased my tight ribs, letting me breathe freely for the first time since I woke. It reminded me of the morning rendezvous with him. Those few minutes after an orgasmic workout when his eyes softened and crinkled at the sides were precious. It made me happy to give Blake that modicum of peace, given everything he carried.

"She put up ten one year." I grumbled. I never understood the Christmas magic, as Mom called it.

"That sounds"—he laughed harder—"awful."

"At least she owned it and didn't care what anyone else thought about her Clark Griswold ways. I adored her snowman collection when I was younger." Maybe one day I would put them out again. Just not this year.

Blake's voice lowered. "I'm sorry, Cyn."

"Yeah. Thanks. Guess you know."

"Suppose I'm doing the same for Sparrow. Probably should have let her stay with her aunt for that same sense of familiarity." Blake sighed heavily. In my mind's eye, he ran a hand through his hair. I wondered if it was down or pulled back and wished I could touch it. "At least I know how to make Gia's ricotta pancakes. It was our Christmas-morning tradition."

"Wow. I forgot she was a pastry chef. Impressive. Our tradition is good ol' Bisquick."

"Did it help?" he asked, his tone hopeful.

"Some. Dad didn't finish breakfast, but his appetite is smaller than I remember. I made sure he finished his egg, so he had protein." I slipped into my mom's chair and watched a flock of wild turkeys march out of the tree row like they were on patrol. My parents kept binoculars on the sill. Hell, they probably named them.

"Wish I could help."

"You've got your own, big guy. Is little chica better this morning?"

Another sigh came through the phone. I also detected a smile in his voice and wondered if it come from my nickname for Olivia. "All of yesterday's travel delays made her grumpiness skyrocket. Acted like I orchestrated them. My cousin wanted us to come early for breakfast and presents this morning, but Liv wouldn't move when her alarm blasted through the apartment. Now she's mad that we're going later. Mostly, I think she misses Gia."

"Jefe, it sounds to me like she's twelve."

"Here I believed only toddlers were rough."

"I'm obviously not an expert, but I remember Kick spending a lot of effort to break her first two of outbursts that were nothing more than a phase. By the time Liam was a teen, she'd learned the lesson and let them roll off her back."

"Interesting. I'll keep it in mind." The line quieted for a moment, and I thought the call had dropped, thanks to living in the middle of nowhere. Then Blake shocked me. "You know, my parents… along with Gia's… expect kids to hop-to like little soldiers. You might be the first person to see Liv's moods as normal. Thank you."

I blinked away looming tears, not that Blake could see them. Still, I didn't want him to hear how much his honesty meant to me. Always the witness to parenting, Blake was the first person I'd ever given child-rearing advice to. He could have easily blown me off, but his acceptance of my observations meant the world. Instead, I changed the subject. "Did she get her present from me?" I made her a necklace and earrings after she had gushed over a similar set I had worn.

"She loves it," he breathed. My ribs relaxed further. "Planning to wear it when we visit everyone."

"Aww." I placed my hand on my heart. Two deer picked their way to the edge of the tree line to stop at the salt lick my dad left out there. "Tell her it made my day to hear. I'm honored."

Blake cleared his throat. "I will. It was… You've been great with her. Can't thank you enough."

My ears heated from the warmth of his tone. His words were like a hug.

"It's hard to, uh… not be smitten with her. She takes after her dad that way."

"Oh really?"

"Do I hear a smirk in your voice, Mr. Brady? A little cocky, are we?" A smile spread across my face as I teased him.

"I don't smirk," he answered dryly.

"Ha. Let me put it this way… a smile, plus brood, equals smirk, sir. Not complaining. On you, it's pretty hot."

"Might be the first time my grumpiness has been called hot," he muttered. "Can you tell my staff? They never read that memo." Next came a hissing noise. "Crap. You're distracting me. Almost burned the pancakes."

"If hearing about your hotness is distracting, I'll keep the choice words about your thick—" I emphasized the K.

"Spark," Blake warned. It was followed by a crash. "Shit!" Then muffled noises. "Miss Cyndi. Why aren't you showering? Hurry up, honey. Breakfast will be done by the time you're out."

"Everything okay over there?"

"Oh, you know…" He chuckled. "Sparrow almost caught me at full mast in my sweatpants."

I giggled shamelessly. "It's never happened before?"

"Not. Once."

"Oh, come on. Even I've spotted my dad's on occasion." I laughed hard. "And bolted from the room."

"Almost slammed it into the cabinet door, thank you," he grumbled. "I only dated when Sparrow was at her mom's. Remember?"

"But you asked me to go on an outing with her."

"Look how well that turned out."

I winced, wondering why he'd still speak to me after what I'd done. Except, he sounded more self-deprecating than grudge-holding. I heard the rush of water from a tap and moved from the topic of erections. "Are the pancakes ready?"

"I dropped the spatula when Liv surprised me." More shuffling sounds and slamming of drawers. "They don't have a decent flipper in this place," he complained.

"I didn't mean to put you in a bad mood." My day just kept going downhill.

There was a sizzle and a click. "You haven't. There. Burner's off. You have my attention and my gratitude. Your voice is exactly what I needed this morning."

"Thank you. Same," I quietly, reluctantly said. It still felt like a bad idea to like this so much, but I couldn't help myself.

"If my blood hadn't dropped into my dick, I would've had Liv talk to you while I finished cooking. She could've thanked you for your present herself."

"That would be nice." The thought of Olivia made me smile. "She'll be about a half hour, right?"

"At least." After more scraping sounds, he continued. "Let's set up a video call. What are your plans again?"

"Tonight's good. I'll get in late, but you're behind me, time-wise. I can stay up."

"Oh right, the musical."

"Uh-huh. Rachel's big debut. Can't wait. It's an early show, followed by a dinner with Kick and Thomas. I'll text you when I get there, and we can firm up a time. But hey… if you need anything at all… remember your promise. I'll pick up. No matter what. That's my promise back."

"Argh." Blake rumbled with frustration. "I'll be fine."

All the fumbling sounds led me to believe Mr. Smooth was a nervous wreck. I would've been. "I'm sure it will be great. Just saying…"

He exhaled loudly. "Thank you, honey. Again."

Blake's promise to turn to me for help had to do with my difficulties with vulnerability, not his. I'd taken it as a sweet gesture, but he could have just said it to make me feel better. "Did you not mean it?" I was glad he couldn't see my insecurities and hoped they didn't percolate in my tone.

"Fuck." The water ran again, like he was cleaning up. His voice softened. "Yes, I meant it. You have to understand… You were cold for days, and I figured history was repeating itself. Then I found out someone drugged you. Put you in the hospital. I had… you know… feelings about it." I imagined Blake moving his hands around, only that was more my style than his. "And you won't let me show them unless we're in private."

"Are you surprised? Have you seen yourself? Especially at work."

"What does that mean?"

"It means… every time you strut into the front of the house, all eyes zero in on you. Hell, I bet the female regulars go to the Garage hoping to get your attention. Being with you in the dining room is like being on the red carpet with an action hero, and I'm the who's-she? date that missed their Botox appointment."

"Jesus. How does your mind… I don't strut," he defended.

"Saunter… stride… swagger. You swagger, Brady." I was grateful he skipped my confession.

"If you say so. Still don't see the problem. I told you the staff is spreading rumors about us. Why not make it official?"

"Grr." It was my turn to have a little fit, mostly with myself. I didn't know what kept me from taking the leap. "I need a bit more time," I whispered, thinking about Deana's advice again. I was almost there but knew I didn't want to make any declarations over the phone. "Let's table this until we're both home."

Blake cleared his throat. "Sure, Spark."

The steps creaked as my dad descended them. Guess he forwent a nap. I lowered my voice. "Hey, sounds like Dad's coming down. He'll want to leave soon."

"All right. I just flipped the last pancake, so… Hope your day gets better."

"Thanks. And pal… I hope yours is everything you've dreamed of. Truly." A rush of air that sounded like nervous energy rang in my ear, squeezing my heart. I quickly added, "If it's not, remember, I'm as close as that small computer you keep in your pocket."

"Thanks, buddy," he said sarcastically. "I'll keep it in mind." Blake's laugh stayed in my ear after the call ended. It traveled south to my belly and warmed me more than the cashmere robe I wore.

"Who was that?" Tatay asked as he entered the kitchen.

He looked deceptively festive in a Rudolph sweater over a

plaid button-down. The wrinkles in his khaki pants gave away his widowerhood. I should've ironed them for him.

He retrieved a glass from the cabinet and poured green tea in it. He kept pitchers of it in the fridge, like Southerners with their sweet tea.

If I told him I'd called a friend, my dad would assume I meant Kick and ask about her. I chose to go with the truth instead. "It was a man from home. He and his daughter are having an interesting Christmas. I wanted to check on them."

My dad's huff let me know he caught on to my euphemism, given the state of our holiday this year. It felt like everyone's festivities were interesting. "A man you're dating?" His tone was casual, but his eyes danced with much enthusiasm.

I spun quickly and reached for another glass. It kept Dad from seeing my face and reading more into whatever showed up there. "Sort of. He wants more, and I'm… I don't know." I filled the glass with water from the sink filter.

"Is he cute?" My father waggled his eyebrows.

Considering it's biologically impossible to swallow while laughing, I ended up in a choking fit. Dad's implication of cute like him hung heavy in the air. Dad's charisma gave him a top-notch bedside manner. Except he and I didn't talk about boys. It had been my mom's job and wasn't lost on me that he was trying to fill the gap.

"I don't think a middle-aged silver fox restaurateur qualifies as cute, Tatay." Under my breath, I added, "The man turns heads when he walks into a room though." I cleared my throat of the residual down-the-wrong-pipe-ness.

My dad squeezed my shoulder. "You should figure it out, iha. Soon."

"Still trying to get rid of me?"

Dad settled on a stool at the island while I dried my hands. I refilled my glass and leaned onto my elbow across from him, hoping a small smile would cover the unease in my tone.

"Still trying to gain a son." He winked and took a sip of tea.

"What about looking after you?" I bit the inside of my cheek to keep my eyes from watering. "Committing to a relationship would make it harder to get away as much as I have this year." When I was married, Joel made sure he was the center of my world and demanded my family come last. Another reason I ultimately considered myself lucky.

"I keep telling all of you… I'm a widower, not an orphaned boy." Dad furrowed his brow and waved me off. "I built a life in a new country and raised you. I can take care of myself."

"That's not what I mean," I whispered. "Why do you think it's been so hard to find the one? No man holds a candle to you."

He clicked his tongue. "No one's perfect. That's not fair."

"I don't mean it's your fault. Honestly, it has had more to do with healing from you-know-who. A friend recently pointed out that I assume everyone will treat me like… him. She thinks I go on the offense to protect myself." I stood up straight and stretched my shoulders. "She has a point." Hell, I knew I couldn't handle another break like that again.

My father grimaced. "I kick myself for not stopping your wedding."

Memories of him telling me to find a good American boy ran through my mind for the millionth time. Except I never blamed my dad for it. I blamed my misinterpretation of his words. "I wouldn't have listened. Joel had been my vision of the American Dream."

"And this new man? What do you envision when you're with him?"

Sheer terror. I sighed. "First off, he's a client."

My dad waved his hand at my comment. "Momma helped

me set up my practice before you were born. It didn't hurt our relationship, and we were together night and day."

I slugged my water, wishing I hadn't called Blake earlier. Dad deserved my focus, and the Brady's could wait until the New Year.

My dad grabbed my hand when I set the glass back down. "We only wanted to see you happy."

Well, shit. Did he think I sent my mother to her grave with unfulfilled hopes for me? I swallowed the lump in my throat. "I love my life," I squeaked. "I've worked hard for it."

"That's not…" He gave my hand a little shake. "We're proud of you, sugar. You can be an accomplished business-woman and find the one person who makes you happy. Who turns a simple breakfast into an adventure. You might think you're too old to start over, but you're not."

I blinked hard to keep it together.

"Plus you will be alone again," Dad added, not helping at all. "Either you'll die first. Alone. Or you'll be left here to live. Alone. If that's your worry, stop it. The quantity of your days together doesn't matter. At the end, you'll still wish for more time, if the love is true. What you don't want to look back on is a lack of quality."

"Dammit, Tatay." I wiped at the juicy tear threatening to unleash a dam full. "If I promise to think about being more with Blake, can we change the subject?"

"Blake is his name?"

I nodded as the corner of my mouth ticked up. Jeez, even his name lifted my spirits.

"Is Blake a good man?"

My smirk became a grin.

Dad tipped his head to the side as he studied me. "Yes, jefa. We can change the subject."

Phew. I couldn't take much more. I pulled an envelope out of my robe pocket. "Since we were talking about happy adventures and things…" I slid it across the counter. "Here's one last present."

He removed the tickets and studied them. "What's this?"

"An open-ended cruise around the Mediterranean."

My dad frowned, surprising me. "Why?"

I shrugged in frustration. "I don't know. You won't commit to visiting me. But you and Mom always talked about seeing Italy and Greece." I pointed at the itinerary packet. "This even goes to southern France and Spain. So you know… take whomever you want as your guest. It doesn't have to be me. We will have to wait until May if you want me to go, which would be awesome."

"Why now?"

"Because you can," I answered. My sarcastic tone sounded like a teenaged girl. "You can't sit around here all day by yourself."

Dad shrugged. "I sure can."

I spread my arms wide. "Don't you want to get away from the memories? Not forever, but for a little while?"

Dad slapped the counter, making me jump. "This is my home. Your mother's home." He pointed at the table. "We sit at that table every morning and watch for the deer twins. If we're lucky, Twerpy, Derpy, and the gang also show up, trudging to the swamp across the road."

His persistent use of the present tense concerned me. "Are you referring to the wild turkey flock?" Of course they had named the turkeys. I was surprised the deer were just called the twins, but they must have been born after Mom died. She had been the namer, not Dad.

"What if I am?" He pointed at the tree line to the left. "An eagle built her nest over there two springs ago. I bought hi-powered binoculars so we could watch her chicks grow. It's an adventure every morning." He walked to the sink and practi-cally threw his glass in it. "That's what I meant about a full life.

Not…" He shook the envelope. "Trips. Your mother wanted to visit those places, not me."

"No one's asking you to sell the farm, Dad," I whispered as my chin quivered.

"Yes, you are." He ran his hands through his hair. "Maybe you don't, but others insist."

Auntie Star. "I see."

Dad stared out the kitchen window while I looked up at the ceiling, willing my tears to stay put. I spun on my heel to head upstairs. My dad's voice reached me before I passed through the archway. "It helps… being here. With her."

I had to respect that. "Okay, Tatay," I said as my eyes landed on the last family photo we'd taken. About ten years back. Mom stood between Dad and me. He might have been comforted by a ghost, but I only felt the hole. The emptiness.

It didn't appeal.

Chapter 25

We Are Family

Blake

The nervous energy did flips throughout my body as Olivia and I stepped onto the front porch of Sherry's house. It was an elegant, hacienda-style home with a pinkish stucco exterior and rustic shutters. Exactly what I expected to see in Scottsdale, Arizona.

My fingers hovered over the doorbell as I counted to three. What are you waiting for? Just do it. My daughter raised an impatient eyebrow at me, mimicking one of my moves.

Suddenly the front door swung open to squeals, tears, and hugs.

"Sherry! They're here," Aunt Donna shouted into the house. She wrapped me in an impressive hug so tight my breath squeezed out of my lungs. "You're really back," she said into my ear, swaying us back and forth.

"Guess I am."

A hitching sob escaped from her throat. Unbridled energy had her shifting from foot to foot. "Okay Stoodis."

I looked behind and only found my daughter. "Who's Stu?"

"Stop manhandling him, Momma," my cousin Sherry scolded as she forced her mother out of the way. She gave me a gentler but equally meaningful embrace.

"Good to see you in person," I told her.

Over Sherry's shoulder, I watched relief settle across Donna's face like the decades of grief she carried in her high cheekbones were healing. The pain hadn't damaged the warmth in her brown eyes, and she smiled as easily as a child. I'd noticed that from our video call.

Sherry stepped back and fanned her eyes. "Don't ruin my mascara. I don't have time to fix it. Gotta make more fry bread." She was a few inches shorter than me and wore her hair in a long braid with a silver butterfly barrette holding back the strands near her ear.

We both laughed since I was also working hard to keep my eyes dry. Liv moved behind me, and I reached back for her. As she shuffled to my side, Donna gently lifted Olivia's chin with her finger. "That web camera didn't do you justice. What a gorgeous girl you are."

Liv shrugged. "Thank you." I squeezed her shoulders into me, needing her support as much as I gave it back.

Donna apparently cottoned on to Olivia's reluctance, because she gave her a gentler hug than mine. At first. Once Liv relaxed and returned the embrace, my aunt turned into a squeeze machine again. This time she peppered my daughter with kisses on her face as well. Fortunately, Olivia laughed and welcomed the affection. I exhaled a sigh of relief. Maybe my aunt was a puberty whisperer.

"Have you always been this rascally?" I asked.

"Not always. I was a serious girl, like this one." She pressed a kiss to Liv's cheek. Aunt Donna jolted, like she had a revelation. Then she hit me with a sparkling smile. "I learned it from my little sister."

I stood breathless, watching Sherry weasel her way in to greet my girl. She whispered in her ear. Before I knew what was happening, my cousin whisked her away into the depths of the house.

"Ahh—" I suddenly felt very alone.

I feared we were underdressed. Both my aunt and cousin wore pretty, long sundresses with patterns on them that made them into works of art on cloth. Sherry's was black and white with red accents. Donna's dress had every color in it and swirled around her feet, mirroring the way her hair did for her shoulders. I was in black Bermuda shorts and an off-white linen button-down shirt.

Aunt Donna grabbed my wrist and pulled. "Come inside." Her eyes dropped to my clenched fist. "Planning on fighting already? You'll fit right in." She winked.

"No, ma'am." I forced my fingers to relax. "Sorry about that."

"At least someone taught you beautiful manners."

Memories that had no business here tried to surface. I chased them away and gave my aunt a polite smile.

"You have nothing to worry about, honey. Everyone wants to see you. We haven't had a Christmas dinner this big in years."

Sweat trickled down my back and not because it was unusually warm for December. While it was a balmy midseventies in Raleigh, Phoenix's temperature cleared the high eighties. As I followed Donna, I heard the rumble of a diving board and splash of a pool. A pool party on Christmas afternoon? Why not? The entire day seemed surreal. Lying around the poolside wasn't nearly as weird as being a reincarnated ghost in my cousin's home.

"Here he is, everybody." As we entered an airy great room, Aunt Donna's arms moved in front of me like she was a game show hostess and I was the door prize.

I caught sight of the back of Olivia. Sherry's daughter, Juniper, had her arm stretched across Liv's shoulder, and they disappeared into another hallway. Sherry and her husband, Gabe, worked in a gourmet kitchen to my right. He waved at me while tending a pot of something stew-like. Sherry placed some dough in a well-loved cast-iron skillet. According to the size of the spread already on their vast island, I suspected dinner was almost ready. The aromas made my mouth water.

Fortunately, Gabe wore a T-shirt under his MR. GOOD-LOOKIN' IS COOKIN' apron. I let out a rush of relief when I saw his basketball shorts and bare feet. We hadn't messed up our first impression. Then I was mobbed.

Donna grabbed my shoulders and turned me toward her grandson, Canyon. "Hey, buddy. Nice to meet you in person," I said.

We gave each other hugs before he introduced his girl-friend, then Juniper's fiancé. Afterward, he announced they were going to change into their swimsuits and told me that's where Liv had gone. Juniper was hooking her up. I hoped it was a one-piece.

Next in line were my Uncle Joe and his wife, Barb. His hair was loose, almost all white on top and still midnight in the underlayers. He wore a Western patterned short-sleeved button-down with faded jeans and cowboy boots. The sharp edge in his gaze told me he had a hard life. Barb was as soft in her visage as Joe was steel. She looked like a woman who'd held on to her kind heart just to spite the tough times. On the outside, she looked a lot like my aunt and cousin, with a flowing dress and braided hair. Her interactions with Donna and Sherry came across more polite than close. I wondered if they didn't hang out much at all.

Joe and Barb's sons, Joseph and Kyle, introduced them-selves next. Joseph's son, Pete, and Pete's newborn, PJ, were right behind the men. The baby's big brown eyes reminded me of newborn Olivia, complete with a massive head of hair. I couldn't help but coo at him.

I'd never seen so many men who looked like me in one place before. I'd found my pocket of genetic relativity. We favored each other, especially Joseph and Kyle. They had dressed like me, had varying degrees of salty hair, and carried themselves like me. There was no denying we shared genes. The thought, there goes a Nez boy ran through my mind. Is that what would've been said about us had we grown up together?

When I was a kid, the Rogers boys lived across the street. Grown-ups laughed about how they could always tell a Rogers boy by the shaggy blond hair, tall build, and bucked teeth. What would have characterized us?

I bit my cheek to keep budding emotions at bay. More cousins came along, only I never caught on to exactly how we were all related.

Finally the crowd dispersed, and Donna guided me to a skillfully carved rocking chair in the heart of the great room, to the person I most wanted to see. I knelt in front of the woman, taking a moment to study her as she did the same with me. Aside from having mostly white hair, she didn't look much older than Donna. She still had plenty of raven strands mixed into her long braid, making a beautiful pattern that reminded me of marble.

This was why I resembled my uncle and his sons. I searched for the echoes of my mother in my grandmother Rose's eyes and found them. "Hello…"

She gripped my hands in hers. "You're back."

"Yes, ma'am." I couldn't stop smiling at her. "Is there a special word I should call you? I mean… what do the others…" I chuckled in embarrassment. "This is new, and I only know a word or two of Navajo." My nose tingled as I spoke. "It's on my list of New Year's resolutions, but there's a lot going on at home." Nothing like rambling during your first impression.

My grandmother leaned forward and kissed my cheek. "Call me Gran." That surprised me. She patted my jaw. "I didn't have our language growing up. They took it when I was a girl. I was already a grandmother when I searched it out again." She shrugged, as if the movement explained decades of complication. "Gran works fine for me." She gestured toward the hallway where the kids were changing. "It's wonderful to hear it from the young ones again." She kissed my other cheek as sweetly as if I was little PJ. "I'm so happy to have you back." She embodied the peace and acceptance I longed for. I'd only felt it recently when Cyndi was around, and now with my grandmother.

Gran pointed toward the island of food. "Go make a plate, then come sit by me. I saw you eyeing that food like you were starving, but I also want to learn about my shitshói."

Grandson. Remembering the Diné word made me smile wider.

"If you had come for breakfast, you would be full. You also missed the big present-opening extravaganza," Donna said. Her tone was humorous, but her face showed a disappointment that made me feel like a kid again.

"I'm sorry, Aunt Donna. Traveling is never easy, but yesterday was one for the books. After missing our connecting flight, Liv and I arrived at our rental really late. We were exhausted this morning."

I picked up a plate and was surprised to see a collection of appetizers from various cuisines. A few empanadas and skewers made up like a Caprese salad would hold me until dinner. There were also multiple dips with what looked like homemade chips and other dishes that looked Mexican.

Sherry caught me staring. "Is everything okay?"

"I don't… sure." Hell, the last thing I wanted to do was insult her menu.

"I forgot to ask if you have allergies," she whispered.

"Oh, we're good. Thank you." I picked up a skewer. "I didn't expect such an eclectic spread."

Sherry laughed. "We serve our traditional food with dinner." She tipped her head at Gabe. "He's working on mutton stew, and I'm almost finished with a second round of fry bread. We made some this morning for a breakfast version of Navajo tacos." She lowered her voice again. "Don't worry about missing it. My mom's just excited to go full auntie on someone new."

I laughed. "Someone explained aunties to me recently."

"Good. You're about to take a master's class in one from my mom," she said as she laughed with me. She gestured toward the food. "As for this… it's a collection of our popular catering appetizers. In fact…" Sherry shuffled over to her pile of cooked bread and brought me a piece. "Slide these off the skewer into this, then drizzle some of the fig sauce on it."

I did as suggested—pulled the stick free, and drizzled. In a matter of seconds, the cheese softened in the warm bread and tasted like heaven when it hit my tongue. My face must have shown my delight, because Sherry beamed.

"So simple but incredible," I said.

"Right? Fry bread makes everything better."

"I guess." I set the wrap down and wiped my mouth. "I forgot you're in the restaurant business. You two sound like mini moguls."

"It turns out we have a knack for fixing struggling establishments. We look for ones that focus on authentic dishes."

"Love that. The food scene sounds a lot like where I'm from but much bigger." I ripped off a corner of the bread and popped it into my mouth. It was like blending the best elements of a buttermilk biscuit and a pita. "It's hard to stand on this side of the counter. I'm used to helping in the kitchen on holidays."

"That's right. You're a chef." Sherry called out to Gabe, "Did you remember my cousin's a chef? How amazing is that?"

"Not exactly." I scratched at my temple. "I started in a kitchen and can still hold my own, but I liked management more."

"Smart man," Gabe said as he wiped his hands on his apron. He dabbed at his forehead. "You won't see me at a grill anymore professionally, but somehow I always end up cooking for family functions."

Sherry rolled her eyes. "That's so you don't have to talk to my family. You pretend to be so busy you can't chit chat."

"Well"—he dipped his chin—"she's not wrong."

The three of us shared a private laugh. Knowing Gabe could empathize with my predicament made it easier to be the new kid in the group. Yet I couldn't shake the idea of how nice it would have been to have Cyndi with us. She would have charmed everyone.

Chapter 26

I'll Stand by You

BLAKE

After an hour of hanging out, we set up for dinner in Gabe and Sherry's courtyard, the focal point of their U-shaped house. It featured the pool, lounge, an outdoor kitchen, and a dining space. A train of tables sat under the canopy of two mesquite trees. It was decorated for a Christmas in the desert theme.

I filled up on Gabe's savory stew, a squash-medley side, various pickled garnishes, more bread, and a family dish called pink elephant salad. It reminded me of the ambrosia concoction my mother used to take to potlucks when I was a kid. Bowls of corn in various shades and preparations filled in the gaps down the center of the long spread. The mush with honey was my favorite.

Halfway through the meal, disappointment set in. The adopted boy in me had expected the day to jar distant memories. Instead, every second brought another new experience. It was a silly notion that I hadn't realized I'd counted on until it stuck around, affecting my mood.

"It's shitty how you were stolen from us, but you have to admit you benefited from it," my Uncle Joe said. He moved into the chair next to me, after the dinner crowd scattered. The young ones returned to the pool, the new moms cared for their babies, and the rest of us formed small conversational bubbles while we picked at the leftovers.

The bite in his words fit the icy determination in his expression. It turned out my uncle was a retired mechanic. He told me all about how he'd hustled until he could buy his own run-down shop, though he didn't have to. It was written on the texture of his skin and on the bends in his fingers. So many sacrifices. He had turned it over to his son, Joseph, a while back but came in part-time to work on his buddies' vehicles when he felt like it. He didn't live as fancy as my cousin, Sherry, but he'd been able to turn a talent into something steady and profitable.

Out of respect, I gave him a smile to hide my objections to his theory about my upbringing. "How do you figure?"

Despite what my adoptive parents told me, my birth family was as American as any I knew growing up. Apparently my grandfather had an alcohol addiction, but so did Kurt Brady. No culture cornered the market on problems. However, when I looked around Sherry's home, I saw all I had missed.

Uncle Joe assessed me critically, as if my appearance answered my question for me. "You were obviously educated, had opportunities we spent years fighting for. Your school probably seemed like heaven compared to ours."

Only if the afterlife was rife with bullies. My schools had bigger budgets and the latest books, but it had been a hellish prison too. Still, I didn't blame my uncle for having wanted more.

Back in the early days after college, Felix and I had done our share of hustling. Memories of the grind in someone else's kitchen flooded me. We worked our asses off to prove our worth. Ninety percent or more of that came from being minorities. Those obstacles fueled our vision. They motivated us to pool our talents and turn what society called a hardship into an asset.

I looked at my uncle, surprised that his eyes seemed filled with challenge. Part of me wanted to point out that I blend in here. Not just in Sherry's house either. Except no one won the game of who-had-it-worse.

I also didn't want to revisit more memories than I already had. The darkest ones didn't belong in the same space as my family. Instead, I gave Uncle Joe my brightest smile and changed the subject. "The drive to hustle must be in our genes. I hope to swing by your shop while I'm here. I've heard great things about your work on classic cars."

My uncle tipped his head back and belly laughed. "You should run for office."

"Quit bothering our nephew, brother. I need his attention." Aunt Donna approached us with Gran following behind. Uncle Joe rolled his eyes. She sat across from me, placing a small stack of wrapped boxes in her lap. "You have presents to open."

"Oh." I jumped up, the chair rumbling loudly as it slid back. "I left yours in the car."

My grandmother was struggling with a heavy chair, so I picked it up. "Where would you like to sit?"

She pointed to an area away from the pool crowd. I placed it down and helped her scoot other ones into a grouping.

"You brought presents?" Donna looked shocked, but Gran smiled, like she'd expected it.

"Not for everyone," I said sheepishly.

I leaned down and spoke to Gran. "I should've told you how beautiful you look, but I was overwhelmed." She wore a soft purple blouse over a light brown skirt. A beaded belt showed off her waist and complemented a pair of intricate necklaces.

"Still a sweet boy," she commented as she patted my arm.

"Your jewelry is gorgeous. Do you know the artist?"

She grinned as she dipped her head toward my aunt. "Donna made it, including my belt."

I thought of Cyndi—again—and her beadwork.

"Your daughter wore a pretty set when you arrived."

I slid my hands to Gran's and helped her sit down. "A friend made it for her for Christmas." My grandmother's smile brightened like I'd confessed a secret. Guess I had. I pretended like it didn't matter.

Donna sat next to Gran and smiled expectantly.

I held up a finger. "One minute, ladies." I walked over to the pool and called Olivia over. "Grab a towel and dry off. Then go sit on the chair by Aunt Donna. I'm going to get our presents from the car."

"Can we not? I'm still—"

"We are. Donna wants to do it now."

As I trotted off, she muttered, "Fine" while climbing up the pool ladder.

"It's so pretty." Olivia lifted a handmade cloth doll out of a carefully wrapped box and held it up.

Aunt Donna preened. "I didn't know if you considered yourself too old, but I kept my dolls, and Juni still adds to her collection. So…" She leaned close and brushed the velvet skirt with her fingers. "This is how I remember your grandmother's doll."

Liv turned to me with wide eyes. "This was your mom's."

My spine tingled at the news of the connection. If it was, someone spruced her up. Her hand-painted face looked brand-new, as did her blue velvet dress and silver trim.

"No, honey," Donna said. "A friend of mine made her based on how I remembered her doll. We don't…" She and my gran seemed to carry on a silent conversation. "We don't keep the things of the dead. It's just—"

"Nothing?" I collapsed onto Olivia's lounge chair, suddenly needing her close. "I was hoping you had photos of her. And maybe me… you know, with my mom."

Gran's expression turned pained. Aunt Donna winked at me before handing my daughter and me each a bag. Mine held an aged envelope. Gran glared at my aunt as I pulled out a small stack of photos. Donna shrugged apologetically, then shook her head and sat up straight as if she'd changed her mind about the penance. "I kept some stuff, okay?" She defended. "She was my only sister."

I held up the top picture so it was next to Gran in my line of sight and raised my brow. She grabbed it from me and inhaled as she looked at it.

"It's your grandfather and me when we were dating." She handed it back, a gentle lift softening the corners of her mouth.

"Olivia looks like you." I handed the photo to my daughter, who oohed over it.

"I was fifteen."

Wow. I couldn't imagine Liv being with her life partner so soon. Then again, my grandfather lived hard and died young, so it probably was good for him. Wasn't so sure about my grandmother.

"You also look like my people," Gran said, her eyes gleaming with pride.

"As did—" Gran smacked Donna's arm. "Oh, come on,"

she retorted. "He doesn't have our memories. We should give him something."

"We've given him this." Gran spread her arms wide.

Oddly, I wished they would just say my mother's name. I understood my grandmother's point of view in my head. To her, it was more than bad luck to speak of the dead. It was blasphemy. Like arguing with the Creator about taking a loved one away. In that regard, I did have a beef with any entity for taking her from me. Besides, I hadn't died, and my mom's body was never found. Great. Now my head swam with new childlike dreams of her living in another country all these years. I shook it off, hard.

Sherry piped up, "I agree with Mom." She sat in a chair on the other side of me, closing the amorphous circle we made. Earlier, Sherry had shared with me about volunteering as a grief counselor. It was a new concept in the community, and helpful. New members were often afraid to speak about their loss, so Sherry created nontraditional ways to help members with their grief while respecting the old ones.

My grandmother lifted her gaze to the sky. She was outnumbered in a highly emotional battle that ran deep. While I felt it, I couldn't relate, which set me... adrift. I shamelessly craved knowledge of any morsel of my past because it helped my present make sense.

"Can he look through the rest, or should I have Blake do it when he's alone?" Donna asked her.

Gran closed her eyes and sighed. Her face still pointed at the sun's rays. "Let him finish."

"May I?" Sherry asked.

I made room for her on my lounger. I was in the middle, with her and Liv flanking me. They oohed and aahed as I flipped through the stack.

My uncle, aunt, and mother as little kids. I swallowed a thick lump in my throat as I saw my mother's face for the first time. She looked about four—a long-haired version of me at the same age. It was weird. Same deep-set eyes. Straight nose —pre-break on my part. I saw where the family tree split into its branches. My mom and Uncle Joe favored Gran, while Aunt Donna looked like their dad.

The biggest difference between me and them was in my eyes. Their brown was deep and warm. Mine was lighter, like my favorite bourbon. I wondered if they came from my real father. It didn't feel like the time to ask about it.

The next few photos were more of the siblings growing up. It told me a lot about Aunt Donna's childhood and more about what she'd lost when my mother and I disappeared. From the way the kids were dressed and the buildings behind them, it was clear the three were raised in a different time and place than what Sherry's kids had experienced. Uncle Joe's comments about my privilege made more sense. Despite growing up poor, these three—my uncle, aunt, and mom— looked happy. Treasured.

In one picture, they were in a large group that looked like extended family. Children were everywhere.

Donna leaned closer. "That's all the cousins." Her voice broke, and she dabbed at her cheek. "I wanted you and Olivia to know where you come from as much as who you come from."

Within the confines of the small squares in my hand, the desert scenery behind the kids looked vast. Delicate yet rugged. Beautiful. A contrast to my time growing up in the woods.

"Sometimes I forget the good parts," Donna explained.

Sherry whispered reverently as I handed the photo to her. "Ooh, it's been so long since we went to the rez."

"Is it far?" I asked.

"Kind of." She passed the photo to Liv. "It's more like… life. We've been busy with work and Juni's wedding plans." She tipped her head toward my aunt. "Mom takes Gran to her appointments."

As she spoke, our grandmother's face formed a scowl. Sherry reached out and squeezed her hand. "You need to get back soon, don't you?"

"Yes," Gran answered, her tone hard and clipped. I hoped my gift would lift her spirits. I decided the rest of the pictures could wait and shifted backward to pick up the box I'd slid under the chair.

"Aww. I've never seen this one." Sherry picked up the top photo in my lap. I dropped the box, straightened, and stared. The picture was of my mother tickling a chubby baby in the middle of a belly laugh. It didn't look how I'd imagined myself back then, yet I assumed the baby was me. I was younger than the first photo Sherry had emailed of us. My mother was definitely the smiling woman from my visions while growing up, confirming it had been a memory and not a dream. My breath fled my body as grief and anger tried to choke me. I wanted more than pictures, but they would have to be enough.

Aunt Donna pressed her lips together as her eyes shimmered. I cleared my throat to keep from doing the same. "I always knew she wasn't a drug addict," I blurted.

"What?" In her excitement, my aunt's feet came up as she rocked back, almost falling out of her chair. A loud screeching of the chair legs caused the rest of the family to stop and look at us.

I shouldn't have said anything, but it erupted from within. They deserved an explanation, and I needed to share my truth. "The story I was given growing up was that my birth mother was a drug addict from Cherokee country in the mountains."

"Cherokee?" Sherry's eyes were wide as she shook her head.

I lifted my shoulder. "From what I can tell, this is the back-story my adoptive mother was given. I have no idea about my… her husband. I never believed them. In my heart… even as a little kid… I knew they lied. Just didn't know why."

I should shut up. Drop this. But Donna kept her hands over her mouth as she shook her head. I hated causing her pain. We had connected instantly, probably because she would have raised me if given the chance. If someone had told them, they would have found me.

"She would have clawed through rock to get back to you."

I pulled Liv to my side and kissed her head. Since becoming a father, I knew Donna's words were the truth. Plus my daughter sniffled quietly. I thought of Gia, regretting my lingering bitterness toward her and resolving to do better.

I handed Gran my box. "Maybe we can lighten the mood. The haircuts alone should make you laugh."

Insecurity kicked in as she carefully undid my amateur wrapping, so my tongue wagged some more. "W-we didn't know what to bring with us, but we hoped these might help you get to know us better."

"Ooh," Donna said as Gran lifted the photo album from its box like she was lifting a newborn. It was a photo book.

"It's some highlights of my life." I kissed Liv's head again, needing an anchor. "Sparrow's too."

Watching my family go through the best parts of my childhood became an out-of-body experience. It had been weird to boil fifty years into a few pages. My parents had only taken photos when it was expected of them, but I made up for it when I left for college. I kept a large box of predigital photos under my bed.

My aunt, grandmother, and cousin vocally celebrated each page of milestones. While Gracie Brady hid this stuff away in a drawer, these women argued over which photo should be framed and who wanted a copy of each.

Olivia once asked me if my parents lived in Florida because we embarrassed them and if that was why they didn't want pictures of her. That had been a fun conversation. I didn't lie. Besides, Gianna's family filled their walls with family photos. Liv had seen the difference her whole life. I tried to make up for it by plastering my walls with our memories. I knew I would add to the collection with the treasures Aunt Donna had given me.

Seeing pride in my grandmother's face at my high school and college graduations was the only Christmas present I needed. Her eyes shimmered at the ones of Olivia's birth. The album ended with a few of her recent riding lessons.

"Who's this?" Gran asked, pointing to Cyndi, who had come along and stood on the other side of Olivia. Cyn had her head back laughing because a horse had stuck her head out of her stall and nuzzled Cyndi's cheek. The picture was currently on the home screen on my phone.

"She's my friend," I answered quickly.

At the same time, Olivia volunteered, "That's Daddy's girlfriend."

I did a double take at my daughter. We hadn't talked much about Cyndi. I figured I'd include her once Cyn and I had worked out our status. In the New Year.

"Girlfriend? You said you were single," Aunt Donna complained. She narrowed her eyes like I'd lied.

Olivia stage-whispered, "It's a secret." Then she grinned at me.

"It's early," I added after a long sigh.

"They talked on the phone this morning while Daddy cooked breakfast. His face looked like this." Liv screwed her features into a grin that was supposed to make her look lovesick as she bobbled her head from side to side.

Sherry snorted and reached around me to shove Olivia's shoulder. "Goofy girl. Don't give your dad a hard time. You'll make that face on your own soon enough."

I grumbled.

"So much for tomorrow's plans." Donna looked ready to pout.

I turned to Sherry. "What plans?" I had visions of some sort of bachelorette auction. Or would it be the bachelor up for sale?

She laughed and patted my back. "Welcome to the family, coz."

Chapter 27

Defying Gravity

"This one goes in Addy's pile."

Aunt Star handed me a shirt box with snowmen on it. She'd recruited me to help make individual gift hills strategically placed around her living room. "I don't mind playing Santa's elf in real time," I told her. This seemed to be extra work for no reason.

She blew her bangs out of her face. It didn't help, considering she was hinged over at the waist, sorting through the name tags. "Then I won't get your presents on camera."

"I'm not a child anymore, Auntie."

I picked up two more Addison presents from her and walked them across the floor to their appointed mark. Literally. Star had taped off color-coded boxes on the carpet. Her unwrapping movies were serious productions. That no one ever watched. She still used a video camera with a gawd-awful light attachment. She had decades of squinty Christmas movies in a closet in her craft room. And none of us were willing to risk the backlash if we protested.

Aunt Star patted my cheek. "You're still a girl to me, iha."

I sighed and returned to the ridiculous sorting ritual.

"You can finish while I set up my tripod."

"Oh goodie," I muttered. At least it was a pretty day. The sun shone in my aunt's south-facing living room. A Santa's Express train choo-chooed in the far corner. The girls quietly rearranged the elves in the village. Star had mentored under my mom when it came to Christmas decor. She'd taken her lessons seriously. The main tree was in here with the presents and soon-to-be paper carnage. A tropical-themed pencil tree stood in the dining room. Another kids' tree was in the family room. Some of the ornaments came from Berno and me. Those were fun. Small ceramic ones finished the rest of the rooms in Star's home.

My father rested quietly in "his" chair facing the tree I currently ducked under. His pile was built at his feet. Something about my auntie keeping to her traditions settled him, which we both needed.

After our fight at home, we spent the drive down in a tense silence. By the time we made it to Star's for lunch, my stomach was too upset to eat much. I'd always hated arguing with my father, and now it was worse without my mom to mediate. I didn't know how to fix it. I hoped Star would bring Tatay out of his shell, but so far, she'd left him to brood.

My aunt finished readying for her Frank Capra impersonation and whispered in my father's ear. He nodded and left the room, heading toward the kitchen. "We might have to slip Pablo a gummy to make him smile," she murmured in my ear.

"Auntie…" No way would I play fast and loose with my father's medicine.

Star bumped my shoulder. "Just kidding." She clicked her

tongue. "Nothing I do or say will lift his mood. What did you do?"

I lifted a finger. "First… he seemed better sitting here." I spread my arms. "The family traditions help, I think. Second… we didn't feel up to go all out at home. Third…" I stepped closer to her and lowered my voice more. "I somehow insulted him by giving him an open-date cruise trip for his big gift."

Star rolled her eyes. "I'll take it if he doesn't want it."

"Auntie…" I made the same nose-flare the women in my family used to silently correct bad behavior.

"Just saying." She gestured at the sofa for me to sit and looked over her shoulder, making sure we weren't heard. "My brother and I had opposite marriages, right?" She brushed her hands together. "For me, it was good riddance. All I can say about Franco now is he was aptly named since he ran our family like a dictator. My proudest moment is getting Bernardo away from such a bad influence."

"Okay," I drawled, wondering where she was going with this.

"I imagine you can relate."

I bit my lip, thinking. "Yeah, guess so. Joel was more of a man-baby, but he did make a sport of taking me down a notch." I shrugged. "Eventually there weren't any notches left."

"Exactly." Aunt Star put her arm around me and squeezed my shoulder. "I still think a Filipino man—like your father—"would have been a solid match."

"You know about Julius, don't you?"

"Who?"

"I dated him after the divorce. He even agreed to do fertility treatments with me. We did two rounds. Mom or Dad didn't tell you?"

My aunt shook her head. "I don't recall."

I shrugged. "Wonder if my mom knew it was a disaster from the start. Obviously, it didn't work out."

"What happened?" Ever the good mother, Star was rubbing soothing circles on my back.

"I'd had enough of the treatments. Joel had a son and daughter by that time, so it was a solid kick that the problem was me."

She squeezed me like an accordion. "Your momma had issues after you were born."

"I know." She'd bravely walked through it again with me, taking on twice the guilt despite what I tried to tell her. "Anyway, the experience made Julius realize he wanted kids. And like Joel, he didn't want to adopt them."

Star let out a long-suffering sigh. "I'm sorry, lovey. I should have been there."

"Ah, no." I wrapped my arms around her and shook her. "I should have figured out what was up when Jules insisted on getting pregnant before he'd propose. He claimed the stress of a wedding was too much. In hindsight, I think he wanted reassurance." I squeezed her again. "I've learned it's all on them, okay? No more guilt."

"I admire how much you've grown from your… because of all that. You found independence."

"I learned to love myself," I added as I rocked my aunt, wondering if she was still reeling from her ex. She'd divorced him when I was in middle school. "I can also tell what you're doing."

"Oh?" Star squeaked innocently.

"Yes." I stopped moving and turned to her, full-on. "You're filling in the gap my mom's left. I love you for it."

She gave me a shy smile. "No one will fill her shoes."

"True. Still appreciate how hard you're trying to. Thank you, Tiya."

My cousin's wife, Luz, quietly approached us. "The kitchen's cleaned, and Berno's entertaining Uncle Paul. They're in the sunroom."

"Presents then?" Aunt Star asked her.

"When you're ready. What are you talking about?" Luz asked as she pulled an ottoman closer to us.

"I was explaining to Cyndi why her father didn't like the Christmas present she gave him."

"You were?"

My aunt threw me some side-eye. "I was getting there."

"Hmm."

Luz scrunched her nose empathetically. "Is that why he's grumpy?"

I opened my mouth to confirm, but my aunt beat me to it. "No, love. He's missing Pat. Pablo wasn't going to have a good day no matter what happened today." She nodded toward the ottoman. "Be mindful of the present piles, dear."

"Sorry." Luz pulled her feet up.

"Would you mind getting drinks before we start filming?" Aunt Star asked her daughter-in-law.

Luz jumped up. "Sure."

I chuckled quietly at my aunt referring to opening presents as if we were on a movie set.

She patted my knee when Luz was out of sight. "So we both know the dark side of relationships. And we've learned to love ourselves first. We can't wait around for someone else to do it. Right?"

I tipped my head from side to side, contemplating her words. "I suppose."

"What we missed out on is trust. Your parents had it. No matter what, they gave each other the benefit of the doubt."

I could see that and nodded my agreement. The images of them through the years settled around my shoulders like my auntie's hug had. Emotions made me unable to speak.

"You know, your momma told me about your other dating adventures," Star added, a sly smirk on her face.

I rolled my eyes. "Great." I straightened my spine. "Listen, I have no regrets—"

"Not judging, iha." Star held up her hand. "If you could trust again, one might stick."

She had a point, but it was wearing on me. Still, I remembered those early days with Blake, wondering if I'd broken it off with him because I didn't trust him back then. More likely, I didn't trust myself. That was probably what held me back currently.

"You haven't explained how this connects to Tatay getting mad this morning."

Aunt Star nonchalantly flicked her hair. "It doesn't."

"Huh?"

She raised her eyebrows like the answer was obvious and I was a doofus. "Pablo is afraid if he makes new memories, he'll lose Pat."

I narrowed my eyes as if that would help me understand her logic. She patted my knee again. "You don't understand because you had to move on in order find yourself."

"So he's afraid if he moves on, he'll lose himself along with my mom?"

She smacked my knee this time. "Now you're getting it."

"But…" I growled in frustration. "I didn't tell him to move on. I wouldn't dare. A vacation isn't moving on."

"It is to him." She switched back to speaking to me like I was her granddaughter. "He met Patricia shortly after starting school at Michigan State." As if this was new information. I raised my eyebrows to get her to make a point. Star threw her hands up out of frustration with me. "All his adult memories are tied to her."

"Aw shit." I sank into the sofa, trying to keep from crying.

"Give it time." Auntie kissed my cheek. "I'll go with him."

"Tiya." I laughed at her, rolling my eyes. "Of course you will."

Luz returned with two glasses of apple cider. "Is it safe now?"

I checked the time on my phone and jumped. It was getting late. We had two hours before we were to meet Kick at the theater for Rachel's debut. "Yeah, we better open these gifts and head out." I turned to my aunt. "Looks like we don't have time to film this year."

She bolted off the couch as fast as a tiny, seventy-year-old Filipino woman could and fired up the spotlight. "The hell we don't."

THE OPULENT THEATER WHERE WICKED WAS PLAYING HAD recently been restored. Walking into the lobby was like stepping back in time to a nineteen twenties Art Deco heaven scape. I looked up at the decadent ceiling and sighed.

Then Berno's daughter's scream brought me back to reality. People around us scoffed and gave us dirty looks.

"Addison didn't get a good nap in the car," Luz explained. She looked on the verge of tears herself.

Kick's husband, Thomas, surprised me by offering to take Addy. He distracted her while we finished having our purses scanned and coats checked. Once inside, Kick and I each held one of Luz's arms and swept her off to the bathroom, telling the rest of our gang we'd see them in our seats.

My dad tapped his watch to let me know it was getting late.

"Shh," Kick soothed as we moved through the doors of the ladies' room. "We've got you." Tears were falling down Luz's cheeks.

"How do you remember me?" Luz asked her. They'd only met once when she and Berno brought the girls down for a visit.

Kick shook her head. "Every mother knows the stress of a baby with a messed-up nap on Christmas Day." Kick bent her knees as she gently dabbed Luz's face with a tissue. "I'm guessing you didn't get a say in the schedule?"

Luz shook her head. "She doesn't sleep well in someone else's bed. Even Star's."

"I'm sorry," I said, feeling like a selfish heel as I rubbed her back. Like that would undo the damage. "What do you need?"

"The first act?" Luz asked. Her lips twisted together like she was afraid she had over-asked.

I nodded sharply. "Done. I'll take her when we get back."

"I should have stayed home." Luz's chin quivered.

"Nonsense," Kick said. "You deserve a nice evening, and we'll all pitch in."

"I don't mind, sweetie," I added. "Honestly. I adore your girls."

"Th-thank you both."

The show held Addison's attention for most of the first act. She sat in my lap with her fingers in her mouth as her eyes followed the story. Even though she was too young to remember meeting Rachel when they visited me, the knowledge alone kept Addy riveted to every move my goddaughter made on stage as Elphaba.

"Wow, baby girl. You sing pretty." Addison shocked me by singing "The Wizard and I" perfectly.

She turned around and touched my face, dampening my cheeks with her little spit fingers. I loved it. "Mommy let me see it on TV." She leaned toward my ear and whispered, "Some parts are scary, but it's okay because it's pwee-tend."

I nodded and kissed her nose. "You're right, brave girl."

Addy grinned and turned back to the performance, her baby butt wiggling in my lap. Halfway through act one, she'd fallen into a light sleep against my shoulder. In the buildup to "Defying Gravity," Addison woke and sang the song along with Rachel. I was proud of them both.

Hearing Rachel, a girl I loved like a niece, sing the defining song of her role moved me to tears. Watching her fulfill a dream was an honor. Witnessing her sing the hell out of the song made me so proud. I shifted to catch Kick's gaze. Her face was drenched with tears as she smiled at her girl. Thomas stood behind her with his arms wrapped around her shoulders. Kick clung to them like they anchored her. I loved that for her. Our eyes met, and we shared a moment as we recognized the same pride in our girl.

As soon as the song ended, Addy's chin quivered.

"Uh-oh." I stood to take her out of the auditorium. Luz and Berno followed close behind us. As soon as we cleared the doors to the lobby, I started pacing her, hoping Addy would calm enough to go back to sleep.

Then my phone vibrated in my purse. I shifted the toddler to my hip and pulled out my phone.

Blake.

Luz held her hands out for Addy.

Berno said, "We're going to take her home."

"Hey, one sec," I told Blake. "Go to Mommy," I said to Addison as I handed off the clingy girl. I blew kisses at the three of them and hustled to find a quiet corner. "Blake? Are you o—"

"Cyn."

The pain in his voice set off my alarm bells. "What's wrong?" I'd never known him to sound so unguarded. I started shaking, my body reacting to his emotion. I wondered if something had happened to Olivia.

He wheezed a moan. "I need you."

Chapter 28

Bent

BLAKE

Olivia ate up all the "little cousin" attention Juniper gave her. When she pouted at my calling it a day, Sherry asked if Sparrow could spend the night. As fun as my aunt and uncle had been, Sherry and I hit it off at a deeper level. Probably because of the should-have-been-siblings air between us.

"I'll take care of your girl like she's my own," she'd said as we hugged goodbye. "Go decompress."

Boy, did I need to. I'd had my fill by the time dessert was served. The added sugar made me twitchy. Irritable. I was missing something despite being surrounded by what I'd been looking for my whole life. I felt guilty—and ungrateful—for bailing on the party first, but I had to go.

I considered Sherry's direction as I parked the car at the condo. It was still on my mind after I changed my clothes. Decompression for me meant working out. Better yet, boxing. Sparring could take my mind off the past and the present. The building had a basic gym but no bags I could hit. Already in a

Garage T-shirt, I was about to pull on sweats when I changed my mind and put on jeans instead. Next thing I knew, my feet were hitting the sidewalk. If I couldn't make the adrenaline run its course, I'd shut it down.

I strolled around the downtown neighborhood, enjoying the evening temperature and the quiet streets of Phoenix. A local bar beckoned me inside as I passed. The bright purple lights of Gerald's intrigued me. It had a sophisticated and welcoming exterior that gave off neighborhood-hangout vibes. I spun on my heel and opened the door.

The dark interior enveloped me like a warm blanket. No holiday tunes played, just an AC/DC song. It was what I needed. I nodded to the handful of guys at the end of the bar and grabbed a stool around the corner from them. Two of the men raised their whiskey glasses in greeting. The first guy looked like Elvis if Elvis had lived long enough to retire to Phoenix. The second guy reminded me of LeVar Burton in a cowboy getup, complete with mother-of-pearl snaps on his shirt. I did a double take to make sure it wasn't actually him.

Another fella had already passed out, his head lying on folded arms. Our reasons for ending up there didn't matter. I was simply another member of the holiday outcasts club.

I had placed an order for a local bourbon when the cloying scent of cheap perfume invaded my nose, making it twitch. I sneezed five times in a row. As gently as I could manage, I removed the hand sliding up my arm, digging deep to make sure I didn't scowl as I looked over my shoulder. God, the girl was… a girl.

I was about to ask her how old she was when the bartender piped up, "Leave him alone, Kara. He's not here for you."

"That true?" Kara asked.

I nodded as my saving angel slid my rocks glass over. Kara huffed and disappeared into a dark corner.

"How did you know…" I asked the bartender, waiting on her name.

"It's Ang and this is my place," she said, hooking her thumb at the lit sign behind her. "A guy like you isn't here for her kind of action. Especially not on Christmas." Ang reminded me of Jamie Lee Curtis, if a touch older.

"The sign says GERALD'S," I said, deciding to skip the guy-like-me comment.

She leaned her hip into the bar, a sweet smile on her face. "He's my old man. We split holidays. Ger did last night. I'm on tonight so the gang has a place to go." She flicked her hand at the men around the corner. I nodded, following along. "Anyhoo," she continued. "You're A… a new face. B… it's Christmas, and a guy like you wants a girl, he doesn't come in here. Not that I'm knocking Kara and her kind." Ang stepped back from the bar and let her head drop. "Suppose I am, aren't I? But they're doing their best."

There was no way to answer her politely, and I indicated so with a smile.

She started wiping the counter. "Want to hear my C?"

Did I? I sipped the whiskey. A smooth, smoky flavor balanced the bite of the grains. I leaned onto my hand. "Why not? Hit me."

"Unfinished business." Ang slapped the counter after I winced. "Knew it. Am I right or am I right, boys?"

The men around the corner raised their glasses. "You're always right, Ang." Their voices were filled with awe, despite their words being slurred, like the barkeeper had side hustle as a guru. What if this wasn't a good idea?

"What's the Garage?" Ang asked, tipping her head at my shirt.

I let another sip slide down my throat before answering, relishing the liquid heat. "It's my restaurant and cocktail bar back home."

"Yeah?" Ang perked up. *Please don't let her want to talk shop.* "Where's home?"

"Oh." I rubbed my temple. "North Carolina."

She pointed at my chest. "Yet that necklace suggests you're Navajo."

I looked down at the jewelry my aunt had made me. All the men in our family had one. *Our family.* They'd been wearing them at our festivities. *For me.* "My aunt gave it to me."

"What made you go so far away from home?"

Now, my bar staff was friendly. I made sure of it. The mix masters enjoyed chatting up any single customer who came in looking for company. One of my bar managers, Brian, found his husband that way. Ang, however, took concern to another level. "No offense, Ang, but... why the curiosity?"

She tipped her head toward the men. "I know why they're all here." She pointed discreetly toward the corner. "Same with the girls in the back booth."

Ang continued wiping the counter like it helped her think. "A man like you comes in. Never seen you before. It's Christmas." She looked up at me. "There's a story here." She stopped her ministrations and plunged her hand on her hip. "You don't really belong here. So I decided you'll get my Christmas gift."

"Aww!" two of the men around the corner protested.

Ang waved her towel at them. "You lot are hopeless." She retrieved Elvis's empty glass and handed back a fresh beer. "Besides, this is the best place for you. It's enough of a present." Ang smiled at all the men, like she was keeping watch of her flock. She turned back to me. "So... what made you go back East?"

All eyes turned to me. I finished the whiskey and set the glass down with a clink. "My adoption."

"Ooh." The men leaned in, ready for more.

Ang's brows lifted. "And you're looking for your birth family."

I raised up the necklace, studying at the intricate beadwork again. "Met them in person for the first time today."

Ang barked a cough like she was about to hack up a lung. "I need another cigarette, but this is too good." She bent toward me with more of that parental attention on her face. "Are they assholes, honey? It's obvious you don't need them if they are."

The coherent male heads nodded in unison.

I slid the glass Ang's way, silently asking for another. Instead of forgetting, what if I just drowned in whiskey? "They were wonderful." I rested my elbows on the counter and dropped my head in my hands. "I think I'm broken, y'all. A broken fuckup."

"What makes you say that, honey?"

"I'm here, aren't I?"

"He has a point," LeVar said.

Suddenly words spilled out of my mouth, like they came from a bottle of cheap whiskey. "I didn't expect them to look up to me, like I'm their answer to the American Dream. They have no clue what it was like. I've hustled as hard as anyone, but I didn't want to dispel their delusion. Didn't want my childhood shit to dirty their beauty either. Then I bugged out early because I couldn't take the guilt."

Old Elvis rocked on his stool as he stared at the bottles of booze. "Family expectations… It's a rough business."

"That simply means the family you've been dreaming about your whole life is human." Ang handed me the second whiskey. "Doesn't make you broken, honey."

The new bourbon was a darker color than the first and a lot smoother going down. "What's this?"

"Top shelf." I opened my mouth to thank her, but Ang shrugged. "Christmas present, remember?"

Lucky me. I tipped the glass her way, adding a grateful smile before taking another sip.

"Anyway, maybe they need to know you're as human as the rest of us."

You'll never amount to shit, boy.

Face it, Gracie, this is the best your kid can do. Don't expect better, you'll just be disappointed.

Once a savage, always a savage.

The soundtrack of my upbringing fired up like it was connected to a switch. I pulled my hair in a futile attempt to make it stop. The first time I'd heard the last insult, I almost peed my pants as I shook with fear and rage. The old man's put-downs motivated me to get where I was, but it didn't mean they stayed in the past. They walked around with me as if they lived in my pockets. They made me feel like I was covered in a shit-film that only I could see. No matter what I did to get rid of it, it tainted everything.

I shook my head vehemently. Forgetting was the better strategy, and it was time to leave.

Ang poured a beer, handed it to guy number three, and returned to me. "You're not broken... What's your name, honey?"

"Oh, uh. Blake. Blake Brady." I reached across the bar to shake her hand.

"Well, Blake Brady, if you ask me... and you seem to be... I think you're just bent. Like that song."

An old Creedence tune currently filled the bar. "What song?"

Ang let out an exasperated sigh and rolled her eyes. "Bent." She cued it up on her entertainment system. "Pay attention."

The guys and I listened to the lyrics as we swayed to the beat. The words left me raw. Wide open. Missing. Wanting.

Old Elvis blew out a meaningful sigh. LeVar tapped his heart.

"Isn't there anyone at home you can talk to?" Ang moved her hands up and down. "You don't get to look like you do by accident, honey. And I mean more than your handsome face. It's obvious you've achieved something good with your restaurant and cocktail bar. People don't do that alone."

Did I have people? Alan Kramer's theft put a wedge between Felix and me. Not that I blamed him for it. It was my fuckup. Gia had been my closest friend, and she was gone. There was one person I longed to be by my side all day. Desperately. But I didn't know if she was about to leave me high and dry again. God, I needed to make changes.

"Maybe I fake it," I told Ang. Except Cyndi kept shining bright like an angel. When we were together, she shooed the demons away. Another reason for her nickname. I wanted to text her like I had promised. More than anything. But she had her own shit to deal with.

"You're thinking of someone," Ang said, pointing at me with an I'm-brilliant smirk.

I scrunched my face and pressed my fingers into my temples. "She's with her family. Taking care of her father."

"Then why did you think of her?"

I found my words in the warmth of another pull of the bourbon. I rarely spoke this much with people I knew, let alone strangers. Obviously. "You guys are great listeners. Did you know that?"

"It's your Christmas miracle." Elvis raised his pint glass in my direction.

"Again, what led you to think about this woman, honey?" Ang pressed.

"Because I promised her that I would text if my visit imploded. Except it didn't. I did."

Ang gathered the dirty glasses and loaded them into the rack. "Does it help to talk to her? Or… is she the real reason you're here? Is she toying with you?"

"No." Our past messed with my head, but Cyndi had been honest since her apology and promise to be straight with me. My spine tightened as I readied to defend her honor. "She's great. Might be too good." I considered all the ways she'd been there for Liv and me recently even though Cyn had her own worries. "It's all on me."

"Sounds like you visited my establishment so you could escape your niggling conscious. Not that I'm complaining."

I raised my hands. "It's fine. I'm fine. I just needed a minute to decompress. My cousin saw it. She even used the word decompress. That's why I'm here."

The fellas shook their heads in unison. Old Elvis lifted his eyes to the ceiling.

"This doesn't feel like much of a present," I muttered as my cheek pressed into my hand.

Ang drummed her fingers on the counter like she was waiting for me to cop to my BS.

I sighed heavily, making a buzzing noise as air passed through my lips. "Y'all are sure I should text her, and not just... I don't know... drown in whiskey with y'all?"

"What do you think, Mr. Blake?" Ang asked. She planted her elbow on the bar top and dropped her chin into her hands, making herself eye level with my grumpy face while waiting me out.

As if adding emphasis to her point, the men chanted, "Text her, text her, text her..."

I swallowed the last of my whiskey and slapped the bar. "All right. I'll do it."

The guys raised their hands in the air and yelled, "Woo-hoo!"

"You won't know until you take a chance. It's the Law of Miracles." Ang smiled smugly. "Merry Christmas, Blake Brady."

"Back at you, Ang." I slapped four bills on the counter.

Guy number three yelled, "It's a wonderful life."

Ang announced to the bar, "I'm taking my smoke break fellas. Working miracles is exhausting."

I walked the block back to the condo, thinking of what to write to Cyndi that wouldn't read as whiny. Or weak. Everything I typed made me sound like a drama king. Still, that had been Cyn's point. I'd jumped in to help her through a vulnerable moment. She promised to do the same.

I stared at my phone for ages as I sat on the terrace overlooking the lights of downtown Phoenix. The determination I'd felt in the bar faded until it morphed into desperation. I didn't need to write to Cyndi. Didn't need to talk to her either. Hell, I needed her. With me.

Could I? Should I? Would she?

Like Ang said, I wouldn't know until I tried. At least we'd talk. I awakened my phone and dialed her number.

"Hey… Go to Mommy," Cyndi said quietly. Next came a shuffling sound, and the background noise quieted. "Blake? Are you o—"

My voice cracked. "Cyn…"

Chapter 29

Breathless

CYNDI

Without seeing Blake's face, I knew he was the silhouetted man pacing the sidewalk in front of the condo a block away. His hair shifted in the nighttime breeze as he'd stop, pivot, and head back in the direction he'd been. His hunched shoulders bothered me. They were a physical manifestation of his pained voice when he called. It was the image I'd visualized on the phone and why I dropped everything to go to him.

He saw my rideshare as it slowed to a stop, and he jogged to the passenger door. As soon as the locks lifted, Blake pulled on the handle and plucked me out of the sedan. His arms wrapped around me in reverence and disbelief.

"You came."

"Not only did I say I would, but the texts I sent you along the way should've clued you in." I added a snarky wink to put him at ease. Shoot, I was also loaded up with nerves. This spontaneous adventure gave me the shakes.

When Blake called me, the catch in his voice twisted my

heart. Made my adrenaline rush. I knew I had to go to him. It wasn't because of an attraction. There was a rightness to it.

My dad and Aunt Star surprised me by backing my disappearance. Both sent me on my way with a hug and a hopeful smile. Fortunately, Thomas's plane had been in town with the pilot on standby. Apparently, Kick's monster mother had shown up uninvited to their family breakfast, and Thomas vowed to leave early if she tried to interfere with anything else.

Since my luggage had been in my dad's SUV, it was simply a matter of transferring my luggage to Kick and Thomas's chauffeured car. Their driver had plenty of time to take me to the airport and get back to the theater during the second act of Wicked.

"Text me when you land," Kick said with tears shimmering in her eyes. "I knew there was more going on between you two," she whispered as we hugged goodbye.

"Did Deana tell you?"

Kick pushed me back to arm's length. "No. Why?" Her brows raised. "What does Dee know that I don't?"

"Uh, nothing?" I bit my lip, loving how both women kept a confidence. I hadn't asked Deana to keep this from Kick, especially since I'd been looking for her when I went to the coffeehouse. "She gave me some advice when you had a dog emergency."

Kick shuddered at the memory. "If you say so. He's the one, chica."

"If you say so," I answered, running my hand through my hair. "All I do know is I have to see."

"Thomas and I committed to each other on New Year's Eve, remember?"

I rolled my eyes in jest. "How could anyone forget? I think the Earth shook."

"That was Halloween night," she said as a blush crept up

her face, referring to their first night together. She bumped my shoulder. "Maybe Christmas is your holiday."

I looked up at the sky and only saw the thick cloud cover. "Sure."

She grabbed both my shoulders and leaned toward my ear. "Defy gravity, chica. It's time." Tears shimmered in her eyes.

The reference to the powerhouse song Rachel had just belted perfectly made my knees go weak. I was ready to put my past behind me and try something new. Something big. I blew out the breath I'd been holding and nodded obediently.

Then we hugged for good, and I fled, changed my clothes in the bathroom while waiting on the pilot, and flew across the country to a sexy, broody man. The whole first-time-flying-on-a-private-jet experience was wasted on me. I ended up spending the time worried about Blake and whether my presence would help. I feared it would end up a monumental waste of time.

Blake shook as he rested his head against mine.

"Hey." I reached up and settled my hands on his face, searching his soulful eyes for clues for what I could do for him. "What happened?"

The driver set my last piece of luggage on the sidewalk and cleared his throat. Blake jumped at the noise like he'd been yanked out of a dream. He stepped over to the man and handed him a few bills. "Thank you for taking care of her."

"My pleasure." The driver looked at his hand and smiled. "Have a merry Christmas."

"I will now," Blake said.

THE RIDE UP TO THE PENTHOUSE APARTMENT BLAKE HAD rented stayed painfully silent. When we finally arrived, he kicked off his shoes by the door and I followed suit.

"Want anything?" he asked without looking at me.

"Water would be great. I'm pretty dehydrated." I looked up at the ceiling, wondering where my nerves had come from.

He parked my bags by the kitchen island, and I let them be. I didn't want to assume we'd stay in the same room or that we wouldn't. With the excitement of fleeing Detroit out of my system, it occurred to me that I didn't have a plan for what happened next.

The lights in downtown Phoenix drew me to the expansive wall of windows. I opened the slider and regarded the ambiance of a big city on a rare, quiet night. A ringing sound brought my attention down to the light-rail crossing in front of the building. The city was surprisingly quiet as the cute train bell broke the spell of twinkling lights. I wondered how different it would be on New Year's Eve. It didn't really matter since we'd be home by then.

"You have a lot of luggage, Ms. Sendaydiego." Blake's voice wrapped around me like the physical contact I craved. He handed me a glass of water.

My shoulders shifted as if his proximity electrified me. I indulged a long drink before giving him a small grin. "I should have shipped them home, considering the clothes I have on are the only ones appropriate for a warm climate." After throwing my sweatshirt over a bench by the front door, I was left in a tank and leggings. I'd packed them for working out. "I have to go shopping tomorrow."

"Mm." Blake's fingers gently grazed my arms.

I leaned into him as he wrapped me in a full-body hug. "Are you going to tell me why I'm here?"

"It's a… Christmas miracle?" I felt his smile as he kissed my neck.

"Blake…" I finished the water, set it down on a side table, and took his hands. "Talk."

He walked us to the U-shaped sectional filling the living

room. As he walked backward, his face crumbled into the visage I'd imagined when he'd called me.

Blake's mouth opened multiple times to start a sentence. He finally huffed a frustrated sigh as he ran his hands through his hair. It gave me an idea.

I walked around the sofa and stood behind him, massaging his scalp with my nails and sifting his glossy hair through my fingers. He closed his eyes and tipped his head back as he let out a groan.

"The words coming into my head make me sound like a whiny baby."

"Hm." I kept up the ministrations, enjoying the silky feeling of his hair in my hands as much as he seemed to like what I did. Something about this evening reminded me of him interrupting me on my back porch. I couldn't explain the confusion and fury roaring through me then either.

I bent down and whispered, "What do you need, Jefe?"

Blake kept his eyes shut. "To forget."

I moved my hands to his shoulders and pressed into a knot on his right side. "How's this?"

"God," he gasped. "Perfect."

"Is this why you called me?" I kissed his forehead and moved down his face.

"I hoped we'd talk on the phone." A grin formed under my lips. "You're the overachiever."

"That's what I've been told." I walked around the sectional to Blake's front and climbed onto his lap under the guise of getting a better grip on his shoulders. Truthfully, I needed to feel more of him.

His hands trailed up my thighs to my lower back. "How did your father feel about you taking off on him?"

"When Thomas offered his plane, Dad was all for it." I remembered the glint in my father's eye when I asked if he minded me cutting our visit short and chuckled. "He had wanted to know about our call this morning since I don't talk about my social life. So I told him some of what was going on with us."

Blake opened his eyes. "You did?" His brow furrowed as he studied my face. "And?"

"Don't sound so shocked," I said, hoping it came across more playful than defensive. "I promised to consider moving to the next level in the New Year, and it's only a few days away. Of course, I've been thinking about you." Blake grinned like I'd given him a present. Maybe I had. "Anyway, my dad practically launched my luggage from his trunk to the Harrison's limo."

"You were thinking about me?"

I sat back on my heels. "Weren't you thinking about me? I assume that's why you called."

"You have no idea." Blake scrubbed his face with his hands. "My family is fantastic, right? Still, I kept thinking they'd like you so much more."

His comment cut me. "Blake—"

"No, hear me out." He settled my hands in his. "What my old man used to say about me trickled in. Like my past and my present were in an epic wrestling match for my mind. It built until I couldn't take it. Then I thought about that afternoon on your porch. I'd never witnessed anyone as vulnerable as you with me. That's how I knew I should call you."

"Is that what you meant by wanting to forget? You meant the negativity from growing up."

"And how it tried to override the good from my family, yes."

Like a switch flipping on, I knew what he needed from me. Blake shifted like he was about to lay me down, and I jumped off his lap.

"What are you—"

I pushed my leggings down and stepped out of them.

Standing in front of Blake, I shimmied my hips as I pulled my tank over my head. He swallowed a lump in his throat as I swiveled in a slow circle for him.

He licked his lower lip. "Is that what you always wear under workout clothes?"

"I spent most of the day in a fancy holiday ensemble that was way too warm to wear here." I looked down my body. "It's not like they match." Both pieces were made of satin, but the demi-cup bra had a red lace overlay—because Christmas—and the black bikinis didn't show under my plaid, wool skirt. Nor the black leggings, come to think of it.

A low grumbling sound came out of Blake. "Right." He shook his head like he couldn't believe his eyes. He reached for me, and I held up my finger as I walked backward, signaling him to wait. I quickly retrieved a medium-sized sack from my luggage.

"What's that?"

"Do you trust me?" I asked in return as I set the bag by his feet.

He gave me a wolfish grin. "Now I'm intrigued."

"Good." I placed a knee between Blake's legs and pulled his shirt over his head. "What you did for me impacted me as much as it did you." I unfastened his belt buckle. "It's time I returned the favor." With the zipper down, I slid my hand into his jeans. My head dropped to his as we both sighed from the contact. Yeah, I needed this as much as Blake did. I slid the denim down his legs with a little help.

"Your turn," he said, reaching for me after I did the same with his boxer briefs.

My pulse tripped as I shook my head. I knew I could do this, but I'd always taken charge of myself. It was never to meet what my partner needed. "No, big guy. I'll take care of you." To make my point, I settled on Blake's lap, my legs bent along his thighs, and I pressed a hard kiss to his mouth. His mouth immediately opened to my tongue. "Relax," I encouraged when he tried to take control. "Let Jefe go for now." I ground myself along his increasing thickness, getting a thrill from the way the gold flecks in his eyes caught the twinkling Christmas lights lining the apartment windows.

"Not sure I know how," Blake breathed.

I bent to kiss his jaw, down his throat. "If I could do it, so you can." By the time I kissed a trail down his impressive chest to his incredible dick, I was desperate for it. I gripped him hard.

"Dammit." His hands slid over my back. "Want your tits, Spark."

"Not yet." I licked my lips as I looked up at Blake. "Let me to take care of you." With my grip still at the base of him, I swept the tip of my tongue over his crown. His dick jumped as I gave it a tight squeeze. "Please."

Blake swallowed hard, then he simply nodded before sinking his head into the back of the couch. He finally relaxed and let me work him like a lollipop. With each pass of my tongue, I eased his stress. His past. His present. My heart jumped into my throat as I swallowed him without warning. Blake had let me go down on him before but not like this. Not when it was all about him. His whispered groans and praises let me know this was the right play.

I pulled him closer to me, to the edge of the seat, to gain better access to his soft sack. As Blake lost himself, grunting scandalous oaths, I cupped his balls with one hand and reached into the bag for the other. By feel, I found what I sought and pressed the On button. Blake's body tightened at the sound.

"Shh. I've got you," I encouraged before taking him to the back of my throat and pressing the small vibrator to his balls. He jerked up, gliding farther along my tongue, forcing me to take a hard breath through my nose. As he settled again, I flattened my tongue, letting it dance along his shaft and swirl over his tip.

The actions brought Blake to the edge. "Fuck." He dragged my mouth off him, but this was different than how we usually played. This was new.

I looked into his whiskey-colored eyes, burning with need. "Mouth or tits, pal."

"Wh-what?" The man was out of his mind.

"You're coming in my mouth or between my tits. Take your pick."

"Fuck… me," he groaned. He gently stroked my cheek with his finger as our eyes held. I saw pure worship in his face and hoped he found the same in mine.

Without saying another word, Blake stretched out, giving himself over to me as he sank back into the sofa. I turned up the little vibrator and pressed it into the back of his heavy sack as I settled my mouth over him once more. By the second time I hollowed my cheeks and sucked back up his magnificent dick, he stilled. With a low, guttural growl for a warning, I hummed appreciation for his impending climax. Then I moved the pulsating massager to Blake's pucker with one hand and squeezed his base with the other. Like a kettle blowing, he released into my mouth, his hips thrusting upward rapidly as I swallowed him down.

"Oh shit. Shit. My Spark. My Spark." His curses and reverence did me in. As Blake calmed, I kissed his thighs before sitting back on my heels. I wiped my mouth with the back of my hand and looked up at him, intending to smile. We achieved one hell of a victory together. I wanted to show Blake how proud I was of him for letting everything go.

Instead, I burst into tears.

Chapter 30

All Through the Night

"It's okay." Cyndi scrubbed her tears with her fingers. "I'm okay. I swear."

The woman wrecked me. Not from the orgasm—although what the hell was that awesome thing? Is that why women often kept a collection of toys? Holy hell. My muscles felt liquified.

No, Cyndi said she planned to do for me what I did for her on the porch. If this was how she felt afterward, no wonder it threw her for a loop. Come to think of it, I now understood her emotional outburst.

"Hey…" I met her on the floor and pulled her into my lap, lifting her chin with my finger. "So my dick's pretty traumatic, huh?"

Cyndi giggled through her remaining tears. Self-deprecation to the rescue. "Your dick is the proper definition of awesome."

"Wow." I wrapped my arms around her and kissed her head. "Then why are you crying? It's scaring me."

"Dammit," she grumbled as I stroked her hair. Her highlights had been dyed green since the last time I saw her. She picked up my T-shirt and dabbed her eyes. It seemed to do the trick to get her to relax. "I didn't want to do that." Cyn floored me with a sweet grin. "I'm so proud of you."

I raised my eyebrow, teasing her more. "For coming? Woman, I can do that just by looking at you. It's more a miracle when I behave."

"No, you dork." She playfully slapped my chest. "For letting yourself go. For allowing me to take care of you."

I kissed her again. God, I wanted to do so much more. Thank her. Worship her. I hated having to wait to fuck again. Stupid fiftieth birthdays.

I closed my eyes as she threaded her fingers through my hair. I loved when she did that.

"You like control in the bedroom, and this was the first time you let me take the reins, so to speak."

"You're just as feisty," I defended. "Not that I'm complaining."

"I totally like how aggressive we get," Cyn agreed. She pressed her lips together. "When you let go... it was beautiful."

I let my fingers tracked down her arm until they laced with hers. "I felt the same way about you." I pulled her hand to my mouth and kissed each knuckle. "Still doesn't explain your tears. Shouldn't we be high-fiving or something?" I pressed her against me. "You're my best medicine."

"That's what I don't understand." Cyndi breathed out an exasperated sigh.

My brows drew together in confusion. "Hmm?"

"What we have now is amazing. Yet..." Cyn scooted off my lap to face me. "After what I did three years ago, I still don't understand why you'd want to talk to me, let alone have this." She gestured between us.

"Oh." I tipped my head to the side, wondering how I could explain she had always been my dream girl without scaring her? "Couple of reasons, I guess… I chalked it up to karma."

"Hmm?"

I shrugged. "I wasn't the best guy to date. Between my girl and moving from a food truck to the Garage, I could be evasive." One sweet yet clingy single mother came to mind. On paper, we had a lot in common, but we weren't compatible. Then there was her ex. "Having a psycho ex quickly became a hard no for me." I hadn't ghosted her, but my abrupt breakup hurt her.

"Can't blame you there." Cyn chuckled. "Those people exist in one of the rings of hell."

"Right?"

"And the other reason?"

My ears warmed as thoughts shifted to the volatile truth. Did I want to go back there? No, but she flew across the country for me. This night was about honesty more than anything else. "That relates to today's meltdown—or was it yesterday's at this point?"

"Ah. You should start there. What happened earlier?"

Hopeful eyes made me want to confess all, but years of self-protective armor were hard to throw off. I stood and reached for Cyn. My head still was fucked up about meeting my family. Sorting it out required comfort, which wouldn't be found on a hard floor. "Would you mind if we move to the private balcony off the main suite? You can grab one of my clean shirts from the closet."

"I'll get my robe."

We rolled her luggage into my room, and I grabbed a small bag off the dresser. "I picked up a pre-rolled yesterday. Want to share?"

"Nice." Cyndi grinned.

I pulled my robe out of the closet and threw it on while Cyn dug hers out of her big suitcase. I couldn't help but swallow hard when she shimmied out of her lacy red bra, letting out a soft sigh as the fabric fell to the floor. She slipped on her kimono, tying the sash around her waist. The woman had no clue what she did to me, which was a big reason we needed to talk.

After settling onto the cushions of a sectional on the balcony and taking a couple of pulls each from the joint, I was ready.

It was easier to talk about our past, so I started there. "When you disappeared, it felt like another one of my mess-ups. More proof Kurt had been right all along. You know, about me being a loser. I figured it was best to focus on Liv and the Garage. Gia and I found our way back to a solid parent partnership, and that had to be enough. Plus I was under the impression you didn't like kids, and I didn't want to put Olivia through anything remotely like my childhood."

Cyndi winced at my last sentence and puffed the cannabis again. "Wow. That wasn't it at all. I love kids. But Blake… you're a self-made, successful restaurateur. There's nothing loser-like about you. Everybody's life has obstacles. How we fight them shows whether we're a loser. And honey… you're one hell of a fighter."

"Argh." I ran my hand through my hair, slumping against the sofa cushion. Peals of laughter from a small group on the street floated up to us. We weren't the only ones up late. I didn't worry about being overheard, but I despised talking about my childhood. "I sound whiny. I'm sorry. Except, it's what the old man said, over and over. It sticks. You know?"

I inhaled the aromas from our joint. The citrusy notes relaxed me more than the smoking itself did. "Besides, how else would I explain my string of disastrous relationships?

Also, I should've known Al was up to something. I should've paid more attention." I slammed my fist on my thigh and looked up at the sky. A few stubborn stars broke through the light pollution. "I let my crew down. If that's not proof, what is?"

"Hey." Cyn scurried to my side and laid her hand on my shoulder. "If you're to blame, then so am I."

"You only recommended the man." I kissed her head and turned back to the clear night. "You didn't know."

"Neither did you." Her stern tone demanded I meet her gaze. "You're doing everything you can. You know, not once have I heard your employees speak poorly of you. They're all desperate to throttle Kramer. But none of them blame you. Not one."

A rattling breath shuddered through me. Cyndi's words were exactly what I needed to hear, what I used to long to hear. I bent down to kiss her. This kiss was slow and reverent. It honored her. "Thank you."

"We both could name people who grew up with adversities." I scoffed in response. She stuck her finger in my face. "See? Describing yourself as whiny suggests you haven't moved beyond Kurtis's abuse because you compare yourself to hypothetical people who have had it worse."

I shook my head at the word abuse. "You have the wrong impression. Kurt left a bruise here and there, but all the dads did back then."

"Honey—"

"No, Spark—"

"Blake…" She pressed her hand to my chest. "The bits you've shared with me were prime examples of emotional abuse."

I kept turning my head left and right, refusing to put myself in the same category as those kids. Hell, the ones I'd grown up with became mirror images of their parents. Kurt's interpretation of guidance pushed me to do better even if it put me in a perpetual cycle where I never measured up.

I picked up the joint and stared at it. "What the hell's in this stuff? It loosened my lips but hasn't helped me forget." I set the damn thing back down.

Cyndi took a quick hit, then snubbed out what was left. She raised my arm and snuggled into my side. The city was eerily quiet as we sat in silence. I almost heard her hand making soothing circles on my stomach as I considered the possibility Kurt had been wrong the whole time. Not just wrong, abusive. What did that mean for me? Was I a victim? That would be worse. I quickly pushed the notion away.

The movements prompted me to continue talking. Still, I changed the subject. "I met my Uncle Joe at Sherry's house."

Cyn blew a thin cloud of smoke. "Yeah?"

"I look like him and his boys." I spoke to the wall of bougainvillea surrounding us. "It was weird. I mean, we favor my grandmother. Aunt Donna and Sherry look more like my grandfather's side. Anyway, there was this handful of men that looked like me—or the other way around, I guess."

"Was Joe a jerk? It sounded like you didn't hit it off."

"No. He was fine. My cousins were great. It's just… Joe implied that my life had been spent on easy street." Like being stolen was worth it because I ended up attending middle-class schools. And I get his point. I've done research. Hell, my aunt gave me pictures that document how hard life was for them. Yet, as Joe pressed his point, I kept thinking of Kurt, my mother's retreat, the teachers who always assumed the worst of me.

Cyndi gripped my robe in a fist, made an angry growling sound in her throat.

"The photos my aunt gave me showed how much they lacked physically, but…" I unclenched her hand and laced our fingers. "They sang of love. My birth family is loud and teasing, but their love is fierce. When I looked around Sherry's house yesterday, I saw the love I'd missed out on. What Joe said, or was it the jealousy in his tone? Anyway, it made we want to snipe back." I rested my head on top of hers, the ugly truth making the day seem unbearably long. "Knew better than to respond, so I held it in and got the hell out."

Cyndi's shoulders tightened. "Your uncle had shitty timing, that's for sure. Some people struggle to put themselves in another's shoes. They only see their difficulties."

"Except he's done great. Joe ran an auto shop, married a fantastic woman, raised good men. Hell, he has an adorable great-grandson. Generations to show for his legacy. He should be proud of it. I'm still trying to check off those boxes at fifty. It's not like I don't understand the hustle either. Why would he think we're so different?"

"I think you're reacting to his unresolved issues, honey. That's not on you. Besides…" Cyn sat up straight, like she was about to deliver tough news. I'd watched her do it with clients. "What you project to the world is quite different from what lives in here, I think." She gently pressed her fingers over my heart.

"What do I project?"

She smiled. "Hardworking. Sinfully gorgeous. Loving father—"

"Scowling asshole," I said, rolling my eyes and thinking of my staff. I called it cool, calm, and collected. A must in business.

Cyn bit her lip. "I happen to like your broody face." I reached over and caressed her lip with my thumb, needing to touch her. She kissed it and said, "It means you're working through a problem, taking care of your people."

I thought of it as my thinking face, but she had a point. "Are you saying my uncle isn't as good at covering as I am?"

"Was he the only boy in the family?"

I nodded.

"Maybe he was treated differently from his sisters. He could've dreamed about escaping too." She stood and reached for my hand as I let the possibility sink in. "I'd give him the benefit of the doubt. Even then, you might have to agree to disagree."

Her advice did more to ease my mind than the joint did. I stood and stretched, the released tension making me sigh. "Where are you going?"

"To the kitchen. Your spliff made me hungry." She opened the sliding door.

Good thing we still had pancakes. I served Cyndi two reheated cakes with syrup and sat on the stool next to her with a cola, grateful that the rental company had stocked the kitchen as part of the deal. I felt more gratitude for the woman next to me, humming her appraisal for my leftover breakfast food. I watched her eat, still in awe that she'd left her celebrations for me.

She caught me staring. "What?"

I wanted to make promises to her. Promises for a future. Hopeful declarations. But a barrier remained between us. We needed to sort it out before I could trust what was happening. "You still haven't explained why you left three years ago." I drank some soda. "You only said my assumptions were wrong."

"Ah, that." Cyndi's face twisted as she stared through the living room and out the wall of windows. I hoped she wouldn't cry again. She quietly started. "You have to know by now I love kids." She turned and smiled. "Especially Olivia."

My daughter's name made me grin back. It was a reflex. Then my brows furled in confusion. "So what happened?" That could only mean I had screwed up. Whatever it was, I'd make it right. Cyn glanced away, her chin quivering. Shit. I might not want to hear her answer.

"Kick recently reminded me that I was ready to walk away

from Joel when he did it first. I just had to grieve another miscarriage first."

My nose flared and my body vibrated with rage upon hearing this. "Fuck."

The sonofabitch left her during a miscarriage. I pounded a fist into my thigh. Had I overlooked this crucial detail? No. One glance at the pain on Cyndi's face let me know how deep she had to bury the memory to move past it. God, I hated her ex-hole.

She placed a steadying hand on my knee. "What I mean is, it required work—a lot of work—to move on, despite knowing in my heart we were wrong for each other."

"All riiight," I drawled, wondering where I fit in with this.

She exhaled audibly. "I learned to protect my heart above everything else. It was the only way to survive." Her nails tapped a nervous beat on the countertop. "I like who I am now and won't apologize for putting myself first."

"Then we're on the same page." Sweat beaded on my neck as I spread my arms. "I also like you. A lot." This still didn't make sense.

The rhythm of her nails filled the space as Cyndi continued tapping. Her eyes closed briefly as if she were wrestling with something. "Do you remember the morning you asked me to go to the state fair?"

"Of course. The famous text you never returned." The sting of the memory made me clip my words.

She pulled her foot up to the seat of the stool, curling herself around her knee. Protective. "The message came through when I was driving to meet a client."

I nodded to let her know I was listening, regretting my earlier tone.

"This business was across the street from Olivia's dance school, and…" Cyn's voice grew eerily quiet. "I saw you walk in together. You in jeans and your boxing gym's T-shirt, carrying her little purple backpack. Liv in a leo and warm-ups." She pointed at her head, lost in memory. "Her hair in a lopsided bun."

I cringed. "Don't remind me." I never got the hang of them.

She smiled but looked like she wanted to cry. "It was the image I'd always dreamed of. What I had hoped for."

The statement should have made me fly, but it felt like a gut punch. "Now I really don't understand." Why didn't she call out to us?

"It scared me," Cyndi blurted and cleared her throat. "You still do."

I almost fell off the stool. "Why?"

She grabbed my hand like she was desperate to press her point. "You could break me."

"Wha—? How?" It's the last thing I wanted to do. Then and now. Did she see us breaking up? Before we started? Then why was she here?

Her silver eyes shimmered. "Have you ever been so used to failure that winning became the real fear?"

No. I always powered through obstacles, letting them motivate me. But she didn't need to hear that. I nodded instead.

She smiled through the tears, her chin quivering. She blew a long breath through tight lips. "Within weeks of being with you, it was obvious you could be my person. Everything I ever wanted. But I didn't trust it." She held up a finger. "No, I didn't trust myself…"

I reached for her hand to keep my temper in check. I hated being compared to her asshole ex, but if she was willing to come clean, I had to let her.

Her tone grew harsh, like she was mad at herself. "I see now what Kick and Deana have been telling me. Back then, I assumed we would break up because by the time we met, it was how I survived. All my relationships had self-protective time limits. But I knew breaking up with you would hurt down to my soul. It was better to walk away before it started." Her voice hitched. "Or so I believed."

I stormed off the stool and circled the island to get some distance. "That wasn't fair." The years we could have shared raced through my mind, making my chest ache.

"I know." She sobbed, and my anger stopped in its tracks. "I'm so sorry. I fucked up, Blake. Not you. You've always been my heart's desire, but I was afraid."

Words that should have made me the happiest man had the opposite effect. I saw Cyndi—truly saw how broken she'd been, and I mourned what we'd lost. "I hate what he did to you. Anyone who disappointed you."

I marched over to her and wrapped my arms around her. She'd let her brokenness hurt us, but I was broken too. If Cyn was ready to move on, I wouldn't let our past keep us from healing. Together. "If you'll let me, I'll love you better than them. I'll give it all I have and dig for more if it's not enough."

Her body shuddered as she relaxed into me. She grasped my forearms as if they were a lifeline and looked over her shoulder. "It was horribly unfair to compare you to Joel or anyone. You've never been like them. Tonight proved it."

"Then why did you cry?"

"The beauty of it. Of you. And us." She sniffed as if she'd been crying the whole time. I bit my lip to keep from doing the same. "You gave yourself over to me without any demands or agendas."

"You asked nicely." I smiled against in her ear.

She grinned against my cheek. "My friends say you look at me like I'm the answer to your prayers. I saw it tonight."

"You are. Over and over. It's why you flying out here rattled me. I called you, expecting to either talk or arrange a time to meet at home. Something to look forward to, to hold me together until I could be with you. Instead, you came to me."

Cyndi pivoted and kissed me, her chin quivering again. "We could've been together for the past three years if it wasn't for my idiocy."

Shit. She'd been wrestling with the same thoughts as me. It had to stop. "What about now? Do you see us going our separate ways in the New Year?"

She looked away then down at the floor. "No, honey."

I lifted her chin with my finger. "Why?" A bud of hope bloomed in my heart, but I had to be sure. For me and for Olivia.

"I've changed. No, that's not it." Cyn's brow furrowed. "I mean… I dealt with my shit, yes. But our friendship means the world to me now. The way it's growing… I've never experienced anything like it before."

"I agree."

She reached for my hand and pulled back at the last second, like she wasn't sure if she had the right. I answered the question by taking hers in mine. "I guess I want our relationship to grow more than I want to protect my heart. The desire burns here." She touched her heart with her other hand. "I don't want it to end."

She voiced what I'd been feeling. I needed to absorb her words before I nodded in agreement. "Then let's not dwell on the past anymore. You weren't ready. For all we know, I wasn't either. How about we consider this our New Year's talk? Do you want to be with me?"

Cyndi muttered under her breath. "Defy gravity." Then she smiled, her eyes glinting at me. "So much." A tear released down her cheek.

I breathed a sigh of relief. "Nothing else matters."

"You forgive me?" she whispered.

"I did a while ago." I peppered her cheek with kisses.

Kisses to heal our foolish mistakes. Kisses for our future. Kisses for honesty. "If you can accept my broken parts, I accept yours. We will heal together but not if it's in secret. I want you out in the open. Officially." My belly warmed with a fire I hadn't felt since our reunion in my office. I should have been exhausted, but our declarations renewed my energy. I didn't want the night to end.

Her voice hitched. "I really want that."

I spun Cyn around, stepping between her legs and pulling her body flush against mine. With only her silky robe and my plush one between us, my dick reawakened. I wanted to drown in her. "My woman," I said against her mouth.

"My man." She giggled back.

Joy overflowed at the sound of a reality so simple, so elemental. The fire in my belly fanned into a flame as we kissed. I pulled away to take a breath. "Gotta touch you, Sparky."

She untied her robe, her husky chuckle filling the room. Letting the sides fall behind her, Cyndi leaned back on her elbows, displaying her spectacular breasts for me. All for me. I might have drooled. Definitely licked my lips. Her posture was one of pride and pleasure, giving and receiving.

"Your eyes glazed over." The corner of Cyndi's mouth lifted as she tapped an impatient tune against the counter.

I bent and drew a dusky nipple into my mouth. Her satisfied hums swept over me as her hands brushed my robe off my shoulders.

"Need inside you," I demanded against her lips. I needed it more than I needed to breathe.

"Same."

I tipped my head toward the living room. "Grab the bag though."

We came together in the king-sized bed in the main suite. After loosening Cyndi up with my tongue and an edible chocolate lube I found in that magical toy sack, I finally slid home with a grunt of relief. God, I craved her more now that she'd agreed to be mine. I wanted to go slow and stay inside her sweet, luxurious body forever.

"Smack me," she begged. Or did she command? It didn't matter.

I laughed, reluctantly pulled out, and flipped her onto her hands and knees. Then I obliged with a slap to her ass as my throbbing dick entered her again. The resulting clench from Cyndi made me see stars. "Slow down, sweetheart. We've got all night."

My hands slid along her spine, around her ribs, up to her tits, everywhere. I couldn't get enough. But I wanted to last, to make this moment as long as possible. I pulled Cyndi up against me. The shallow angle let me hit her clit just right.

As her moans grew louder with each thrust, I brought her wrists up behind my head. She was stretched out, giving my hands full access to her perfect body. I filled them with her breasts, massaging each one and gently twisting those tight nipples. Cyndi's cries changed in a way I recognized now.

"So close," she panted.

I turned her head to me. "I know." The flutters of spasms started in Cyndi's core. I kissed her as the fire built, my tongue stroking, thrusting, promising. Like my dick in her pussy.

The light seeping in from the sliding doors made Cyndi's skin glow. To savor the moment, I let my free hand slowly trail down her front, through the valley of her tits as they bounced with each surge. I made note of the feel of their weight before tracing lower to her belly button, outlining it.

"I could do this forever," I rasped as I held still inside her, struggling for control. "You feel so damn amazing. Always amazing."

"Please, Blake." Her ask sounded harsh, like an order.

I thrust harder, gripping her hips so I could go higher. As

the spasms twisted tighter, Cyndi let go, chanting, "Yes, yes, yes…" I pushed on her clit with my finger and detonated us both. She let out a throaty scream as I came with a series of guttural expletives. I blew so hard I was dizzy from the way her pussy gripped me. This was more than ecstasy. I'd finally found heaven.

After we dropped to the bed, I couldn't stop touching her, like part of me was still afraid she'd run. Her hands also stroked my skin, almost making me purr.

"We're really doing this?" I asked after we'd cleaned up and slipped back into the bed.

"Well, yeah." Cyndi chuckled as she snuggled into my side, her leg draped over my thigh, her finger looping circles on my pecs. "Just one thing…"

"Hm?" I asked, my eyes already closing from contentment.

"What will we tell Olivia?"

Chapter 31

Learn to Fly

Cyndi

I shoved my head under the pillow when Blake's phone blasted a notification throughout the bedroom. He humphed and tapped my shoulder.

"No wakey," I demanded. "More sleepy." We hadn't slept for more than a few hours. Even then, it wasn't a deep sleep for me or Blake. He seemed to be startled each time our limbs touched, like he was surprised I was still in his bed. Honestly, I was too, considering how far our relationship had jumped ahead in the past twenty-four hours.

"Dammit. I forgot about meeting the girls at the mall. Sorry, Spark." He lifted my pillow. A guilty expression fell across his chiseled features, making me wince. "I'll go alone. You rest."

After witnessing his euphoric face earlier, I would do anything to get it back and keep it in place. "Never apologize for sorting through feelings. Or for giving orgasms. Especially orgasms." I sighed as memories of the previous night and early morning cleared my sleep fog. "Yours are extra special, honey." I reached over and messed up his hair. Still a beautiful mix of salt and pepper, it didn't tangle like mine. Not fair. "I'll come with you. I need to buy some shorts anyway." I vigorously rubbed my face. "Please tell me there's decent coffee in the kitchen."

Instead of smiling at my compliment, he frowned. "Sorry, again. It's the pod stuff. Not a good brand either. However, Sherry mentioned her favorite coffee chain has a place about a half mile away. It specializes in drive-thru orders or something. Should be easy in and out. Will you be all right getting ready before your fix?"

It was my time to pout as I silently protested the lack of decent java. It wasn't Blake's fault that Kick had turned me into a latte snob. "Fine." I sat up and jolted. "Argh." Sunlight practically smacked me across my face. Now I knew how vampires felt. I rubbed my eyes. "Need drops."

"What, honey?" Blake's big palm made soothing circles on my back.

"Dry. Eyes." I blinked rapidly while swinging my legs to the side of the bed. "Need my drops." No surprise I'd been a little preoccupied the night before.

He kissed my shoulder.

My vision improved some and purple dots caught my attention. On my skin. I looked down at them. "I have hickies on my boobs."

Blake peered over my shoulder and grinned. "Sorry about that."

"No, you're not." I lifted one breast to inspect the colors above my nipple, deciding I liked them. They were proof of our new status.

He gave me a wolfish smile of pride as he gently touched his "art." He lifted the sheet, checking out the rest of me. "Gives new meaning to the term hot flash."

"You pulled the sheet away, not me," I protested, trying hard not to smile at his bad joke. "I didn't flash you."

He popped his brows at me. "Wouldn't be upset if you did." He reverently kissed my shoulder.

"At least you don't hold middle age against me."

"You were beautiful when we first met." Blake moved my hair off my neck and kissed me there. "You're still beautiful." The light kisses traveled down my shoulder blades, making me shiver. "You'll be beautiful when we're old."

It sounded like he saw a future for us. I exhaled into the concept, and it didn't scare me. On the contrary, instead of wanting to bolt, I wanted to celebrate. I also failed to stifle a yawn.

"There are protein shakes in the fridge. Would one help until we can get your latte?" he asked.

"It would. Thanks." I turned my head, intending to kiss his cheek, but Blake caught my lips instead.

"Good. Now hurry." He squeezed my boob and backed away. "Your naked body is making me forget about my new family obligations."

I looked up in time to see Blake pass in front of me in the buff. My bronze adonis. Mine. This time blinking had nothing to do with dry eyes. He displayed impressive morning wood as he… it… they… strutted out the door. His fine ass flexed with each step, like he was making sure I noticed him both ways. Oh, I noticed.

"Wow." Talk about a hot flash. The man was perfection. My perfection. I cleared my throat, which suddenly became as dry as my eyeballs. "Umm… Are you just planning to bob around the condo?"

Blake turned around. The wolfish smile was back, brighter than ever. I swear one of his teeth glinted off the morning sunlight. He hooked his thumb over his shoulder. "Figured I'd use the bathroom in Liv's suite, unless you want me…"

I caught the visual of us peeing together and waved my hands. "Nope. You're right. We're good. Thank you. Very thoughtful. I'll just…" I pointed at his bathroom and stood.

Blake drawled "hot flash" under his breath, then turned. He was chuckling down the hallway when reality hit me. I was about to meet his family.

"When's the wedding of… what's her name?" Despite my lack of caffeine, I suddenly couldn't stop talking. As the clock ticked closer to meeting Blake's family, my stomach did somersaults.

"It's early summer sometime, and her name's Juniper." Blake made a left turn. "Goes by Juni."

"Juni. Right. Okay." My thought salad flew through my brain faster than the downtown Phoenix scenery going past the window of Blake's rental SUV. The farther we traveled from the secure bubble of the apartment, the more my anxiety ramped up. "How old is Sherry again?"

"About five years older than us."

"You or me?"

"Spark." Blake quickly turned toward me and frowned. "We're the same age."

"Not anymore. You're really fifty, remember? A year older than me."

He stopped hard for a right turn and growled. I didn't know if it was because of me or almost missing our destination. We drove to the middle of the parking lot and found ourselves at the end of a long, double line of cars waiting for coffee. A young man and woman took the orders at the driver's window instead of using a squawk box.

"Line seems to be moving fast," I observed.

"What's happening right now? You won't stop talking."

I bit my lip, not wanting to admit my issues to myself, let

alone Blake. The car moved forward a length, then Blake lifted my hand and kissed my knuckles.

"They're going to love you." He held on to me as we rolled again. "I told you the whole time I was at Sherry's, I kept thinking how much everyone would love you."

"Technically, you said you would've been more comfortable with me there. Like I was an emotional support accountant. Not that your family would love me."

"You're my woman now, not my—"

Before he could say more, we moved up to the young blond barista. Blake put his window down. A slight breeze blew my hair back.

"Good morning, you two." The enthusiastic fella's nametag read "Cal." "What can I get you this fine morning?"

"A large Americano," Blake muttered.

"Hot or cold?" Cal asked, his finger poised over a button on his pad. Blake rolled his eyes.

"Hot please," I answered for him. "I'll have a large hot peppermint latte with oat milk." I gave Cal a smile to make up for Blake's grimace. I wondered when that had shown up. He'd been happy earlier.

"Perfect…" Cal cheerily punched more buttons. "Any add-ons?"

Blake sighed as he handed over his credit card. "Just. Coffee."

"And how was your Christmas?" Cal inquired as he ran the card.

I opened my mouth to tell him about my day, but Blake gritted out, "Fine."

"Wonderful. And what are you up to this morning?"

"We're going to the mall to meet his family and get some clothes for me. I just flew in from Michigan and need shorts and a pair of sandals," I explained.

Blake did a double take and screwed up his face.

"I wouldn't buy a lot," Cal said as he handed back the card with a smile. "Looks like temps are falling tonight. When are you—"

Blake pulled the window button, making it go up and cutting off our perky server.

"Hey!" I blinked, shocked he would do that. Then I leaned across him, yelling, "Sorry! Blake has a lot on his mind."

I settled back in my seat. "That was rude."

Blake narrowed his eyes to slits. "We're. Here. For. Coffee. You know, the stuff that makes people sociable." The low, guttural noise he used to speak made him sound otherworldly. Threatening. Hot.

Suddenly I wanted to take him back to the condo and spend the day in bed more than I wanted to breathe. Except it wasn't totally about his broody sex appeal. In desperate need of a distraction, I made Ls with my hands and fitted them together like a rectangle.

"What are you doing?"

"Framing out your lips," I answered like it was obvious. "It's an art thing."

"Why?"

Not so obvious then. "Do you know you have the right lips to be the Dark Knight? I didn't recognize it until you growled like him." Funny, since he growled often, but this time was different.

One of his brows lifted. "Excuse me?"

"Batman lips. They're a thing since the mask-helmet or whatever covers so much of the actor's face. They're even ranked."

"Where's that coffee?" Blake muttered, shaking his head like his ears were ringing.

"Why are you so grumpy? You were chatty enough this morning, with your" —I waved my hands over my crotch area — "bobbing and smirking and kissing."

"Did you just mime my morning wood?"

I ran my hands through my hair and realized I should've put it up. I never like it limp. "You were chatty then." I grabbed my purse and dug through it.

"That was sex adrenaline. It wore off when you started stressing about my family." We pulled forward another car's length. "What are you doing?"

I was still unzipping and rezipping pockets. "Looking for a scrunchie to put my hair up."

"Why? You look great."

"I couldn't shower since we ran late, and my dry shampoo isn't cooperating." I found the hair tie and set it in my teeth before flipping the mirror up. At least the green and silver highlights looked pretty with my hair pulled back.

"And what happened to you since we left the condo? You were barely functioning after I woke you. Now you're shaking." He gave me the concerned dad exhale I'd watched him give Olivia. "Do you think more caffeine is a good idea? Maybe a drink to calm you down would be better," Blake foolishly suggested as we pulled up to the order window.

"You did not just tell me to calm down."

"Oh shit."

I JUMPED THREE FEET—OR IT FELT LIKE IT—WHEN TWO fingers jabbed my sides from behind. When I spun to see who the attacker was, Olivia hopped in front of me, a mischievous grin on her face.

I blew out a relieved breath, only my nerves stayed as raw as ever. "You scared the crap out of me, little chica." She stepped back and looked at her feet, leaving me feeling like a heel. I pulled her in for a hug and whispered, "Sorry about snapping. It's so good to see you."

The bright light filling the mall food court reflected off the gold flecks in her eyes. So much like her father's. "I can't believe you're here."

"Same, kid. Same." Sweat trickled down my back as I pivoted, searching the food court for where Blake had gone. I was supposed to meet him here after using the restroom. My eyes landed on an animated foursome—Blake and three women of different generations. From the way they favored each other, I guessed they were his cousin, aunt, and the bride-to-be. Their resemblances were uncanny.

Blake's family.

"Come meet my family." Olivia waved me in their direction.

Blake stopped talking when he caught sight of us. A grin split his face as he reached out. I didn't know if it was for me or Olivia, so I slowed and let her reach her dad first. He pulled her in with one arm, kissed her head, and murmured something in her ear.

"It was big," Liv answered enthusiastically.

Blake chuckled then raised his arm for me. "There you are," he breathed. He turned toward the women. "Ladies, meet my... Cyndi." Tipping his head in each woman's direction, he introduced me to Donna, Sherry, and Juni.

"Hi." My voice sounded like Minnie Mouse to me. Blake gave me his amused eyebrow lift.

Sherry invaded my space, wrapping me in a warm hug. As much as I wanted it to, her sweet, vanilla scent did little to ease my whooshing nerves. "So nice to meet you. Olivia told me about you." She did? Sherry leaned closer and added, "He needed you."

I still didn't trust my voice as I was handed off to Juni, who gave me a gentle hello hug. The young woman was the embodiment of grace and beauty—everything I lacked at the moment. Blake beamed as he watched us. I wanted to shine for him, but my annoying nerves wouldn't cooperate.

His Aunt Donna said, "Hello," with a polite smile. She immediately turned to her daughter. "Stoodis. Where to next?"

Blake pointed at his aunt. "You said that yesterday. I thought you were looking for someone named Stewart."

"It's slang," Sherry answered. "It means let's do this. You know… stoodis."

Made perfect sense to me, but I had grown up in a family that used words no one in my peer group knew. It was cute.

Then she looked up at the directional signs. "Nordstrom's." She clapped her hands, adding, "Skoden" with a warm grin.

"Let me guess…" Blake tapped his chin.

Donna sighed and swept her arm forward. "Let's. Go. Then."

Blake chuckled as we moved forward. Sherry patted his shoulder.

And I babbled like an idiot. "We parked in the Nordstrom's lot," I said, pointing down the hall we'd come from. Yeah, no one cared. I stayed in the back of our group and let myself get lost in the shuffle of people, the holiday decor, and the leftover Christmas music as we moved toward our destination.

"Here's that men's store that Gabe likes," Sherry said to Blake. They veered to a small boutique with colorful button-downs in the window.

I'd moved to follow, but Donna intercepted me. "What are you?"

The temptation to answer "an accountant" was so strong I swallowed a few times to make the words go back down. My next impulse was to tell her I put the Asian in Caucasian. My nerves made me feel punchy, and this was a sure way to shut down inappropriate clients. The thing was, I knew exactly what Donna meant. The words potential in-laws rushed into my mind, and the reason my hackles were up became perfectly clear. Well, pooh. That wasn't fair to Blake's family. I wished I could crawl back into his bed at the condo. Instead, I told my insecurities to go away, gave her my best smile, and recited my well-rehearsed answer. "My mother liked to call herself an American mutt, though most of her ancestry came from German immigrants. My father is from the Philippines. He came here for medical school, met my mom, and set up a family practice near her hometown."

"Huh."

I couldn't tell if my answer was acceptable or disappointing. That was also a common experience. So I smiled more and added, "I think of myself as a transplanted Michigander."

"And how long have you been with Blake?" Donna pulled her long braid over her shoulder, as if the movement helped her process information. "Your name never came up until yesterday."

I didn't realize she'd steered us back toward Nordstrom's until the last set of stairs were in front of us. Juni and Liv were way ahead while Sherry and Blake seemed to have disappeared. "We've known each other for over four years."

"You weren't dating that long. He would've told us."

"True." I didn't know how much Donna knew, especially since it felt like she was fishing. For what, I didn't know, but I suspected. I had an auntie myself after all. One who was obsessed with my marriage prospects. Or lack thereof. Just didn't know if I wanted to tackle it head-on or let it go considering this was our first official outing as a twosome.

Blake wouldn't have mentioned me when I insisted we see each other in secret. He respected my wishes, but he also had his pride. That would make Donna protective of him, something I could get behind.

The man himself cleared his throat, saving me from taking the wrong tack. "I keep losing you."

I slipped my arm through his elbow. "You'll have to try harder for that to happen."

We found Olivia and Juniper in the women's special-occasion area of the store. Juni brought over a floor-length gown with an asymmetrical neckline in georgette. "What do you think, Mom? It's amethyst, like some of my bridesmaids' dresses."

The confident artist in me awakened, chasing the anxiety away. "Oh, Sherry, it would be lovely. Do you have silver shoes?"

"That's a great idea," Juni said. "My girls are also wearing silver shoes." She practically vibrated with enthusiasm. I remembered how searching for each item on my bridal checklist had felt like an epic hunt. And that was at the beginning of the big, crazy wedding era. The girl had my empathy.

"I don't know." Sherry held up a more subdued, beige, knee-length dress. "What about this?"

"It looks like what I'm going to wear," Donna said, rolling her eyes like she was bored.

"What does that mean?" Sherry asked.

Juni spoke into her mother's ear as Donna and I awkwardly stared at each other.

Blake cleared his throat. "Is everything all right?"

I gave him my best smile. "It's great." In no way would I make a scene. Better to keep my head down and let Blake be the star.

Fortunately, Juni appeared with another gown slung over her shoulder. "Come on, Momma, let's find a dressing room."

Sherry ended up trying on several dresses. The personal shopper, Juni, and I brought over several. As much as I loved playing stylist for Blake's cousin, I also didn't want to sit in the waiting area with Donna. Not that I had a problem with her, per se. After spending the day with my auntie, I knew where Donna was coming from. In fact, she was currently beaming at Blake and Olivia, and I didn't want to break their bubble.

After about a dozen dresses, Sherry declared she'd had enough, so I settled next to Blake on a leather settee. Each time

Donna pseudo-glared at us from the sofa on the other side of the space, I moved a few inches away. Then my man would pull me back into his side, like a human yo-yo. His fingers not so subtly walked along up my leggings-clad thighs. I grabbed his hand.

"Behave," I warned, leaning into him. "You're a grown-up, not a teenaged boy."

His eyes narrowed. "Exactly. We don't have to sneak around. We can do what we want."

I gritted through my teeth. "I just met your family."

He bent toward my ear. "So did I."

"Ugh." I rolled my eyes and grabbed his wandering hand. "I'm bored."

I chuckled. "No shit."

Olivia overheard from her slumped-postured position next to Donna. "Same."

The laugh grew in my belly. They looked like mirror images.

"Didn't you want to buy some things?" he asked suggestively.

I lowered my voice. "I wasn't going to buy a bikini. Just a pair of shorts." I held out my foot. The thick socks with hiking boots were making my feet hot. "A pair of sandals too."

"You sure you don't need new underwear?" He dropped his forehead to mine and smiled. A bored Blake was a frisky Blake. "I can wash what I packed." He sighed and pretended to pout. "Is it really that bad?"

"It's torture," he whispered. "Brings back memories of shopping when I was a boy." He shuddered like a little kid.

"You know what I think?" He raised an eyebrow, looking skeptical. I stretched my neck. Boy, I wanted to get away from the stress. Even from Blake for a minute. A lot had been dumped on me—albeit willingly—in the past twenty-four hours. "You should stop focusing on yourself and talk to your aunt."

"I don't know what to say." He sighed and gave her small smile.

"Surely you don't know her life story yet. Ask her about your mom."

"Here?" Blake's voice cracked and his expression looked shocked.

He had a point. "Right. Then ask her about herself. Where she went to school." I swallowed as my mind raced to think of ideas for him. "Ask him what Sherry was like growing up."

He finally sat up straight, his shoulders dropped and loosened, going back to the man I was used to. He nodded. "Yeah. All right." Then he swatted my ass as I stood, and I folded my arms.

"I'm going to check on your cousin." Blake smirked as I walked backward toward the dressing rooms. I caught sight of Olivia and Donna staring at us. Liv had a smile plastered on. Blake's aunt looked like she might cry. It was fine. That would change as soon as they had time alone. The loving protectiveness of auntie energy didn't scare. Not really.

When I turned on my heel, Sherry and I almost bumped into each other. I stepped back and gasped. She wore a silver chiffon maxi dress with an empire waist. All the anxiety regarding bored boyfriends and new family fled as the group collectively awed at her.

"Yeah?" She made a tentative face. "But it's not purple. And what about my arms?" The dress was sleeveless, and I'd quickly learned that Sherry didn't like her upper arms—the scourge of middle-aged women everywhere. It had a just-right low-cut neckline to show off her cleavage without being scandalous. Or one of those attention-seeking mothers of the bride.

"You could wear amethyst jewelry and a purple shawl," I suggested.

Juni and her mom put their heads together, comparing the dress to photos of the rest of the party, when Blake cleared his throat. "Excuse me, ladies." He kissed Sherry on her cheek. "This dress is the best one, though you look beautiful in all of them." His cousin beamed. "Cyn needs to pick up some light-weight clothes, and then we're going to check out the store you mentioned. How far is it again?"

"Under ten minutes." Sherry gave him a hug. "Thank you for putting up with us. I know it wasn't fun."

Blake rumbled something near her ear that had her preening. Donna's eyes shimmered as we said our goodbyes. After a quick purchase and change into linen shorts and cute platform sandals, Blake, Olivia, and I headed to the parking deck. This wasn't our first outing together, but it felt different. He laced our fingers as we walked. Like a family.

Chapter 32

A Girl Like You

Blake

Cyndi relaxed on the quick drive to Old Town while my nerves kicked up as we entered the Native American gallery. I didn't know why. Everything was beautiful. Inspiring. Maybe it was another reminder of what I'd missed.

The beaded jewelry stole Cyn's attention. No surprise. Her gray eyes sparkled as creative wheels spun. She moved from necklace and bracelet sets to the earring display, oohing and aahing.

Her hands fluttered around her head. "So many ideas sparking up in here." She picked up a ring. "How cool would this look with an opal as the center stone and this turquoise design surrounding it?"

"What are opals again?" I bit my lip to keep from smiling like a goof. Watching her mind work fascinated me.

"They're my birthstone. They come in a variety of colors, but my favorite is the Mexican fire opal. It's orange, has a gorgeous flaming look to it." She sighed. "And is unfortunately rare."

I tipped my head, studying the ring she held. "It sounds gorgeous. I wonder if this artist could make it."

"Ah. No worries." She whispered, "Something like that would be very expensive. It's just my brain freewheeling."

"Hm. Do you see anything here you'd like?" A turquoise necklace stood out that would look perfect against her golden skin. "What about this?"

Cyndi's eyes softened. "It's gorgeous."

I laid it on the counter, asking the cashier to hold it for us, and Cyn gasped hesitantly. "You don't want it?" I asked.

She touched the center stone and pulled her hand away like it was hot. "It's an artist's conundrum… We have a pile of stock in our studios and endless ideas in our heads. Makes it hard to justify wearing someone else's piece. Yet we also know the importance of supporting each other."

"But I want to buy it for you."

"It's… why?" Cyndi grabbed my hand, looked over her shoulder, and pulled my knuckles to her lips for a kiss.

I shrugged. "To commemorate this trip. It's kind of a big deal. Don't you think?" It had all been fucking life-changing for me.

"I…" She touched the piece as it lay on the counter, then whispered, "Yes, it is." She squeezed my hand as I stared at her beautiful gray eyes. They looked like a combination of shell-shocked and awed, like how I felt. "Are you okay? You seem pensive again."

I leaned against the counter. "We have more to talk about later. But yeah. This place… this trip keeps catching me by surprise." I kissed her hand back. "Having you here helps more than I can explain."

"Okay." Cyn looked behind her again, then gave me a quick kiss. "I'm glad. Thank you for reaching out to me."

This woman. If I didn't change the subject, I'd drop to my knee and ask her to marry me in the middle of the store. What the hell was she doing to me? Cyn's darting eyes helped me pull myself together. She was tracking Olivia's progress through the store, but I didn't think it was for protective reasons.

"You can kiss me in front of my daughter, you know." I waggled my eyebrows. "That's the point of being official."

Her eyes narrowed at me now. The look was supposed to make me cower. Instead, I shivered. Feisty Cyndi turned me on.

"You can't assume with a preteen in the best of times, let alone after the year she's having. We should sit down with her and find out how she feels. I'm not saying ask her approval, but it's important to show her we honor her feelings."

"Sparky, she's the one who told my family about you. And that I 'like, like' you." I kissed her forehead. "She knows."

"It's disrespectful to assume."

She folded her arms. Still so cute. "Are you speaking from experience?" Cyndi's father was recently widowed, so what did she know about single parents who dated?

"I remember being twelve," she pressed.

"Weren't your parents together for decades?"

She rolled her eyes. "Yes. I had friends with divorced parents. The dads tended to be particularly out of touch when it came to dating and their kids." She touched my chest. "It will go a long way if we check in with her in a safe-space way."

"You're a wise woman, Ms. Sendaydiego." I didn't know my attraction to the woman could grow. My daughter's well-being was as important to her as mine. It was hot. "Got it. Let's talk with her when we're done here."

The cashier finished with another customer and found us again. "Are you ready to check out?"

I spotted my daughter in a far corner. "We're still looking."

"Great." He pointed at the necklace. "Excellent choice. Shall I box this?"

"Please," I answered.

A small smile reached Cyndi's eyes. "Thank you," she whispered, her hands rubbing secret circles low on my back. She spotted my girl and hooked her other thumb in that direction. "I'm going to see what Livvy's up to. You coming?"

A display of Navajo dolls held my daughter's attention. After seeing Juniper's substantial collection, Olivia probably wanted one of each. I shook my head. "You go. I'll poke around the other room."

The store looked like it had expanded into a neighboring space. This room was set up like a traditional gallery, with paintings and pottery. I stepped across the threshold, spotted a painting to my left, and saw myself on canvas. All right, it was not that mystical of a moment. Not like a religious experience or anything. But somewhere out there, another Native American man thought like me. What hung on the wall was a Stormtrooper helmet from Star Wars covered with native symbols.

In a way, all the parts of me were represented in this funky painting. My past as an outsider growing up, the imaginary family who helped me through it, and the real one recently found. Fiction blending with reality. Contemporary mixing with traditional.

"Ooh, how cool is this?" Cyndi said, her arm sliding around my waist.

I pulled her in closer. "I'm going to hang it in my office."

"Makes sense." She looked up at me, a knowing smile on her face. "If only there was a piece representing Luke, like a painted light saber." Wow. She knew me well.

"Naw. This works." I'd probably search for that very thing eventually. When I had time.

"Liv found a doll. Well, four," Cyn said with a chuckle. "I

had her narrow it to one and told her collections aren't fun if you buy it all at once."

"Smart."

"Anyway, it's a hoop dancer doll that reminds her of Juni. She filled me in on what that is. Sounds beautiful. I'd like to see her compete sometime."

I liked the idea of visiting when we weren't the center of attention. "Great idea." I looked around the store. "Where is Sparrow?"

Cyn tipped her chin toward the other side of the wall. "Learning about Kachina dolls."

"Great." I rolled my eyes, hoping my credit card wouldn't max out before we left. On the other hand, I loved spending it on local, native artists.

She laughed harder. "Don't worry, honey." She patted my back. "Let's get the owner over here for your painting and a couple of horsehair pots I can't live without. He already told me they'll ship them for us." She pivoted away from me, sniffing the air. "Is that handmade soap? It smells amazing."

At least we weren't dress shopping anymore.

"These succulents are so pretty." Cyndi swooned at the plants around us. "I wish I could bring some on the plane."

After a quick lunch, we visited the Botanical Garden.

When we told Olivia about wanting to officially try a relationship, she glowered and said, "Can you not?" Then she dissolved into a belly laugh at the panicked look on my face. So that was fun.

The day was cloudless with a slight breeze hinting at an eminent drop in temperature. By the time we left the restaurant, I wanted to spend another day as a threesome. I justified it as learning about the area since we didn't have time to drive up to Flagstaff. It didn't feel right to go there without my family anyway.

"This twisted one looks like coral," Liv said. "Remember when we went snorkeling, Daddy?"

My mouth twitched. "The one-horned buttfish? Yeah. You're right." The one-horned buttfish had been a tongue-in-cheek name for snorkeling tourists when we vacationed in the Caribbean.

Gianna had been a huge fan of the beach or anything to do with water. In fact, this was the first time I'd been to the desert. That part still blew my mind. I kept waiting for the moment I recognized something, but it was all still new and wonderful.

"I love the movement in this Queen of the Night cactus," Cyndi said. She walked around the pot like she was deciding where it would fit in her house.

I leaned down to her and murmured, "You know it has to stay here, right?" Then I received a playful elbow to my gut.

"I love how much is in bloom in the winter," Cyn added. "It's so alive. Wish I had my good camera." She walked around us, taking shot after shot with her phone. Sometimes crouching low, other times zooming in on the plant tag. I assumed it was for reference. "Wish I could bring you home," she cooed to a pink plant.

I tapped her on the shoulder. "Take a photo of the big cactus for me. I've never seen a pattern like it before."

"Why don't you take one?"

"My phone is old. The sky doesn't look as blue as yours do."

Cyndi crooked her finger for me to bend down, and she kissed me. "My photographer's fee."

"Works for me," I said, smiling against her lips.

"Ugh," Liv scoffed, making Cyn jump back. My daughter

rolled her eyes. "Relax. I'm supposed to say that stuff. It keeps you in your place."

"Really?" Cyn asked me.

I shrugged, clueless. "My entire life is new at the moment." On the inside, I was floating with pride.

"Stinker." Cyndi tweaked Olivia's nose. Then she positioned us in front of the cactus, knelt and took photos, looking up, with the perfect blue sky and the plant in the background. A couple came by and offered to take some of the three of us. One of those ended up being my phone's new wallpaper.

Chapter 33

Finally Woken

CYNDI

"You're sure you won't mind seeing me around more?" I asked Olivia. We had stopped for snacks on a patio in the Botanical Garden. Blake had dashed off to the restroom, so this was my first time checking in with her. "Your feelings are as important to me as they are to your dad, you know."

"Well… I presume you're staying in the condo," she said sketchily.

I pressed my lips together to keep from laughing. "You presume correctly," I deadpanned.

"Does this mean you'll spend the night at our house when we go home?"

I watched some fancy-ass pigeon-looking birds peck around for crumbs. They looked like they were sporting fascinators. As much as I wanted them to, they couldn't give me the right words to say. "Would you mind?"

Olivia played with an earring I had made for her. One of

the fancy pigeons bobbed its head at us, like it was on board with my budding relationship.

"What would that mean?" Liv bit fidgeted with her lip. "You'd sleep in Dad's room, right?"

I glanced at the restrooms, wondering how long Blake planned to be gone. "That's how dating works. With grown-ups, I mean. Not teens… or preteens." I adjusted my short ponytail. "Hasn't your dad had girlfriends over before? What about your mom's boyfriends?"

Olivia popped a chip into her mouth, her face twisting as she chewed. "When Momma and Derek got engaged, he sort of moved in. Then they broke up, and that was it. Daddy never invited a girl over with us, but I've smelled perfume in his bathroom before. When I asked Momma about it, she admitted he was dating someone. I just never met anyone."

The significance of Liv's words hit me hard. She couldn't have been referring to me. She was too young to pay attention to such things the first time around. When he'd invited me along on an afternoon with Olivia back then, it had been a monumental ask. And I had freaked. I blink fast to keep from crying.

I cut to the chase and leaned in, my hands flat on the table. "You and your dad are so important to me. I would never want to upset you on purpose. That said, grown-ups kiss when they're dating. Hold hands. That sort of stuff. I do want to know how you feel about all this, because hiding it is disrespectful. You know?"

"You know I'm not a baby?" She stretched toward me and lowered her voice. "I know what happens when people date."

Well pooh. "Sorry, little chica. I'm just nervous about—"

"Wow, you ladies looked deep in conversation," Blake said as he bent and kissed his daughter's head. Then he settled in the chair between us and squeezed my hand. "Everything all right?"

Olivia slouched nonchalantly into the back of her chair. "Chill, Daddy-o. I was feeling out what life will be like after we go home."

"I hope Cyndi will be around as much as possible. Since you already like her, I don't see any problems."

"Hang on, you two… Ack." The wind picked up and blew a few specks of dust in my eyes. I wiped at them with the collar of my tank top. "My busiest time of the year is the winter. Also known as tax season. Business picks up in January, but in February, March, and early April, I rarely see anyone that's not a client." I'd lost relationships over it in the past and was nervous about it now. I slid my sunglasses onto my nose.

"You still eat, don't you?" Blake spread his hands. "We can plan meals with you." He turned to Olivia. "We'll figure it out. Right, Sparrow?"

She shrugged.

The weight of new responsibilities hit me harder than the wind in my eyes. I couldn't guard against it with protective glasses either. It was time to embrace these two or push them away forever. The last thing I wanted to do was disappoint either of them. My, how times were changing. I was changing.

"Anyway," Blake said, his fingers tapping on the metal tabletop. "Sherry texted while I was in the men's room. She wants Sparrow to spend the night again. What do you think, my birdie?"

"Sure," Liv said, a little zoned out. I was afraid I'd given her the impression I didn't care about her very much.

"She wants you to show her how to make zeppole in the morning," Blake continued. I wondered if he noticed Olivia's sudden distance. "I didn't know you knew how. I assume Gia taught you?"

Olivia planted her elbow on the table and cupped her chin. "Zeppole's probably the third real recipe she taught me."

"If you ever want to make anything… and I mean

anything, honey… let me know. The kitchen is yours as much as mine." He ran his fingers through Liv's hair, and she gave him a small smile. Blake sighed. "Anyway, we're going to meet Sherry and Gabe at their Italian restaurant for a late dinner. They want Sparrow's input on the food and mine on the cocktails." He shook his head. "I don't know why. These two are killing it out here. Every restaurant is a home run." He drummed the table and stood. "So what should we do next?"

"I want a selfie inside the dwellings, then go chill at the condo," Olivia said. I was all for vegging out.

BLAKE AND I FOUND OURSELVES WOUND UP AFTER DINNER WITH his cousin and her husband. Gabe brought an air of ease to the remaining anxiety between Sherry, Blake, and even me. They already loved Blake very much and held no hesitancies about accepting him into the family. It was weird how they both treated me like his partner when I hadn't accepted the label. Yet.

A quickie on the barstool in the kitchen didn't do enough to spend our pent-up energy, so we re-dressed and walked around downtown Phoenix. With the temperature dropping fast, I wrapped my arms around Blake's biceps and snuggled close.

As we passed a friendly-looking bar with magenta signage, he said, "Let's go in here."

I was surprised to hear the bartender say, "Oh hey, Blake. You found your miracle."

What the hell was that about?

"Evening, Ang. I did." He pulled a stool out for me and hung my purse on a hook under the counter.

I muttered, "What's going on?"

"Went here yesterday to think." Blake tipped his head in

reverence. "Angie helped me sort through my bad mood. Then I called you." He looked around. "Where are the guys?"

The bartender poured Blake a glass of whiskey without asking him what he wanted. The color reminded me of his eyes, especially with the glow of the signage shining through the glass. "Still sleeping it off, I guess."

"It's quieter tonight."

"Some people shouldn't be alone on Christmas. The day after's more tolerable." She reached out to me. "Hi. I'm Angie."

I shook her hand. "Cyndi Sendaydiego." I bumped Blake's shoulder. "Thanks for helping the big guy, I guess."

"It was truly my pleasure." She tipped her head to the side. "Sendaydiego. That's… Spanish?"

I offered her a big smile, letting her know wherever this was headed, cowering wouldn't be involved. "Filipino."

"Oh yeah." Some kind of recognition sparked in her eyes. "You're very exotic."

I shrugged it off. Blake squeezed my knee, giving me the sense that he understood. Of course, it could also have been a plea to stay calm, letting me know just how much we had to learn about each other. I winked at him and felt his hand relax.

"What can I get you?" Angie asked, seeming oblivious to the subliminal conversation she'd started.

I pointed at Blake's drink. "Is that bourbon?"

Angie nodded. "A local one."

Blake offered his glass for a taste. "I'm going to see if my rep can order some for the Garage."

"Ooh." I licked my lips, savoring the smoky, mesquite flavors. It reminded me of a good mezcal. "I'll take one on the rocks."

"Nice." She turned toward the back shelf.

I sipped from my glass when it arrived, swallowing the warm relaxation, letting it settle in my belly. The air smelled of beer and spirits, but the room had haze, like the ghost of smokers past lingered in the corners. It made me want to stay awhile. Still, coming in didn't feel like an accident now that we were settled on the well-worn stools. "Why are we here?" I asked Blake.

He set down his tumbler. "Guess there are more things to talk about."

"Like?"

He sighed. An hour-long conversation in one breath. "The restaurant… my family here… how much it's going to take to get out from under what Alan Kramer did… how pretty it is out here." He shrugged off the whirl of his thoughts.

"Do you want to move out here?" I asked, my voice higher than normal.

"Thirty years ago? In a heartbeat." He rubbed at his temple.

I swallowed hard, my back tingling.

"Hell, I would've relocated twenty years ago. But now?" He shook his head. "I won't take Sparrow away from her mother's family." He reached for my hand, his thumb rubbing circles on my palm. "Now there's you." He kissed the back of my hand. "I mean it about seeing where we can go."

My eyelids fluttered furiously as I wondered where the emotions had come from. I was relieved to hear he wanted to stay in Raleigh and didn't know what I would say if he asked me to uproot my life.

He continued, "Liv's questions from earlier have me thinking… We're official now, but we shouldn't leave it up to chance what this looks like when we go back home. I want more of you."

"More how, exactly?" My foot started bouncing on the crossbar on the stool.

"Easy." Blake pressed a hand on my leg. "That's why we should talk. Your schedule ramps up, which means there's time to plan us into it. At the same time, I'm at the mercy of the court's schedule as well as my daughter's. I don't want to limit ourselves to those midmorning quickies."

The room felt like it wanted to press in on me, squeeze my ribs. "But if that's all there is…"

"Spark… Don't get me wrong, I love our getaway moments." Blake pushed my hair off my face, letting his fingers slowly trail along my jaw. "I also want sleepovers, quick meals, long days, outings as a threesome." He brought my hand to his lips and kissed my knuckles. "I want a chance to treat you better than he ever imagined."

"You already do." I brushed away a threatening tear. "I stopped comparing you to him." I chuckled into my glass. "There never was anything to compare."

"Hey." He leaned in and kissed me gently. The bar wasn't crowded, but we were technically in a public place. And it didn't matter. "Can the three of us put our schedules together tomorrow?"

"Sure." I exhaled a ragged breath and struggled to bring in a new one. This stage in our relationship was wonderful, yet my instincts set off warning bells that I should back off. It was only a reflex. My heart knew better and told me to accept it all. With gratitude.

To keep from dissolving into another emotional mess, I changed the subject. "So… what's up with Star Wars?"

Blake barked a laughed and raised his hands in surrender. "Other than growing up in the seventies?" He pushed his empty glass across the bar for a refill. I leaned onto my elbow and raised an eyebrow. "Yeah." He chuckled. "There's more."

An older man came into the bar and patted Blake on the back as he passed us. "It's the Christmas miracle fella."

Blake tipped his chin. "How're you doing?"

"Same ol', same ol'," the man said. He slid onto a stool two down from us.

"Hi." I waved at him, thankful for the interruption. He winked at me like he had a secret. It wasn't much of one at this point.

Angie set a fresh glass in front of Blake and moved to the new guy.

"Anyway…" I restarted our talk.

"First off, understand I've never been to one of those Cons. It's not about that for me."

"What is it about, honey?"

"So, Luke's an orphan, right? Then it turns out his dad's the second worst asshole in the galaxy…" He lifted a shoulder. "It hit a nerve."

I laughed at his description of Darth Vader and stopped short. "Wait, did you find out who your birth father is?"

He scoffed. "No. My grandmother hinted at it or has a theory. But I don't think my birth mother told anyone. During one of our first interactions, I asked Sherry, and she didn't know. I can only guess based on my DNA test." He leaned onto his forearm, curling toward me. "No surprise daddy has shown up in my inbox, like Sherry did. Still, my adoptive parents' story about my origins sounded like Luke's." He cleared his throat. "Thing is… the rebels were the good guys and the underdogs, right? I mean, the bad guys were modeled after the German Army, but it reminded me of growing up. A lot of the good guys in the series were indigenous. The Empire was clearly intent on suppressing and not celebrating the variety of cultures they controlled." He gave me a tight smile. "It hit home."

"Wow. I never looked at it like that."

The corner of Blake's mouth lifted. He didn't know how sexy that was. "Then there was Leia."

I sighed into my hand. "She was badass."

"You were into the movies?"

"Of course. Everybody was. I liked how the characters

were multilingual, like my family. Plus every girl I knew wanted to be Leia." Enough water had melted off the cube to open the bourbon flavors the way I liked them, and I took a large sip. "The battle over good and evil. She fought alongside the guys. Everyone loved a Space Western."

"That's just it… I hated Westerns. The neighborhood boys loved having a genuine Indian to be the bad guy and take their beatings."

I gasped at the visual, rubbed his back as mine tightened for him. My hand settled above his waistband. "Little shits."

"The old man found it hysterical." He spoke to the swirling liquid in his glass as his hand moved in circles. "It's why I learned to box."

My creative wheels started spinning in my head, and I gasped.

Blake seemed to pull out of his memories and lifted an eyebrow. "What?"

"An idea for a piece for you just popped into my head. I didn't give you a present. Yet." In my excitement, I drummed on the counter. "It'll be perfect."

"Beg to differ, Sparky," he said, his voice full of amusement. "What you did coming here—along with that toy and such—was a wonderful, heartfelt gift."

The tips of my ears heated. "It wasn't meant… Okay, it kind of was—" I swallowed my tongue, still uncertain how I ended up in Phoenix with him. I only knew I didn't have regrets.

Blake chuckled quietly as he studied me. "So, jewelry ideas just pop into your head?"

"Sometimes." I touched his wrist and stroked it. "Would you be okay with a bracelet?"

He glanced down at my finger. "I'd love whatever you made me."

We looked up from the bubble we'd created and found

Angie staring at us, an approving grin on her face. "You two are adorable. I don't understand why you weren't together last night. You look like you've known each other for years."

Interesting choice of words. I patted Blake's arm. "In a way, we have." Then I leaned my head on his shoulder. It belonged there. My instincts settled down and let me relax into his body. "But this is new."

She leaned onto the counter. "It really was a Christmas miracle then?" Then she addressed me. An unnerving sense of knowing in her features. "You know, they say Dolly wrote both 'Jolene' and 'I Will Always Love You' on the same night."

I looked at Blake, who shrugged, and said, "I'm sorry. We don't get it."

"Only saying that lightning strikes for a hot minute, but the effect can last a lifetime."

I shook my head, still confused. "And…"

Angie sighed heavily, the way my mom used to when I frustrated her. "How about this one… Piss or get off the pot?" Then she brought the dish rack over and set our glasses in it. Her tone settled down with the rhythmic movements. "Just because life changes can happen quickly, it doesn't automatically make them bad." She tipped her head at me. "You look like a scared bunny, but this one…" She hooked her thumb at Blake. "He wants the best for you."

Wow. I swallowed hard, accepting her rebuke. The songs she mentioned did so much for Dolly. Also, for millions of other people. Can the amazing gifts in life simply land in your lap without a struggle?

Blake pulled me tighter as he cleared his throat. "Cyndi's been through a lot."

"Makes it time for something incredible then," Ang retorted, rolling her tongue in her cheek.

"What about me?" he asked as he pulled out his wallet.

Angie accepted his credit card and tapped it on the

counter. Her brow lifted as she assessed him. "Your family wants to help you. Let them."

His eyes widened as he swallowed hard. "H-help me?"

She rolled her hands like it was obvious. "With your… money problems." She looked up at the ceiling. "I'm getting too old for this."

I blinked. Twice. This was so familiar. My bestie, Kick, had premonitions that came true. This kind of encounter wasn't entirely new, but…

Blake signed the bill. "Thank you, Angie. For everything."

He helped me off my stool and continued holding my hand as we left Gerald's. About a block away, he stopped and faced me. "What the hell just happened?"

How the woman knew precisely which button we both needed pushing, I couldn't fathom. I didn't want to. "Another Christmas miracle, I suppose."

"You don't… believe. Do you?"

I shrugged and told him about my experiences with Kick. "The first time I noticed it, she and I were at lunch and she suddenly we insisted leave the restaurant. When we pulled up to her house, Liam had just broken his arm. Obviously we were able to drive him to the emergency room. There have been other times. Her husband's death, her father's too."

Blake rubbed his temple. "How did you two end up drugged then?"

A couple passed us, and the woman stared at me, her eyes wide with surprise, then sympathy.

"Shh." I elbowed Blake. Keeping my voice low, I added, "I don't think it works as well on Kick; it's more about the people she loves."

Blake grimaced. "That's awfully inconvenient."

.   .   .

"Wow-ow-ow! Look at you." Blake lifted his blanket for me to slide in beside him. "How did I get so lucky?"

We made it up to the apartment an hour earlier, and I made a bath while he caught the end of a basketball game. I needed time alone to process the past two days. After I toweled off, I thought, what the hell, and pulled on a black satin nightie with strategic cutouts.

Angie the bartender's earlier wisdom had stuck with me. Whether it was the bathwater, her words, or both, I relaxed and allowed myself to picture a future with Blake.

As I drew closer, instead of scooting over for me, he stood and pulled off his clothes except for his boxer briefs. His eyes stayed glued to my body until he had to draw his shirt over his head. "There." He brought me down to the couch with him, a playful glint in his eyes.

He hummed his approval as his hands roamed over my skin. "What the hell were you planning to do with this in Michigan?" He pushed my hair off my neck, and his eyes continued to roam over me. The incredulity in his voice made me laugh.

"Nothing." I leaned close and kissed his nose. "I bought it in Michigan. An old friend owns a lingerie shop. It's also where the bag of toys came from. She was clearing out inventory and practically gave me the stuff."

Blake pressed kisses down my side. "That's a big bag of toys."

"And lingerie… but they're not all for me," I said, giggling at both his tone and the way his kisses tickled.

"Another side hustle?"

"No, Big Guy." Blake gasped when I squeezed his… bigness and winked. "Most of them are for Kick and other friends." I pulled his braid over his shoulder and started taking it out.

"Look at you being all considerate," he said against my lips.

"I try."

The basketball game ended, and I felt around for the remote, not wanting to take my eyes off Blake. Whatever he was thinking in there, it looked dangerous. And fun.

"Do you want to put on a movie or…?"

"Yeah." I shifted to check out the channel guide. "Ooh, Say Anything is starting." I sighed, thinking about my favorite parts. My new favorite part involved Blake's daughter. "Liv and I watched it together when I kept her company."

Blake groaned. "Doesn't the dad go to jail for tax fraud in that?"

I winced, making the connection between the plot and real life. Then I tapped his shoulder. "In this scenario, you are Lloyd."

"The kid with no future?" He chuckled sarcastically.

"He had a future. He just didn't know what it involved. Yet."

Blake's groan turned into a whine.

"Fine." I scrolled down some more and found Star Wars. His face split into a wide grin. I pressed the button and let the movie roll.

He settled behind me, one hand on my stomach while the other explored my pussy. "Leia and you… my wet dreams come true. Life doesn't get better than this."

Chapter 34

All For You

BLAKE

I woke up from the best night's sleep, longing to convince Cyndi to move in with us. My head stopped the rumination as soon as it surfaced. We weren't ready. Only, it felt like I'd chased this woman for years. I decided to appreciate our new moments instead. Seriously though, I could get used to spooning her. I already had.

We took our time showering together, making use of the wide bench and the side jets. When we arrived at Sherry's house for breakfast, I was a happy man. Delighted. Humming with the rightness of the world. A note taped on the front door told us to let ourselves in.

The aroma of Gianna's famous zeppole threw a momentary wrench into my contentment. Memories from living with my former fiancée-turned-co-parenting-partner sucker punched me. The newness of my cousin's home mixed with my past had me so discombobulated I expected Gia to round the corner from the kitchen and greet us instead of Sherry. It had slipped my mind that she asked Olivia to show her how to make the pastries.

Cyndi squeezed my hand. "You okay, honey?"

I blinked, her voice pulling me out of my head. Cyn shifted from foot to foot like she was nervous about being there. Then Sherry and Liv appeared, bright smiles on their faces. Globs of vanilla custard dotted my daughter's apron like Gia's did. The sadness was immediately replaced with pride. Whether she followed in her mother's entrepreneurial footsteps or not, Gia's recipes would live on through Olivia.

I gave her a careful hug and scooped up some of the custard with my finger. After a quick taste, I grinned. "You did good, kid. Tastes just like Momma's."

Olivia's eyes dropped to her stocking feet. "Thanks, Daddy."

"It smells amazing," Cyndi added, stepping close to me. "My stomach is growling."

"Come on in then." Sherry waved us over for a welcome hug and hung up Cyn's jacket.

The temperature had dropped hard overnight. Not exactly as cold as it had been for Cyndi in Michigan, but no one would swim in my cousin's pool today. I pulled my sweatshirt over my head and gave it to Gabe after our slap-the-back greeting.

"Miss Olivia could be a pastry chef if she wanted," Sherry said. She removed a hairnet and hung it on a hook by the mudroom, along with her apron. "We had such a fun morn-ing." A cheerful glint shone in her eyes. "My kids aren't into cooking or baking, beyond the basics." She pulled Olivia's apron over her head and set it on the counter. "Thank you for letting me have her another day."

I sensed my face was beaming, my chest puffing out like the proud father I was. "She's great at whatever she does." I kissed Olivia's head.

"Da-aaad." Liv's tone filled with complaint, but she failed

to hide her smile. "Auntie Sherry promised to teach me how to make fry bread, but we might have to do it over a video call at home."

I rubbed my hands together. "Then I can join in." I wanted to perfect the recipe before introducing it to Felix. The Auntie Sherry reference settled in my heart with a warmth and rightness. Once again, I was reminded how close Sherry and I probably would've been if I hadn't been taken away from the family. The idea made me smile.

I was discovering how it felt to not be alone, both in my family life and in my love life. I had business partners and friends, but I'd never had anyone back me personally.

"I can't wait to try these." Cyndi clasped her hands together at her waist, then let them drop to her sides, her fingers flexing. I wondered what bothered her.

While Gabe and I set the table, Sherry pulled Cyndi aside and spread out some papers on the counter by the coffee station.

"Now I see it," Cyndi declared. Her finger traced something. "She's going to be so gorgeous." She held up one of the papers, but I couldn't see what was on it. "And you… Sherry, your dress is perfect."

"What's going on over here?" I stepped close, and both women jumped like they'd forgotten others were around.

Cyndi pointed at what looked like printouts from a website. "Sherry was showing me Juniper's wedding dress. It's on order now. She had described it to me at the mall, but the photo is…" Cyn made a chef's kiss gesture. "I love how different it is." She leaned toward Sherry. "I'm not a fan of traditional wedding dresses either."

I peeked over her shoulder and saw differing angles of a mostly white dress with a purple skirt that faded upward. Om-something, I think the term was. Gia had used it before. I could see what Cyn meant about the nontraditional part. A dress like that would be just what I'd expect her to pick. What I knew of her past pulled me up short. I raised an eyebrow.

"What?"

I scratched my temple, wondering if it was a safe topic. Cyn's mood had lightened significantly—thank you, Sherry—so I just said it. "I can't see… you-know-who… allowing you to wear something with this much color. Or just nontraditional at all."

Cyndi scoffed and told Sherry, "Blake's referring to my ex-husband." She looked back at me. "Nope, you're right. My dress was all white—you-know-who's grandmother snickered about that… as if. And the only other word to adequately describe the getup was poofs." She made an exploding gesture with her hands to help the visual.

Sherry laughed. "Same, girl. Same."

Cyndi's laugh sounded like fairies to my ears. Seeing her at ease in my cousin's house made me smile along with them. This was the woman I knew and, uh… Never mind. Not going there now.

"Olivia said you're coming back to see Juni hoop dance. The big competition is Valentine's Day weekend," Gabe said. "Better get your plane tickets now."

I winced at his words. We were sitting around Sherry and Gabe's dining table, enjoying a second cup of coffee. Olivia was in their backyard playing with the dog, who had been kenneled because of family allergies during the Christmas party.

"I can't get away in February. For some reason, I thought the competition happened during Spring Break."

"Ah. Juni has a local event in April."

I rubbed my chin. "To be honest, I don't exactly know when Spring Break is. Other than it's the week before Easter."

"Ooh, it's late this year. After April fifteenth, so I'll be free," Cyndi said. It pleased me to hear her automatically joining us. She was invited as far as I was concerned anyway.

"Sounds about right." Gabe scrunched his face and looked up. "Sherry has a better head for dates than I do."

"You got it, babe." She tapped his hand. "It's the Saturday of Easter weekend."

Gabe tipped his head inquisitively, almost like he knew. "What's going on in February?"

I rolled my head to the side, stretching my neck, not wanting to answer his question directly.

Cyn stroked my arm. She leaned in and quietly said, "Remember what Angie said. It'll be okay."

"Who is Angie?"

"A bartender at a place near the condo. I think she's an angel or witch or some such." I sighed heavily. Resolved. "All right… I have my first court date in February. You might as well know… the Garage is in trouble. Or I am. At least I shouldn't have to worry about jail time anymore."

"Jail time?" Gabe's eyes widened in surprise. Sherry gasped.

So much asked and implied in two words. It propelled me to come clean fully and let them see what a fool I'd been. They'd cotton on eventually anyway. "My last accountant stole a significant amount of money from me. Then he disappeared right as the government realized my tax bill had been shorted for three years."

"Blake," Cyndi drawled. "Stop being so hard on yourself." She shifted toward Sherry and Gabe. "Alan stole from five other restaurants too. He and his cousin rigged their POS software."

Gabe whistled and raised an eyebrow. Sherry's hands covered her face, but I caught her disappointed expression right before they came together.

I swallowed hard. The Old Man's voice shouted in my head, and I repeated what I knew he would have said to me. "I'm still the dumbass who didn't look at the paperwork close enough."

"I've heard of schemes like this." Gabe shook his head. "Everybody thinks they can outrun the government."

I wanted to shrink inside my T-shirt.

"How much are you on the hook for?" Sherry asked, a sympathy I didn't want or need in her tone.

I watched the wind blow through their mesquite tree as I calculated the unknown.

Cyndi answered for me. "It depends on penalties... and what the lawyers can negotiate."

"We need to find Alan Kramer. If he hasn't spent the money and his hidden accounts can be recovered." I tipped my coffee mug back and gulped the last of my Americano. "It'll be several hundred grand at least."

"Oh, sweetheart." Sherry looked like she could cry.

I turned to Cyndi for an escape, but she wore the same face. Her chin even quivered. Dammit. I pulled her against my shoulder. "It's not your fault either, Spark."

Sherry's shoulders drew back, her spine straightening. "What did you do?"

"Nothing," I insisted.

"I recommended the asshole," Cyn said, her voice tiny. Guilty. The only guilt was mine.

Olivia broke the tension by opening the sliding door. She and the dog coming inside sounded like a stampede. The wind followed them in, fluttering Juni wedding prints. Sherry brightened at the activity. It didn't take a genius to theorize that she missed having young kids around.

Liv coughed aggressively as she unzipped her hoodie, triggering my dad Spidey senses.

"You all right, Sparrow?"

As she shuffled to the back bedrooms, she choked out, "Fine. Getting… inhaler."

I popped up. "Need help?" After a smaller cough, she gave me a thumbs-up. I exhaled my panic and eased back down. I rubbed my chest. "Sorry, y'all. Since her mother died from an asthma attack, I've been on edge with hers. Every time she sneezes, my nerves jump."

Cyndi grabbed my hand. Sherry looked ready to cry as she refilled my cup.

"Thank you, Sher. It's all right. Really."

Gabe leaned toward the center of the table, his voice low. "Does Liv know?"

I shook my head as I caught sight of her heading to the mudroom with the dog. She gave us a smile and two thumbs up. She looked well and had stopped coughing. Thank God.

"Let's go sit by the fire," Sherry suggested as she gathered the empty cups. She glanced at her husband. "Can I talk to you for a minute?"

Gabe rose and followed her into the kitchen.

Taking advantage of the privacy, Cyndi grabbed my face with both hands. "Get this through your thick, handsome skull —Kramer is the criminal, not you. You're a victim—"

I flinched at the word, and her hands dropped to my shoulders. "Right. Survivor. And you'll survive this. You hear me?" She squeezed me reassuringly. "We will." Relief rushed out of my lungs like I'd been the one gasping for air. She pulled my forehead down to hers. "If you want to take on my baggage, I can certainly do the same. All of it."

"I'd do whatever I can to keep you out of it. All of y'all."

"Stop being silly." She kissed my temple and stood, holding her hand out to me. We walked with our fingers laced into the living room and shared the love seat next to the fireplace.

Sherry set a tray with four glasses of iced water on the sofa table. "We want to help, and before you blow it off, we have an idea…" She snuggled against Gabe, her eyes bright. He rubbed her back as she spoke. "We want you to join G&S Hospitality."

"That's not…" I ran a hand through my hair. Were they asking me to move? If I couldn't work out an agreeable arrangement, I'd have to declare bankruptcy and close the restaurant. Except I had responsibilities. My people. I'd fight for them. There were days I wished I was an employee again, but it also meant defeat. "I can't move here, y'all. I have people to take care of. Thank you so much, anyway."

"We didn't mean—" Sherry started.

Gabe cut in. "We want to invest in your restaurant and expand G&S Hospitality by bringing you into our portfolio. Since you don't need guidance on the day-to-day, it wouldn't matter so much that you're across the country."

"We've been looking for a restaurant outside the valley." Sherry continued, "We could make it an East Coast expansion instead. Since it's in the family."

In the family… we hardly knew each other, but Sherry and Gabe were ready to take on my debt. I lost my breath. Rubbed my chest. Cyndi put her arm around me.

"Out of matter of habit, I guess," Gabe started, breaking the spell. "I looked up your place early on and was impressed. Of course, we'd have to go over the books and get a clear picture of what happened. Plus we'd want access to your recipes. The market for Southern food is expanding, and we'd like to open a restaurant featuring your chef's dishes in Phoenix. It would take a couple of years to actualize, obviously."

Sweat beaded at the back of my neck. What the hell would I say to Felix? He would have to agree to everything. And those recipes… They were his grandmother's.

Chapter 35

I'll Be There For You

BLAKE

I parked the SUV, cut the engine, and sank into the seat. Desertscape views from the parking lot extended in all directions. It was gorgeous. But I wasn't ready to hike yet. Cyndi patted my thigh, soothing and supporting me. I shifted my gaze to hers. "What do you think?"

Her nose scrunch told me she knew exactly what I referred to. "There's still my offer. And our local connections. I'm sure Kick—"

"No." I rubbed my temples and groaned in frustration. If Cyn and I were going to work, I didn't want to muddy it over money.

"Mrs. Howard says the smartest people know when to accept help. That's how they get smarter," my little fount of wisdom piped up from the back seat matter-of-factly. Mrs. Howard was her social studies teacher, I think.

I looked over my shoulder. "That so?"

Liv shrugged, like I was missing the obvious.

"Let's go." Cyn snapped her fingers. "Exercise will help you think."

The wind whipped underneath the SUV, rocking it. I turned around fully. "Sparrow, do you have a hairband in your backpack?"

"Sure." She dug through the bag and handed one over. Thankfully, it was black and not pink. I made quick work of a ponytail. I hated it when the wind whipped my hair around my face.

As we exited, Liv's bag fell out of the car, and I ran around to her side to help the ladies pick up the escaped items. Once it was zipped again, Olivia threw the backpack in the car and slammed the door. She let out a growl. "I'm so clumsy."

I lifted her chin to meet my eyes. "Everything's fine, honey. That was an easy fix." I pulled her into a hug. "Ready?"

Halfway to the trailhead, I noticed Cyndi wasn't with us and turned around. She was getting up from a crouch by the SUV, saw me searching for her, and smiled. She broke into a jog and quickly caught us. "Sorry." The wind gusted, and she zipped her jacket up to her chin. "Let's go."

Olivia found a brochure at the information kiosk by the restrooms. It contained a map of the trails, along with information on the plants and animals in the area. She wandered up the hill, stopping in spots to read up on a plant or critter. Cyndi and I were happy to pick our way up the rising path. We were in no hurry.

Sherry and Gabe had suggested this preserve, with a loop overlooking the valley. It was their favorite spot for pictures with Phoenix in the background. They had planned to come with us but were called away by a restaurant emergency. The time apart would help me think about their offer without their hopeful enthusiasm anyway.

We visited with them for another hour after their proposal. Gabe shared with me how they revived struggling restaurants, but the system they'd developed didn't apply to the Garage. With the small renovation almost done, we were ready to level up on our own. If it weren't for the cash problem hanging over my head, I would have been my usual cocky asshole self, angling to secure the Beard award for Felix. The money situation had given me a monster dose of humility.

No, the Garage needed a safety net so it wouldn't crumble if I landed on the wrong side of the judgment. After explaining my side to Gabe, we agreed to a video conference after I returned home and talked to Fee.

Cyndi bumped into me, pulling me out of my head. "You okay?"

"I…" Looking down and seeing her concern shook something loose in me. Both of us had to lighten up. I pulled her into a hug. "I am. You?"

She shifted up to her toes. "May I?"

"You better." The tension in my body floated away when I bent to meet Cyn's sweet kiss. Her eyes darted around, searching for Olivia. "She's fine, Spark. We can kiss."

Cyndi blew out a long breath, her body softening in my hold. "If you say so."

I dropped my forehead to hers. "She likes you."

"Sorry. I'm still not used to this." She tipped her head back and kissed me again, like she was test-driving the permission I'd given her. "It's all good." She snuggled into me. "Really good."

It was.

Another burst of wind swirled around us. "Ew." Cyndi brushed dust from her eyes. Then her arms circled my waist again, where they belonged. Her bright eyes sparkled when she looked up at me, reminding me of why I came up with her nickname.

"There you are." I grinned, relieved.

She looked around. "Did I go somewhere?"

"Sort of. You were tense at Sherry's." I shrugged. "Thought it might have to do with me."

"Oh." She twisted her lips but stayed quiet.

"Did I do something?"

"No, no." She bit her lip, like she was psyching herself up. "I wasn't sure if your family liked me."

That didn't sound right. "You mean Sherry?" She wouldn't answer, so I squeezed her. "I won't be mad. I want to know."

"It feels stupid now." She tipped her head back. "Your aunt wasn't exactly welcoming at the mall. Then Sherry told me about Donna's plans to parade you in front of eligible bachelorettes, hoping she could entice you to move here."

I shuddered. "Yeah." I chuckled, remembering how disappointed my aunt had acted on Christmas Day. "I hoped she would let it go when she found out about you. I'm sorry, Spark."

She scrunched her nose. "You didn't do anything."

"I should have checked with her. I gave Donna the wrong impression about my availability since I didn't exactly know where you and I stood." I stepped back to meet her gaze. "Is that why you asked me about moving here?"

"Yeah." She pushed her hair back, looking sheepish. "Yeah. You answered well, hon." She held my hand. "You do fit in here, you know?" Her hand swept the valley. "Like you belong."

"There are plenty of Native communities in North Carolina, and I haven't moved to any of them either." I had connections in Charlotte, in the western counties, in Robeson County too. If moving to an Indigenous community had been what I needed, I would have done it years ago.

I turned and admired the surrounding scenery. Low-growing plants displayed blooms in pinks and blues. The beauty of the desert was a new experience. I loved it. It reminded me of my family, new and familiar at the same time.

I couldn't wait to learn more about it and them. Still, the desert didn't call out to me in the present. It was more of an echo from the past. Maybe in the future it would lead me back here, but not now. It was enough to know it was here for me. "I like what I've built at home. It's why I'm working so hard to keep it."

Liv rounded the bend, running back to us. "Can you guys stop canoodling? I found the overlook, and you have to see it."

"Where did you hear 'canoodling'?" Cyndi laughed.

"From one of the recess moms." Olivia grabbed her hand.

"Oh, okay. Do we want to know the context there?" Cyn asked.

"Probably not," Liv said, laughing.

Cyndi held on to her hood as she went ahead with my daughter. "We should sing a hiking song." Liv made a face at her. "Like this…" Cyndi slipped her arm under Olivia's and started singing the Rembrandts' "I'll Be There For You." Off-key. Obviously.

I slowed my pace to listen to the two of them snark at each other about the Friends theme and how old it was. Olivia hadn't joked that much since losing Gia. My girl had been an expert shade-thrower before. And Cyndi gave it right back, without taking offense. Instead, she laughed her ass off, called Liv a stinker, and tickled her.

Seeing them like this was a glimpse into the future and all its possibilities. I wanted this life. My women laughing and playing, enjoying our threesome. It didn't matter that the sky was cloudy; they brightened the world. My world.

This trail wasn't as crowded as I had expected, thanks to the cooler temperatures. We wound up a steep part of the hill and hit the plateau Liv mentioned, the valley in front of us. Saguaro cacti spread out down the slope, with those prickly plants and their delicate flowers spacing themselves between the old giants. Mountains in the distance rose in formations of varying blues under the gray sky. Sunrays broke through the cloud deck, and I snapped several photos.

Cyndi spotted a mother owl nesting in a saguaro and shot pictures of her. The protective bird never took her eyes off us. Her camera's zoom lens caught what looked like a cataract in the bird's eye. "She's an older mom," Cyn observed. "I bet she's raised many. What's the word for baby owls... batch?"

"A brood," I said. "Owlets come in a brood." I often carried binoculars with me to our greenways, where owls were a common sight, especially in the spring. I hadn't expected to see one in the desert.

"Guys..." Liv spun in a circle with her arms out. "Isn't it big? I love it up here."

"It's the largest city in Arizona. It's supposed to be big." At least I didn't call her Captain Obvious.

Cyn bumped my shoulder. "Big means awesome."

"Really? How do you know?"

Olivia shook her head at me like I was hopeless.

Cyndi slipped her phone back in her pocket. "My godson uses it." She raised her hands and spread her fingers in an arc like she was making jazz hands. "You know, it's... big. It's our awesome."

"Sure." I rubbed my temple, wondering if Liv would still use the term thirty years from now. We moved farther along the path. It skirted a low ridge, then headed up to another peak.

"It's so quiet out here," Cyndi commented, a sense of awe in her voice. "My backyard is noisier than this. The birds poking around in my woods sound more like their dinosaur ancestors. Here, it's just the sound of the wind." She wiped her eyes with her cuff after a cold gust made them leak.

"Look around. There aren't as many animals and hardly any birds," I said. The realization hit me suddenly. "Our woods are thick with animals because there's more to eat."

We took more photos with the three of us, then stood still and stood in awe of everything around us. It was eerily quiet. Until it wasn't.

A cloud of dust made Olivia cough while we were on our way back to the car. The coughing turned into wheezing and escalated to her gasping for breath so fast that it seemed to happen in an instant.

"Daddy…" She gasped, her eyes wide with fear. My biggest fear of late flashed before me. I could tell my girl was also thinking about her mom.

I grabbed her shoulders. "Where's your inhaler?" Why hadn't I double-checked that she had it? She should have puffed before we left the parking lot.

She squeaked, "In the car."

"No, no, no." My heart thumped out of my chest. I could pick her up and run to the SUV, but it was still a quarter of a mile or more. Between the rocky terrain and my boots, I didn't know how fast I could do it.

Tears streamed down Liv's face, and I crouched to pick her up. Panic as I faced my biggest fear was the only thing keeping me from crying.

"Oh!" Cyndi jumped and shuffled through the pack she wore on her waist. "Here…" She shoved an inhaler into my hand. "It was on the ground… by the tire… didn't want her to lose it." Cyn spoke like she was also out of breath.

The initial pump of medicine took forever to administer as Olivia struggled to open her mouth for me. She reminded me again of a little bird as her body sucked in the life-saving aerosol. I shook it and held it to her again. Her lungs began to ease with the third pump. Liv's coughing turned productive, and I wrapped my arms around her, giving her control of the inhaler. The sound of her chest clearing was more beautiful than any love song. We dropped to the ground, my baby sitting in my lap as she cried. My tears fell as I rocked her, sitting on the rocky path.

I'd almost made my biggest screwup of all.

"Shh." Cyndi crouched with her arms around us, sniffing. A tear dropped onto my head. I opened my arm and pulled her in. She sat against me and held on to the both of us.

"You saved her." My voice croaked with emotion. "You saved my baby." I kissed Cyndi, then my daughter, and dropped my head against hers. "Thank you."

"The dust has been irritating my eyes and nose. A-and I remembered th-the asthma…" Cyn's breath hitched. She tenderly brushed Olivia's hair off her forehead. "The car had already locked, so I figured it was better to bring it."

"So glad you did." I kissed my girl's head again. "God, we need you, Spark."

"Shh." Cyn brushed the tears off my cheeks before kissing me and my daughter. "We would have figured it out."

"We didn't have to because of you." I almost declared my love for her right then.

"Daddy… can't breathe."

I started and fumbled for the inhaler.

"No." Liv pushed against my arms. "You're smothering me."

We started laughing, which turned into another coughing fit for Olivia. I stood and brushed off the dust from her. "We need to find you a doctor."

Cyndi pulled out her phone. "There's an urgent care nearby."

I spotted the parking lot at the bottom of the trail. It was farther than I'd originally thought. "You shouldn't walk down to the car, Sparrow."

She lifted an eyebrow. "Are you going to carry me?"

"Yep." I crouched down. "Pretend you're little and hop on my back." We walked back to the car without talking. I listened for Olivia's breaths, making sure each inhale had a matching exhale. The wheeze had improved, but the attack had taken its toll on her. She was so tired that she collapsed onto my shoulders. For a moment, it felt like she had fallen asleep.

I didn't sleep that night. I kept thinking about what I'd almost lost. And how much I needed Cyndi. The song she'd sang became an earworm as I stared at the black ceiling. She was the missing piece I'd been looking for this whole time. I hoped she would always be there for us, like she'd been that afternoon.

Chapter 36

Follow You Follow Me

Cyndi

The asthma attack wiped out Olivia. No surprise. The doctor at the urgent care center had a lot of experience with asthmatic patients and gave her the right medicine, according to Blake. However, he itched to take his daughter home and to her own doctor. That led to more anxiety about how we'd get there. All flights to Raleigh were booked until after the New Year. I had already been stressing over whether I'd find success on a waitlist, but Blake didn't want Liv sitting on a packed plane with potentially sick passengers for hours.

The experience wiped out Blake. The bed in Olivia's room was a queen, so he stayed with her. The poor guy only relaxed when he heard her steady breaths. Part of me wanted to bring Liv into the king-sized bed so I could be there for both Bradys, but everything was still so new. Instead, I left the bedroom door open and checked on them a few times during the night.

In the morning, I made a run to the drive-thru place for coffee and cocoa. The most amazing breakfast aroma hit me when I returned to the condo, making my stomach growl. I placed the cup carrier in front of platters of bacon, grits, biscuits, and gravy.

The amount of food made me chuckle. "Planning to feed a crowd?"

Blake blew at an errant piece of hair. He wiped his hands on his apron and fixed his ponytail. The shadows under his eyes told of how little he had slept. The looseness of his shoulders showed how much cooking helped him relax. "Sherry's bringing Donna and Gran over to see Sparrow. They'll be here any minute."

"Are they taking the food somewhere?" I didn't see the three of them making much of a dent in those platters.

A small grin broke through the worry on his face. "Once I started, I couldn't stop."

I bit into a piece of bacon and rolled my eyes. Heaven. "It's a wonder you aren't a chef."

"My talents lie more in the short-order realm." He removed his cup from the carrier and picked up a bacon strip, nodding his approval as he chewed. "Unfortunately, there's no money in short-order cooking. Not like what I do now." He pointed at the dishes on the island. "Make yourself a plate. My family's almost here."

I smiled at him. "It's nice to hear you say that."

"What? Family?" Blake dipped his head as the grin held a shy, boyish charm.

"Yeah." I moved around the island and stroked his back. "It's almost like they've always been there."

"I texted them this morning, and Sherry immediately called back. She wanted to bring food, but we need to clear out the fridge."

"I love that for you."

"Thanks." He popped another strip into his mouth.

"Have you heard from your mother?"

"I texted her as well. She has a cold." I must have scowled, because Blake shrugged it off. "She's afraid of Sparrow's asthma. Right after the diagnosis, I showed Ma'am how to do a treatment, and she stopped babysitting instead. Said she couldn't handle it."

Boy, there were days my patience with that woman spilled out of the container I kept it in and splattered all over the floor. I was glad we weren't in the same room. Or town. Gracie Brady had let fear control her life and almost ruin Blake's. In the process, she became irrelevant to her child's life. It made me respect him more. I squeezed his waist. "Glad you found your birth family." I remembered my dad and made a note to check in with him.

"And you." He kissed my head, then sprang back. "Oh, Uncle Joe called."

A lot happened during my errand. "Did you text him?" I asked, feigning a breezy curiosity. After our talk about his uncle, it shocked me to think Blake would contact him already. I grabbed my coffee and drank after removing the lid.

"No. Donna told him. He immediately called to check on us." Such an auntie thing to do. I wondered if she'd chewed out Joe for what he'd said at Christmas. As if he could read my mind, Blake added, "Once he was assured Olivia wasn't in danger, the topic of his dad and mine came up. Guess I have my auntie and cousin to thank for that. Anyway, we decided we appreciate how hard we've worked and who we became."

"Look at you… using 'auntie,' coming to a healthy understanding with your uncle." I threw my arms around his neck and hugged him tight. "I'm proud of you."

Blake's eyes glowed with warmth when I pulled back. I hoped it meant he was proud of himself, but he didn't say more. Maybe he wasn't comfortable with the emotion yet. I would find a way to fix that. Instead, I removed Olivia's cocoa from the drink holder.

"Better take this to Sparrow before it gets cold," he said.

Yeah, he didn't fool me. I swatted him on the ass. "You do that… and I'll make those flight arrangements."

He stopped outside Liv's room and heaved a sigh. "Thank you."

"Look at you… delegating." I squeezed his juicy buns as I passed him on the way to the primary suite. "This trip has changed you."

"Don't I know it?" he muttered as he entered Olivia's room.

After talking through our options earlier in the morning, I convinced Blake to let me charter a flight home. If my plan worked, Olivia could see her doctor in two days and keep her stranger exposure to a minimum.

TWO LONG DAYS LATER, I WAS FINALLY HOME. MY PRETTY, BLUE cottage with a red door looked like it had missed me as I pulled into the driveway. Sheesh, I'd missed her too. The excitement about being back in my space overwhelmed my senses, so I didn't notice what was wrong until I saw my succulents. My babies looked sad. No, they looked awful. A new pot of string of pearls caught my eye. It was dead.

The reason for the "mass killing" became clear in the next moment. My house was freezing. In fact, I could see my breath. I zipped my jacket up and checked on the thermostat. It worked, but my system refused to ignite. Fortunately, I knew an HVAC specialist.

An hour later, my plants were warming up around my fireplace. At least I had gas. The furnace expert, Georgia, planned to squeeze me in the following afternoon. While the weather in Arizona had cooled locally, an ice storm followed by four inches of snow had hit Raleigh. Georgia warned me the part she suspected had broken would be on back order since she'd run into the same issue already. Daytime temperatures were rebounding, but the sun had already set. I was looking at a freezing night.

After pulling my favorite chair closer to the fireplace with my babies, I settled under several blankets with a new book. A space heater ran in my bedroom to warm it up before bedtime. Unfortunately, I only had one compact unit.

My phone rang where I'd left it in the kitchen. I reluctantly crawled out from under the blankets to answer it in case it was my father. He seemed good when we spoke. Still, I worried about him, especially in the winter. He didn't do much when it was frigid outside.

Instead, Blake called.

"Hey, Jefe. What's up? How is your girl?"

"She's downstairs picking out which show we're going to binge for the rest of her break. I'm making popcorn." His voice quieted when he added, "Missing you. I know it was only a few days but… it was nice. Really nice. Just wanted to hear your voice. How's your house?"

I filled my kettle to make instant cocoa. I didn't want to wait for proper hot chocolate in this cold. "The driveway was cleared, thanks to my awesome neighbor. But there is a snafu…"

He made a growly sound. "What kind of snafu?" I wondered if he'd developed a radar like Kick had. Then again, hers wasn't foolproof. Otherwise, she would have known about my plants and saved them.

"My furnace broke during the storm." I sniffed at the dead plants still sitting in my kitchen window. "Several of my plants died."

"I'm sorry, Spark. You take pride in your collection." He soothed me with an empathetic tone I wasn't used to unless it came from my best friend.

"They're like my babies, yes—"

"Wait… is the furnace out now? Are you there in the cold?"

I shrugged, then remembered Blake couldn't see me and rolled my eyes at myself. "The gas fireplace is on, and a space heater is running in my bedroom. Add to that leggings, sweats, a thermal top, a hoodie, wool socks, and mittens. It'll be fine." I only hoped my butt didn't stick to the ice-cold toilet seat and made a mental note to buy a heated one soon.

"How old is the unit? When's it getting serviced?" His microwave dinged, sounding like my answers were being timed.

I tried to remember the age of my HVAC system. "You know, it might be kind of old. My HVAC person is coming by tomorrow afternoon. She's been working round the clock since the storm passed."

"I don't like this."

My kettle whistled, and I poured the hot water into the mix. "It'll be fine. At least the outside temperature is back to normal winter conditions." It would still go down into the twenties before dawn. My breath steamed in the kitchen and not from the cocoa. It was why I needed the drink. "I'll talk to her about a new unit. The part I need is on back order anyway. A new system might get me up and running faster."

"How long of a back order?"

I picked up my mug and blew on it, ready for the warmth to fill my belly. "Couple of weeks?" I risked burning my tongue and took a big sip.

Blake blew out a ragged breath. "Come stay with us. Right now. We miss you already anyway. Stay until the heat's fixed." I gasped, choked, and ended up spewing the cocoa all over my cabinets before dissolving into a coughing fit.

Chapter 37

Head Over Heels

CYNDI

The first morning back in my house reminded me of the Christmas breakfast with my dad. Something was missing—or some people. My heating unit's part was back-ordered. Then the install caused another part to fail. Eventually it was easier to replace the system, which required more waiting. And more time at Blake's condo. I ended up enjoying playing house with him and Olivia in Raleigh more than I had in Phoenix.

Blake spent the mornings seeing Olivia off to school while I "recovered" from our late nights. Not that I slept in. I listened.

To their laughter. To their sparring. To their encouragement and reliance on each other. Olivia missed her mother desperately, but it was obvious in those moments that Blake softened her pain the way a father should.

After the second delay at my house, I joined them for the morning routine, often helping Olivia style her hair. She didn't know how happy it made me to come up with unique ways to arrange her beautiful, shiny hair.

In the evenings, I helped Liv with her homework and made dinner. Then we binged a show as a threesome when Blake came home. We were starting the third season of Stranger Things when my furnace was finally ready. Now I didn't want to finish the show alone. It was fun reminiscing with Blake about the clothes, music, and other aspects of "those days" while Liv engrossed herself in the kids' adventures.

I washed my dish and cup by hand since my dishwasher was empty. I never minded waiting for it to fill before. Now it seemed silly.

I used to treasure my mornings alone, centering myself before heading out for the day. Now I was just alone. So much had changed in a few weeks. I placed the plate and mug on the drying rack when my phone rang.

It was Blake.

"Were your ears ringing? I was just thinking about you."

"We have an emergency," he said solemnly.

The hairs on the back of my neck stood up, my worries going straight to Liv's health. "What's happened?"

"Sparrow's p-p…" Blake huffed into the phone, then cleared his throat. "Her period came."

"Oh." Relief washed over me until I remembered how we'd all been not so secretly awaiting this big day. "Oh! How's she doing? Did she use her kit?"

"I-I don't know." He cleared his throat again, and I wanted to reach through the phone and hug him. "She wants you. Only you. Do you remember your promise about spending the day together?"

I did. "Isn't it finals week? Can she get away?"

"Today and tomorrow are review days. She swears she can miss one." Blake dropped his voice. "I'd do it, but I'm meeting with the lawyers and have interviews for the event coordinator position. Besides it's—"

"It should be a ladies' day," I answered for him.

"Yeah."

"Hang tight. I'm on my way."

THE DOOR OPENED AND BLAKE PULLED ME INTO A RIB-squishing squeeze. "Hey, big guy. That bad, huh?"

He mumbled into my hair. "I'm kinda freaking out."

"Imagine what Livvy's going through." I pulled back and stroked his jaw.

"She's whimpering behind the bathroom door."

"Well, shit. We can't have that." I nudged Blake back and hung my jacket on a hook. I gave him a reassuring kiss and pointed at the stairs. "I'll go up."

Blake's soulful eyes gleamed with relief, like I'd just delivered world peace.

I knocked on the door to her bathroom. "Liv? It's Cyndi. Can I come in?" The silver knob turned and red, puffy eyes greeted me. "Oh, honey." I shut us inside and sat on the edge of the bath. "What do you need? Where are your supplies? I can set it up for you and give you privacy."

"No." Olivia leaned against her sink counter, her head down. "I did all that." She shrugged. "I tried a pad first."

"And…" I rested my arms on my knees and dropped my voice. "Did it go okay?"

"I think so."

"So what's next? How can I help?" When Liv's chin quivered, I reached for her.

"I don't want it." She dropped down next to me. "I thought I did because all the other girls already have theirs. Some even called me a baby for not getting it yet." A tear trailed on her cheek. "But it hurts."

"Hey," I drawled and held out my arms. "May I?"

She scooted against my side and let me rock her. "Shh," I soothed. "I bet those nasty girls had the same reaction to their first time. The thing is"—I sighed hard, forcing myself to remember where my head had been in those early days—"periods are part of life. The muscles involved haven't moved before, so that's your source of pain. It should lessen. Plus there's medicine." I pushed back and looked into her eyes. "Did you take medicine for the pain?"

Olivia bit her lip. "I forgot."

"First things first then." I found the meds in her linen closet and handed her the pills with a glass of water. "Give it about thirty minutes. Until then, we can set you up with a heating pad while you eat breakfast and I reschedule my day. After that, I'm all yours."

Liv's face finally formed a small grin. "Thank you." She hugged me tightly.

"You're doing great, little chica," I soothed, brushing her hair off her face. "Now let's boot your dad out of the house so we can do our ladies' day."

FOUR HOURS LATER, WE WERE SITTING AT A TABLE AGAINST A window overlooking downtown Raleigh, having lunch. Olivia's wide grins made my heart soar. My efforts to turn the day into a positive one for her had worked.

When the heating pad, breakfast, and medicine had quieted her cramps, she'd brightened and requested a grown-up lunch in a rooftop restaurant. The place we picked had glass walls on three sides. Add in a sunny day and it felt like we were dining alfresco. Cream linens with orchid centerpieces and bas-relief sculptures on the walls made the place feel sophisticated—exactly what Liv needed. Me too, to be honest.

It helped that we'd done her hair in an adorable bun. Liv wore a ruby-red velvet dress with a cropped black sweater and black combat boots. I swiped a bit of my cranberry gloss over her lips, letting her indulge. She looked lovely, and I could tell she felt it. I was sure it helped ease the pain when the cramps cycled. Instead of scrunching her face from the pain, she winced a little and kept talking.

We had parked in a deck before our reservation and stopped in the nearby shops. I hoped Blake wouldn't accuse me of spoiling Olivia, but as far as I was concerned, the point of the day was to celebrate her as well as her new stage in life. Our four bags of goodies sat in a chair between us.

"You're really good at this," Olivia observed.

"At what, honey?"

She waved at our packages, then at me. "Mom stuff, I guess. You knew what to do this morning. And this place is…" Her nose wiggled, then she drank some of her mocktail and changed the subject. "Why didn't you want kids? You're fun."

"I wanted children. They just weren't in the cards for me." I shrugged it off, thinking she wouldn't want more of an answer.

"What do you mean?"

I swallowed hard. Tread lightly, Sendaydiego. Don't scare the girl. Or piss off Blake. "Uh, well, I had a lot of miscarriages."

"What about the medicines for that?" Her sweet brown eyes, so like her father's, were wide with the incredulity of ignorance.

I stared at my mocktail, wishing I'd ordered a real one. "They do." I started laughing sarcastically at the memories of all those "medicines". "I was probably prescribed all the ones available back then." Her brows furrowed in question, reminding me of a puppy. I wanted to give her honesty within reason.

"What about paying another woman to have a baby? My friend Lola was born that way."

I choked on my soda concoction and started coughing. Because of the cost. Because my husband took matters into his own hands and slept with his assistant. Because… "Some plans just don't work out. By the time my ex and I would've been at that stage, our marriage ended instead."

She played with her necklace. It was a locket containing a picture of her and her mother. I'd encouraged her to wear it this morning, thinking it might help her. "You could have been a single mom."

"True, but…" How did I explain to a twelve-year-old how wrecked my identity had been back then, let alone my self-esteem? I survived by telling myself it had been for the best.

Olivia interrupted my train of thought. "The world is different now, you know. For kids. We talk about stuff." She leaned in. "My friend Kimmie was born from a sperm donor. Her mom didn't want to get married."

"Kimmie? That was my best friend's name growing up. You don't really hear that name for girls anymore."

"She was named after her grandmother." Liv innocently bit into her sourdough roll. "Wouldn't it be funny if her grandma was your friend?"

Ugh. Gut punch. Then again, some of my old friends were grandparents. "She did move south after graduation." I buttered my roll and placed it on Olivia's plate after remembering I was ordered to cut back on carbs. "As to having a baby on my own… When my marriage ended, I needed time." I finished my drink and looked around for our server. "Plus I didn't have the money to keep up with the treatments. I didn't just have to start my personal life over, my career also had to begin again. I didn't have a corporate insurance plan anymore." I gave Liv a bright smile. Meant as much for me as for her. "Life is great anyway. Don't feel bad for me."

The conversation stalled as our meals arrived. I wanted to tell her about all the lessons I'd learned from my low times and hoped the days ahead would allow for such conversations. That time definitely wasn't now. I placed an order for a pomegranate martini and picked up my fork.

Before I could dig in, Olivia said under her breath, "I didn't mean to upset you."

I reached for her with my free hand. "I'm not upset, honey. You can ask me anything." I waved the fork. "The hard part is remembering what's age appropriate… and what your dad will be okay with. We're still…"

"Getting to know each other?"

"Exactly."

"But you've known each other for years. Daddy said you guys dated before."

I nodded, hoping she didn't ask about our breakup. I suddenly felt like I'd been lured into an interrogation. The kid would make a good detective if she wanted to be one.

She ate some of her shrimp and grits while I shoved my salad in my mouth. Chewing was a great way to keep from answering questions.

"Guess I'm trying to say I like you a lot. You and Daddy are big. In case you were wondering. I wouldn't mind if you did more. Together."

Oh jeez. The martini arrived right on time.

"How did it go?" Blake asked cautiously. It was late when he came home. He slowly lowered onto the sofa next to me, wincing and rubbing his knee.

I was in the media room, catching up on Stranger Things after discovering they were two episodes ahead of me. I paused the show and reached for his back, rubbing between his shoulder blades. "You okay?"

"I tweaked my knee." He inhaled deeply. "Feel old."

I chuckled at his words. "You should cut back on late shifts."

"Argh." Blake stretched out his legs and sank into the sectional. "I twisted it this morning, sparring with a twenty-something kid trying to make a point." He turned his head my way. "This shit sucks."

"Are you talking about being fifty?" I asked saucily.

He narrowed his eyes. "Don't remind me."

"Hey." I patted his thigh. "All your legal documents say you still have two and a half months yet."

At the mention of legal issues, he grumbled.

I changed the subject a little. "Maybe go easy for a few days. Let yourself heal."

He gave me another round of side-eye. "Do you have any idea how much shit I'd get if I"—he made air quotes—"took it easy at the gym?"

"Well." I leaned against him and ran my fingers through his hair. "You could use my home gym until you feel better. I have enough machines upstairs to rehab you and keep your heart in shape."

Blake sighed under the ministrations of my hands. Then he raised his brows. "Not a bad idea. I might take you up on it. Can you join me tomorrow?"

I tipped my head as I mentally ran through my schedule. "Think so. I have an early appointment in Oakville. I can meet you after. Can you go with me to the Perked Cup after?"

He nodded. "Sure."

Is this how couples shared a life? It was nice. I remembered the early days of Kick and Thomas's relationship. She had reworked her schedule at the coffee shop to match his teaching days. For the sake of her youngest—a high school senior back then—they stayed at her house during the week and at Thomas's farmhouse on the weekends. We could probably make a similar arrangement if Blake and Olivia wanted. The picture in my mind made my insides warm.

His firm hand stretched to my thigh and squeezed, grabbing my attention. "You didn't answer my question about your day."

"Oh, well... Olivia's already sleeping soundly. The heating pad is by her bed, but you'll need to have her pain meds ready in case she still needs them when she wakes up."

"Sure, but how did your day go? Together?" He sat up. "Or are you deflecting because it was a disaster?"

I pivoted toward him, pulling up one of my knees. Before I knew what was happening, my eyes flooded with tears.

"Shit. Sorry, Cyndi." Blake turned toward me, mirroring my position. "I was afraid she'd be in a mood considering... you know."

I pressed my lips together and vigorously shook my head.

He tucked some hair behind my ear. "What then?"

"She's..." I swallowed hard as tears still fell. "She's amazing."

His face softened, making his earlier fatigue disappear. "Yeah, she is."

"No. You don't understand." The emotion-avoidant part of me I'd been trying to hide behind for weeks suddenly poofed like magic. It left me with nothing but my truth. "She's..." I dropped my head and whispered, "I love her, Blake."

"Yeah." Blake dropped his forehead to mine as his hands cradled the back of my head. "I know."

I tipped my head back. "Did you just Han Solo me?"

A sexy grin spread across his face. "You do remind me of Leia." As I scoffed, he chuckled.

"But how?" My mouth gaped as my brain struggled for words to justify my surprise. "I've done my best to—"

"Sparky..." Blake interrupted me, gently brushing my hair off my cheek. It instantly calmed my pulse. "You flew across the country on Christmas Day, for Christ's sake."

My skin heated. "Yeah, I don't know what got into me."

"Then you saved my girl's life." His finger traced the outline of my cheek. "Not to mention how you lay yourself bare when you come." The corner of his mouth twitched. "Pun intended." The grin morphed into a smirk. "It leaves an impression."

Talk about being laid bare. "I—"

He pulled me closer until I straddled his lap. Then he held my face, showing me all he kept inside. The happiness. The fear. The excitement. The I—

"We love you too."

"Y-you do?" I breathed. We. Not I. Blake and Olivia loved me?

"When you crashed into me at the Garage, the chemistry between was still there." Blake huffed a laugh. "If I hadn't needed your help with the books, I still would've chased you down. Made you be mine again." He kissed me slowly, letting his lower lip linger as he pulled away. I leaned forward to chase it. "I love you, Cyndi, and I won't let you disappear again."

"Promise?"

He chuckled. "Yep. I'll tie you up if you need it."

I shivered before lifting an eyebrow. "You still could do that." The TV screen shifted from the paused scene to the screen saver, bathing the dark room in a mix of swirling colors.

"Please don't make me chase you." Despite being shaded by my back, I could see the vulnerability move over Blake's features. "Stay. Choose us."

Having both our walls completely dropped should have scared the bejeezus out of me. Yet I didn't want to take it back. Not a word. Instead, I wanted to celebrate. I smiled widely. "I do choose you. I love you. Both of you."

Blake released a sigh of relief and brushed my hair off my face. His hands felt strong and caring. Safe.

Home.

We smiled at each other as ambient light danced around us.

"You're staying tonight."

"Are you asking?"

He slapped my ass. "Hell no. I need to fuck you now. Worship you." Blake pressed kisses along my jaw and down my throat. "The prettiest girl in the world just said she loves me. Hell, I'm the luckiest idiot on the planet now." He undid buttons on my cashmere sweater and kissed down my cleavage, murmuring pleasantries.

"Girl? Really?"

Blake stopped and tipped his head back, catching my gaze. "No matter how old we get, you're my girl. Being with you makes me feel like a boy again."

If this were all a dream, I didn't want to wake up. His words practically melted my panties into oblivion. "Oh. Well then. Carry on." When I'd taken my things home the day before, I left most of my toiletries and a few outfits, figuring I'd spend the night on a semiregular basis. Along with all our life-changing declarations, I enjoyed being able to make a last-minute decision to stay over. Like our pieces had clicked into place and we were making a real life together.

Blake tried to stand with me wrapped around his waist and fell back when his knee refused to hold us both. "Hell," he grumbled. "So much for being a kid."

"Hey, boys hurt their knees too." I jumped up, pressing my weight into the furniture and not him. He stared at my outstretched hand. "Let me help. Promise I'll make it better."

With a chuckle, Blake laced his fingers with mine and stood. We walked upstairs side by side, our arms wrapped around each other's waists. He found his strength and energy as we spent the rest of the night celebrating each other. And love.

Chapter 38

Come As You Are

Blake

I entered the Perked Cup and sensed Cyndi at the counter before I saw her. It didn't matter that she always sat there so she could chat with Kick. My body had developed a kind of electrical attraction tuned to hers, like a magnet.

She spoke some Tagalog mixed with English on the phone. I assumed to her father. I didn't know but a few words Cyn had taught me, but I recognized the intonations. Plus her voice softened when she spoke to her dad.

I kissed her on the temple and ordered a pour-over coffee. She was texting when I sat next to her. "What are you doing?"

Cyndi gave me the prettiest smile, making her golden skin glow. "Sending my dad a picture of Olivia's last riding lesson." She bit her lip sheepishly. "You don't mind, do you?"

"Not at all." My face spread into a grin, and sarcasm filled my tone. "Can't blame the man for wanting to see who dragged his daughter away at Christmas. If it were me, I'd have flown down already."

Cyndi's expression clouded. "That's what I'm trying to get him to do."

"Check on me… or visit you?"

"Smart-ass." My lousy joke did the trick, and she smirked. "I was hoping he'd spend a month here. Sunshine will do him good." She took a big drink of her coffee. "I can't convince him, so maybe Olivia will do the trick."

"You're bribing him with my daughter?"

She downed her latte like she was mainlining it. Then again, I'd kept her up late. "He loved being a girl dad and really wanted to be a grandpa." She made a cute, nervous face. "Not to assume more than we have. I'm hoping they would hit it off." Cyn blew out a long breath and dropped her gaze to her phone.

I reached for her chin, turning her face to me. "Assume away, Sparky. I get it. If a dad as wonderful as yours wants to take a grandfatherly interest in my girl, I'm there for it. She was shortchanged in that department."

Cyndi relaxed and snuggled into me. "That's what I thought. Thanks, honey." Her phone dinged.

"Did it work?"

Cyn read the text. Her shoulders dropped as she set her phone on the counter. "Still being evasive." She tucked her hair behind her ear. "Stubborn man."

"Now I know where you get it." I wrapped my arm around her and drew her back in.

Kick finished with a customer and stepped over to us, laughing at my words. Before we could say more, her husband, Thomas, interrupted us. He'd emerged from the back area, his face pulled into a worried moue as he approached his wife.

"What's wrong, Cowboy?" she asked him.

He sighed in frustration. "Betsy let the new kid exercise Ed despite telling her the boy wasn't ready to handle him."

I quietly asked Cyndi, "Who's Ed?"

"His horse," she whispered back.

"Like the TV show?" Memories of Kurt watching Mr. Ed came to mind.

"No, like Black Beard."

After a minute, I remembered the name of the infamous pirate who'd settled in the Outer Banks had been Edward Teach. It shouldn't have. His story was well known throughout North Carolina.

"What happened to the rascal?" Kick asked, her face filled with concern.

"He ran off." Thomas made a rumbling noise of annoyance in his throat. "I checked the neighborhood page, and someone saw him running down Main Street." He kissed his wife. "Going to nab him. Hopefully before he gets hurt. Just not sure who gets the ass-whooping."

The neighborhood page? The horse could be anywhere by the time Thomas made it to Main Street. "How do you track down a horse?" I wondered.

As he passed, Thomas tipped his chin in greeting, muttering, "You follow the trail of shit." With that, he flew out the door.

Kick watched him get into his car, then turned back to us. "He's running a big experiment this evening. He didn't need this." I related to that feeling.

Cyndi grabbed her friend's hand. "Thomas goes with the flow better than anyone. He'll be fine."

"I suppose." Kick blew at her mass of curls before sighing and pulling them back into a hairband.

I huffed, looking into my cup, thinking I could use a lesson in go-with-the-flow. Officially seeing Cyndi was expanding my circle as well. Thomas had recently invited me to a poker game he regularly attended. I wasn't comfortable gambling with my current money issues, but when it ended, I planned to go. If they ended in my favor, that was.

Cyndi reassured her, "Seriously, Kicky. Thomas will find Eddie, and he'll rock his experiment."

Kick nodded. "You're right. Yeah." She pulled a cloth from the back counter and started wiping down the surrounding area. "So what are you doing the rest of the day?" She turned to me. "And what brings you to our side of town so early?"

Cyndi answered first. "Preston's meeting me here"—she checked her phone—"in twenty minutes. I ran through a pretax checklist with him this year, so we should avoid the job-that-never-ends scenario this time."

"Good thinking." Kick folded her arms in thought. "Let me know if you see him pull up. I'll get his order ready. You can use my office if you want."

"That won't be necessary. Thanks anyway."

"Speaking of..." I started. "We need to chat about our schedules. I have a couple of ideas that could give us more time together."

Cyn raised an eyebrow. "Yeah?"

"Wait." Kick planted her hands on the counter, leaning toward us. "I knew there was more to the furnace mishap."

I was about to make a quip about how Cyndi borrowing Kick's husband's plane should have clued her in when Cyn cut to the chase.

"We love each other, Kicky." She threw her arms around me and laid her head on my shoulder.

My arms automatically wrapped around my woman.

"Yay!" Kick's face lit up. She raised her arms in the air like we'd scored a touchdown. "Finally." Her expression turned serious. "At least we don't have to pretend you're friends anymore." She made air quotes with her fingers for emphasis.

I rolled my eyes. "You have no idea."

Cyn swatted my stomach with the back of her hand. "You sure you don't miss the cat-and-mouse in front of your staff?"

She leaned toward her friend. "He made an art of trying to accidentally out us."

"For the umpteenth time…" I raised my brows at her to make my point. "They. Knew." I blew out a breath. "It's a relief to be out in the open." It so was.

Kick and I belly laughed as Cyndi shared stories of how I teased her. I didn't mind since I knew she loved every second of it. Before she finished, Banger McHenry strolled in, instantly cooling the atmosphere. This wasn't bad, per se. I simply wondered if the man ever joked. He jerked his thumb over his shoulder. "What did he tear out of here for?"

We all humphed, but Kick explained about Thomas's horse escape. Banger shook his head. "How many times have I told him to buy a motorcycle?" He counted off his fingers. "No paying for boarding. No one getting up at the ass-crack of dawn to feed it. It sure as hell doesn't take off down the road by itself."

Kick tsked. "But handlebars don't nuzzle you with affection either."

"Says who?" Banger smirked. So he did smile. Who knew? Then he nodded a greeting at Cyndi. He placed his helmet under his left arm and held his right hand out for me. "Hey, man."

As we shook hands, I said, "I didn't realize you and Thomas were close."

"He's the reason I know this lot," Banger said as nodded at the coffee shop.

Kick giggled. "You're bonus family."

Did that make me bonus family too? What if it did? I would like it, that's what.

Banger rolled his eyes before sending Kick a warm smile. He turned back to me. "I went to your restaurant, and your people said you were here." He blew out his breath. "It's what I get for not calling, but this is in-person news."

My blood pressure spiked with anticipation as I simultaneously tried to keep from getting my hopes up.

"We caught the bastard," Banger declared. While his expression stayed its usual grim, his eyes danced the tiniest bit. And they called me broody.

"Alan Kramer?" Cyndi squeaked with excitement.

A weight like an eighteen-wheeler lifted off my shoulders with those four words.

"Is there another bastard who stole from his restaurant?"

Chapter 39

Stellar

Blake

The next month passed like any other, with a mix of highs and lows. The highs included adding an event planner, an intern to take care of social media, and an office assistant for Jay and me to the Garage's team. Cyndi, Jay, our assistant Bridget, and I set up specialized practices regarding our money management to guard against anyone else stealing from the company. Felix was kept in the loop with monthly reports so he'd never be blindsided again either.

Our event room booked up fast, including an evening catering to a local gluten-free support group. After that night, new reservations came in nightly based on the recommendations of the attendees. Cyndi and Kick hadn't been kidding about how connected those people were.

The lows included a scare for Cyndi's father, Paul. He'd caught a virus and spent a couple of nights in the hospital. He and Cyn argued over her going up to stay with him, but Dr. S. knew all about his daughter's tax season schedule. He wouldn't let her risk her business to "play nurse when I know exactly what do."

Cyn's raised voice set off alarm bells in me. She was feisty but not with her father. It was fear speaking. So I stepped in, and we video chatted with him twice a day until Dr. S. was back to his routine.

I also had to disappoint my cousin Sherry by turning down her offer to take over the Garage. Felix deftly refused the deal and threatened to dissolve our partnership if I moved ahead with it. I didn't mind agreeing with him either. I had researched the G&S Group since our trip. My cousin specialized in fixing dilapidated restaurants, but the Garage was doing great. It would be a waste of their talents. What we needed was a loan to pay the penalties and lawyers when the judgment came down in April.

Banger McHenry's people found Alan Kramer and his cousin, along with their two largest offshore accounts, but it didn't add up to the full amount they'd stolen. Banger said more banks were involved. Add in the fast-approaching deadline from the state and the burden became crushing. I doubted his team would find all the money in time.

The light through it all was Cyndi. My Sparky. We shifted our schedules to take Wednesdays off together. She stayed at my condo through Saturdays and used the spare office at the Garage for meetings with clients in town. She spent Sundays through Tuesdays at her house in Oakville and worked with the clientele up there. We were both shocked by how everything snapped together once we believed it would work.

Gianna had been a fantastic parenting partner, but Cyn was showing me what a life partner could be. We collaborated on—and complemented—every aspect of our lives.

That's why she currently sat next to me in her favorite booth at the Garage with Banger across from us. The deep V between his brows indicating he'd brought bad news didn't scare me with my Spark by my side.

I spread my hands. "Just say it."

"We found another account in the cousin's ex-girlfriend's name. They'd grabbed her signature at some point, so the deposits looked real." He wrote something on a tablet. "We're tracking down all their family members—kids, siblings, etc.— and a long trail of girlfriends." Banger scratched his buzzed head. "We'll get them."

"Before the state's deadline though?" I asked him, lowering my voice as a customer passed our table. "It's next month."

Banger winced. "Yeah, can't say."

The man acted like he had all the time in the world. I found it irritating. The possible amount of the impending judgement always made my heart race.

"We should talk about loan options," Cyndi said as her thumb whisked over my hand.

I rubbed my temple to hold off a threatening headache. "That's more interest payments."

"Eventually most of your money will be returned," Banger said. "I just can't guarantee when."

My phone buzzed with a text from my lawyer's office. "Wonderful," I groaned sarcastically. "At least it's timely."

"What's wrong?" Cyn asked. Her earring reflected a glimmer of light from the rustic lamp over our booth.

"Three of the restaurants Kramer stole from are owned by the Gennaro brothers, right?"

Cyndi nodded, and Banger's eyes narrowed.

"Well, they're suing me and the other two restaurateurs for the money that's been recovered. They claim it's only ten grand shy of their part of the theft, and it should all go to them instead of splitting it between the six restaurants." I perused the end of the email. "They claim their burden is greater than ours and it would be a"—I looked back at my phone, my eyes struggling to read the words—"bigger detriment for the community if their company shut down."

"Unbelievable." Cyndi vibrated as she scoffed. "A judge will throw that out."

Adding on more legal fees didn't help. Our new employees were part-time, but their work was already pointing to more hours. Then there were my daughter's riding lessons. It was foolish to think I could keep this from touching Olivia. My shoulders tightened like an old-fashioned clock spring. "It'll still mean more billable hours at the law firm." I dropped my phone on the table like it was at fault. "The court date's in three weeks."

"I'll fan the flame under my people." Banger sat back and folded his arms, as calm as ever. Did anything rock the man? "Plus, I'll send a bill to these asshole brothers. If they want to reap the rewards of my work, you're not paying for it."

I chuckled. "Thanks."

Felix approached then, a stressed look on his face. I hoped the beef supplier hadn't shorted him again. We'd recently switched to buying directly from a local ranch. They'd sworn it was a newbie accident when the first order messed up.

As he hovered over my shoulder, I snapped, "What?"

Fee shifted from foot to foot. I worried he was in pain. I immediately went over which sous chef could take over for him while he was out sick.

"Listen, B, you gotta tell the staff to quit sending me out to talk to those allergy moms."

I shook my head as if I'd heard him wrong. "Is something wrong with their training? We can add it to our next meeting."

His eyes darted around the dining room, like he hoped no one would notice him in the front of the house. "No. I mean… the women want to thank me after their meals." Fee twisted the hell out of his chef's coat as he spoke.

I rubbed my temple. "I don't understand. You've never complained about compliments before."

He looked like he'd spotted a ghost or revisited a scary memory. "They cry. Big tears, B. No one does that."

"Aww," Cyndi cooed.

"Let me guess… you have a dedicated fryer," Banger added, a rare smirk crossing usually dark expression. "I do know that makes a woman smile wide."

Cyndi giggled, and I laughed with her. "We upgraded the kitchen to have a dedicated prep space for allergens."

Banger looked up at Felix, his brows locked down again. "Take it like a man, my friend. It won't last forever."

I gestured across the table. "Banger has a point." Felix wheezed a sigh, making me turn to him again. "Didn't you just interview a chef to take responsibility for the dedicated area?"

"She starts on Monday."

That lifted some of the day's burden. The woman was great during the interview. I shrugged. "Make the hug-and-kiss part of her duties. I'll have Meredith run interference until then."

"Thanks." Felix moved away then turned back, his shoulders dropping. "They just keep interrupting my flow. You know?"

I raised my hand. "I gotcha. Isn't it odd for a mother and kids to have lunch here on a weekday? Or was it a little one?"

Felix twisted the hat now. "It's teacher conferences or whatever today. Early release."

"Oh shit." I checked my phone. My appointment with Olivia's teachers started in twenty minutes, and I'd forgotten to set an alarm.

Chapter 40

Ain't Nobody (Loves Me Better)

Cyndi

That night, I was the one arriving home late. Well, home as in Blake's condo. Both his place and mine were home now. Being at my house wasn't even about getting in my "Cyndi time" anymore since I brought Olivia over occasionally. Blake continued to work out there until his knee improved enough to box again. We had become a couple who had two houses.

Unfortunately, I hadn't learned the art of leaving my work at the office yet. I'd never been good at it, but it didn't matter when I only had to rant to my plants. This day had been hard, ending with my most difficult client—read misogynist asshat. After slamming the front door and yowling in frustration, my face warmed with shame, hoping I hadn't disturbed Blake or Liv.

Days like this were common at the height of tax season. A good yell usually made the frustration go away so I could relax for the rest of the evening. When I reached the top of the stairs, a glass of red wine—I took a slow sniff of the earthy

Malbec—appeared in my vision, followed by the sexy man holding the glass of goodness.

Forget yelling. My body relaxed at the sight of Blake and his outstretched hand. "Thanks, honey."

"Was it a box of disorganized papers?" He cleared his throat. "Or a misogynistic asswipe?"

"Both, rolled into one." On his growl, I held up my free hand for him to wait. "It's—"

"Yeah, yeah, 'part of the job.' Doesn't mean I have to like knowing it happens to you. And under my roof. You'd think meeting the men at the Garage would make them behave… I'm getting you a bodyguard for when I'm not there."

"Stop." I tried to reassure him. Soothe him. "Jay chased him off when he got handsy."

"Handsy?"

Really, Cyn, what did you think he'd do? I put my hand on Blake's chest. "I handled it. Then I fired him. This is the last time I do his taxes. However… you can't put an anti-male-toxicity force field around me. I can take care of myself." I finally tasted the spicy wine, closing my eyes to savor the swallow. "Wine helps." My hand traveled up and around his neck, pulling him down for a slow kiss. I licked my lips after, relishing the taste of the Argentine countryside mixing with the smooth whiskey in Blake's mouth. "Mm. As does this."

He pulled me into a full-on body press and gave me another kiss, his tongue tasting and dancing with mine. He hummed. "You're right."

It made me lightheaded and aware of my need to undress. "I need to get out of this damn shapewear." I shifted from foot to foot. "Can we go up to our room?"

"Always. Have you eaten?"

I gave him my best side-eye. "Seriously? Your staff is afraid you'll fire them if I go home hungry. Especially after a long day. Jay wasn't the only person checking on me." It was sweet, really. Their loyalty to Blake had transferred to me.

"True." He waggled his eyebrows and playfully swatted my constrained ass. I just shook it harder as I led the way upstairs.

I let out a blissful sigh once I'd pulled the long brief off me. The release of my bra equaled heaven. Washing my face and brushing my teeth reset my evening as water circled the drain. I slid a silky magenta chemise over my head, preferring to wear them to bed at Blake's. My phone rang, and I jogged into the bedroom to answer it.

"Mm-hm… Yep." Blake was talking to someone. "Sure. Sounds good. It'll be the first item on my list tomorrow. Thanks." I checked to make sure he was on his phone and not mine, but it was his. "All right. Hey… thanks for helping Cyn earlier… He did what now?… Fucker… We need to— Yeah. Thanks, man. I mean it, never again."

Oh shit. I knew that clipped tone. Blake was irritated. He tracked me across the room, his gaze darkening. Murderous. He must have been speaking with Jay, who shared some things he shouldn't have. Bet he saw my client grab my boob. For an unhealthy old man, my client had a fast reach.

Blake ended the call and placed his phone on the nightstand. "Cyndi…" He growled at me, head tipped down and reminding me of bull.

"Why do you have my ringtone?" I deflected.

"I liked it."

"It sounded like the call was for me. It's confusing. Pick another one, please."

"All right," he drawled as he walked over to me. The full force of the Brady glare landed on me. "Were you going to tell me Glen stuck his hand in your blouse?"

"I told you he'd been handsy."

"Cyn, that's assault. You can press charges. You have a witness."

"And be blackballed for future work? You can't be serious. Most of the old boys' club members behave themselves. I look militant and I'm done. Told you I fired him."

"He's banned from the Garage. Jay already spread the word." Blake dropped to the edge of the bed like he was exhausted. "We have your back, Spark."

My heart swelled at his words. I knew this, but hearing it meant a lot. I stepped up to him. "I know, and I love all y'all for it."

He smirked at my use of the Southern term. When he looked down, his smile grew. His head moved up and down as he perused my body again, stopping at my feet. "What are you wearing?"

Despite knowing what was still on my feet, I looked down. "They're compression socks." Cool ones with cacti on them. Considering my wanting stature, they came up over my knees. Combined with the chemise, it probably made a sight. My ears warmed. "I sit so much this time of the year my legs tend to swell. So my doctor suggested them." I raised up my hands. "Yay hormones."

Blake raised an eyebrow. "Hormones?"

"It's all part of the road to menopause."

The smile tilted. "You look like a schoolgirl."

I leaned in close to him, examining his irises.

"What are you doing?"

My gaze continued moving between his eyes. "Looking for signs of early dementia."

"Rude." His brows furrowed. "Don't yuck my yum."

I rolled my eyes, wondering where he'd heard that phrase. "Earth to Blake." I snapped my fingers in his face. "I have silver streaks in my hair."

He winked. "They make you sparkle." He grabbed my hand and pulled me between his legs, then placed my hands around his neck. "You'll always be my schoolgirl."

"Does this mean you're not mad anymore?" I kissed his forehead. "Are we good?"

"We're so good." He flicked his hair off his cheek. "I wasn't mad anyway. I was…" A range of emotions played across his face as his hands found the bottom of my slip. "I'm a beneficiary of your competence. And you're right about the political game even if it's not fair. What you've built by yourself… it's inspiring." He placed a gentle kiss between my breasts. "Sexy."

"That might be the nicest thing you've ever said." Other men had a way of making me feel like earning their respect was a never-ending uphill climb.

He pulled back, his eyes narrowing. "I hope not."

"Well…" I bent and kissed him. "You do say a lot of wonderful words."

Blake hummed when he discovered my bare ass, as if I'd put on fresh underwear after jailbreaking from the compression brief. As he played with my sex, he asked, "Do you have to take the socks off?"

"Uh-um." His kisses and fingers made my brain fritz. "N-no. N-not yet."

"Good." He lifted the lingerie over my head. "Leave them on."

Chapter 41

Confident

Cyndi

"They can't be serious," Kick said. "I can't believe a judge wouldn't laugh the case out of the courtroom."

"That's what I told Blake, but the Gennaro Brothers are connected. They aren't kidding about being mainstays in the Triangle."

I'd been stewing for weeks over the new lawsuit against the Garage and the other restaurants. The idea of two plaintiffs being more important because their restaurants had been around longer was ridiculous. If anything, their industry experience should have made the brothers more culpable. When I handed Blake off to Alan, the restaurant was doing great, but it was still new. He had a better excuse for being duped. Hell, I was duped.

Not that the law worked that way. Blake's stress grew with each day, and I spent our time together easing his mind, feigning confidence he and the restaurant would be fine. So I took a break from my work and talked to Kick. The sun filling the dining room of the Perked Cup helped, like Mother Nature was smiling at me.

Kick clicked her tongue. "You won't find me in any of their restaurants. Those idiots claim to have gluten-free options on their website just so they can show up on a search. The number of people who were sickened by cross-contamination..." She shook her head in disgust.

Olivia came up to me and tapped my shoulder. "Can you watch my stuff? I have to go to the bathroom."

"Sure, honey." She pivoted on her heel and bounced away, disappearing behind the wall that led to the restrooms.

"Does she know about the restaurant?"

"Nope."

Kick narrowed her eyes. "Are you sure that's a good idea?"

"I'm following Blake's lead on it." I drank some of my flat white—my order for the month. It steadied my nerves. "It's his third rail, so to speak... Olivia realizing he's human."

"Pretty sure she knows. Twelve is a brutal year on parents."

"Naw." I shook my head. "Not yet. She still thinks he hung the moon."

"A parent can be both real and awesome." Kick filled a customer's order, then came back to me. "I do understand being skittish. Thomas walked on eggshells around the kids at first. Especially with Dylan and Rachel. He was overwhelmed by how close the four of us were. Then he discovered one of my parenting blind spots and had to speak up for me."

I sighed and rested my elbow on the sleek wooden counter. "It's so important to Blake that he does a great job with her. Being a good dad isn't enough. He has to be the best. You know, the man who raised him had the nerve to call him a loser. Every chance he got. Never praise. He was a boy. Can you believe it?" I checked behind me for signs of Olivia's return. "Blake used the negativity to prove his father wrong. It's how he's come so far on his own. When it comes to parenting… He gives himself no quarter with his daughter." I blew out a sigh of anger. "What I wouldn't give for a chance to tell off his parents."

Kick slid another coffee in front of me.

"Oh, I don't think I should—"

"It's half-caf," she said.

"Ooh. Nice." As I took a sip of the warm brew, Kick tipped her chin, looking over my shoulder. Olivia was stomping toward us. Her eyes shimmered with tears. I held out my arm. "What happened?"

She didn't have school because of a teacher's workday. Since her neighbor, Carol, was in DC visiting her daughter, Liv joined me for the day. So far, we'd had fun working from the coffeehouse.

"My period came again," she whispered in my ear. "I forgot to refill my kit."

Kick was busy with a customer, so I gestured to Deana to come close and quietly asked if Olivia could get a pad from the back.

"Sure, sugar. We keep a stash for anyone who needs it." She waved toward the back offices. "Come with me. I'll show you where they are."

"Uh, thanks," Liv said to her boots before she met Dee at the end of the counter.

I spent the next few minutes yelling at myself for not checking her backpack. Or at least teaching her the importance of resupplying it. I had been busy with work and let her down. More proof that I would have been a terrible mother.

"She okay?" Kick asked. I explained the situation again.

Liv and Deana emerged from the back. One hustled back to the bathrooms while the other joined Kick and me.

"How's she doing?" I asked Dee.

"Your girl's fine," Deana said in her usual warm tone. "She'll have this down in no time."

But the time wouldn't be today. When Olivia returned to her table to work, her sweatshirt was wrapped around her waist. She wiped furiously at her eyes. The sniffles broke my heart.

I went over to her table and sat beside her. "Hey, every woman in here has done wrapped a piece of clothing around her waist to hide a spot. More than once." I grabbed her hand, soothing the top of it with my thumb. "You're doing great."

"I thought you said it would take a while to be regular," Liv grumbled, then sniffed again. "It's been exactly four weeks." She wiped her nose with her sleeve.

I squeezed her hand. "This is good, honey. It means you'll probably be able to plan your schedule around it. Soon it'll be an automatic part of life. Like brushing your teeth." Unlike me. "Have you talked to your aunt or grandma about theirs?"

"No." She bit her lip.

"You should consider it." I pushed back the hair that fell on her face. "Your mom's family might have their own traditions about this."

Liv shook her head. "They deny I'm growing up. When I asked my aunt to take me bra shopping, she said I wasn't old enough for one."

Another tear fell down her cheek, and my heart broke for her. I wished Gianna had been here. "Well, I'll do whatever I can. You know that right?"

The corner of her mouth quirked up. "I do. Thanks. It just... fucking sucks." Olivia's eyes widened, and her hands covered her mouth. "Sorry."

"Did it help?" I asked, chuckling.

She giggled. "A little."

"Then we can make an exception." I patted her hand. "I

think your dad would understand anyway." I squeezed her shoulders. "Do you think you can focus on your project again?"

She shrugged.

"I have an idea…" I bolted for my bag, pulled out my headphones, and gave them to Olivia. "Pair your phone to these. You'll get lost in your homework before you know it."

Her smile finally reached her eyes again, making me feel a foot taller. "Thanks, Cyn."

"I've been thinking…" Kick began when I returned to my stool at the counter.

"Uh-oh." I laughed.

Kick stopped polishing the counter and narrowed her eyes. "Seriously. First, what if you reached out to a journalist about Blake's struggle? I know he's trying to keep the struggles quiet, but that strategy isn't working. There's a metric ton of buzz about the Garage on the gluten-free pages on social media. People should know how hard he's fighting for them." I was mulling the idea around in my head when she added, "After what happened to the Perked Cup—and me—because of our local paper, they owe me."

"What's the second item?"

"Huh?" she asked.

I tapped my nails in a rhythm on the countertop. "You said 'first,' which implies a second. What is it?"

"Oh right." Kick stopped working and stared eerily into my eyes. "How's Tatay?"

I leaned away from her. "Why?"

She shrugged. "He's been on my mind. Is he doing better?"

"He was." I hated it when people were on her mind. Kick's premonitions made my spine run cold. I picked up my phone and sent him a text. When he answered, I laughed out loud before turning the screen around for Kick to read.

At least my dad was in a good place. I watched Olivia work as I finished my cup.

"There's a third one," Kick said, leaning onto her forearms and lowering her voice. She tipped her head toward Liv. "You could help Olivia understand there's more to a period than pain and blood. Help her see good things will come."

I blew out my breath as I spun back to Kick. "Like what you did with Rachel?"

"That's one way. What would Blake say about it?"

I rolled my eyes. "He's overwhelmed. So he's following my lead regarding her time of the month."

"Are you sure?"

I nodded. "Definite—" My words were cut off by my phone ringing. A client had an "emergency" and wanted me to rush over.

A COUPLE OF WEEKS LATER, I ACCOMPANIED OLIVIA TO HER afternoon riding lesson. The friend she usually carpooled with stayed home with an illness. I jumped at the chance for some alone time with her. Aside from her stressing over her period, we had a blast when we hung out on her day off.

"What are you doing?" Olivia asked after she'd settled in the saddle.

"Sending pictures to your dad and Tatay," I answered as I sent the first photos.

She leaned so far forward she looked like she was about to fall off the horse. "You know Taylor Swift?"

"What?" It took a minute for me to sort through our crossed wires. I started laughing. "No, honey. Tatay is how I say daddy. Remember? My father was born in the Philippines."

"Right." Her head shifted from side to side as she contemplated this. The move looked adorable, with her riding helmet on. "Why are you sending him pictures?"

My father quickly sent back a note complimenting her posture, and I showed her the text. "He's taken an interest in you since you joined me on some of our video calls. It reminds him of when I had riding lessons." Dad was talking more about visiting when my work slowed. He wanted to meet Olivia and Blake as much as he wanted to see me. Any means necessary.

She nodded. "Big. Can you film us in a canter?"

"Absolutely."

Liv smiled before directing her horse into the arena. I filmed them for several more minutes.

Instead of working bent over my laptop while sitting on a bench in the observation area, Betsy, the stable owner, let me use her office to finish my work. In my early freelancing days, I couldn't imagine juggling my crazy schedule with raising a kid, especially an older one who had their own activities. My how times had changed. Now have laptop, will travel was my motto.

Liv ran into the office after her lesson, bouncing on her feet from the excitement. "Can we go to the Perked Cup?"

"Does this have to do with a certain night manager over there?" She had developed a crush on Jake, Kick's right hand in the evenings. If I told her about him scouting spaces near the Garage to open another café, she'd be insufferable.

Olivia blushed.

"It's better if we pick up a real dinner, honey."

She made a pouty face. "Okay."

"I have a surprise for you in the car. Will that help?"

Liv's mouth ticked up at the corner, reminding me of her father. "Maybe."

Out in my car, I blasted the heat to warm us up while I gave Olivia a little box.

"What's this?"

Sweat trickled down my spine, despite the chill hanging in the air. "You'll have to open it and see."

She tore off the wrapping. "A lipstick?" She pulled on it, accidentally hitting the On button. "Why does it buzz?"

As I explained how the little vibrator worked, her wide-eyed expression ticked up my nerves. "I hoped this might help you understand…" I shook as words fled my brain.

How the hell had Kick done this with Rachel? When she'd encouraged me to help Olivia see the positive side of a period, I remembered that Kick had done this with her daughter. She'd been adamant that Rachel wouldn't learn about her body at the hands of a man, the way most women of our generation had. I'd been proud of her for it. Rachel seemed to trust her mom more after that and often came to her with the hard questions. I hoped I could do the same for Liv.

Keep it together, Sendaydiego. If Kick did it, you can. Think of Judy Blume… "Periods aren't just pain and blood. Good things also come with it."

Olivia let out a frustrated groan. "I know about boys and… that." She made a face that would have delighted her father.

I used it as an opening, raising my hand. "There's my point. You're not ready to date, but you can help yourself feel good."

Olivia's tongue rolled in her cheek as she studied the little blue device. I'd made sure to buy her favorite color. "I've been waking up in the middle of night tingling… down there. Is that what you mean?"

I nodded, a wide smile blooming on my face. This was a sign I'd done well.

"You use this?" She shifted toward me as she asked the question.

"Sometimes. I have other toys too." I raised my hands. "They come with time and… experience."

"You mean sex, don't you?" Liv's face scrunched. "Some kids at school already do it."

"When I was in your grade, I knew kids who were sexually active. That's not a good reason for you to be. You know this, right? You decide when. And if you're not sure, come talk to me. I'll do my best to listen and not judge." My heart pounded with the hope I was being the person she needed. Was this motherhood? Because it kind of hurt.

"Okay." She grabbed her braid and twisted the end. "It's just… how my teacher explained sex"—she swallowed hard—"doesn't sound fun."

"It didn't when I was your age either." I tapped the box sitting on the console between us. "This is not a pretend penis, honey. That's why it doesn't look like one. It's for your clitoris. Did your teacher explain what that is?"

"Uh-uh." She shook her head, eyes filled with curiosity this time. "Only that we have one."

What the hell? Then again, I learned about it from Dr. Ruth. "Hold on." I reached into the back seat for my bag and pulled out a notepad and pen. Then I drew a vulva as best I could. "Your vibrator goes here." I starred the area where a clit would be. "When I was your age, girls relied on their fingers, but some bodies need a little more. You can experiment with light and hard pressure. It doesn't have to go into the vagina unless you decide you want it to. Understand?"

She kept her eyes on the device in her hand. "I think so."

Silence filled the car, and my nerves took flight. I reached for her shoulder. "Was this a bad idea?"

More silence. Liv's lips twisted with thought. No matter what any of us wanted, time was marching fast within her body. She was a perfect blend of her mother and father. High cheekbones, thick lashes, warm brown eyes, like Blake. Roman nose, pouty mouth, wavy hair like Gianna. The curves were also blooming. Lord, help us.

The inevitability of time made me sink into my seat. I swallowed hard at the realization. "My body's been changing too, honey. To be honest, it has scared me." I threaded my fingers through my hair. "You're handling your situation better than I have mine. At least you admit what's bothering you."

She tilted her head to the side. "What's happening to you?"

"It's the opposite of puberty." I looked out the windshield at the empty parking lot. Everyone had scattered so quickly. My little crossover car didn't seem like the refuge it had been when we first shut ourselves in. Now we were simply alone. Except we had each other. I inhaled deeply and made a decision. "Women have a bad habit of pretending the harder parts of life don't exist. Or we're weak for acknowledging them." Because of that, I often felt hopelessly alone during my fertility journey. "When you get to be my age, perimenopause shows up. Similar to what's going on with you, my body feels like everything is changing. Pretty much because it is." I gave her a small smile. "Maybe we can support each other."

Olivia leaned back against the door. "I don't have answers about getting old. I don't even know how to kiss."

"That's not what I mean. I'm sorry, sweetie. My point is, sometimes what we really need is someone to listen and help us see that we're still us despite the crazy changes going on inside. You know? Hell, menopause isn't even about getting old. Not anymore. That's kind of the problem. By the time you're my age, women will probably have more decades without their period than they did with it. We need to figure out what it means and how to help each other through it."

"More listening sounds nice." Liv smiled back at me. She turned the vibrator on again and giggled. "This is so weird, but I also wish Sofia was here. We asked her mom about periods and dating and stuff. She says we'll know when it's time. Except it feels like it's time now."

I rubbed my chin as she spoke. "Wise words, young one. I

know what you mean. Some days it seems like I turned around and what I used to know about myself has changed."

"Yes." Olivia shifted in her seat. "Right." She leaned forward and gave me a tight hug. "Even if I still had Momma, I would be glad Daddy has you."

My nose tingled as I squeezed her back and kissed her cheek. "Thank you, honey." I pushed her back to meet her gaze. Yeah, I'd fallen hard for both Bradys. "Now… any ideas on what we should do for your dad's birthday?"

Chapter 42

Ain't No Rest for the Wicked

Blake

"What is this?" Cyndi asked as she removed her earbuds. She was working in the office next to mine—her office now—and despite how busy she was, I couldn't stay away.

"What does it look like?"

She pulled the stapled paper edges apart and gasped. "Three. Oh, Blake."

That right there. Her smile made my day. Made all the expense to track down the succulents worth it.

"They're from the botanical garden, aren't they?"

"You recognize them." It worked. Cyndi hadn't forgiven herself for the plants that had died when her furnace broke. She lost five of them, and the nursery I worked with could only find three. They promised they could get more when the weather warmed.

"I've been hunting them down for you. No better timing for them to show up than Tax Day. Congratulations, Sparky. You did it." She still had clients who were late to file, but from here on, they would be on her time. Meaning more time for me.

Her mouth ticked up in a shy grin. "For not freaking out and ghosting you during my busy time?"

I bounced back on my heels. "Ghosts stick around, remember?"

"Right." She tapped her nails on the desktop. "I didn't poof."

"We can do hard things."

She closed her eyes and inhaled. "I love doing your hard thing."

"Walked into that one," I said, chuckling.

Cyn followed the twisty arm of a plant with her finger. "This is such a sweet surprise. Thank you." She wrapped her arms around my neck after meeting me at the end of her desk. This was where she belonged.

I hated how hard and how late she worked the past few months. I didn't want her to quit but wished I could lighten her schedule. She promised it was no big deal, but the dark circles under her eyes told another story. Except I had no business trying to take care of Cyndi when I wasn't sure the Garage would make it.

Cyn settled back on her feet and placed her hand on my chest. "What's wrong?"

"Can't a guy give his girl a present?"

"Blake…" She folded her arms, waiting.

This is what happened when you let someone in. They ended up knowing you. Too well. I pinched the bridge of my nose. "Fine. I needed to see you smile and couldn't wait for you to take a break."

"Aww." Those arms moved back around my waist, and she spoke into my chest. "Is it the lawyers, Felix, or family that's getting to you?"

My body melted into hers. "All of them. Part of the

problem is Felix is family." My oldest friend. "Gabe understands our reluctance to sign over the restaurant. Now he's interested in licensing Felix's recipes. Instead of raising a lump sum of money, it would be an income stream, but…"

"Let me guess. Felix bristled."

I stroked Cyndi's back to settle myself more than her. "He's thinking about it." Fee didn't do well with change, so I wasn't surprised when he didn't jump at the offer.

"Hmm. I heard Heavy D coming from the kitchen this morning, which meant he was in a good mood."

I chuckled at her observation skills. "Yeah. That was before we spoke. Despite the money issues, the restaurant is doing great. We've decided to go for the Beard." Word of mouth had already spread to the point we were booking reservations for weeks in advance.

"You totally should. You two deserve it." Cyndi tipped her head back. "That's why I think the public needs to know about what's happened behind the scenes. Your fans will want to help."

"Is that why a journalist called me today?"

"He did?" She jumped back and clapped. "Talk to him please. Trust me, it will help. The journalist owes Kick for his role in almost running her out of business. He'll take your side."

I groaned and sat on the edge of her desk. "It's embarrassing. Besides, isn't this guy supposed to be objective?" Not to mention I'd basically have to tell the world my old man had been right about me. I ran my hands through my hair. "I'm not ready for this."

"Are you kidding?" Cyn stepped between my legs. "What you need is a distraction."

I undid her top button, and she slapped my hand away. "Not that kind. Well, not right now. We need to plan your birthday party."

"Oh, let it go, Sparky." I wheezed out a breath of annoyance. "I'm not in the mood, and it's not my birthday anymore."

"For all intents and purposes, it is. Turning fifty deserves recognition."

I raised my eyebrow. "For not killing myself with stupidity when I was younger?"

"No, Mr. Snarky. For how you've persevered and how much you've built." Her fingers did a flirty walk up my thigh. As if that wasn't distracting. "I'm sure the staff wants to celebrate you. How about closing the restaurant for the night?"

"Absolutely not. We're already booked." I wasn't canceling the potential income. How did Cyndi not know that? I pulled her against me, squeezing her ass. If I couldn't undress her, I'd settle for this. "If you won't let up, we're at least keeping it low-key. The jazz group we like is booked for the night. Let's reserve our booth and call it a party. All right? Besides, this morning I found out I'll be in court on the day of my supposed birthday." God, everything about the upcoming day made me want to growl like a bear. Except for Cyn.

"Then it will be a doubly good reason to celebrate."

Or make me more miserable. I raised my eyebrow. "Highly doubt it."

"What if you reschedule the reservations and I paid for the night?"

I scoffed. "Seriously?" Then I kissed her forehead. "You're gorgeous, so don't take this the wrong way…" Her scowl darkened the shadows under her eyes, proving my point. I tucked a piece of her hair behind her ear. "I'm trying to tell you that you look tired, honey. I don't want to burden you with more." I tipped her chin up with my finger. "Time spent playing in my bed beats planning a dumb old party by a mile."

"You don't think I can do both?"

"I don't want you doing both." I pressed a slow kiss on her

full mouth and melted into her. It wasn't near enough, but it would have to hold me over until we found our alone time.

My phone dinged, and I pulled it out of my pocket.

MEREDITH

Yo Boss. Alan Kramer just walked in.

Should we boot him?

Or do you want the honors?

I blew out my breath. "Well, hell."

Going by the disgusted look on my hostess Sara's face, Alan Kramer was so busy offending her as we descended the stairs he didn't notice us. He followed her gaze, eventually turning his body and smirking at me. His face broadened into a lewd grin when his beady eyes landed on Cyndi behind me. I wanted to send her back up to her office, but she'd never go.

"Well, well, well. I heard you'd hooked up with your old squeeze. Still shitting where you eat, I see, Miss Sendaydiego."

My spine stiffened as my plan for Kramer almost flew out of the central skylight over the dining room.

"You son of a bitch!" Cyndi stormed past me and stomped on Kramer's foot, making him grunt and double over. The baseball cap he wore flew across the space. Then she clocked him with a right hook to the nose. A snap echoed around us.

"What the hell?" Kramer's hands flew to his face, but it didn't stop the gush of blood running down his T-shirt and onto my floor.

"You're my biggest regret, and that's saying something, asshole." Cyn stepped back, her fists held high, ready for another swing.

For a moment, I stopped breathing. No woman had ever defended me before. Not with words, and certainly not physically. She'd acted on instinct, telling me any hidden doubts about her feelings for me were unwarranted. She'd taken ownership of us, of me. Suddenly the need to protect her inflamed my anger. Still, I had to keep cool, defuse the scene, and implement the plan I'd set in motion upstairs.

I pulled Cyn against me, caging her with my arms. "Easy Spark. Another step and he'll press charges. Those legal fees are high enough." More importantly, I didn't trust the bastard to not hit back, even in front of me. From the moment our eyes met, he held the squirrely look of someone with nothing to lose.

"You broke it. You bitch!" Kramer screeched while probing his nose.

"You deserve worse," Cyndi bit back.

Sara handed him a towel for the bleeding, then gave me a what should I do look. I tipped my head toward the back to take her away from any danger.

I forced Cyn behind me and faced Alan. "Not another word to her or my staff."

"Blake…" Her arms slammed into a folded position.

"Thank you, honey, but I've got this." I kissed her quickly, then grabbed Kramer by the shoulders, guiding him into the space under the stairs with a false friendliness. It was the area people hung out in while they waited for a table with leather benches at the perimeter. Aside from the privacy, it moved him away from the door.

In my periphery, Meredith kept a sight line on us while a wall of plants screened her. Seeing the plan we'd quickly concocted upstairs working helped calm me down. It gave me another idea.

Kramer's nose wasn't the only thing on him that changed. Before, he had kept his hair short in a businessman's distinguished cut. Now it was badly dyed a dark brown and grown out. Stringy.

He pointed in the direction Cyn had gone. "Control her, or…" His demeanor shifted, shoulders falling as if some sense had finally settled in his brain. "Never mind." He touched his nose and whimpered, saying more about his desperation than words could.

Having the upper hand allowed me to keep a cool head. "You know you can't come near me or my staff, so why take such a risky chance?" I casually asked.

Alan's face twitched as he spoke. It was turning black and blue before my eyes. Solid hit, Sparky. He lowered his voice. "Get me out of the country."

"Why the hell would I do that?" An incredulous chuckle erupted from my throat.

"No, listen"—Kramer grasped my shirt—"I can get you money. Enough money to pay off the government. And… and a bonus."

As if the miraculous appearance of the missing funds plus penalties wouldn't look suspicious. Not to mention leaving my fellow restaurateurs in the lurch.

Kramer turned his head, looking for Cyndi, I suspected, but she was hiding with Meredith. "For your woman… and your daughter. How old is she now?"

I warned, "My daughter doesn't exist to you." Playing both an adversary and an ally proved trickier than I imagined. Nothing he said tempted me, but he'd basically confessed to having active bank accounts. At the same time, my hands twitched with the desire to hurt him. My phone sat heavy in my pocket. It better be doing its job. "I was inadvertently wrapped up in your illegal exploits. Why the hell would I entangle myself on purpose?"

"I told you." He clicked his tongue like I was stupid. "It's about money, dammit. A lot of it." He tried to twist his swollen face, but it looked more like a pucker. "I can't do time. You're only on the hook to the state. The feds are after me, man. The feds! You know what that means?"

"Yeah." I tipped my head. "Butner doesn't sound too bad," I said, referencing the federal prison about an hour north of us.

Kramer made a wheezy noise, sounding like a balloon with a leak. Collapsed onto the lobby bench like one as well.

"Why me?" I asked. This whole time, I'd been kicking myself with visions of Kramer laughing at me, calling me a sucker. It's what I envisioned when I hit the bag at the gym.

"Those Gennaro Brothers were supposed to get me somewhere safe, and they flaked at the last minute."

I sat next to him, leaning in. "Are you telling me those bastards are suing me for the recovered money and were planning to take more money from you? Exactly how much is still out there?"

"Well… wait—" He inched closer, lowering his tone. "Are you helping me or what?"

I rubbed my chin. "Maybe." I heard a small squeak behind me and knew it was Cyndi. Meredith needed to keep her in line, or I'd have to fake a fight with her.

My response seemed to relax Alan. "I might have been embezzling for a while, yeah? Small stuff to practice with, you know? A thousand from one client over several months here. A few more from another there. Like I said… practice."

Well, shit. "How much in total?"

"Minus what they seized from me?" He tilted his head from side to side. "Six million, three hundred sixty-nine thousand and eighty-three cents."

Seized from him… nice. I inhaled deeply to keep from punching him. Only needed a couple more minutes. "Eighty-three cents?"

He smiled. "I'm an accountant."

I settled my forearms onto my knees, using the bending

move to look for action outside the restaurant. Everything remained quiet. "What do you want me to do exactly?"

Alan pulled his Hurricane's shirt away from his chest and fanned it as a satisfied grin spread across his face. Sweat stains spread down the material from his pits, making the areas where it mixed with dried blood a darker brown. The Alan I knew wouldn't have been caught dead in a Cane's shirt. He was from Pittsburgh and a devoted Penguins fan. It must have been part of his "disguise."

"It's easy. Rent me a car but in your name. I'll take care of the rest."

Good God. "Let me guess… You know a smuggler in"—I pinched my lower lip—"Beaufort." It had to be somewhere close. He didn't have time to dawdle down to the Gulf Coast this time.

He shrugged. "Something like that." The bleeding had slowed, so he scooched over to his Yankees cap, quickly stuck it back on his head, and returned to the bench. "The less you know, the better. For your own safety."

"Right." I pointed at his hat. "This is your disguise?"

"Simple but brilliant."

If you say so. I smiled and nodded. Where the hell were the police?

"So you gonna do it? It's a huge payout for a few minutes' work." His hands made a blow-up gesture to portray something large.

"You know the rental company would come after me, right? You'd be better off paying cash for a used car."

"Ooh." Kramer snapped his fingers as those beady eyes lit with joy. "Great idea. Let's do that."

The sound of a distant siren finally reached my ears. Thank heaven. I still had to keep him distracted. "Do you have cash? Because my savings are frozen thanks to an annoying legal situation I'm experiencing."

"Ahh…" He shoved his finger in my face. "You're funny." He tipped his chin at me. "I don't remember you having a sense of humor. More like buttoned up and… stuffy."

Fuck you too. "People change."

The siren noise grew exponentially and finally caught Alan's attention. "You called the cops." He had the audacity to look hurt.

I jumped him as the Raleigh police filled the street in front of my restaurant. "Like I told you, you're not supposed to be here." He struggled against my hold, making several failed attempts to flip me. I pressed tighter, pulling his arms behind his back. "Stop moving or I'll deliver a kidney blow." My body vibrated with the urge to make the asshole pay physically for what he had done to me and mine.

Kramer wheezed about charges, but the drumbeat of my pulse in my ears drowned out what they were exactly. As if I cared about a misdemeanor at that point. My fist raised over his midsection when Collin and Ryder, my assistant bar manager, grabbed Kramer's legs.

"We're here, Boss," Collin said. The knowledge they had my back relaxed my limbs. In the next moment, the policemen ran through the doors and arrested Kramer's ass. I collapsed onto the bench in the waiting area and willed my breath to slow.

"You were brilliant today." Cyndi sat in my lap on the love seat in my bedroom, feeding me a lumpia she'd made in celebration of Kramer's capture. Since he'd fled the country once, he had to stay in lockup through his trial.

I swallowed and licked my lips. "You worried I'd gone over to the dark side, didn't you? Kramer didn't hear your squeak—thank God—but I did."

"Sorry, honey." Cyn sheepishly dipped her head.

"Meredith set me straight." She lifted her eyes and smiled. "Recording him on your phone was a genius move."

My lawyers were thrilled. They immediately informed the prosecutor on my case about how I'd helped the government get more evidence against Kramer. Plus the Gennaro Brothers' lawsuit was thrown out. My team planned to argue that they shouldn't receive any of the recovered money instead, now that they were implicated in a conspiracy with Kramer.

I still had to raise money for my reconciliation, but my hope grew that the court would show me mercy with the penalties. Moreover, I didn't feel like such a dumbass about the whole incident anymore. From what Kramer had implied, he still had clients out there who had no clue he'd stolen from them. I expected his former accounts would hire an audit of their books as soon as possible.

As the police put Alan in a cruiser, Stan Roberts, the journalist Cyndi urged me to speak with, and Banger McHenry walked into the scene. Stan had been arriving for our planned interview. Cyndi had texted Banger when she was hiding with Meredith. I showed them Mer's video and let them listen to Kramer's confession on my phone—I planned to have my lawyers give them to the police after they were done with them. It practically made Banger giddy as he had better ideas on where to search for money and how far back the accounts went.

The information did the same for Stan since he now had a real investigation to pursue. For a small paper, this was the lead of a lifetime. I couldn't wait for it to end up in the news. I smiled, hoping it would make Kramer's case a slam-dunk for the prosecutor. I would probably sit in the courtroom if I could watch him hauled off for good.

"What?" Cyndi asked. She swiped at crumbs on my T-shirt, then her hands drifted down to the hem, and she pulled it over my head.

She parted her robe and pressed her body against mine. Her soft skin gave new meaning to the word home. The warmth of her body promised more than a happy ending to our day. I let my wishes drift to beautiful ones of us together permanently, with no lawsuits hanging over us. My Sparky and Sparrow and me. An idea blossomed in my mind. She nudged me, and I realized I'd left her question hanging. I didn't dare tell her my idea. It would work best as a surprise. So I said, "Thinking about that asshole eating his just deserts."

"He really will." She wrapped her arms around my waist and snuggled against my chest. "I'm proud of you."

For the second time that day, my breath caught. Had anyone ever said that to me before? I couldn't conjure up a memory of it. "You know, I'm proud of me too." In the end, that's all that ever mattered.

Chapter 43

Don't Dream It's Over

CYNDI

Blake pocketed his phone and tapped the table to get Olivia's attention. "Go upstairs and get your backpack, Sparrow. Time for school."

I pivoted from my spot at the sink and grabbed her breakfast dishes. The legs on Liv's chair squeaked as she pushed it back, but she didn't rise.

The hesitant look on her face made me sit. I reached for her hand, hoping it wasn't another rough morning. She'd only had a few since January. Since I'd started staying over. I liked to think it had something to do with me. We had grown close in the past few weeks. "What is it, honey?"

"Umm…" She swallowed hard. "Remember the dance tomorrow?"

Blake nodded. "Uh-huh."

"Well"—she twisted the hem of her sweater—"Sofia is going with Grant and Brett is Grant's best friend, so…"

Oh Lord, I had a feeling I knew where this was going. I reached for Blake's hand, giving it a squeeze.

Blake rolled his free hand as Liv bit her lip.

"I think Livvy's trying to tell you this Brett boy asked her to go to the spring dance tomorrow night."

Blake stiffened, his grip on my hand like a vise.

Olivia nodded before waving it off. "It's a formality, really. We'll be in a group the whole time. Just… everyone is sort of a couple, so it made sense to go with Brett. Just not together, together."

"How do you feel about this boy?" I asked her.

She shrugged. "It's more about Sof. She really likes Grant." She leaned toward me. "They kissed."

Blake growled like he was imitating Roy Kent.

"Stop it," I pleaded with him, then turned back to Liv. "We're talking about you and Brett."

She tucked her hair behind her ear. Since I'd given her better conditioner, she wore it down more. "He's a good dancer, which should be fun."

"No kissing. For either you or Sofia," Blake said, looking at me for approval.

I rolled my eyes and nodded.

He rubbed his temple. "Go get your backpack."

"Thank you, Daddy." Olivia ran around the table and kissed Blake on his cheek, then be-bopped up the stairs. "I have to text Sof."

Blake sank into his chair, moaning like he was in pain. "A date? In seventh grade? How?"

"It's not a real date, honey. The only cars involved are mine and Sofia's mother's. The kids will all stay at the chaperoned gym at school. Like Liv said, it's more of a formality."

Blake settled his head on his elbow. "If you say so."

"I do." I rubbed his back. "You should be happy she opened up to you. The kids could've kept it a secret. She obviously wants your support. Giving her trust will go a long way toward her making good decisions. If it will help, I'll remind her of it in the car."

"Thank you." He continued, pressing his thumb into his head. "Except we don't know what this boy is really thinking. His hormones are probably running rampant in his brain." He wheezed. "And other parts. I should've taken the night off and chaperoned."

"It'll be fine. Olivia knows about hormones—boys' and girls'. We've talked. She's uncomfortable with Sofia's interest in this Grant kid, but she doesn't want to lose their friendship. Liv knows she's not interested in relationships yet."

Blake's head snapped in my direction. "Who talked about relationships?"

"Oh, Jefe." I wrapped my arm around his shoulders. "It's time to let our girl take more steps toward growing up."

"What does that mean?"

"It means she has enough on her mind and doesn't want to fill it with boys." I took his hand and kissed it.

"You mean grieving Gia? Living with me full time."

"She'll always grieve her mother." I ran my fingers through my hair. Blake still cringed at talk of Olivia's period, not to mention other proof of her changing body, but it was time he got over it. "She wasn't thrilled about having periods—most girls aren't. So we've been talking it through. I'm trying to emphasize the positive points about growing up. Anyway, she's made it clear boys are not on her radar. It would help if you reasonably clarified her noninterest in this boy, but I'd be happy to do it. For your peace of mind."

He tipped his head back and scoffed. "Peace. There's no peace." He squeezed my hand. "How have you been helping her feel better about growing up? I should take a cue from you."

"Ooh." I sat up straight, still proud of myself for how our

talk had gone. "Most of it has been sharing about the mystical aspects of hormones and menstruating. How she'll come to see the cyclical benefits of her body. To help her along, I gave her a little lipstick vibrator." I waggled my eyebrows at my brilliant gift. "You see, Kick did this for—"

Blake went eerily still. "You did what?"

The lack of movement on his part made me shiver. "It's okay," I reassured him.

Instead, he burst out of his seat. It made me lose my balance, and I grabbed the edge of the table for purchase. "Shh. It's all great. Sh-she liked it." I raised my hands to calm him, but it had the opposite effect.

He laughed diabolically. "You gave a twelve-year-old a vibrator, Cyndi. A sex toy. What the hell is okay with that?" He pulled at his ponytail. "God, I hope no one at the school finds out about this. They'll take her away from me. Shit, what if Gia's family finds out? They'll file for custody."

I stood and rushed to him, to both quiet him down and reassure him. "No one's taking her away from you." I stroked his arm. "It's not a sex toy either. It's just a small, low-powered clit stimulator. Fingers rarely do the job right. She should know—"

"Do you hear yourself? You're talking about a little girl," he roared.

"Keep your voice down." I looked over my shoulder for signs of Olivia. At the same time, my ire was rising to meet his. How dare he. I was doing everything I could to help. Both of them. "I'm trying to tell you… Hell, we're both trying to tell you that Liv's not little anymore. Hell, she's growing faster than her hair is. She should learn about her body now, so she doesn't have to learn it at the hands of a future boyfriend." I shoved his shoulder. "Or worse." But he stopped listening.

Blake walked away from me, his hands running through his

hair, messing up the ponytail. "What if… it broke, and she's lost her virginity already?" His hands balled into fists. "I should've been paying closer attention."

I stomped up to him and stuck my finger in his face. "Stop yelling and stop thinking about yourself. This isn't about penises. That's been my point… She's not interested in them."

He gave me a death glare.

"Knock it off! The whole hymen business is a bullshit myth."

Blake looked confused, like he doubted me. Damn patriarchy.

I didn't care if he understood. I pressed on. "As if it's the sum of her value. You are supposed to understand. You're supposed to be different." My arms slammed across each other as I faced off with him. "Besides, she's been riding horses for how long now? Trust me, it broke already. Stop acting like an Antebellum father. Your job is to raise her into a modern woman, not some antiquated Southern Belle. I was only trying to help. You know… give the next generation a better experience growing up than we had? That's what I'm trying to do."

He stepped into me, over me, using his body to intimidate. "You're teaching a twelve-year-old how to orgasm."

I stomped my foot. "News flash… she already does. You know how boys get wet dreams?"

He rolled his eyes, giving me the quintessential look for duh.

I held my ground. "Fine. Then why are you surprised to learn that girls get them too? Huh? Except while everyone thinks it's a hilarious rite of passage for boys, girls are kept in the dark about it until years later—when they finally understand what's been happening because their partner shows them —and the light bulb goes on." I made a flashing motion with my hands. "So that's what has been going on down there. Is that what you want for her? Because I don't. It's all I was trying to do." I leaned my hip against the counter. "It's not like I opened my toy drawer and told her to pick one. But my experience let me know what was appropriate for her. And it's not about her being a good girl or a bad one."

"I didn't say it was." He might not have intended to, but as far as I was concerned, he had. Blake pivoted away from me and stared out the kitchen window. His grip on the counter was so tight his knuckles lightened.

A heavy cloud cover had descended over the city, typical for the back-and-forth of April weather. It seemed appropriate for how fast this morning had gone wrong.

I silently pleaded with his back. Please understand. Please.

"I'm her parent. You should've asked me."

I sniffed. "Probably. Yeah. It's just—"

"No, Cyn. No excuses. It's all on me. The past year has been…" His head dropped between tense shoulders. "I can't screw her up too. I won't. Do you understand? I can't deal with surprises like this. She has to come first."

My eyes welled with tears. "What do you mean?"

He sounded so cold and shut down when he lifted his head. "I need time to think."

"About Liv. Or"—my tears fell as his meaning hit home— "you want me to leave. Over this? I promise, Blake, this isn't the mountain you think it is."

He stared out the window. "If you say so."

The dead tone of his words slapped me across the face. I swiped my cheek. "Fine. Think about it. I want you to consider this… It's easier for boys." He scoffed, but I pressed on. "Seriously. Her changes are on the inside. They're not easy to see like a boy's, with random hard-ons. They're felt in some mysterious, empty, 'in-there' place."

Blake flinched. "I can't right now."

"Obviously." My breath hitched as I moved to the kitchen

archway. "She deserves to know her body isn't only mysterious, it's also enjoyable. Before anyone else does. That's all I was trying to do. Think about that."

As I stomped past the stairway, I caught sight of Liv sitting at the top of it. Crying.

I murmured, "Sorry, little chica."

Chapter 44

Fighter

Cyndi

When I pulled into my driveway after fleeing Blake's, I was a worthless mess. It had taken all my energy to keep my eyes clear for the road. It was a good thing tax season was done and I had scheduled an easy day to relax and catch up with my cleaning. The dam broke wide open when I stormed through my front door.

I wished I had a cat to snuggle with. Then again, I'd probably be a bad pet parent. That's what Blake basically confirmed. He said I had horrible judgment when it came to Olivia.

I tossed my jacket on the hook in the entry, turned on Vivaldi, then padded to my sofa and collapsed. I put my feet on the tufted ottoman-slash-coffee table and settled in for a thorough sob. The woodsy plug-in air freshener that usually helped me find peace couldn't fix this despair. The "Winter" concerto added to my whirlwind of emotions. I turned off the music and embraced silence. My loneliness.

This is why the IVF never worked. The voice in the back of my mind—the one sounding a lot like my former mother-in-law—screamed into the empty room. You would've ruined my grandchildren. Joel's affair was the best decision he ever made. Okay, that was an actual quote. One I wished had rolled off my back but never managed to.

I grabbed my head and howled, convinced my biggest fear was true. When my throat sounded hoarse, I pressed into the soft cushions. My gaze flitted around my house, my sanctuary. However, it didn't feel like home anymore. My home was a man, currently furious with me.

Movement in the upper corner of the living room caught my attention. A small house spider worked on a web with admirable diligence, oblivious to my crumbling life. How dare it. Then again, I wished I could focus on something besides heartbreak. The smooth, efficient movements of its legs lulled me into a relaxed state until my eyes closed. They flew open a few minutes later when my phone rang. I hoped it was Blake.

My shoulders fell when the caller ID read Joel. "Are you kidding me? Now?" I yelled at the phone as it continued to ring. The man possessed a talent for finding me at my weakest. He was the absolute last person I wanted to speak with. Except ignoring his calls wouldn't make him go away. Like a period pimple, he had to be dealt with immediately, or he would erupt. I straightened my spine and pressed the green button. "Joel."

"Hey, Cynthia," he soothed before clearing his voice, his tell for nervousness. Odd.

"Now's not a good time," I snapped.

"It'll only take a minute," he pressed, and I rolled my eyes. The man never took no for an answer. "I… want t-to apologize."

I swallowed hard. "E-excuse me?"

"Yeah." His voice lowered to a whisper. "I'm sorry, baby girl."

Suspicious, I asked, "For what exactly?" My gaze traveled back up to the spider carefully adjusting a section of the web.

"For all of it. The affair. Letting Mother run roughshod over you." There was a long pause after I scoffed. "Yeah, I kind of did too. You can say the apple didn't fall from the tree."

Oh, I definitely did. No surprise Joel's apologies were all about him. "Then why did you call me Cynthia when you knew how much I don't like it?"

He chuckled lightly. "A sophisticated woman should have a sophisticated name. I am still me."

Yeah, he never knew the real me. My stomach flipped. In the middle of one of my worst days in recent history, Joel was giving me what I had needed most from him. It wouldn't be right to stay mad just because I was arguing with Blake. Unless… "Is this another attempt to get me back?"

"I wouldn't say no if you wanted to." He blew out a long breath. "Naw, that's not right. Truth is, I was seeing someone, and it ended in a disaster. Again. She told me to get therapy like you did. Guess I finally listened."

"Wow. Okay." The news gave me a burst of energy. I stood and moved through my living room and kitchen, stopping at the sliding door to look out over my backyard. It was my place of peace. "You like this therapist then."

"I've seen a couple, but this new one is good. He uh… While digging through the crap in my head, he kind of helped me see our relationship from your perspective." He sniffed. "I fucked up, Cynth… Cyn."

I scoffed. Adrenaline spiked, and my chest hurt. Like someone picked the edge of a scab on my heart. I didn't know if I could live in a world where I didn't despise this man. Part of me wanted to run away and hide. If that was the case, then I hadn't healed from him after all. If you're going to do this, be straight with him. "Yeah, you fucked up big time. Made me think everything wrong in our marriage was my fault, including your affair."

"You know, I wouldn't trade my kids for the world. But in hindsight… I should have calmed the fuck down. Mother had… No, can't use her as my excuse anymore either." A long pause followed, and my heart felt like the scab was being slowly ripped off, only I didn't know what I would find underneath. My hands sweat, and my phone almost fell to the floor. He mumbled something like, "You can only change yourself." Then he said, "I allowed the pressure of family expectations get to me, and I lost sight of what—no who—was supposed to be my priority. You should've come first, and I made you last. Then I dumped it all on you."

"I felt like a broodmare. A broken one at that." I tried to stifle a sob when he whimpered at my words. It inelegantly burst through anyway. We both cried quietly for a few minutes. Whether it helped him, the honesty came as a relief for me. I discovered the wound underneath my heart's scab was gone. Healed. Renewed. In the revelation, I also recognized Joel's sincerity. "I-I forgive you."

He whispered, "Thank you. It means the world, gorgeous."

The words settled over me like a warm hug. Joel had used the word gorgeous as my nickname when we dated. It became a second name, like how Blake called me Sparky. When Joel stopped using it, I knew our marriage was in trouble. The name, however, didn't excite me the way it had when he was wooing me. It remained a fond memory of days gone by.

Sparky was who I wanted to be now, who I had become. I liked the woman Blake saw. He didn't have to be corrected about who I was. He recognized me.

Then I knew I needed to tell Joel. "You should know… I'm seeing someone. Blake, actually… from the restaurant when you drank yourself into oblivion. We knew each other before that night. We'd dated a few years earlier and got back together a few months ago. At least, I think we're together." My voice cracked. "We had a fight this morning, and I left."

"Did… did you break up?"

"No. I don't know." Dammit, I sounded so mousey. Insecure. I couldn't believe I was telling Joel this, except he played a huge part in why I ran out of the condo. "Blake said he needed to think, and I didn't want to fight in front of his daughter." Joel inhaled sharply, and my heart squeezed from the pain. An old pain. The beats felt off, like they were skipping. "We fought over her. Over something I did. I…" I turned and paced through the house as emotions filled my throat. "I would've made a terrible mother."

"N-no," he gasped. "Is that… is that why you never had your own or… or adopted?" He cleared his throat, then yelled a muffled, "Fuck!"

Fresh tears fell as if I'd never cried over this before. Jeez, I wanted the waterworks to stop, but they cleansed me deep inside.

With a new, quiet resolve, Joel said, "You would've been the best mother. Sometime… a lot of times I wish we could go back. Bet you're wonderful with this guy's daughter."

"Apparently not, but I want to be." Joel's words were the gift I had needed for years. "Thank you."

"I mean it. I'm kicking myself, realizing I made you feel this way." His voice wobbled again. "Does he at least love you better than I did?"

I pondered the question for a minute. "He does." Even in an argument, he did. In my heart, I knew what he said had come from his fears and not from a judgment against me.

As if he could read my mind, Joel said, "Then Blake knows what a treasure he has. Your love is… He better not take it for granted like I did."

"Thank you. That's very kind. And Joel… thank you for calling. It means the world."

"Didn't expect it to be so…" He chuckled lightly before sniffling hard. "Yup, that was a dumb assumption."

"Clearing away all the garbage is a lot of work." And huge relief. "I hope you finally find your person."

The line went quiet, and the little spider caught my eye again. It crawled across the crown molding, looking for a new place to spin a web.

I started when Joel spoke again. "A part of me will always love you, C-Cyn."

Thanks to his call, the wounded parts of our relationship, memories so painful my brain couldn't focus on anything else, dissipated with the scab. In their place were the fond memories, ready for visiting without needing protection from more heartbreak. "You'll always have a place in my heart."

"We had some great times, didn't we?"

Great days and smiles I had suppressed for years roamed free again. A peace settled over me. "We had some amazing times."

Exhaustion washed over me after we hung up, despite my gratitude for this new turn. The day had been a lot to take. I collapsed into the spot on the sofa where I had been when Joel called, rewinding the morning's events, hoping what he said was true.

Blake didn't say we were over. He asked for time. He didn't tell me to go home either. I ran. Again. I feared escalating an argument in front of Olivia, because every time I had tried to stick it out with Joel, our fights whirled into a vicious tornado of hurt and accusations. But Blake didn't play those games. He had already proven he loved me better.

Damn, I was bad at relationships. The past me would have viewed our fight as a glaring sign of our incompatibility. Presently, I felt like—I groaned at the spider as it seemed to gather energy and spun away to a new corner to weave a clean new strand.

Blake didn't know how to see past his fear to forgive me. Yet I was afraid to repeat past pain to explain myself, especially since our fight had hit my rawest nerve. At least my talk with Joel helped heal that open wound. Renewed and resolved, I gave Blake his time and planned to call later, hoping we could meet for breakfast in the morning. I'd fight for us and show Blake how he was still a fantastic father.

Spent from the emotional upheaval, I fell into a light sleep when Kick burst through my front door. That's what I got for giving her a key. Her intrusion jolted me upright.

"Oh, sweetheart." Kick knelt next to me. She brushed my hair off my face. "I rushed over here as soon as I saw it… Look at your puffy eyes. Am I late?"

"Apparently." Kick and her blasted visions. A warning yesterday would have been nice. Last night had been perfect. "It was more of a big fight than a breakup." I reached for her cheek to reassure her. "Don't know why your vision seemed so traumatic." My breath hitched. "Then again, it was a doozer of an argument."

She sat back and scrunched her nose. "An argument?"

"Yeah. Blake and I were talking about whether Olivia could go to a dance with a boy, and… yada, yada, yada… I told him about the lipstick vibrator." I sighed and tugged on my small ponytail, pulling the end over my shoulder. "He lost his shit. Said he needed time to think. So I left." Guilt swept over me at the memory. "We made Livvy cry."

"Are you telling me"—Kick shifted onto her heels—"this morning was the first time Blake heard about her gift?"

"Well, yeah. It was a girls' moment." I leaned onto the armrest. "I was trying to be there for her. Like you and Rachel."

"Feck." Kick spat under her breath. She looked up at the

ceiling and chuckled sarcastically. "Guess I left out the part of the story where it took me two weeks to convince Shane that Rachel's bullet was an appropriate gift for his little girl." She rolled her eyes while she made air quotes.

"Now you tell me." I dropped my head into my hands and made a grumbling sound.

"I'm sorry. It's just—"

"You never talked about your fights with anyone. Including me."

Her hand came up and rubbed my knee. "I didn't want to be like my parents airing their dirty laundry all over town. You had enough on your plate after moving here and recovering from him-who-isn't-named. Plus Shane and I had been together for years by then. We'd built up trust in each other's judgment the hard way. You and Blake are—"

"New." I looked up, catching her warm, sympathetic smile. It helped more than her thumb circles did. If worse came to worst, I still had Kick and her family. Except I wanted my own. Somewhere along the way, I began to think of Blake, Olivia, and me as a family. It was beautiful. I wasn't afraid of it anymore either. "Speaking of Joel, he called me about an hour ago. He apologized. For everything."

"What?"

The part that meant the most, that I'd needed the most, came to me. "H-he thinks I would've been a great mother."

"Of course you would have…" Kick's expression darkened. "Have you believed you wouldn't have?" Her voice cracked. "This whole time? L-like you were punished?"

A tear dropped onto my cheek as I nodded, overcome by emotion.

She muttered, "If that were true, by your logic, I shouldn't be here." Her parents—particularly her mother—put her and her brother through hell growing up. I understood immediately what she meant. She looked up, tears matching mine, descending from her hazel eyes. "All this time, I believed you stopped pursuing motherhood because your desires had changed."

I sniffed. "They did because I made them. I wasn't pining over it, just…"

"Shit." She wrapped me in a hug. "Do you know how much you helped me with my kids? How much you mean to them?" Between Kick's health issues and grieving, the years following her husband's death had been hell on her.

"They also had your parents."

Kick pulled back. "What did we just say about my parents? Daddy tried, but he had to run interference between my momster and me. And the kids. It exhausted him. You filled in the gap, chica. You. When the kids grew sick of me or my advice, they turned to you. Still do." Her breath hitched as she tried to manage a sob. "Jaysus, have I never thanked you?" She swiped at her eyes.

"You have, in many ways." I dabbed at my eyes as well. "You had the kids buy me Mother's Day presents. They still send cards."

"Really? I didn't know." As she smiled, her expression filled with pride. Then she hugged me again. "Please kill the thought you would've sucked as a mom. No… don't kill it… abolish it. Obliterate it."

I chuckled at her indignation. "Okay." We laughed together for a few minutes.

When we quieted, she whispered, "The kids and I never would've made it without you."

God, first Joel, now Kick. Except the person who held my heart was still up in the air. I sniffed hard. "What should I do about Blake?"

"You still love him, right?"

"So much." My chin vibrated before the tears flowed again. I growled at myself, frustrated with them.

"Oh, sweetie." Kick let me cry on her shoulder like the thousands of other times we'd done this since our freshman year at Michigan State. "Remember when Thomas and I broke up?"

"Mm-hmm." I nodded on her sleeve. "But that was his stupidity, not yours."

"Good point." She sat back and grabbed my hands. "What about this? Do you regret giving Olivia the present?"

"Nooo," I drawled. "That's the thing. I wouldn't redo that. Going through this with her has brought back those memories. A little bullet would've helped when I was her age."

Kick dipped her chin in agreement. "Exactly." She shifted onto the sofa and faced me. "Now, what did you do wrong?"

I propped my elbow on the back of the sofa, dropping my head into my hand. "I should've cleared it with Blake first."

In my periphery, I caught my neighbor walking past my front yard with her little grandson. She watched him three days a week. I wondered what that would be like, helping Liv with her future child. Or supporting her if she didn't want one.

I wiped my cheeks. "I hurt his feelings, Kicky. Since we hooked back up, I've wanted to fix all his problems, make his life easier. And I scared him instead because I was afraid that he'd say no to the bullet."

"You realize Blake's a big boy, right? He's responsible for keeping his shit together."

"Of course, but he's had a hard—"

"No buts. When Blake found himself in a world of trouble, he turned to the person he knew would help him best… You. Help is the operative word there. He didn't ask you to take the burden away. That's him taking responsibility. Also, when he needed you at Christmas, he called you."

"Doesn't mean it was easy."

Kick squeezed my knee. "Blake chose to yell at you. He let insecurity or whatever the hell is his Achilles heel overtake him.

That's not on you. Also, I don't believe he wants to break up either. But you should expect an apology from him. You deserve to receive one as much as you need to give one."

I stared at her in awe. I had never experienced this dynamic with a man. Well, maybe my dad. Blake reminded me of Tatay more than Joel ever did. I scoffed at Kick. "You make it sound like it's possible to fight and not yell."

"You and I have been frustrated with each other countless times without raising our voices." Kick shuffled her curls at the back of her neck before giving me a soft smile. "We talk it out."

I stretched my arms over my head. Emotions were wreaking havoc on my back. "That's different."

"Not really. We give each other the benefit of the doubt, assume the other one had the best of intentions. Or at least a good reason for doing what we did. You and Blake need to learn how to do that." She leaned into her hand. "You had to see it in your parents. They were awesome together."

I waved her off. "My parents never fought."

Kick raised her brows impatiently, giving me pause.

"You think they did?"

She blinked. Then asserted. "Everyone does, chica."

"But they never yelled."

Kick tapped the edge of her nose, like we did in Charades.

"You think they argued without yelling." Her face brightened, and she rolled her hand for me to continue. "Annnd they gave each other the benefit of the doubt in their arguments."

She clapped like I'd won a prize.

"I should call Tatay and ask him for advice." Except I would have to keep the vibrator out of the conversation. I winced. Oh, how I wished I could talk to my mom again. I was grateful for her being at peace, but there were days.

Kick snapped her fingers. "That reminds me... my vision. It wasn't about you and Blake. Or Joel. It was Tatay." She rubbed her forehead. "I probably misinterpreted it."

A chill skated down my spine. "What about my dad?"

My phone rang, and I picked it up, expecting it to be my father because Kick's visions didn't play. Instead, my cousin's photo was on my lock screen.

I answered hesitantly. "Berno. What's up?"

"Uncle Paul's in the hospital. He had a heart attack, Cyn. He needs you to come home. We need you."

Chapter 45

And So It Goes

Blake

Each time I listened to her voicemail, I kicked myself for not answering the phone when Cyndi called. Her breath hitched before she spoke in a tiny voice. I wasn't sure which sound tore the bigger hole in my heart.

"Hey, honey." She gasped a few more times before gathering herself. "I didn't want to text, so this is me calling. I'm not running. But there's been an emergency." Then she broke into a sob that ripped my soul. "My dad had a heart attack, a- and I have to go to him, Blake. I'm so sorry. I'll call as soon as I can. Promise." After a pause, she added, "I wish you were with me, even still mad. But don't worry. Focus on your court date. I'll be okay." Her voice broke on the last word. If she lost her father a year after her mother, Cyndi wouldn't be all right. Not by a long shot. She needed me, and I was stuck in Raleigh. After a few stuttered breaths, she whispered, "Love you. Both of you. And… I'm so sorry for running out and not talking to you about… you know."

And now my woman was probably sitting in a cold, antiseptic-smelling hospital room with a twice-broken heart, hoping her father would wake up. If that didn't set my shit straight, nothing did. I listened to the message again, twisting the knife a little more. Because I hadn't dealt with my issues, I hurt the woman I loved. I called her right after listening to the message and several more times since, but she must have been busy with her father. God, I hoped they were all right.

The alarm on my phone rang, breaking me out of my navel-gazing funk. I had a lot to make up for, starting with my daughter. I called up to her, "Hustle up, Sparrow. We're leaving for Sofia's soon."

It was the night of the spring dance, the kickoff to her school's spring break and the impetus for my fight with Cyndi. She was supposed to take the girls to the event, and Sofia's mom planned to bring them home. So I switched shifts with Jay and filled Cyndi's shoes for the night.

Originally, the three of us were supposed to spend the next week in Phoenix, celebrating my fake birthday and watching Juniper's hoop dance competition. Then my accounts were frozen in the lead-up to my last court date. Cyn and I quickly adjusted and planned a staycation with Liv. Now it was just my daughter and me for a week. Only she wouldn't speak to me.

Olivia came to the top of the stairs in her pajamas. "I'm not going to the dance. Sof knows, so her mom's taking her and taking Cyndi's shift as chaperone."

Fuck. I padded up the steps and gestured for Liv to sit on the top step with me. "Is this because of the argument?"

She scowled at me. "You mean the fight? Yes."

"Sparrow, honey—" My shoulders fell.

"I don't want to go with a boy if it upsets you. I don't feel like going anywhere." Her chin quivered. "I want Cyn back."

I stretched out my arm, pulling her in for a hug. "We still have her. She just needs to take care of her father while he's in the hospital. It's not like when he had the flu. Heart surgery is a major operation."

"But I didn't get to apologize before she left."

I moved back and looked down to catch her eyes. "For what?"

"I don't know." She squeaked as a tear fell from her lashes. "I spied on you."

"During the argument? You heard what we were talking about?"

More tears flew as she nodded. "You were yelling, not talking."

"I'm sorry." I pulled her in to my side and kissed her head. "You didn't do anything wrong."

She sniffed. "I've been mad… about my period and stuff. If I hadn't freaked out about it, Cyndi wouldn't have tried to make me feel better with that…"

I scratched my temple, wincing. Cyn was right about me manning up. Liv was growing up despite my wishes. "It wasn't your fault. Nothing was."

"Doesn't matter. I threw it out. Now you can get back together."

Double fuck. I tipped my head back, taking the verbal gut punch, seeing my assholery in full. "You didn't have to do that. The more I think about it, the more that… t-toy"—I swallowed hard—"s-sounds all right. L-like a good idea, I mean."

Why did parenting have to be so painful? I rubbed my chest, wishing Cyndi was here. If anyone could teach Olivia to be strong and brave, it was her. And I had almost run her off. I squeezed Liv's shoulder. "Besides, Cyn will be back."

"But I want to be there with her. You know, like she came to us in Phoenix? Why can't we go to her in Michigan?"

Because I didn't have the funds. Except Liv didn't know about that. I'd kept it all from her under the guise of protection. Only, it wasn't her I was protecting. It was my fucking fragile ego, wishing I could always be the best dad. I blew out a long breath. "It's time to let you in on what's been happening at the restaurant."

"Hello?"

I reached Cyndi after an exhausting talk with Olivia. Despite the emotional drain that comes with a confession, she had listened with grace and maturity. Her anger over what happened and the promise she still loved me, letting me know I'd done the right thing. It also gave me the courage to call my lady.

"Were you crying?" I asked her.

"No, I haven't slept much." Then her voice cracked. "He looks so fragile. Blake, I'm scared."

"Oh, honey. I'm sorry. About all of it. Not that we can talk now, but…" I bit my tongue. Cyndi shouldn't be thinking about that. Not until Dr. Sendaydiego was out of danger.

"I want to talk about it. I'm sorry too. So sorry."

God, I wanted to hold her so badly my arms ached. "Don't apologize. It's all on me."

She sniffed and cleared her throat. "No. I overstepped. I should've talked to you first." Her voice squeaked. "I'm sorry for taking liberties I don't have. It was presumptuous."

One of the succulent plants I bought her sat on the night-stand that was now Cyndi's. It seemed to reach out to me. Or my head was all screwed up with emotions. I settled against the headboard on her side of the bed. "Please presume with Liv. Do I wish you had explained it to me first? Yes. But I've been a stubborn ass about her puberty experience. In denial, you know?"

Cyndi made a noise of agreement.

I cut to the chase. "I need you, Sparky. So does my girl. If

Gia were here, we'd still need you." The phone filled with the sound of light crying. "Please don't cry, honey."

"My emotions are raw." She lowered her voice to a whisper. "Are you sure? Don't you think I would've sucked as a mother? I think that's why…"

Ah, hell. "Are you kidding me?" I rubbed my temple with my free hand. "You would've been the best mother. God, to have a baby with you…" Instantly images of Cyndi with a baby bump came to mind. With my hand on her stomach, she smiled up at me, glowing. Just as fast, I realized we were younger—the age I was when Olivia was born. And that was that. We had enough in our lives. No crying over what could have been. I cleared my throat. "I need you, Spark. So does Sparrow. She loves you. She was scared—"

"Because I left again?"

"I explained what happened, and she understands about your dad."

"That's good. Tell her I love her, okay?"

"Sure. She's sleeping now."

"How was the dance?"

I reflexively made a face even though Cyndi couldn't see it. "She didn't go."

"No—" She sounded on the verge of crying again. I resolved to never put her in another situation where she might cry. It was the worst sound ever.

"It's all right. We had a talk instead. You'd probably say it was long needed."

"Yeah?"

"I told her about Kramer." Cyn hummed with sympathy. "Yeah… she handled it well." I laughed. "You probably wouldn't have been surprised, but that's what you've been telling me, isn't it?"

"I suppose." A smile filled her tone. "What did Livvy say?"

Emotions overtook me, and I couldn't speak for a minute. "She's on my side."

"Of course she is. Why do you sound surprised?"

"I worried she would look at me differently." I cleared my throat. "Disappointed. My biggest fear is that she'll see me as a loser."

"Blake…" Cyndi sighed heavily.

We didn't have to talk about the origins of that problem. We already knew. Knowing it didn't make it evaporate. "The way they look at you when they're babies, like you're a god… it's addicting. I'd do anything to keep that look on her face."

"I know. I've seen it. It doesn't have to go anywhere. I didn't lose that with my dad, even after he became human." Her voice broke again. "That's why this heart attack business is so hard."

I slammed my fist into my thigh. "Dammit. I'm sorry. I shouldn't have burdened you with this. We can talk later."

"No. It helps to work out our disagreement. It is better, right?"

"Hell, yeah. You are and have always been perfect."

She chuckled. "We should talk about your skewed perspective. Or you're lying so I won't cry anymore."

"Never. I mean it."

"Thank you."

The hum was back in her voice. It traveled to my core. I wanted, no, needed, her at home with me, but I wouldn't voice it.

"What's going on with your dad?"

There was a shifting sound on Cyndi's end, like she was getting up from one of those vinyl chairs in a patient's room. "He's okay. We'll go home in a couple of days as long as nothing new happens."

"That's a relief. I'm looking forward to meeting him in person."

"Dad asked about you and Liv. He felt bad for taking me away. I didn't tell him about… you know."

"Because you didn't want to upset him." I ran my hand over my head, desperate to hold her. To help.

"I would love that," she whispered. Apparently I had spoken the words. "Oh…" More movement came across the line. "Shh. I'll get her."

"What?"

"Oh, hey. Tatay's up. I have to talk to the nurse."

Selfish idiot. "Sure. Go, honey. Keep me posted all right?"

"Yeah. Thanks for calling."

"Call me anytime, day or night. Got it? Love you."

"Love you too. Thanks, big guy."

Chapter 46

Courage

Blake

Olivia sat on a stool in the back corner of the bar at the Garage. Technically, it was illegal for her to be there, but we were between the lunch and dinner crowds, meaning we were officially closed even though the doors were unlocked. The staff complained about our grumpiness, so I played with the bar ingredients and made Liv mocktails. It was our way of hiding in the corner, and I hoped it would cheer my daughter up a bit. When we made cocktail pairings with Felix's menu a focus of the Garage's mission, my curiosity about the science of mixology was piqued. Lately, I unofficially apprenticed under Ryder to relieve stress. He was on his lunch break, so I experimented.

I set the glass in front of my daughter. She tasted it carefully.

"Well?"

Liv pressed her lips together. "Too much elderflower syrup."

"She has a sensitive palate. Too bad we can't give her alcohol yet," Ryder said.

Where had he come from? I narrowed my eyes. "No, it's not too bad. She's twelve."

He raised his hands in surrender. "Just saying… the kid would be an asset behind the bar. When it's time, of course."

"What brings you back so soon anyway?"

Ryder shrugged. "The delivery driver texted that he's running early."

"Then why aren't you at the dock?"

He gave me some serious side-eye. "When's Cyn coming back? You two are ogres supreme without her around."

Liv sniffed, and I sighed. We'd become a mess without our Spark. "She's getting her father ready for rehab down here, but she needs to settle the property. Apparently he's…" I searched Olivia's face for the word.

"She calls him a gentleman farmer." She slid her glass back to me.

I snapped my fingers. "Right. Anyway, her father has animals and land." The image coming to mind made me shudder. That had never been my desire. "He can't be stressed, so it's all on her." Cyn needed rest before she left in a rush. Her voice sounded more tired every time we talked. It was killing me to have to stay away. So I did what I could for the moment, which was to add a touch of soda to Liv's tumbler before handing it back for another taste.

A man clearing his throat captured my attention. He had entered through the patio door, and I didn't see Thomas Harrison approach.

"Oh hey, man. What brings you in?" A panic dropped over me. "It's not Cyndi, is it?" I pulled my phone out of my pocket and made sure it worked. We texted multiple times a day in addition to our video chats. But she also stayed in constant contact with her best friend.

Harrison's answer surprised me. "You have a persuasive daughter." He winked at Olivia. "Congratulations on making the principal's list this quarter."

"How do you know——"

"I… ah… might have called Miss Kick." The corner of her mouth ticked up in a sheepish smile.

Thomas chuckled. "You have good instincts, young one. Kick demanded I give you this."

"What…" He handed me a business card. "Is this?"

Harrison leaned against the counter. "That's the number for my pilot. He's waiting for your call."

"Why?" My eyes narrowed when I caught Liv's wide grin. What the hell was she up to?

"Kick already knew how hard the past week has been for Cyndi, then she talked to Miss Brady, here…" He slid onto the stool next to her. "The plane's available, and we're planning to use it to bring Cyn and Dr. S. back down already. The airfield is about thirty minutes from the hospital, so you'll have to rent a car or order a ride."

"Please, Dad. Pleeease." Olivia bounced so hard she almost fell off the stool.

Harrison and I laughed at her, breaking the tension and lowering my automatic resistance to help.

I rubbed my temple, contemplating the schedule. I still had a court date in the morning. "I'm aware of all this but——"

"You'll be doing me a favor," Thomas cut in when he sensed my hesitation. He tapped the bar. "I know you're closed, but is it possible to get a soda?"

"Are you kidding?" I poured a tall glass. "I'll make you a meal myself if you're hungry. I still don't see how I'm doing you a favor."

He took a pull of the drink and sighed in relief. "I owe Kick. Plus she's worried sick about Cyndi, but she can't get away. Then Olivia"—he looked at her and smiled—"mentioned that she's on break. Well, happy wife and all that." Harrison spread his hands like loaning out a jet was no big deal. He breathed in and closed his eyes. "Is that pulled pork I smell?"

"Fresh from the smoker." The sweet, woodsy aroma equaled the Garage to me. My head swirled from the back-and-forth of subjects. "Want me to have Felix fix you up?"

"Would it be any trouble?"

I tipped my head back and laughed. "You're offering the use of your plane to me. What else do you want? Fee's banana pudding should be ready."

"Any chance it's gluten-free for Kick?" He leaned onto his fist.

"Uh, no. But our gluten-free baker brought in a carrot cake this morning."

"Yes, to all of it. If it could be to go." Thomas's hand flew to his heart. "I've had a taste for barbeque for weeks. Thank you."

"Yay!" Liv threw her hands in the air.

I shook my head in disbelief. "It's a generous offer. The problem is… I have a court date tomorrow. How long will your plane be available?" My shoulders fell at the idea of disappointing my Sparrow. Myself as well. Not to mention how much Cyn needed us.

Thomas rubbed his chin. "The sooner you can go, the better. I can't tie up the crew for long."

Liv's chin quivered, and mine felt like doing the same. "I'll call my lawyer."

"Let's talk, Daddy-o." My bed bounced when Olivia flung herself on it. She looked up at me expectantly.

I dropped a rolled-up shirt into my suitcase and folded my arms. "All right. What's up?"

The good news was my law team didn't need me in the courtroom. I earned brownie points by recording Alan Kramer, giving my team undeniable proof that I wasn't a part of the embezzling scheme. They were fine with explaining my absence as a family emergency. They planned to ask for a delay, but it would be fine if they had to proceed. At least we would have the final judgment. Peace had settled over me, and I trusted everything would work out. That's what the right priorities can do for a man.

Getting to Cyndi was my focus now. Liv and I were so excited we hardly ate any dinner. We were leaving right before dawn. I wouldn't sleep much either.

"What're you gonna do when we get there?"

I shrugged. "Ring the doorbell."

Liv narrowed her eyes. "Can you not?"

"Fine." I plopped down beside her and mussed her hair. "What's cooking in your brilliant mind?"

She held up a trench coat, her face filled with excitement. "Well…"

Chapter 47

I Was Made For Loving You

CYNDI

A hard driving beat interrupted the morning news as I washed breakfast dishes. The Kiss song playing in the background of an economic report didn't make sense. I turned off the news, but the song played on. In fact, it came in through the windows in the breakfast nook. Dad had been home for two days, and we planned to leave for North Carolina tomorrow morning.

Tatay didn't listen to Kiss, plus he was in the bathroom. He didn't have any reason to be in the driveway either. His job was to rest up for the flight.

When I moseyed over to the bay window, my hands flew to my mouth in shock. Blake was leaning against the hood of an unfamiliar car, holding a speaker above his head while wearing a trench coat. Olivia folded her arms in disappointment.

I laughed at the comical sight as I opened the side door. My very own Lloyd Dobler from Say Anything. This had

Olivia written all over it, especially given the pained look on Blake's face.

"Interesting song choice." I raised my voice to speak over the crisp, spring wind, then pressed my lips together to keep from laughing. Except it didn't work. I ended up doubled over, giggling at the two of them. The song ended and moved on to "Build a Bitch," and I barked a laugh before Blake shut off the speaker in a panic.

Olivia threw her hands in the air and stomped her foot. "He wouldn't listen." She ran to me as I descended the steps and wrapped her up in a hug. Her strawberry shampoo mixed with the scent of wet mud in the air, making her seem more childlike. "It's a grovel. Like Lloyd from our movie."

"I see that." I kissed her head and tugged on her braid. "Nice touch, little chica." Her smile beamed up at me. "What happened to the song from the movie?"

Blake trudged over to us, grumbling, "My grovel. My song."

I raised an eyebrow teasingly. "But… Kiss?"

"It's what worked for young Blake. That's the point, right?" He straightened his back. "No wimpy love songs about eyes and shit."

I bit my tongue, loving the chance to mess with him. Needing to after the torture of leaving with our relationship in the air.

He hugged me and made a rumbling sound in his chest. "Do you want a do-over?"

"Not on your life." I wiggled an arm free and brought his face close for a kiss. "Thank you. I missed you both so much."

To my surprise, Olivia didn't complain or make a face. She stayed within our circle, smiling at us. I gave her another squeeze. "It means the world."

"Who do we have here?" my father asked, stepping

through the screen door. His eyes landed on Liv and a smile appeared, replacing the painful looks I'd grown used to seeing in the past week. We walked over to him, and he reached for Blake's girl. "Cyndi has shown me many pictures of you."

Olivia shyly tucked some hair behind her ear. "Hi."

"Dr. S." Blake shook Tatay's hand. "Good to meet you in person. It's also a relief to see you on the mend."

My dad had the look of someone who'd won the lotto after years of hoping. "Mr. Brady."

"Call me Blake, sir. Please."

Dad put his arm around me and spoke into my ear in a stage whisper. "I knew you would find a good American boy."

Sunrays broke through the cloud cover as my gaze landed on Blake's. Despite standing on the land where I'd grown up, he was home. His full lower lip hung slightly, like he'd been dumbfounded by my father's approval. The high cheekbones and set shoulders showed off his pride about being accepted. I wanted to do inappropriate things to him but restrained myself given our company.

I settled for stroking his hand. "He really is." Without looking away from my man, I added, "Livvy, why don't you go inside with Tatay? We have pancakes leftover from breakfast. Bet they're calling your name."

Olivia snickered.

"What's so funny?" my dad asked. "Her pancakes are delicious."

I had a feeling about what had tickled Liv's funny bone, and I answered for her. "Taytay is the nickname for her favorite singer, Taylor Swift."

She nodded and laughed harder.

"Is this Taylor boy famous? A super handsome cutie?"

"Can you not? My stomach's going to hurt from laughing." Olivia held her middle while she pulled herself together. "She is the most famous singer in the world. The best singer-songwriter of our generation."

"Your generation?" I looked up at Blake, who simply shook his head. He had promised to get them tickets to a concert the next time the singer came within driving distance. They didn't know I had already bought some for the Detroit concert for the three of us, plus Berno's daughter, Willow.

My dad waved Liv over and turned for the door. "Tell me about this young woman, and I'll introduce you to Robert Seger. Now there's a singer-songwriter." He laid his arm across her shoulder and turned his head back. "Let's give these two some privacy. Oh, and why don't you call me Lolo?"

As they disappeared into the house, it hit me that I wasn't the only one receiving a lifelong wish. "He's in grandpa heaven. We might not get her back."

Blake raised an eyebrow in question and muttered, "Lolo?"

I went up on my toes and whispered, "It means grandpa."

"Mm." Blake engulfed me in his trench coat, hugging me tightly. "He's really sweet. Can't say I'd mind if he entertained Sparrow for a bit. Dr. S. did a fantastic job with you." My arms stretched around his waist as we gave each other strength. I inhaled his woodsy scent and relaxed for the first time in what felt like forever. I had the impression he was doing the same. "Need some time with my woman."

After a minute, I tipped my head back. "You know, there's a newer song called, 'I was made for loving you.' Bet you'd like it as much." Despite my deadpan face, I hoped he heard the mirth in my tone.

"Again, with the song." Blake chuckled, letting me know it landed how I intended it. "How about we agree to disagree? Which leads to my point." He looked around. "Is there some-where we can talk?"

I pointed to the closest outbuilding. "Mom's greenhouse is

behind the shed." We walked with laced fingers across the gravel drive. A whipping wind made it hard to speak, but words could wait for the refuge of the hothouse.

After I entered the code, Blake opened the door and gestured for me to lead the way again. I steered him to a table where my parents used to eat their lunch in the spring, when my mother tended her seedlings. Now the space seemed… expectant. I sat in one chair and Blake used the other.

"I should have cleared Olivia's gift with you first."

"I overreacted," he said at the same time. We laughed at ourselves and started again. "I'm sorry, Cyn."

I reached for his hands. "Me too. So much."

He let out a relieved breath. "I'll do better. However, your joke about my song choice reminds me"—he kissed my knuckles—"I'd rather fight with you every day for the rest of our lives than pretend I can live without you. Especially since fighting with you makes me a better man."

"Oh, honey." I pulled his hands against my heart. "I can't live like that—"

"But—" Blake's hopeful expression fell.

"Hear me out…" I cleared my throat. "We should learn how to fix our bad habits so we don't jump to negative conclusions. What about couples' counseling?"

He thoughtfully stroked his chin. "That's… heavy. Are you sure?"

"You're heavy. I mean, important. You and Liv are the most important. I want to do right by both of you."

"You have." He leaned into his hand. "You do."

"Our fight said otherwise. You knee-jerked yelled because of your insecurities. I knee-jerk fled for self-protection. We can do better." I moved around the table, settling in Blake's lap. I brushed his hair off his forehead. "Have you had a bad counseling experience?"

"No. It's just"—he snuggled into my shoulder—"the old man always said head shrinkers were for the weak."

"And what do we think of his advice now?"

He smirked. "All of it was shit."

"That's right." I bent and kissed him. "Mm. I missed you."

"So you said." Blake shifted like he was preparing for a deeper kiss.

I leaned back, determined to get one last point in. "I promise to never overstep with your daughter again."

"No, honey." He sighed. "I listened to what you said… about Sparrow growing up, and… you're right. I should trust your judgment. Girls should get the same respect young boys do. What came out was my fear."

"We should talk about her more. Be purposeful about these years."

"We will. I'm grateful she has a wonderful woman to guide her again." Blake kissed me quickly. "Can we add one more item to our agenda?"

His words and faith in me had me floating on a cloud. I'd promise him anything. "What's that?"

"I get what you said about not wanting to be a Brady—"

"Blake… that was also my fear speaking."

He pressed a finger to my lips, stopping further protest. "I don't need a signed contract for you to be mine, but I would like it if you… moved in with us." He scrunched his face, looking so vulnerable I wanted to give him the world. "Or we could buy a house together. One with a yard."

"Whoa."

"It's too early. I'm sorry."

"Not at all." I shifted to straddle Blake's lap and tapped my heart. "I'm surprised how perfect it feels in here. Besides, I love the neighborhood by Olivia's school." I draped my arms over his shoulders and played with his hair. "You might be brilliant."

The sweetest smile spread across his face. "Might be?" Blake grabbed my ass and made me grind against him. "Mm… Yeah… I just… don't want to split up the week anymore." He closed his eyes. "Need you in my bed every night."

"Ooh." My breath caught as he hit the spot that had been aching for him. "Wha…" I reached for his hands, stilling them. "What about Tatay's rehab?"

"Damn. Right." He clicked his tongue. "When Dr. S. is back on his feet, you're all mine. Deal?"

"I'm already all yours." I slowly undid the buttons on his shirt, taking time to appreciate each revealed inch. When my fingers followed the trail my eyes made, Blake's pec muscle flinched like he was in pain. I felt tape from a bandage and raised my brow in question. His jaw flexed when I lightly traced the square. "Are you hurt?"

He shifted uncomfortably. "You can pull it back and see for yourself."

The area shone with a healing salve over his tattoo. He'd added to the sparrow representing Olivia. The branch the bird perched on had been changed. My eyes filled with tears. "You added sparks." The thin branch looked like a lit sparkler now.

"It's you." Blake relaxed when I gently replaced the gauze. Then he added, "It's also how I see the two of you. The bird is resting on the spark, getting ready to take off. That's what you've become for Olivia, and I'm grateful for it, Cyn. You're not only my refuge. You're also Liv's."

My tears landed on my lips as I smiled at him. "You know, you had me with the Kiss song." I finished with his shirt and swept it off his arms, going to work on his belt and pants.

He lifted for me, a broody smirk crossing his face. "Here?"

"You just tattooed me on your body. Damn skippy, we're getting it on." I leaned back. "Unless it'll bother your skin. We can wait or—"

"Don't you dare." He set me on the table and shifted down to his knees. "But I get first dibs."

As I wiggled off my lounge pants, his lids dropped to a sultry half-mast, watching me. "God, I love you."

I stopped moving and cheekily said, "I know."

Blake tipped his head back and barked a laugh at the Han Solo reference. Then we steamed up the greenhouse.

Epilogue

Home

Cyndi

The news made me so giddy I burst into Blake's office before my brain registered his phone call. I tried to stand in the corner, patiently waiting for him to hang up. Emphasis on tried. More likely, I looked like a cat about to pounce. In a futile attempt to be quiet, I ran back to the hallway and smiled at Carol Page, waving her closer.

"I should let him work," she whispered.

I grabbed her arm, then let go, afraid I'd squeezed her too hard in my excitement. "Please wait. He'll want to hear about it from you."

"But you did all the work."

I scoffed. Carol came up with the brilliant idea that I should have had.

"Can I call you back, Eric? My lady needs me," Blake said. He ducked his head into the hallway and eyed us suspiciously. "Thanks, man." He put his phone in his pocket and chuckled. "Why are you so antsy?"

I woke up my laptop in my arms and carried it to his desk.

His gaze lasered in on my mile-wide grin as he looked between Carol and me. "What's this?"

"A GoFundMe page." He gave me a look saying, duh, so I continued. "For the restaurant. Well, for you, really, but for the restaurant. You know?"

He rubbed his temple, like he didn't compute.

I put an arm around Carol's shoulders and pulled her close. "You know how regional newspapers picked up the Oakville Weekly's article on your embezzlement case?"

"Of course. My phone's ringing off the hook from the exposé's momentum."

Not only that, Blake had increased his assistant's hours to full time to handle the extra attention. She helped me convince him to do an interview with a local TV reporter. That made the Garage so popular reservations were booked out for months. Not that I blamed anyone. He'd been swoony as hell on camera. Caught up in memories of my man on TV, I stopped talking.

Blake snapped his fingers, startling me.

Carol spoke up instead. "Cyndi set up the page to help with your tax penalties."

"But it was your idea to begin with," I insisted. Blake raised his brows at both of us. "Anyway…" I made a convention-show-model-demonstrating-a-product move with my hands. "It's more than funded. Isn't it great?" I jumped up and down in a not-so-sophisticated-show-girl way. Blake's eyes following the movements of my boobs suggested otherwise. "It's like a modern day It's a Wonderful Life."

Carol watched us with a beaming smile on her face. I had grown to love her in the past few months and really loved having her nearby.

Blake put on his reading glasses and read the screen. When his brows shot up to his hairline, I knew he'd discovered the important part. "You did this?" he asked Carol, leaning back with his hand over his mouth, taking it all in.

Carol blushed as emotions filled the office. "Like I said, your lady did all the work."

The money raised ended up big enough to cover the tax penalties and buy the space attached to the Garage. He and Felix had been dreaming about purchasing it to expand the kitchen and open a separate tavern. I wrapped my arms around Blake as he shuddered with emotion.

In a gravelly voice, he said, "You eat free for the rest of your life."

"Bless your heart." She chuckled.

I kissed his cheek. "She already does."

"Right. Then you get free parties... whatever you want." Blake leaned back and looked up at me. "How did it come about?"

"Carol asked me for help with it." I squeezed her hand. "The story enraged her as much as me."

"You left out important details when you confided in me, young man."

I giggled at Blake's guilty expression.

"It's not like I—"

I cut him off with a kiss. "We know. Your customers were eager to help. The television appearance didn't hurt either." I popped my brows at him.

"Stop." He grinned and dropped his chin. "Good thing I have Sparrow. She won't stop complaining about how embarrassing my interview was." We all laughed at that. Older girls had been steadily coming up to Olivia to tell her how hot her dad was.

I wrapped my arm around his neck, the desire to touch him overwhelming me. The feeling hit me a lot since we'd come back from Michigan.

"Are there tax implications for this? Don't people use the site for medical and funeral expenses?"

I kissed his cheek. "I'll handle it."

"Yes, you will." Blake brought me around to his side and hugged my waist. "Kramer inadvertently did me a solid." I moved back and met his gaze, confusion surely on mine. He shrugged and said, "He gave me back my Spark."

Carol cooed at his words, and I preened. My body felt like it was floating.

My broody grump had become a swoony mush ball.

"Here, gentlemen. Thank you for taking care of the delivery."

"Wow. Thank you, Mr. Nez. It was our pleasure," one of the delivery men said.

Hearing someone else say Blake's original last name plastered a grin on my face. It sounded so right. All the legalese completed a week ago, making Blake officially a Nez again. His eyes shimmered yesterday when we signed the mortgage documents on our new home. It was the first big thing we'd done together and with his rightful name.

Out of respect for the Bradys, he kept Kurtis as a middle name. It showed more grace than I would have given them, but that was Blake.

The other delivery driver cleared his throat. "My anniversary is next month. Can I use this to surprise my wife?"

"Absolutely. Congrats, man," Blake answered. The men stood in the foyer of our new house, around the corner from the dining room where I was listening. I wished I could see what they were doing, but I couldn't take my eyes off our new table and chairs. "Tell you what, call this number and tell Meredith that Boss said to give you table ten. It's my favorite."

"Boss, huh?"

"You know it."

I chuckled quietly, imagining Blake giving the driver a wink and the driver—I think his name was Eddie—puffing out his chest at the idea of being Blake's special guest. Months after his interview, the story still circulated the internet. All summer long, producers reached out to him for more show bookings. Others offered words of support. Needless to say, he'd become locally famous. Blake handled it with grace, but it wore on him. He hated the continuous reminders of what he still saw as a failure. My mantra to him stayed steadfast that it was a lesson learned. Also, Gabe and Sherry's company ran an audit of Blake and Felix's business-management style to make sure any other weaknesses were resolved.

Still, Blake couldn't wait for the spotlight to move away from him. Considering how much the restaurant's revenue had grown from the previous year, the rest of the staff didn't mind the fuss over my guy. Purchasing this house helped distract him as well. We had signed the papers on our new home in the morning and moved out of the condo in the afternoon.

When I volunteered at Olivia's field day in late May, Sofia's mom told me their next-door neighbor wanted to downsize. We jumped at the chance to be so close to Liv's best friend, not to mention living in one of the prettiest areas in Raleigh. Like the other homes around us, ours was about a hundred years old, in a deep lot. It was a Charleston low-country style, painted in a cream color with a black door and shutters. I couldn't wait to drink coffee on the upstairs porch and look out at the trees in the boulevard running down the center of our block. When I first moved here, I'd drive down these streets and dream about living in one of these beauties. I now owned my favorite one. So much had changed in a year.

I currently stood in front of a custom-made dining set from a local furniture maker—another bucket list item of mine. It's what the men had just delivered and set up for us. I ran my hand along the raw edge, running the length of the walnut top. Raw was kind of a misnomer. The craftsman made sure it was smooth to the touch. He used epoxy to simulate a dry riverbed running down the center of the table. The effect looked like the desertscapes in Arizona and was an homage to Blake's family. The table base was made of wrought iron. Mismatched chairs gave the room a rustic-meets-industrial feel. It was masculine and artsy.

The dining room itself faced the street, but no one would know at the moment. Overgrown bushes covered the windows up past the sash. I folded my arms as I stared at them menacingly. "I can't wait to cut these down," I said to Blake. Between the quiet at the entry and his yummy cologne reaching my nose, I knew he'd joined me. "Or pull them out altogether. What about low-growing gardenias?" I glanced at him over my shoulder. "They'll make the room smell like heaven next June."

"Whatever you want." He circled his arms around my waist. "It smells like heaven anytime you're in it."

I spun around and placed my hands around his neck. His eyes shimmered like mine. "Why are you emotional?"

"Why are you?" Concern quickly dried up his expression.

"Guess I'm still not used to hearing you called by your proper name." He nodded in agreement. I sensed it overwhelmed him and added. "Really cool how great Mrs. Brady's been about it."

Blake's shoulders softened as he sighed. "It's like a weight was lifted off her. She called and told me she was proud of me the day after the papers were filed. Then she asked about Sparrow."

"Wow." I wouldn't need to pop her one after all. Unfortunately, the topic of Blake's adoptive parents still triggered me. The visual of the lonely little boy in desperate need of a champion would live in my heart forever. The various blues in the epoxy glinted off the table, reminding me that his life was better than good now. The little boy had found his family… and me.

I brushed my fingers over the surface. "How awesome is this?"

"It's great." Blake held me at arm's length, letting his eyes slowly follow my body. The hungry look made previous thoughts flow down the proverbial river.

I pointed at his head. "What's going on in there?"

A wolfish smile tugged at his lips. "I love this dress."

"Wh-what?" It was a nothing-special sundress. I chose it for comfort since we moved on one of the hottest days of the year. He started unbuttoning it. "Oh… Really?" Our bed hadn't been set up yet, but Blake's determination to make it through all my tiny buttons told me he wasn't planning to go upstairs. "Here?"

He finished with my dress and spread it open, sighing at the sight of my underwear. The summer weight ensemble didn't leave anything to the imagination. "Let's celebrate."

"Again. Here?" I moved back, my hips bumping into the table. "On our spanking new custom build?"

He lifted me onto the top, slid my dress off my arms, and laid it out like a blanket before reaching behind me to unclasp my bra. "Now that you've put spanking on my mind, we'll add it to the celebration."

I squeaked. I'd been in a celebratory mood all week and planned a big surprise for my man in the evening. Olivia was staying with my dad, and they wouldn't be back until the morning. As Blake bent to suck a nipple into his mouth, my happy vibes turned into a sexy hum in my core. I grabbed his head and let the sensations from his tongue float through my body.

Blake pushed me back, kissing his way down my belly as he pulled off my underwear. "This is the first of many surfaces we'll christen." He pulled a chair under him with his foot. He licked through my sex and stopped to catch my gaze. Hunger in his hooded eyes made my breath catch. "Years from now, when we're old and gray—"

"We're gray now."

"Hush." He kissed down my thigh. "How about when the room is filled with grandchildren—"

"Filled? Do you have more kids besides Livvy?" I bit my lip in anticipation of Blake's reaction to my sass.

"Behave." He accented the order with a slap to my ass.

I hummed. "Never." The kisses traveled back up to the apex of my thighs. I hissed and shifted to give him better access.

"That's better." Blake added a finger to his play. "Now… when we're serving dinner for our extended family…"

The image he painted put a smile on my face.

"I'll look down the table… you in your seat…" Another lick and circle of my clit with his tongue. My body jolted with need. "Despite the guests… the loved ones… I'll think of you here. Now. Laid out before me."

"Oh my God." My core sought his lips, fingers. Release. Love.

"My favorite appetizer, meal, and dessert." Then he earnestly set to work until I was screaming in bliss.

We did all the things on our new table until Blake collapsed on top of me. I pushed him back into the chair and curled into him, straddling his lap as we gasped for air. He peppered my forehead with kisses, whispering praises for our present and promises for our future.

We stayed in each other's clutches, relishing this moment, until my foot cramped. I gingerly stood and reluctantly dressed again, wishing it was practical to unpack a house while naked. It would motivate us to quickly finish the move. The images made me giggle as I rebuttoned my dress.

"What's so funny?" Blake asked as he zipped his shorts. His shirt still lay on the floor in the opposite corner of the room.

"Oh my God!" Olivia shouted from the archway. Tatay stood behind her, an embarrassed smile on his face.

BLAKE

"You honestly expect me to consume food in there now?"

Despite moving to the sofas in the family room and away from the scene of our "crime," my daughter stayed furious. Cyndi and I sat together on the love seat that came from her living room, like two children awaiting their punishment.

Olivia recoiled when Cyn reached for her hand. She sighed and looked at her father, holding a mediator role between the three of us. "Dad?" she pleaded with an exasperated sigh.

It didn't help that Dr. S. kept snickering. He bit his lip, giving himself a moment before addressing Liv. "Iha, you must understand something very important…"

Using the endearment grabbed Sparrow's attention. It helped that Cyn's father was now her favorite grown-up. During Dr. S's rehab here, he and Liv developed a tight bond. So much so that when he recovered, he returned to Michigan to sort through his belongings and sell the farm. While he was gone, Cyndi did the same with her house and moved in permanently with us. Then her father bought her home in June, giving my daughter carte blanche to redo the upstairs to her liking.

He had spent the summer fully devoted to grandfather duties, like he was making up for lost time.

Olivia groaned. "I know Lolo… it's their house."

"Yes, but that's not my point," Dr. S. said. He raised his finger for emphasis. "Sex is how adults play." He patted the cushion in front of him. "As a doctor, I know this. As a man, I lived it."

"Oh Lord." Cyndi folded over from embarrassment, her arms on her knees.

"Tell them they're supposed to be in… you know…" Olivia pointed at the ceiling, where our bedroom was.

Dr. S. leaned toward Olivia. "Do you play only in your room?" She opened her mouth to answer, but he continued. "One day you'll understand how important it is to change things up with a partner."

Cyndi moaned as if she was in pain. "Mercy."

Her father smiled, enjoying himself. "The dining room will still be a dining room, like a greenhouse will still be a greenhouse, etc."

I barked a laugh. Dr. S. had known what we'd gotten up to the afternoon of our reunion. It made me wonder how often he'd done the same in the old outbuilding.

Cyndi turned her head toward me and murmured. "Make him stop."

"See? She gets it." Olivia pointed toward Cyn, making me laugh harder.

I KISSED SPARKY AS SHE LAY SOUND ASLEEP IN OUR NEW BED, A satisfied smile on her face. Considering I'd given her another round of orgasms, it was no surprise. After our scolding, Olivia found the laptop and riding helmet they had come back for. Then they left, giving us three days to set up the house and "play" in more rooms.

Above Cyndi's supine form hung a painting she surprised me with when we unpacked the bedroom. It was a reproduction of Gustav Klimt's The Kiss, but with Han Solo and Princess Leia as the couple. The muted colors reminded me of the Stormtrooper art I bought in Arizona. I considered hanging this painting alongside it in my office, but Cyndi reminded me so much of Leia it had to stay in the house. I kissed her temple and slid out of bed, too excited to sleep.

Navigating boxes in the hallway, I stopped at Olivia's new bedroom filled with cardboard and a bed I still needed to build. Her room would soon be decked out with equestrian decor, featuring the horse Cyn's father gave her. She was an American Paint with a sweet personality that had been Cyn's mother's. Aside from that, I just knew she let me pet her and feed her treats.

Between Cyndi, Carol Page, and Dr. S., I could now sit back and enjoy Liv's lessons. Dr. S. had fought with me to pay the fees until Cyn begged me to let him. According to her, he was making up for lost time. It lifted my heart to see them together. With my Gran, Aunt Donna, and Dr. S., along with Gianna's mother, Olivia was surrounded by loving grandparents.

Moving downstairs, I lifted a bottle of Grand Marnier from a box and padded into the kitchen. It was my mother's drink of choice, and she used to sneak me some when I was little. I found it perfect on a hot summer night. After pouring the spirit over ice, I kept moving. The weirdness of reorienting myself to a new place didn't bother me as much as it usually did. But this wasn't just a house. It was a home. A forever home.

We were already on my contractor's calendar to update the kitchen. During Liv's summer break, we deepened our bond by cooking together. I envisioned the new, bigger space. We planned to knock down a wall and turn the galley layout to a full U-shape with a center island. Cyndi clapped when she saw the plans for a walk-in pantry. The renovations at the Garage didn't put as big a smile on my face as her simple glee had.

The breakfast nook, however, was perfect as is. It reminded me of the one at the Sendaydiego's in Michigan. Only, instead of looking over a field, it opened to a backyard garden. I lifted the sashes of the bay windows and inhaled deeply before sitting on the built-in bench to relax. A full moon illuminated our private oasis. Flowers that Cyn said were coneflowers impressed me with their ability to thrive in the August heat with colors in white, pink, and purple. While they seemed to sleep at night, the late-blooming gardenia bushes filled the yard with a wonderful scent.

I couldn't wait to build a vegetable garden at the back of our lot. Gia's mother promised to show Olivia and me the secret to growing her prized tomatoes next spring.

As a fox made its way around the bushes, I wondered about kismet or serendipity or whatever. I called it life working itself out thanks to perseverance and the willingness to grind. A healthy dose of luck also helped. Take this house, for instance. Thanks to Cyndi receiving her insider's tip, it never went on the market.

Still antsy, I scooted out of the nook and moved to the screen porch. The warm, orange liquid tasted smooth on my tongue and complemented the floral scents floating on the night breeze. I checked the time on my phone and dialed it.

"Hey, coz." Sherry's greeting halted the marching ants in my stomach.

This was why I couldn't sleep. My news didn't want to wait. "Is this a good time?"

"Sure. I walked in the door a minute ago."

"Shit." Should have known better. "You're probably tired. I'll call back tomorrow."

"Don't you dare." I loved how she talked to me like a big sister—or how I imagined a big sister would. "Silly me drank an iced coffee this afternoon, so I'm awake. Sounds like you have tea, so you better spill it."

"You know… when I was a kid, I wanted a big sister."

"Blake…" Sherry's voice wavered. "Somewhere, deep down… you remembered." She sniffed. "Hope you didn't call to make me cry. That would be a mean little cousin thing to do."

In the months since meeting in person, Sherry and I had grown close. My auntie and Gran too, but I could talk to my cousin about everything. And I was bursting to tell her this. "My new ID arrived yesterday. It's official."

"You're a Nez again," she breathed into the phone.

I sipped my drink and swallowed the lump in my throat. "Yep." My inability to stop smiling made my cheeks hurt as I signed my proper name on all the mortgage papers earlier in the day.

"Dammit, you are making me cry." She sniffed as she laughed. "What about Liv? Did you get her name worked out?"

"We did." The lawyers must have performed magic or did a voodoo ritual to make that happen. "Gianna's family had no problem with it when I offered to hyphenate her last name. Sparrow's thrilled with it, although yesterday she complained about how long it is now." The ice clinked against my glass as I swirled the remnants around. "She's officially Olivia Rose Ciccio-Nez."

Sherry squealed, and I pulled the phone away from my ear, laughing. "She'll have to decide what to do with all that when she marries." If she does.

"We need to celebrate with everybody. When can you come out?"

I blew out my breath. "School starts in two weeks, and we'll be knee-deep in renovations for a couple of months." The school calendar flipped through my memory like an old Roll-a-Dex. "There's a long weekend for Columbus Day."

"You mean Indigenous Peoples Day," she crisply said.

I smiled. "Exactly." Something else I wanted to do came to mind, and I asked, "Can you send the information to your jeweler friend?"

Sherry chuckled. "Which one?"

I didn't know there was more than one, but I didn't remember a name. I cleared my throat. "The one who uh… makes rings." My voice cracked on the last word as my stomach flipped.

"Rings?" The line went eerily quiet. The hum of neighborhood air conditioners filled the air, as if they cycled in sync. Sherry finally cleared her throat. "As in engagement rings?"

"Sort of?" I swallowed hard as my heart rate sped up. "Definitely special rings. Important rings." Cyn's description of a ring with turquoise and opal had stayed with me since our shopping trip to the Native Art Market. She had said Mexican fire opals were rare. "A custom one. It… it might be expensive."

Sherry squealed in my ear, making me laugh. I also checked the area for blood. It felt like she'd burst the drum. "Do it out here."

"That's my plan, but it might not be an engagement. You need to slow down."

"Why the hell wouldn't you want to marry Cyndi? She's wonderful."

Didn't I know it? "I'd have married her already, but she's gun-shy. I'm thrilled you like her. When she first met you, she was… intimidated."

"Yeah, thanks to my mom." Sherry clicked her tongue. "I loved her from the start. Mom thinks she's perfect for you now. You can tell her that."

"I will."

"So what's the ring for if there's no wedding?"

I scratched my temple as a light breeze blew hair across my forehead. "I didn't say there wouldn't be a wedding——"

"Coz…" Sherry warned.

"Fine." I laughed, wishing I had more liqueur to quell my nerves. "You know we're both in it for keeps." Sherry made a sound of agreement. "Well, last week, Olivia accidentally called Cyndi 'Mom'." Sherry gasped. "It was a slip, but it felt right for all of us, and it hit me… we are a family. If Sparky still doesn't want to sign a legal marriage contract, I'm fine with it. But I want to commemorate becoming a family. Does that make sense?"

"Stop making me cry." My cousin sniffed. Cyn had cried too. Hell, I teared up. "She's going to marry the hell out of you."

In the initial stages of buying our house, Cyndi mentioned it's easier to own property as a married couple. She blamed it on the religious influence of our state lawmakers or some such. I wasn't sure if it made her want to be compliant or more rebellious.

"If someone can make the ring in time, I'd like to give it to her when we visit." I wanted to do it on the trail we'd hiked last Christmas. Despite almost losing my little girl there, my memory of the place was a happy one. It's where my feelings for Cyndi clicked into place. When she saved Olivia, I knew I needed Cyn as much as I wanted her. We needed her. Liv and me. And Cyn needed us. It was right to celebrate there.

"Trust me. She'll get it done in time. I'll make sure of it."

I didn't want to hurt any friendships over a ring. "Well—"

She cut me off. "This is going to be the party of the century." Sherry murmured words, sounding like she was sharing my news to Gabe.

"Hey, remember to keep it a surprise, all right? We're officially coming out to celebrate the name change."

"You got it." Her voice filled with mischief. "As long as you bring everybody."

Dr. S. and Felix were first on my list. Fee already wanted to meet Sherry and Gabe in person. Then I wondered if the Harrisons would come. I envisioned this enormous party in

Sherry's yard, and the words "I'll bring the whole family" spilled from my lips. Cyndi's people and my people. Together.

Our people.

Our family.

*****

Thank you for reading Cyndi and Blake's story. Did she say yes to everything Blake offered? Sign up for my newsletter, and you'll receive a *Love You Better* bonus scene to find out. It was a fun extra bit to write from Olivia's point of view.

If you haven't read about Cyndi's best friend, Kick, yet, you can click here to find her first book. Kick and Thomas' story is covered in a romantic suspense trilogy.

The next series on the horizon is Oakville Next Gen. It's the stories of Dylan, Liam, and Rachel McKenna. You can find more information on the series here.

- Scanning this QR code will also let you sign up for my newsletter and find my social media links. Or just go to www.kallynjones.com and start there. Newsletters are sent monthly. Frequency picks up in the run-up to a book release or for occasional promotions. You can unsubscribe at any time.
- **You can make a difference in an author's career by leaving a review.** Seriously. Writing a few words with your retailer of choice or at Goodreads.com or Bookbub.com, helps readers like you find their next favorite book. Links to my pages at these sites can also be found when you scan the code. If composing a review makes you uncomfortable, a rating is a wonderful gift too.
- *Love You Better* has a public playlist on Spotify that you can find here (also with the QR code). Couldn't let all those songs in the chapter titles go to waste!

Author's Note

I've been asked if Blake will ever find his mother, and the answer is no. Indigenous women are three-and-a-half times more likely to experience violent crime than other women. The statistics on sexual assault and domestic crime against indigenous women and girls are outrageous.

The simple fact is too many Indigenous women have vanished the way Blake's mother did. Our world is less rich for it. I encourage you to look up the Missing and Murdered Indigenous Women's (MMIW) movement. We need a world filled with culture and varied experiences. Moreover, we need all women to live healthy lives.

When I researched 20th-century Native American adoption practices, I was shocked to learn that the idea of an Indigenous child being plucked from a crime scene and given to a white couple without looking for his family wasn't merely plausible. It was part of the horrific crap that happened regularly in the community.

Acknowledgments

- As I begin this year with yet another flare, I am ever grateful for the things I *can* do. My thanks go out to the medicines and caregivers who keep me going and keep me improving.
- To sweet Sophie Sue (12/1/2012-12/17/2024), the inspiration for Macushla in Oakville Obsessions. Thank you for your unconditional love and adventurous spirit. You will be forever loved and missed.
- To my Jones crew: As our relationships evolve into the next era, I'm so thankful for each one. For your support of my writing adventure, the laughter you bring to my life, and your wisdom. Watching you grow is my life's joy.
- To Jeanne and Shannon for helping me with Blake's character. This story is richer for what he brings to Cyndi's life.
- To Louis for tax law guidance. I still took a lot of liberties with it. No mistakes are Louis'. He's brilliant.
- Thanks to D. A. Sarac for fixing the words and for your encouragement. Even more for your friendship.
- To my coffeehouse crew, Beth and Laura: Thank you for the book talks and sprints and for getting me out of the office. You make writing a joy.

- To my budding ARC team: I'm indebted to you for helping spread the word about my little series.
- To my readers: So much gratitude to you for taking a chance on my books. There are endless stories to choose, and I'm honored you picked mine. Hugs to all of you. XO KJ

About the Author

Kallyn Jones returned to her roots as an author after a successful career as a brand specialist. She brings the same passion for diving into unique stories as she writes about her sexy, down-to-earth characters and their offbeat families. She delights in finding heroes and heroines in unusual places and believes hard-fought happily ever afters are the sweetest.

Kallyn lives in her adopted hometown of Raleigh, North Carolina, with her own hero and their three sons. In her spare time, she enjoys trail walks, DIY projects, digital painting, and testing out new, "healthy" recipes. She's proud to say her fellas usually like her experimental dishes. *Usually*.

Follow Kallyn Here:

Website: www.kallynjones.com
Facebook: KallynJonesAuthor
Instagram: KallynJonesWriteNow
Goodreads: Kallyn Jones
BookBub: Kallyn Jones